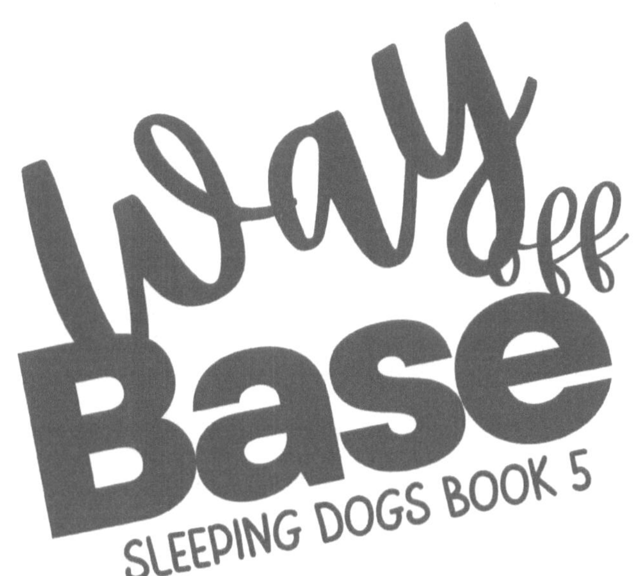

CHANTAL ROOME

Book Cover by Chantal Roome

2nd edition 2023

Print ISBN 97817777076682

ebook ISBN 9781777707699

Back to Basics

Travis

"Are you heading home already?" Johnny asks when he looks over and notices that I'm packing up my stuff.

We're in the studio today and we should be working on a new album, but Connor, lead singer of Sleeping Dogs and one of my oldest friends, has been too preoccupied to get much done. Ever since reconnecting with his childhood sweetheart and love of his life, Alex, when our last tour ended a couple of weeks ago, he's been spending every spare minute with her, so we've been messing around in the studio. We're not doing anything serious enough to warrant my attendance for a full day, that's for sure. Plus, Ryder didn't even bother to show up, so I refuse to feel bad about leaving early today. At least *I* was here for a bit.

And right now, I need to get the fuck out of here. At the end of the tour, I thought being back in the studio would give me a sense of relief, but these days, being in the studio feels nearly as stifling as being on tour.

Sometimes I think about what it would be like to walk away from it all. To tell everyone I'm done and refuse to record anything or play music at all. And as more time passes, that thought becomes more and more appealing.

I'll never act on it, though, because the guys need me. I couldn't let them down like that. And I do love making and playing music. It's mostly touring that gets to me.

"Not home," I say to my older brother, Johnny. "Heading over to Mom and Dad's. They've got some shit they need done around the house and I said I would work on it this week."

"You're making me look bad." Johnny packs up too, but I know he's not planning to join me at our parents' house. He thinks I don't know, but he's been pining after Alex's best friend Becca since the night he met her. They've been spending a lot of time together, even though they both insist they're just friends. I'd bet anything that's where Johnny goes when he leaves here today. "At least let me know if I can help buy materials or anything. I might be shit at actually doing the work, but I can swipe my credit card like a pro."

I have to laugh. If only he knew that Mom and Dad ask me to fix things around their house because they know I enjoy working with my hands and being in the band doesn't leave me much time to do it. Johnny has always focused on creating art, whereas I've been more interested in building and fixing things. When I would spend time with Dad in his workshop, building stuff out of wood, Johnny would be off somewhere drawing in his sketchbook, or in the kitchen baking with Mom. Not that my woodworking projects aren't artistic, it's that few people can appreciate the art in a well-made piece of furniture the same way they do when looking at the tattoos or paintings Johnny has created.

"Yeah, yeah. You know how Dad feels about that."

"You'd think having two successful musicians with a shit-load of money in the family would be a good thing, but not for our folks. I wish he'd let us at least pay for the repairs on the old house since he's never let us buy them a new one."

"You don't need to convince me. But you know how they feel about that place."

"Yeah, I know. That's where they raised the seven of us, and that's where they want their grandkids to visit them. "It's not just our house, it's our home". Mom gives me that same tired line whenever I offer to buy them a new place." Johnny quotes our mother in a high-pitched falsetto that would get him slapped upside the head if she heard it. "At least she let me tattoo her for free after the double mastectomy. That's the only thing she's ever accepted from me, and that's because I refused to take her money after the tattoo was done."

"It's not like she could have returned it and given you the money back like she does with gifts she thinks are too expensive."

"Right? Such a stubborn woman. Let me give you some jewelry, dammit. I can afford it. At least the other women I tattoo give in a little easier than Mom did. Not by much, though. Something about surviving cancer makes women extra fierce."

Besides being a famous guitar player, expert baker, and exceptional tattoo artist, Johnny is also an incredibly kind human being. He doesn't tattoo regular clients. He only works on mastectomy patients, and he only ever does it for free. He says the feeling of giving a woman back her sense of beauty and femininity is worth more than money to him. The only other tattoo he's done in recent years was one for Becca, and that one helped her recover from trauma stemming from a childhood injury.

And he didn't charge her, either.

"I'm sure she'll still try to pay you somehow, even though it's already been years."

Johnny and I walk out of the studio together, tossing a wave to Aiden and Devon on our way out. I try to hide the sigh of relief that escapes me when we walk out those doors. The older

I get, it seems the less I enjoy being in the band and every-thing that entails. Truthfully, I'm loving that Connor is so distracted right now. It gives me a chance to finally relax. Maybe I'll work my way around to enjoying the music again, or at least to hating it less.

I know, I know. I'm such an asshole for feeling this way, because who doesn't want to be famous? I'm out here living a life most people dream about and I can't even appreciate it.

"I'll see you later," I tell Johnny as I climb into my beat-up truck. Yet another way that I'm not much like a rockstar. I drive a big truck and use it for hauling stuff, not showing off. "Tell Becca I say hello." I pull out past Johnny and give him a two-finger wave before heading down the driveway.

Johnny looks over at me, with his eyebrows raised and mouth open in shock as he watches me drive away. He no doubt thinks I read his mind with the fake twin thing we have from being born ten months apart, but really he's so transparent when he's in love. He's such a romantic he's practically floating on air with hearts circling his head. It would have been impossible for me not to guess that he was going to see Becca. I don't even need to read his mind for that. I think it might be the real thing for him this time, though, so I hope it all works out. He's been looking for *the one* for so long, he deserves to find her after all this time. Not only that, Becca is cool as shit, and we'd be lucky if she joined our family.

Me, on the other hand, I've given up on the idea of finding someone to share my life with. Like the other guys, I spent time at the start of my career messing around with the groupies and assorted models and actresses who wanted to hook up with young musicians, but that got old fast. I want something like my parents have, but I can't see any way to do that while still being a full-time touring musician. I don't want my wife to have to come on tour, and I really don't want my kids to live a life in the spotlight. What would I do if I weren't in the band?

Who am I kidding? I know what I would do if I weren't a musician; it's what I was planning to do before I followed Johnny into this whole music thing in the first place. I wanted to work with my hands like my dad. Building things, creating stuff out of raw materials, fixing stuff. That's the real reason my parents call me instead of Johnny when something needs to repairing or renovating at their house. It's because they know I enjoy doing that kind of stuff. They know it's that kind of work that fulfills me. Playing bass guitar in a famous band is cool and all, but it doesn't light me up like it does the other guys. So yeah, if I ever want to have a family, I won't be doing it while I'm still in Sleeping Dogs. That wouldn't be fair to me, my wife, and any kids we might have.

But that's all a fantasy, anyway. I can't see myself walking away from something that gives me the resources to take care of my parents for life. Even if they won't accept it, it's nice to know that I could help them if they needed it. And it's not like I can let the rest of the guys down. Sure, they could find someone else, but I'm not going to think about that. There's no sense in worrying about it since I'll never leave the band. Problem solved.

MOM AND DAD LIVE on the opposite side of Westborough from Connor and Alex, in one of the older neighborhoods. It's not that far, but it takes a little longer to get there because I drive through the middle of the city.

When I finally pull up to my parents' house, I notice a moving truck across the street, and disappointment hits me, a palpable weight on my chest. That house has been vacant for a few years, and I've been playing with the idea of buying it myself so I could fix it up. It was never a solid plan though, more of a daydream I entertained when trying to distract myself from the day-to-day of being in the band. I shouldn't feel a sense of loss now that someone else is moving in. Even so, I can't help but wonder what I could have done with the place if I'd taken that chance.

I hope these new neighbors work out better for my parents than the last ones. The previous tenants weren't exactly what my parents considered good neighbors. Lots of parties, lots of fights, some screaming kids, and an unkempt yard did nothing but make my parents crazy. They still refused to move away, though. There's no scaring them away from this home.

Maybe these new neighbors will do something to fix the state of the house. As it stands now, it looks like it's falling apart, even though I'm pretty sure that's not the case. If Dad were still in the business of taking clients, I'd say he should offer his services as a handyman to help them get things fixed up, but he's pretty much retired and mostly builds for fun now. Kind of how I do it as a hobby.

I park on the street in front of my parents' place and take an appraising look at their house, trying to guess what it is they want me to work on. From what I can see while standing on the sidewalk, the fence needs painting, as does the trim around the windows. I think they need some work done on their roof, as well. Looks like I'm going to have a lot to keep me busy during this break from touring. I can't wait to get started.

"Hey there," Dad calls out as I'm grabbing my tools from the back of my truck. "Ready to do some proper work for a change?" he asks with a chuckle. He thinks that being in the band isn't hard work. He's not entirely wrong. It's not as physical as construction, but it's difficult in its own way. Still, it's easier to let him think what he wants.

"You bet," I say, patting my toolbox. "I even brought some quality tools, so I don't have to use your old, shitty ones."

"Pshh," Dad scoffs and shakes his head. "Didn't anyone ever tell you? It's not the tool that matters, it's how you use it." He waggles his eyebrows and thrusts his hips, really driving home the innuendo. "How do you think your mother and I got all you kids?" he adds with a booming laugh.

I cringe. The thought of my parents having sex is not something I need right now. "Yeah, okay. I don't want to think about that ever again. How about you tell me what needs fixing and let me get to it already?"

He's still snickering when he leads me into the house. "I have it all written down for you here. Come in and sit."

Dad and I go over the list and before I know it, I'm out in the backyard repairing his tool shed. The first task is underway, with at least twenty more to go. I couldn't be more excited.

2

Moving On In and Spank Bank Surveillance

Finley

"THAT'S THE LAST ONE, sweetie," Mom says as she carries in a small box marked "kitchen". "Let's get this stuff unpacked now."

Unloading the truck took a little longer than expected because we had to be extra careful on the stairs up to the front door. The first step has some rot, and we didn't want anyone falling through. That means it's getting late, and we're all getting hungry. And cranky.

Okay, maybe I'm the one getting cranky. But it still counts.

"I have a better idea," I say, pulling a stack of paper plates out of a box marked 'open first'. "Let's order pizza, get some beds set up, and have dinner. I can always unpack the rest of the stuff tomorrow, but if we don't get some food into these kids soon, they're going to revolt."

Braden, Sarah, and Austin have been little troopers all day, but there's only so much patience you can expect kids to have when doing something as boring as moving. If I didn't need Mom and Dad's help to move, I could have had them babysit so the kids wouldn't be in the way. Or if their idiot father had picked them up for the weekend like he was supposed to, I could have had help and no kids.

The divorce has been hard on them in lots of ways, but having to move in with my parents, and share bedrooms and space with each other, has probably been the hardest thing. When my grandmother suggested I move into her old rental property in Westborough, I jumped at the chance. And that was before she told me she was giving me the house, not only letting us move into it.

The house is a bit of a fixer-upper, but luckily for me, I've spent most of my working years doing construction with my dad, specifically doing house remodels. Grandma probably had that in mind when she thought of giving me this place. I am uniquely qualified to fix it up, after all. And I needed a place to stay. A place to escape to. At least here the kids will have their own bedrooms.

"So, does Emilio already have the address?" my dad asks. "When is his next weekend with the kids?"

My soon-to-be ex-husband and I have an unofficial arrangement that gives him every second weekend with the kids. However, in the last year, since we split up and made this arrangement, he's never spent an entire weekend with them, and he's only had a handful of overnights. It takes its toll on the kids, as you can imagine.

"Yeah, I texted it to him. And I reminded him several times that we were moving in this weekend. He agreed to take them this weekend, but his scheduled weekend is next weekend. If he even bothers to show up," I add in a whisper.

Living with my parents for the past year has given them a front-row seat to the drama that is my divorce. Emilio had been distant for a while, but when I found women's underwear in his car, underwear that didn't belong to me, I decided I'd finally had enough. Mom and Dad were happy to let me move in with my three kids, but I'm sure they're more than ready to have their space back. And to not have to witness the kids' disappointment every time Emilio lets them down.

My dad pulls me into a hug, squeezing me before he lets go.

"One day, kiddo, those kids will have the dad they deserve. Emilio had us all fooled for a while, but I think it's probably a good thing that he's out of your life now. And I don't think it would be so bad if he bit the bullet and disappeared from the kids' lives altogether. If he doesn't grow up and take some responsibility soon, these kids are going to suffer for a long time."

I swallow, dad's words coming too close to the way I really feel for my comfort. If he knew how many times I wished Emilio would sign over full custody and disappear forever, he'd be shocked. And it's something I refuse to say out loud. If Emilio ever disappears, I want to make sure no suspicion could ever be cast my way. Call me superstitious if you must, but I've watched enough true crime to know better. As the ex-wife, I would be the first suspect. I don't need to add any questionable comments as fuel for that fire.

"Okay," I say, clapping my hands together. "Kids. I'm going to order pizza. Go get the air mattresses and sleeping bags and pick a room that we can all share for the night."

The kids scramble to the pile of boxes in the living room, digging through them until they find the air mattresses and the pump.

"Gramps," Braden, my oldest, calls out. "Can you come help me blow these up?"

My dad goes upstairs with Braden while I pull out my phone. I turned it off in my pocket, somehow. That's been happening a lot lately. I should probably try to replace it one of these days. Yet another thing to add to the list of things that need fixing that I can't afford. I get it powered back on, pull up the app, and get our pizzas ordered. My mom has already enlisted the help of Sarah and Austin, and together they are now getting the kitchen unpacked. Mom's never been one for putting things off, so I'm not surprised that she didn't want to leave things for me to work on tomorrow.

I, however, am more than happy to wait until tomorrow. I grab myself a bottle of water and go out to the front porch. Well, I suppose since it runs along the entire front of the house, it's more of a veranda than a porch, but porch is much easier to say.

It needs a little work, but it's still a nice place to sit.

I have no patio furniture right now, but I can already picture a hanging porch swing and maybe a couple of overstuffed all-weather armchairs.

Sitting on the floor with my back against the wall of the house, I open up my water and take a drink. I'm desperately in need of some time to myself, and this brief foray onto the porch is merely the start. It feels like I haven't been alone with my thoughts since I moved my kids out of the house I shared with Emilio.

It's been both the longest year of my life and the shortest one, too.

I inhale deeply and settle against the side of the house, looking around at the houses neighboring mine. I definitely have my work cut out for me if I want to bring this house up to the standard set by the neighbors. They clearly care about their houses, and this one, mine, is the eyesore of the neighborhood. It needs a lot of work, maybe more than I have time to take on myself. I might need to look at hiring a handyman.

A noise cuts through my thoughts, and through the half-broken spindles on the porch's dilapidated railing, I glimpse a man going into the house across the street. A definitely shirtless, clearly muscular, possibly good-looking man, and a flash of desire blasts through me. Ugh. You know it's been too long when the barest glimpse of a man's attractive body gets me a little hot and bothered. Not that I'm going to bring a new man into my bed, even one as sexy as Mr. Across-the-street. I am looking forward to some private time with my battery-operated boyfriend, though, now that I'm not living in my parents' house.

Even before Emilio started staying out all hours of the night, working on his 'band', we weren't very affectionate. I spent so much time mothering him I had no interest in sleeping with him. Maybe that contributed to his cheating, and maybe it didn't, but either way, he never made it easy for me to be interested. He's one of those men who couldn't understand how needing me to take care of him like he was a child made him less attractive to me.

So yeah, it's probably been almost two years since I've been with a man since I would never cheat on my husband. Not that I ever had enough energy to even consider it, but still. Plus, it's also been at least a year since I've even given myself a proper orgasm, since not only have I been living in my parents' house, I've also been sharing a room with my seven-year-old.

Needless to say, B.O.B. is coming out of retirement and getting a good workout when I finally get a bedroom for myself again.

And, as if the thought of my battery-operated boyfriend summoned him, the sexy guy across the street appears again.

Hello neighbor.

I sit up and adjust the glasses on my nose to get a better look at the glistening hunk of man-meat coming out of my across-the-street neighbor's house. Yup, he's good-looking, as I suspected. So good-looking it should be illegal. That's too much sexual power for one man to have.

He's carrying a toolbox and wearing a tool belt over his low-slung jeans, his muscles rippling with every step. Seriously unfair. I crawl to the railing, attempting to remain hidden while I continue to stare. What? I just finished talking about my year-long dry spell. A woman needs to have spank bank material before she gets her B.O.B. buzzing. And this man has the goods to become a regular feature, I think.

He stops at the truck parked at the curb in front of the house. I can't see him as well now, since he's on the other side of the vehicle, but after a moment, he turns and walks back to the house. He's still shirtless, but he's lost the tool belt and toolbox. And I have to say, he looks as good from the back as he did from the front. His back muscles ripple with each step, and his ass flexes as he walks. The late afternoon sun lights up his red hair, showing it to be more copper than auburn.

Oh, yeah. He'll definitely be a repeat performer for the old spank bank.

"What are you doing out here, sweetheart?" Mom whispers in my ear, making me jump. "Checking out the local wildlife?"

"Shit!" I say a little too loudly, jumping up and away from the railing. "You scared me."

She stands up and crosses her arms over her chest, a knowing smirk on her lips. "We're all done putting away stuff in the kitchen. Would you like me to work on the bathroom next?"

"Sure, Mom. Thanks," I say, resisting the urge to put my hand over my pounding heart. I can't believe she caught me ogling that sexy man across the street.

She gives me a nod but doesn't turn to leave. "You know," she says, before walking back into the house, "there's nothing wrong with moving on. It's been over a year since you left Emilio, and even longer than that since he left you emotionally. No one would blame you for wanting to find love again."

My cheeks heat at the thought of trusting myself like that again. Looking is one thing. Actually trying to find someone new is another thing altogether. Emilio had me fooled for so long, I don't think my trust meter works properly anymore.

"Thanks, Mom. I'll keep that in mind."

I wait for her to go back inside before risking a peek back across the street. The sexy redhead is gone, leaving me with nothing to stare at but an immaculate lawn and a fence that needs a paint job.

This reminds me, I need to add a new fence and new sod to the list of repairs for my new house. At the very least, I need to mow down the weed patch that currently lives in my front yard. I pull out my phone and add those to the ongoing list of repairs, as an unfamiliar car pulls into the driveway and a young guy hops out with our pizzas.

Perfect. I'm starving.

But thanks to that sexy redheaded beast from across the street, I'm not so sure pizza is what I'm hungry for.

3

In Hiding and New Jobs

Travis

WHEN DID EVERY SEASON in Westborough become summer? I pull off my shirt and use it to wipe the sweat from my forehead. I've been painting my parents' fence for the last hour and it's so hot I'm thinking about coming back after dark to finish. It should start cooling off by this point in the season, but it's as hot now as it was at the height of summer.

Time for a quick break.

I walk up and let myself in the front door of my parents' place. The house is weirdly quiet. Growing up here with five sisters and one brother, it was always crowded and loud. Now that most of those sisters have husbands and kids of their own? Let's just say that Nana and Poppa's house is as full as ever most of the time, even though all of us kids have moved out.

Right now, though, it's silent.

I grab two bottles of water from the fridge, cracking one open and drinking it all back while standing with my back to the sink. It's so cold I can almost feel slivers of ice sliding over my tongue, and I've never been more thankful for my parents' insistence on keeping their ancient fridge.

"Oh, there you are Travis," Dad says, coming in the front door. "I was just out looking for you. How's the fence coming?"

Considering you have the biggest lot on the block, and the longest fence to go with it? "Oh, you know, Dad. Couldn't be better." I say, wiping water from my lips with the back of my hand.

He laughs. "Well, don't stay out in the sun too long, my boy. We gingers aren't made for prolonged sun exposure." He reaches out and lifts a strand of my sweaty, copper-colored hair.

"You're not kidding. I have my sunscreen out front. I'll reapply when I get back out there."

"Good thinking. Okay, I'm heading out to the hardware store. Do I need to grab anything for you?"

I've been doing woodworking projects with my dad for as long as I can remember. I think I was using a handsaw before I could properly hold a pencil. You should have seen it when my dad tried to teach me to use a chainsaw. I was ten years old, and it weighed as much as I did. My mom was not impressed. My dad thought it was hilarious.

"No, Dad. I don't really have anything on the go right now. I've got a few things in mind, but I can pick up materials when I settle on a project." I twist open my second bottle of water and take a huge drink.

"Suit yourself." He waves and heads out the door.

I finish my water and grab another bottle from the fridge before heading back out to continue work on the fence. Stopping at my stuff, I grab my sunscreen and slather some more on. Dad's right. Gingers are not made for the sun. I wipe my hands off on my shirt and stuff it back in my pocket, ready to get started again.

I bet the paparazzi would love to see me now. Covered in sweat, my shirt tucked in my back pocket, and jeans hanging low. They'd get decent money for those pics, I'm sure. I'm not covered in tattoos like Johnny, but I keep myself in good shape. The paparazzi stopped coming around a long time ago, though. The guys of Sleeping Dogs stopped being interesting the minute we stopped doing outrageous rockstar stuff. And since we're sort of fading into obscurity instead of going out in a blaze of glory, they don't care as much about us anymore. Ryder still gets some attention, because he still parties all the time, but the rest of us are pretty tame.

And you know what? That suits me fine. I was never really into music for fame, anyway. I only learned how to play bass because Johnny joined a band, and I always did what he did. Partly it was my way of watching out for him. Even though he's the older brother, I've always felt responsible for him. That and if I didn't join the band with him, I'd have been stuck home with my sisters. Not that I don't love being in the band, but I would have been just as happy working with my hands like my dad. I've always pictured myself with my own woodworking shop. The smell of sawdust, the feel of the wood grain under my fingers. I love making custom furniture and I'm sure I could do it long-term. There's something amazing about creating something tangible and real.

Not that music isn't real, but it's not like you can grab it in your hands and hold on.

I blow out a breath and grab my paint roller. No sense in dreaming about that again. It's not like I would ever leave the band and start any sort of building or furniture business, anyway. It's best if I push that aside and get back to work on the fence.

I've actually gotten a lot done already, and I should finish by this evening. Dad pressure-washed everything a few days ago, so all that's left is for me to slap on the paint. I almost feel like Daniel-san in The Karate Kid with Mr. Miyagi standing behind me, telling me to 'paint the fence'. I chuckle to myself as I take a half squat and mimic the movement he used in the movie. "Paint the fence. Up, down. Up, down. Don't forget to breathe." Something like that, anyway. It's not exactly the same using a roller instead of a brush.

"Excuse me. Hi. Hello?" A tap on my shoulder snaps me out of my daydream, and I turn to see a woman trying to get my attention.

When she smiles at me, all the breath leaves my lungs, leaving me suddenly lightheaded. I try to swallow but my mouth is suddenly dry despite all the water I just finished drinking. None of our fans have ever had this kind of effect on me before.

Her dark-rimmed glasses give off a sexy librarian vibe, and her graphic t-shirt, ripped denim shorts, and Converse sneakers look comfortable and effortlessly sexy. The thing that stands out the most, though, is her hair. It's colored a dark forest green, and it's piled up on her head in a messy knot.

Fuck, she looks good.

"Hey. Uh, hi," I say, finally getting it together enough to respond. Fuck. That sounded stupid. Fix it, asshole. You've never had a problem talking to fans before. "Can I do something for you?"

"Actually, yes. Maybe? I'm Finley," she says, holding out her hand for me to shake.

I extend my hand in return.

With the paint roller still firmly in my grasp.

White paint smears over her hand, part of her arm, and a little of her shirt. *What the hell, Travis?* I've accosted a fan with a paint roller. *Shit.*

"Oh, shit. I'm so sorry." I drop my roller back in the paint tray, splashing paint on the sidewalk, and pull my shirt out of my back pocket. I wipe the paint off her hand before lifting the bottom of her shirt and attempting to clean it as well. My fingers brush the skin of her stomach and an electric shock shoots through my hand. What the hell was that? "Fuck. I can't believe I did that. I'm so sorry. I can replace it." *What the fuck is wrong with me? Why am I being such an idiot?*

She laughs and gently pushes my hands away. "It's no big deal. It's not the first time someone attacked me with paint, and I'm sure it won't be the last."

She shoves her hands in her back pockets and licks her lips, and my dick stirs. *Now is not the time.*

"I'm Travis," I say dumbly. *God, she's beautiful.*

"Still Finley," she says with a laugh, pointing at herself.

I can't help but chuckle at her subtle teasing. *Right. She already told me her name.*

I can't help that I'm so distracted. She's cute. And sexy.

"Um, so anyway. I was wondering if you have a card or something?" She pushes her glasses up her nose with a finger, a move so adorable I want to kiss her. *What? That's ridiculous. Come on, Travis, get your shit together.*

I must look as confused as I feel because she elaborates.

"I've seen you doing a lot of work around here. I moved into that house over there." She turns and points to the old place across the street. "My grandmother was using it as a rental property, but she's signed it over to me now. How could I say no to a fresh start in the city I grew up in?" A look crosses her face and I can't tell if it's sad or angry. "But as you can see, it needs a lot of work."

"Okay?" *I'm still confused, which could have something to do with still being in awe of how beautiful she is. Actually, I'm sure it's exactly that. She's too beautiful and I can't concentrate.*

Has that ever happened to me before?

"So, I was wondering if you had a card, so I could call you to set up some time to get a quote on some repairs? You're a handyman, aren't you? Or a general contractor? I've seen you here at the Donovan's house fixing the fence, and doing a lot of other work around the place, so I figured..."

Wait. She thinks I'm a handyman?

She thinks I'm a handyman, and she wants me to do some work at her house. *She doesn't know who I am. She's not a fan?*

"Yes!" I shout, making her jump. "Sorry," I apologize, forcing my voice to a lower volume. "Yes, I'm a handyman, but I don't have any cards on me. Can I give you my number?"

"Sure, yeah, that would be great." She pulls her phone out of her pocket and gives it a funny look, before muttering, "Again? You stupid thing." She presses a button on the side and hands it over. "I could do most of the work myself, but I don't have any time."

"Oh?" Usually when a homeowner says that, they don't really know what they're doing, but I believe her when she says she could do it. I look down at her phone to input my information, and it's just finished turning on. That must be the button she pushed. I navigate to her messaging app and send myself a message, so now I have her information, too. The idea that she might not contact me after all made me feel a little panicked, so I sent the message before I considered she might think it's a little weird of me to do so. Oh, well. It's not like I haven't been weird with her already.

"Yeah, I remodel homes with my dad, and I'm getting my real estate license before he retires. So I've been studying for the licensing test, and then between moving, and... everything else, well, it's been a lot. I thought if I could hire someone to do some of it, I'd save myself some time."

I pass her phone back. "What about your husband? Are you married?" Of course, she's married, stupid. She's too gorgeous for someone to not have snapped her up yet. And she remodels houses? Yeah, she's got to be married.

I learned my lesson a long time ago not to mess with married women. Her husband's fists weren't especially forgiving, not to mention how shitty I felt about it afterwards. Not that I actually knew about the husband when I first hooked up with her. She had told me they were divorcing, and I believed her.

"He won't be my husband for much longer, thank god." She laughs and tucks a loose strand of hair behind her ear. "At least, he won't be once he signs the divorce papers and agrees to terms. I don't know why he's dragging his feet. We've both made it very clear that we don't want to be married anymore. He'd rather be off with his 'band'"—she uses air quotes with the word band—"playing shitty music and chasing girls, and I'd rather be anywhere else but with him."

Shit, so now she's going through this completely alone? And it sounds like she's not a fan of musicians. Why does that thought scare me?

"Are you new to town, or…?"

"Sort of? I lived here when I was younger, then I moved away before high school. I stayed there with my husband after we met in college, but then one day he decided he didn't want to be tied down anymore. When my grandmother heard about the divorce, she insisted I come back to Westborough. How could I say no, especially when she threw this sweet, and definitely not run-down, or haunted, house in with the deal?" She laughs. "And with the original shag carpeting still installed, and in terrible shape? *Of course* I said yes right away."

I look back across the street. The house is an older style two-story, with a porch running the full length of the front. It's a nice-looking house, but it definitely could use some work. It's got a bit of a 'crazy cat-lady-who-is-also-a-witch' vibe. It needs fresh paint, some new siding, the shutters are hanging on for dear life, a couple of boarded-up windows, and I can see some broken spindles on the railing around the porch, but it's not too bad. At least from the outside. But this is all stuff I already knew since I was thinking about buying it myself.

"It looks decent. And you're right, I'm sure it's not very haunted at all," I say with a chuckle. "What all needs doing on the inside?" I don't need to know right now, but I really want to keep talking to her. I want to know more about her.

Am I really going to take on a project like this? Something this big could take longer than I have. We're supposed to be starting a new tour after we finish this album we're working on. A thought that I've been dreading, not that I've said anything to anyone.

"Do you want to come take a quick look? It's a bit of a mess, but I'm sure you've seen worse than empty boxes and dirty dishes in your line of work, am I right?" She laughs and touches my arm. "I can't tell you the horror houses I've seen in my time working with my dad."

"Um, sure. I've got a few minutes." I'm not a handyman. *What are you doing, Travis?* Leave this poor woman alone. Let her find a real contractor to help with her house.

"Great, come on." She turns and crosses the street, leaving me scrambling to catch up. I'm torn between lagging behind to see her ass in those shorts and walking beside her because I'm not really an asshole. "Watch this step." She taps her foot on the first step up to the porch. "I need to get this replaced right away."

I take my phone out and make a note. If I'm taking this on, I'm going to do it right. Besides, this could be fun. I get to fix up the house. Maybe not exactly like I wanted to, but I still get to work on it. And anything that gets me closer to Finley can't be all bad. A giddy sense of excitement builds in my chest.

I've got my head down, putting my phone back in my pocket, when Finley spins around in front of me, and we collide.

"*Oh,*" she says, her hands coming up to rest on my chest. She licks her lips and looks up at me, sending a flash of heat through me. *Kiss her,* I think.

I've almost got her backed against the door, and I want to push a little further. I want to push myself into her and feel her body against mine. I want to kiss her. My eyes flick down to take in her lips and I hear a sharp intake of breath. She wants me, too? No. That's not possible. Is it? Her hands flex on my bare chest and I lean forward and put my hands on her hips. I press her gently against the door, tilt my head and bring my face to hers. I shouldn't kiss her. I can't be in the kind of relationship she deserves. She is getting divorced, though. Maybe she'd be interested in something temporary with me? Something fun? That's it. I'm kissing her. I'm close enough to feel her breath on my lips when the door suddenly flies open behind her and she frantically pushes me away.

"So, anyway," she says, her voice a touch too high. "The door sticks sometimes. Oh, hi Braden. This is Travis. He might fix some stuff around the house for us. Travis, this is my son Braden."

She has a kid?

Braden is looking at me with disgust. He's not a fan either, it looks like. But he does look to be about my nephew's age. I know how to interact with kids. "How's it going, Braden? Good to meet you." I stick my hand out for him to shake, thinking that a little respect will go a long way with a kid this age.

"Yeah. Sure. Whatever. Where's your shirt? What were you doing with my mom?" He ignored my hand completely, so I let it fall. Guess I was wrong about the respect thing.

"Braden," Finley warns. "Manners."

"Whatever," Braden says, before stomping away.

Finley blows out a breath and pinches the bridge of her nose. "So, that's my oldest, Braden," she says with a fake smile. "He's twelve going on seventeen, with the attitude to match. The other two are around here somewhere, too."

Oh, shit. She's got three kids, and she's fresh out of a divorce? That settles it. Leave it in your pants, Travis. She's hot, but she's off-limits. She's got enough to worry about. And I really can't be the kind of guy a single mom with three kids needs.

"I have a ton of nieces and nephews, so I know what it's like. Don't worry about it. I'd probably have a lot of questions too if I found my mom in a compromising position with a strange shirtless man."

"Yeah, sorry about that." Her face reddens, and she forces a laugh before taking another deep breath. "Okay, then. Should we look at the rest of the house?"

"Let's do it." I may not be able to get as close to her as I would have liked, but I can help her out with her renovations. I can keep my distance and do that, too.

I think.

4

Stupid Exes and Eye Candy

Finley

"BRADEN, YOU GET YOUR little butt down here, right now!" I yell up the stairs after Travis leaves to go back to painting the fence. And after I have a minute to calm myself after being in his presence.

I'm surprised I kept it together as well as I did in front of him. What would he think if he found out I've been watching him every chance I get, ever since that first day when we moved in here? That's not why I approached him, though. Not really. He's been doing a lot of work at the Donovan's, and Mrs. Donovan has had nothing but great things to say about him. With her recommendation, I know I can trust him to do the work around my house. His insane hotness is a bonus.

And holy shit, is he masculine or what? Nothing like my ex, who takes that skinny rockstar look to the extreme. Not that Emilio's a rockstar or anything, except for maybe in his dreams. Travis looks like a regular, hardworking guy. A super sexy, incredibly fit, regular guy. Exactly the kind of guy I should look for. If I ever decide to look again, that is. For now, I'm happy to keep him in the spank bank file.

He's been performing his duties there very well, too. I haven't had to change B.O.B.s batteries in ages. My Travis fantasies make my orgasms almost instantaneous.

Not that anyone wants to take on a woman with three kids, anyway. Especially when one of them has been acting like a little asshole ever since his father and I split up. Not that I blame Travis. Or Braden, for that matter.

Braden finally stomps down the stairs. "What?" he huffs, arms crossed over his chest, with all the snark he can muster.

"You know darn well what." I reach out and tip his chin up so he's looking at me. "You know that was rude. I've been waiting for the chance to talk to that man for a while now and your attitude wasn't helpful. It's hard to find a handyman who comes recommended. You know I don't want just anyone coming in here and fixing this place up. Mrs. Donovan spoke highly of Travis and I would really like for him to take on the job."

"I don't understand why you don't do it," Braden pouts. "You're probably a million times better than that guy, anyway."

I have to smile. It's nice to know my kid has faith in me. "I very well might be, but I don't have time to do everything myself while I'm studying for my real estate licensing exam. And even if I had the time, I don't even have all my tools here." Because, for some reason, my ex decided he wanted to keep them. That man couldn't operate a hammer if his life depended on it, let alone something with moving parts, like a drill, or a table saw. Lord knows what he thinks he's going to do with my tools. I pull Braden in for a hug. "Now I want you to go across the street and apologize for being rude."

"Aww, Mom. Really? Do I have to?"

"Yes, you do. March over there and say you're sorry." I walk over and open the door, pointing out to where Travis is painting.

"Ugh, fine." Braden stomps out the door, grumbling what is sure to be some not-very-nice things about me. As long as he doesn't say it to my face. He's having a hard time with the divorce and I'd rather he direct his anger at me than at his little brother and sister. It would be even better if he would direct it at his father, but I refuse to say anything to make that happen.

No matter how shitty Emilio is, I will not be trash-talking him to the kids. Even if he is a no-good, lying, asshole, cheater.

"And watch out for that bottom step," I remind Braden as he reaches the step in question, causing him to awkwardly jump it at the last second. "I really need to get that fixed," I mutter to myself when he's out of earshot.

I make a mental note to stop at the hardware store later on today, to grab some lumber to fix the step. After I've gone to visit my grandmother at her retirement community, that is. I try to visit her every couple of days, at least. After she was nice enough to give me this house, visiting her is the least I can do.

Even if the house needs a major overhaul, I was so glad to have somewhere to land when my idiot ex-husband decided he'd rather be off chasing fame and girls in short skirts than supporting the family he signed on for when we got married. If it weren't for my grandmother's generosity, we would have been stuck in a tiny apartment or still living with my parents. No, I'd much rather have an old, drafty house in need of some cosmetics than a cookie-cutter shoebox of an apartment any day, thanks.

"Mommy, Sarah said I have to sleep in the attic. Is that true?" I pinch the bridge of my nose under my glasses, partly at the question and partly at the one asking it. You'd think a kid would be scared at the thought of sleeping in the attic, but you'd be wrong. He's practically vibrating with excitement.

Austin is standing in front of me in his usual outfit of all black, with a skull on his t-shirt, and his grin almost as wide as his face. He's the cutest little goth kid ever, if goth kids had white-blond hair and bright blue eyes. Sarah loves to tease her little brother about his fascination with all things creepy or spooky. And, since Austin is only seven years old, he usually believes whatever nonsense she tells him.

"Do you think it's haunted? Can I have a ghost best friend? Is that okay, Mom? Do you think there's already a dead body up there, or will we need to put in our own? Can I have a coffin?"

Austin can also be a little on the creepy side. Mostly he's cute, but sometimes...

"What if I promise that we'll be quiet? Can I have a sleepover in the attic with my new ghost friend?"

I release a sigh. "If you make a new best friend who also is a ghost, then yes, you can have a sleepover. But not in the attic. It's not safe to walk around up there. It doesn't have a proper floor."

"Maybe you can get that naked guy you were playing with to build one? Then I can walk on it. My ghost friend will float, so that won't matter. And we'll need the floor before we can bring the dead body and the coffin in."

I choke on a laugh. Braden obviously told his siblings he met Travis.

"Travis wasn't naked, buddy. And we weren't playing. He's going to fix some stuff around the house for us because I don't have time. After we fix everything, maybe we'll see if we can put in a playroom up there. How's that? But no dead bodies. They're unsanitary and they stink up the house." Add that to the list of things I thought I'd never have to say to my kids. Parenting is wild.

His little shoulders slump, letting me know this wasn't really the answer he was hoping for. "I guess that's okay. As long as we can paint it all black."

"We'll see." I rely on the classic, time-tested, mom non-answer, which we all know means "no way". It's bad enough that he wants an attic space to hang out with ghosts in. Painting it black, too, would be too much creepiness for me to handle. Luckily for me, Austin hasn't caught on to the true meaning of "we'll see" yet.

"Why don't you go up and tell your sister to get ready? Your dad is going to be here soon to pick you guys up for the weekend." My ten-year-old daughter is taking forever to get ready. She's been experimenting with makeup, a hobby that I am fine with, as long as she doesn't wear it to school yet. I'm not quite that ready for her to grow up. Evenings and weekends are good enough for now.

Austin turns and runs back up the stairs, already yelling for his sister.

I walk over to the living room window to check on Braden. I didn't get any weird vibes from Travis, and Mrs. Donovan seems to think the world of him, but I'm still not about to leave my son alone with a strange man for long.

I expected Braden would run over, mumble sorry, then run right back, so what I see outside shocks me. Somehow, Travis has enlisted Braden's help. Now they're both over there, shirtless, painting the Donovans' fence. I think I can feel my ovaries twitching as I watch.

He's hot as fire *and* good with kids? How am I supposed to resist that? How could anyone?

Emilio has never been very involved in the kids' lives. Beyond the standard greeting whenever he saw them, he almost never interacted with them at all. In the last couple of years, he's been spending every evening rehearsing or playing shows at bars, so he didn't get home until late. And then he'd be passed out until after the kids and I were out of the house. Really, the only reason I didn't ask for the divorce sooner was that I didn't see him enough to realize there was a problem. I was too busy doing everything by myself to even notice that I was doing it alone.

Emilio has even been terrible about visiting the kids. He's spent very few of his many weekends with the kids, thanks to all his shows with his band, even though he's been arguing with me for them. Not as hard as he's fought to keep my tools, mind you, but he still insisted on two weekends a month. And in the last year, he hasn't used even one of them. Well, he's used parts of them, but that's all. I'm not expecting anything different today either, but I have to keep a positive attitude for the kids' sake. I won't stop them from having a relationship with their dad, but sometimes it's hard to keep my mouth shut about what an idiot he is. I never thought my family would end up this way. Divorced, with the kids shuttling back and forth for visits with a dad who isn't even interested.

I wish I'd seen Emilio for who he really was before we got married. But I was young, and dumb, and believed whatever he told me. So stupid.

But now, seeing Travis out there working with Braden, I know that divorce is the best for my family. If I'm going to do it all alone, I may as well actually be alone.

Plus, I found out that not only was Emilio not doing his part in our family, he also wasn't doing a very good job of keeping it in his pants all those nights he spent away from home.

Thank god all my tests came back negative, or I'd have had to kill him instead of merely divorcing him, and who would look after my kids while I was in jail? My parents still work and they wouldn't have much time.

I suppose my Grandma could look after them, at least for a little while. I'm not sure what kind of influence she would end up being, though. She's got the kids calling her G.G. Money, for crying out loud. I thought G.G. was cute, you know, short for Great Grandma, but she said it wasn't 'hip enough' and that it would scare all her boyfriends away, and so G.G. Money was born.

I'm getting divorced and my eighty-five-year-old grandmoth-er has boyfriends, plural. The world sure is an interesting place.

Phew. That's depressing. Good thing I can resume my admiration of shirtless Travis. I'm watching him teach Braden how to come along behind him with a paintbrush to get the spots he misses with the roller. Even at this distance, I can see the muscles bunching in his back, the sweat dripping down the waistband of his jeans. It's been a long time since anyone has grabbed my attention this way. Since well before I asked Emilio for a divorce. It's hard to feel sexy with someone who you have to look after like they're another child.

My phone buzzes in my back pocket.

Please don't be Emilio canceling again. I cross my fingers for my kids' sake as I open my messages. I snicker a little when I see Emilio's name. I changed it when I found out about his cheating. It's childish, but it makes me laugh when I see it.

Asshole Emilio the Cheater- I'll be about an hour late.

That fucker.

Finley- You're still coming, though, right? The kids want to see their dad.

Asshole Emilio the Cheater- I'm not fighting with you right now. I'm busy. I'll be late.

Finley- Fine. As long as you show up. I'll let the kids know.

I wait a minute for an answer that I'm sure won't come, and then I take a screenshot of the conversation and put it in the file I'm keeping for my lawyer.

"Let me guess. He's not coming?" Sarah stands at the bottom of the stairs, backpack in hand, a frown on her face. "Why doesn't he want to see us this time?"

She has her brave face on, but I can hear a hitch in her voice. She's noticing the pattern too, and she's too smart to believe any of Emilio's lies about why he can't spend time with them. Ten-year-old girls are very perceptive, and this one is especially so. She's very observant. Hell, she noticed before I did her dad was never around anymore, and I'm the one who was married to him.

"No, baby," I say, walking over and pulling her into a hug. "He's just going to be a little late. He got held up at work." I feel bad lying to her, but I feel worse not giving her some sort of reason. It's not like I'm going to tell her that her father is being an asshole. I'm sure she'll figure it out on her own soon enough.

"Yeah. Sure, Mom," she says, pulling away from me and heading into the kitchen where she drops her backpack on the table. "Can I have some juice?"

I sigh and nod. "Sure, honey."

Fucking Emilio.

5

Moms Never Let You Get Away With Anything

Travis

"Nice work, dude." I hold up my fist for a bump from Braden. "You cut hours off my day by helping me out like this."

The grin on his face tells me he's proud of himself, and he should be. This kid works hard. Together, we knocked out the rest of the fence in under two hours. He originally came out on what was clearly a mom-directed mission of apology, but he didn't hesitate to jump in and help when I asked if he wanted to. He's a good kid.

"So, what are you and your family up to for the rest of today? Can I take you all out for ice cream or something, as a thank you for your help?"

He laughs humorlessly and shakes his head. "My dad is *supposed* to come and pick us up to go to his place for the weekend."

"Oh, that's cool. You must have some fun stuff planned with him."

He looks over at me. We're sitting on the front step of my parents' house drinking icy bottles of water, trying to cool off after working in the scorching sun. The kid looks a little better than I do, even though we both did the work shirtless. He's not as pasty white as I am, though, so that makes sense. He's got dark hair, and slightly darker skin, so the sun didn't do as much to him as it did to me.

I stupidly forgot to reapply sunscreen to my back earlier, and I can already feel the redness creeping in. I'll have to get someone to put some aloe vera gel on me later. Mom still keeps a bottle of it in the fridge for the gingers in our family. Dad and I are the worst of us, but I have two sisters and some nieces and nephews are also blessed with ginger hair and pale skin, so it pays for her to be prepared.

"I doubt it." He heaves a huge sigh, shoulders slumping, clearly struggling under the weight of something serious. "He hardly ever shows up when he says he will. We'll probably stay home with Mom this weekend. Maybe see our crazy great-grandma. She's pretty funny, at least."

"Shit, dude. That sucks." I mentally slap myself. "Sorry, I shouldn't swear in front of you. Your mom probably wouldn't like it."

Braden chuckles a little. "She swears a lot, too."

"Still," I say.

I hate deadbeat parents. I'm so lucky that I've never had to deal with that personally, but my buddy Connor has never even met his father, and Ryder's mom left when he and his brother were kids. It changes a kid when someone who's supposed to love them shows how little they care. Of course, Connor's mom has never been much of a mother, either, so who's to say how different things would have been even if his dad had stuck around?

"Well, his loss might be my gain. If you're around and up for it, I have a lot of stuff to do around here this weekend. My mom's keeping me doing projects for her." I gesture around us to the house and yard. "She's always coming up with new things for me to work on."

"Mrs. Donovan is your mom?" Braden looks surprised. "I thought you were a handyman?"

Oh, shit. Yeah, I guess I did say that.

"Oh, yeah. I am. I'm doing some favors for her in my downtime," I say. "She enjoys having another handy guy in the family. Saves her a lot of money and my dad a lot of time." I laugh.

"I like your mom and dad," he says. "They've had us over for dinner a few times. Their house is so loud."

I burst into laughter. "Oh yeah, it is definitely loud. Have you met the other kids yet? My nephew, Tyson, is the same age as you."

"I met him. He's pretty cool. He's going to be in the same grade as me. I hope we're in the same class."

We sit for a bit longer, talking about school, sports, and video games before his mom comes out of their house and starts over in our direction.

"See that look on my mom's face?" Braden says. I look up and see a sad smile on Finley's face. "That's how I know I'm right. My dad's not coming."

I give him a sweaty, one-armed side hug before his mom gets to us. I feel bad for the kid. He deserves better than a dad who can't even be bothered to be around every second weekend. If I had kids, I would need to see them every day.

Probably a good thing that I don't, then. It's not like I could bring them on tour with Sleeping Dogs. I know lots of guys in other bands do it, but I wouldn't want that kind of life for my kids. Children need more stability than that.

Having kids is a dream for the Travis who really is a handyman. The Travis who plays bass in Sleeping Dogs, won't be having a family. It sucks, but it's for the best.

"Hey guys," Finley says, sitting on the step next to Braden. "The fence looks great. Very fresh."

"Thanks," Braden mumbles, looking at his feet.

"So I was telling Braden, if he's not busy this weekend, I could use some help around here. My Mom's got me doing all sorts of stuff while I don't have any other projects on the go, and Braden is a quick learner. He saved me so much time today."

She grimaces and exhales loudly.

"It's okay, Mom. I know what time it is. Dad should have been here hours ago. Let me guess, he's not coming, is he?"

Finley wraps her arms around Braden and kisses his head. "No, he's not. I'm sorry, kiddo."

"It's fine," he says, standing up. "I'll help whenever you want, Travis. You know where to find me." He walks over to their house without looking back.

I pass Finley a bottle of water. "He's a good kid," I tell her. "He jumped at the chance to help when I asked. And he completed his apology mission, in case you were wondering."

She chuckles a little. "I wasn't sure how it would go, to be honest. I thought he might say the word and then run back home." She opens the water and takes a long drink. Is it possible for someone to drink water sexily? Because if so, she is nailing it. "Thanks for letting him help. He's been having a tough time. Moving away from his friends has been hard."

I nod. "He said he's met my nephew, Tyson, already. Maybe they'll end up being close. He said that they're going to the same school?"

"The neighborhood school. It seems that most of your family lives nearby." She laughs. "Thanks for letting me think you were only their handyman, by the way. You could have told me you're the Donovans' son."

"Hey," I say, hand to my chest in mock outrage. "You can't blame me for that. Beautiful women so rarely walk up to me on the street and start asking me questions. I was completely flustered."

Finley's cheeks turn a gorgeous shade of pink. "Oh come on now, I don't believe that for a second." She looks at me. "Have you seen you? I'm sure plenty of women approach you."

"Well, sure. But never any who are as beautiful as you." I waggle my eyebrows at her to add some levity to the moment. "So thank you. You've been a *major* boost to my ego."

She laughs and smacks me on the arm. "You ass," she says, still laughing. "You had me going for a second there."

Yeah, too bad I actually meant it. The part about her being beautiful, anyway. Women approach me all the time. It's a hazard of the job. There's something about Finley, though. It makes me want to know more about her. And since I know her ex isn't coming to pick up the kids, maybe now's my chance.

"So, before you came over here, I had asked Braden if you all wanted to go grab some ice cream or something. To say thank you to him for his help, and to you for lending me your kid. Are you up for it?"

"Oh man, that sounds amazing. Especially on a day like today. But I already promised my grandmother that I would go visit her at her retirement home today. I can't cancel on her now. Can I get a rain check?"

"Oh, yeah. Of course. Anytime." I stand up and dust off my pants before offering my hand and helping Finley up. "It was nice to meet you, Finley. And if Braden wants to help this weekend, send him over. I'll be here around eight in the morning."

"We'll have to see. Braden is rather fond of sleeping in. I practically have to dump ice water on his head to wake him up before noon."

I chuckle. "If it weren't for work, I'd be the same way," I lie. My actual job happens later at night. Mornings are usually for sleeping in unless there's press. Or working in the studio, like we are now. That's the life of a musician. It sucks sometimes because I really like mornings.

"Not me," she says. "I like to be up with the sun. I don't want to waste a minute of the day. There are way too many things to get done to sleep the day away."

I don't know how long we stand there looking at each other, but I know I don't want her to leave yet. I'm about to ask if I can invite myself along to visit her grandmother, to get a little more time with her, when I hear someone clear their throat.

"Ahem. Travis, there you are." My mom is standing in the open doorway, a grin on her lips. I don't know how I didn't hear her coming. "I see you met Finley. Did she ask you about her house?"

"I sure did, Mrs. Donovan. He's going to put together a quote for me." She leans over and elbows me a little. "How come you didn't tell me he's your son? He let me believe that he's a hired hand."

Shit, Mom's going to tell her what I really do. I don't want her to know that. Not knowing what I know about her feelings about musicians. "I finally told her I'm doing stuff for you while I have some downtime with my regular contracting work. Right, Mom?"

Mom gives me a funny look before she turns to Finley. "Yes, that's right. It's lucky for me he's not all booked up. It seems like most years he's gone for months and months at a time."

"Haha, good one Mom," I say, my voice strained. I turn to Finley. "Well, I don't want to keep you any longer. I'm sure your grandmother is eager to see you."

"Oh yeah. I'm really late now, too."

"Did Emilio make it this time, dear?" Mom asks.

"Ugh, no. That prick," Finley says. "He keeps letting the kids down. I hate watching their little faces fall every time he disappoints them yet again. Braden and Sarah are old enough that they've started expecting it, but Austin still gets so excited every time."

Mom steps out and pulls Finley into a big hug. "I'm sorry, love. It's hard when you get caught up with the wrong man, and it's even harder when there are children involved. You bring those kids over here any time you like. We always have a half dozen or so wandering around. Three more are no problem. Anytime you need a break, let me know. Okay?" She holds her out at arm's length, hands on her shoulders. "That Emilio Is an idiot for letting you get away. One day, you'll meet a smart, handsome man who knows what he has as soon as he sees you. And he'll make sure you and your kids never want for love ever again."

Finley sniffles a little and tries to sneakily wipe her eyes. I pull my shirt out of my pocket and offer to her to wipe her tears.

She laughs. "That t-shirt has seen a lot of action today. You're probably better off throwing it out than you are washing it at this point."

"You're not wrong," I say with a laugh. "But it makes such a good rag that I can't bear to get rid of it."

"Oh, give it here," Mom says, snatching it from my hand. "You know it's going to end up in my washing machine anyhow." She looks at Finley. "Bye-bye, dear. Say hello to your grandmother for me. And remember, my offer to watch the kids is good anytime. I expect you to take me up on it." She turns and marches into the house, no doubt throwing my shirt straight into the wash.

"I'll let you go, too," I say. "Send Braden over tomorrow, anytime." Before I can think it through, I lean in and kiss Finley on the cheek. "I really enjoyed talking to you today."

I turn to follow my mom into the house. The last thing I see is Finley touching her cheek, right where I kissed her.

I've never wanted to be a simple handyman more than I do right now.

"Well?" Mom stands by the kitchen with her arms crossed, her foot tapping an irritated rhythm. "Are you going to tell me why you're letting that lovely woman believe you're a handy-man instead of a famous musician? Or are you going to make me force it out of you?"

I cringe. It doesn't matter how old you are. Mom's never let you get away with anything.

6

Not So Peaceful Pines

Finley

THE PARKING LOT OF Peaceful Pines is quiet when I pull in today, which is surprising. This bunch of seniors is as active as any sorority or fraternity I've heard of, except I think these seniors get into more trouble than any member of a Greek letter organization ever has, outside of a movie. The other day when I was here, the parking lot was overrun with senior citizens drag racing tricked-out, souped-up, powered mobility scooters. It was like a Fast and Furious movie, but with octogenarians instead of Paul Walker and Vin Diesel. I didn't even stay to visit Grandma that day because they were all planning to drive their scooters to a diner downtown to have milkshakes and pie. Probably a good thing too, since I had the kids with me, and they'd have wanted to hop on and scoot out for a milkshake too.

I planned ahead this time, though, so I know Grandma is expecting me, and the kids are at school. Whether that's a good thing or not remains to be seen. There's always a chance that I'll walk in on some crazy naked yoga, or something equally scarring.

My grandmother is what some people might call eccentric, but I think she's just this side of bat-shit crazy. That's one reason I love her so much, though. She doesn't give a shit what anyone thinks, and she lives her life how she wants to live it. After so many years of Emilio slowly chipping away at my confidence, and stealing my happiness, I need someone like my grandmother to help me shake things up a bit, to help me get back to myself.

I don't think it would surprise anyone if I told them she's the one who helped me dye my hair green the first time. Her give-no-fucks attitude helped me realize it was something I could do, no matter what anyone else thought of it. So I did it, and I've had green hair ever since.

I grab the coffee I brought myself and walk the short path to Grandma's cute cottage. She lives in number five, right next door to her best friend. The two of them together are troublesome enough on their own, but when they get together with the rest of the residents of Peaceful Pines, crazy things happen.

"There you are, Flipper." My grandmother nicknamed me Flipper when my parents gave me the name Finley. Apparently, Flipper was a more acceptable nickname than Fin, even though it's clearly the more ridiculous of the two. "I was wondering if you'd stood me up for a little afternoon delight." Grandma stands on the front stoop of her cottage, waggling her eyebrows salaciously. "You know that I'm talking about dick, right?"

"Yes, Grandma. I know you mean dick. And no, that's not why I'm late. I stopped to get coffee so I have something to drink other than that tea' you keep trying to foist on me. I don't need whiskey this early in the day. What's Delores up to? I figured she'd be here. You two are almost never away from each other."

"That tea will put hair on your chest." She waves me inside. "Delores is off with her grandson today, shopping or something of the sort. That boy has more money than he knows what to do with, and he's not afraid to spend it on her. He's in a famous band, you know. You should find yourself one of those successful musicians. Maybe you could date Ryder?"

"I'm not really looking to date, Grandma." Besides, even if I wanted to date, I'd be more interested in someone like Travis.

He's been working at my place off and on for the last month or so, and it's taken all the willpower I have to stop myself from jumping him. It doesn't help that he usually shows up during the day before the kids are home from school. It's not as hard to stay away from him when the kids are there to act as a buffer, but when we're alone? Yikes. You could cut the sexual tension with a knife. "Plus, I think Emilio will be my last musician, successful or otherwise. They're too unreliable, always on the road, going where the shows are. I have three kids to think of. The last thing I need is to introduce another disappointment into their lives."

Grandma reaches over and pats me on the knee. "I always hated Emilio," she says. "He gives off such dirty little scumbag vibes."

I snort coffee out my nose, spilling it down the front of my t-shirt. Ugh. I *had* to wear white today. "Grandma, you never told me that."

"Well, I couldn't very well tell you on your wedding day, could I? And I wouldn't risk our relationship for anything. I figured I would stay quiet and let the marriage run its course." She leans back in her rocking chair. "Unless he'd been abusive. In that case, I'd have come running with my stun gun and a shovel. And Delores would come too, with her rope. She's getting pretty good at tying those fancy knots."

Delores and my grandma like to spend some of their time going to kink conventions where they purchase interesting items, like teacups with curse words on them, or take up interesting hobbies like Shibari, the art of Japanese rope bondage. I guess that's more eccentric than anything else.

"That's great. It's not quite the knitting and crochet that I'd expect ladies your age to take up, but it's similar, I suppose."

Grandma gets up and looks out the front window. "Bah, that stuff's for old people. We're not old, we're well seasoned." She walks to the door and opens it. "Hey, hot stuff. Get over here and show me that dick. I mean, come meet my granddaughter, Flipper. Ain't she a looker?"

"Grandma, what are you doing?" I ask in a harsh whisper. "I told you, I don't want to date anyone. And I'm covered in coffee. I can't meet someone looking like this."

"Oh, hush now. You're only saying hello to him, and besides, you look gorgeous. You can't date him until I see his dick, anyway. And let me tell you, he's one tough nut to crack. He has a death grip on that dick, so to speak." She's still laughing as Delores and her grandson walk in.

"I thought I told you to stop talking about my grandson's dick," Delores says to my grandma. "He won't show it to you. Let it go."

"How can I let it go when I haven't even had the chance to grab onto it yet? I just want to know what it looks like, for crying out loud. That's not a crime, is it?"

"No, it's not, Gladys. But the way you're always sexually harassing me is," the man says to Grandma, giving her a kiss on the cheek before walking over to me. "Hey," he says, holding out a hand. "I'm Ryder."

"Finley," I say, shaking his hand. "Not Flipper, no matter what my grandmother tries to tell you."

He laughs. "Yeah, I think both of our grandmothers are firmly in the 'not to be trusted' category. They get up to some interesting stuff around here. Have you witnessed any of the many activities that require bathing suits yet? Those are especially damaging to the psyche."

"Oh, nonsense," Delores says, playfully ruffling Ryder's hair. "You know you aspire to be me when you grow up."

"Sure, Gran," he says, ducking away from her hand. "Whatever you say. I'll agree with anything, as long as you don't do me like you did Hunter with those firecrackers. The scent of burning hair still lingers around Peaceful Pines' basketball courts."

"That's what that smell is," I say with a snap of my fingers. "I couldn't place it that day you were first showing me around, Grandma." I laugh.

"My brother still has only a few patches of hair growing on his body. There's a small patch on his right pec, and another on his left knee. It's hilarious."

"Hey now, we didn't do that on purpose. You know it's hard for me to mix explosives properly when I don't have my reading glasses on," Grandma says in her own defense. She waves a hand, changing the subject. "Let's forget all that and have a drink. Ryder, will you stay and have some tea?"

Ryder and I both shudder.

Ryder shakes his head and takes a step toward the door. "As much as I'd love to have a big cup of whiskey with you, Gladys, I need to get going. The guys are probably losing their shit because I've been skipping out on them so much."

"You're missing out, big guy. I got some new glassware to serve in. Each one has a good-looking beefcake on it, and when you fill it with cold liquid, he gets a gigantic boner. With veins and everything." My grandmother's face lights up like a kid at Christmas. "It's reverse shrinkage."

I can't hold my laughter, snorting coffee out of my nose, yet again, and this time Ryder comes to my aid, patting my back until I get the choking under control. He passes me a napkin from the coffee table and I wipe my face. I grab another napkin and pat my shirt down, trying to clean some of the mess.

"Grandma!" I scold her when I finally get myself together. "Again? I'm going to have to go home and change before I pick the kids up from school. The other moms at the after-school pickup are vicious. They gossip about me enough, like I need to give them another reason."

"They don't even know you. School hasn't been in long enough for anyone to form an opinion. It's only been a couple of days." Grandma reasons. "What could they possibly have to say about someone they just met?"

What don't they say? I've heard many things whispered behind my back, including words like divorced, cheating husband, those poor kids, free house, and green hair, amongst other, less flattering, descriptions of me. They all fit a certain mold, and I don't fit in with them. At all.

But the kids have been making friends. That's what matters.

"School started over a month ago. But it doesn't matter, Grandma. I'll deal with it." I stay out of their way as much as I can and leave it at that. "It's cliquey, like high school all over again. But it's nothing I can't handle." And one day, when I make some of my own friends, we'll go stand outside the school waiting for our kids and talk shit about them. Because I'm mature like that. Ha!

"Well, now that we have that under control, I'm actually leaving." Ryder gives a little wave. "Nice to meet you, Flipper," he says with a wink. "Bye Gladys, bye Gran. Try to stay out of trouble. Scratch that. Try not to get arrested. I know asking you to stay out of trouble is a lost cause."

After Ryder leaves, I get up too. "I need to get going, too. I want to check on the progress my handyman made today before I go get the kids."

"You'll have to bring us over when he's working one day," Grandma says, with Delores nodding in agreement. "We need to be sure he's up to our sexiness requirements."

I laugh. The last thing I need is for these two to come and give their opinion on Travis. "Oh, he's scorching hot alright. But the last thing I need is you two distracting him with dirty talk. Or propositioning him until he quits."

They give me a 'who me?' look of incredulity before bursting into laughter.

"Yeah, you're right," Delores says. "But make sure you invite us before he finishes up completely. All the hot young studs we know are friends with my grandsons, and I want to branch out. rockstars and tattoo artists are fine, but nothing beats a fine-ass blue-collar man who works with his hands and gets dirty for a living."

She's not wrong there. I picture Travis sweaty and covered in sawdust like he was when I left earlier today. I nearly convinced myself to skip visiting Grandma to stay home and help so I could watch him work, but you can only do that so many times before it gets creepy. And I'm pretty sure passed that number about three weeks ago.

"Okay," I say, gathering up my coffee and keys. "I promise you can come and ogle him when he's nearly finished. At least if you scare him away right at the end, I should be able to pick up the slack and finish myself."

"Oh, no," Grandma says, walking me to the door. "Don't finish yourself. You let that sexy man do that for you." She wiggles her eyebrows, letting me know her mind is back in the gutter. "The thing with men who are good with their hands is that they're really good with their hands. Know what I mean?"

I shake my head and step off her front stoop. "Yes, Grandma. I know what you mean." And I would give anything to never have to hear her say anything like that ever again. "See you soon. Bye, Delores."

The thing is, though, I think as I walk to my car, *Travis looks like he'd be fantastic with his hands.*

7

Sledgehammers and Sensitivity

Travis

THE THREE DONOVAN MEN, me, my brother, and my dad, are standing in the front yard of Finley's house discussing work that needs to be done.

"This porch needs to go," Dad says, pointing out some boards that have rotted away completely and others that are well on their way. "We don't want any of these kids to fall through if they accidentally step in the wrong spot. Halloween is right around the corner."

Shit. I forgot about Halloween. This neighborhood loves to go all out for it. "It's on my list," I tell Dad. "I'm working on getting the inside more livable first. It's like some of the previous tenants gouged out pieces of flooring on purpose. You're liable to get slivers if you walk around barefoot. Not the little kind that needs tweezers, either, but the big, nasty ones that require a visit to the doctor and some local anesthetic. And the spots that aren't full of slivers are covered in fifty-year-old shag carpet that's never seen a steam cleaner. I'm considering hiring a hazmat team to remove it."

"This is why you run out of every studio session like the devil himself is chasing you?" Johnny asks. "To come and do manual labor for a neighbor who thinks you're a handyman?"

I punch him in the arm. "Shut the fuck up," I whisper harshly. "If she finds out I'm in the band, she won't talk to me ever again. Something about her ex-husband chasing short skirts and fame. She hates musicians."

Johnny pretends he's offended. "Even me? But I'm such a sweetie." He laces his fingers under his chin and flutters his eyelashes at me. "I'm harmless."

"Yeah, sure. Whatever you say, man." I laugh. "As long as you're harmless without giving away my secret."

"What secret?" Becca, Johnny's friend, surprises me. "Can I be in on it? Is it a good one?"

Johnny turns to her with the sappiest look on his face to explain. How she can't tell he's completely in love with her is beyond me. It's obvious to literally everyone else who sees them together.

"Travis is letting Finley believe he's just a handyman—"

"—Hey!"

"Sorry, Dad," Johnny apologizes. Sometimes Dad can be a little sensitive when people act like the trades are less worthwhile careers than other options. "He's letting her believe he's a handyman because she hates musicians. She doesn't know he's in the band, and we can't tell her."

Becca raises an eyebrow at me, her judgment palpable in the air. "You honestly think lying to her about it is your best option? What are you going to do when she finds out you've been lying this whole time? It only takes her seeing one interview, or one slip of the tongue, one public appearance that she sees advertised before she realizes you're not who you say you are."

"I will tell her, but not yet. Her ex-husband has really messed with her head. He's not even successful, and he's been running around on her and letting her down for years. Let me prove that I'm reliable before I spring the whole 'surprise, I'm a famous musician' thing on her."

She gives me a look that says she thinks I'm full of shit, clueless, and stupid, but she nods. "Fine, I'll do what I can. But you better tell her soon. No one likes to be lied to."

I release a relieved breath. "Yes, I promise. I will tell her soon." I'm nearly done with all her renovations, and I figure that will be a good time to tell her. We've become better friends while I've been working at her place for the last couple of months, and she's become a fixture at my parents' house, too. It's like she's already part of our family. She won't be able to give all that up, will she?

"Back to the matter at hand," Dad says, stepping up to us. "I think you need to move the porch to the top of your list. It's almost Halloween and you know how this street gets. We don't want any injuries. Get some friends together and we can do it this weekend."

Johnny and Becca both laugh. Dad's never been impressed with the band or the guys in it. He'll call us all over to help with whatever because we're younger than he is and should know how to do hard work. Ask him to tell you how he had all five members of Sleeping Dogs, plus our head of security, Devon, replacing the toilets in his house a few years back. He loves that story.

"This is great. I'm calling the guys. They all need to get in on this. I'm going to make them do it." Johnny steps away and pulls out his phone, leaving Becca behind shaking her head. "Don't worry, I'll make sure they know about keeping your little secret."

"I can't wait to see how this turns out," Becca says, a glint in her eye. She's enjoying this.

"How what turns out?" Finley has forced her front door open and is carefully picking her steps as she walks across the rotting boards.

I definitely need to get that door done, too. But the porch needs to come first. Dad's right. The thought of Fin or any of the kids hurting themselves is twisting me up with guilt at having put it off for so long. I walk up the rickety steps to help Finley down. I'd rather I fall through than her any day.

"Dad pointed out that this porch needs to move up on the list of priorities," I tell her. "With Halloween coming, we need to make sure it's safe for not only you and your kids but also the neighborhood kids."

"I don't know if I'm able to do that yet," Finley says, chewing her thumbnail. "I'm burning through my savings pretty quickly while I finish up these courses for my real estate license. I don't have the budget for that size of a project right now."

"They're in." Johnny comes back as Finley confesses she doesn't have the money to finish the work. "Everyone will be here early tomorrow to help."

"Let me go get my measuring tape and I'll call in the order to the hardware store." Dad hustles back across the street to his place.

"Make sure they know I'll put it on my card when we pick it up," I yell to Dad before he makes it into his house. "And don't you dare try to put it on your account instead." Dad waves me off without a backward glance. I won't be surprised if I have to sneak in to pay off his account after this. He's not impressed with the band or our money.

"Travis," Finley says loudly. "I said I can't afford it right now."

I turn to face her, taking hold of her upper arms. "I should have insisted we do it first, Fin. It's not safe for you and the kids to be tiptoeing around the old boards every time you need to go anywhere. We can square up later."

"I already owe you so much. You've been working on my house for a while now. I can't believe that you had this much free time in your schedule." She takes a deep breath. "But you're right, it's not safe. I'll let you pay for this, but I'm not letting you do anything else in the house until I've paid everything I owe you. Got it?" She pokes me in the chest.

"Yes, ma'am," I say with a snicker. She's so much smaller than me it comes across as cute when she tries to look tough. "But you're getting the family discount. And the employee discount, too. I wouldn't be as far along as I am if it weren't for help from you and Braden."

Ever since that first day when Braden helped me finish my parents' fence, he's been helping every chance he gets. And he's gotten lots of chances since his father hasn't come for any of his scheduled weekend visits. I almost want to get my lawyers involved in Fin's case because there's no reason she needs to be sharing custody with such a deadbeat. As far as I can tell, he doesn't even pay any child support.

"I accept," she says, smiling up at me. "I don't know what I would have done without your family. You and your parents have been so welcoming to us ever since we moved in."

"Hey, what about me?" Johnny butts in. "I arranged for an entire crew of muscular guys and smart women to help with this build tomorrow. I'm basically a handyman now, too." A huge grin crosses his face as he looks at Fin for approval.

Fin laughs and pats Johnny on the cheek. "Yes, Johnny. You have also been a big help."

"I knew it. I'm indispensable. Just wait. Tomorrow I'm going to build this thing myself. It's going to be epic."

Becca shakes her head at him, a soundless snicker on her lips. "I'm going to see if your mom needs any help," she tells Johnny. "You hang out and congratulate yourself some more."

"You bet, babe." He waves her off and turns back to Finley. "Should we head over to Dad's tool shed and grab some sledgehammers? I don't know about you, but I'm feeling a little destructive today." He holds his elbow out, which she grabs with a laugh.

"That's the best idea I've heard all day," she says. "Can I imagine the boards are my ex, or would that be too violent?"

"*Au contraire, mon cher.* I think that's the exact right amount of violence for such an occasion." Johnny makes a little bow and holds his arm out for Fin to link hers through. "Let's go get the smashy-smash tools." If he weren't my brother, and if I weren't absolutely positive he's madly in love with Becca, I'd be forced to act on the rage that's suddenly coursing through my veins. But because I know, I'm able to stop myself. Barely.

I watch as they cross the street and walk around the side of my parents' house. Most dads would have their tools in the garage, but not mine. Oh no, when he retired, Dad had his garage converted into the ultimate beer den and moved his tools around back to a separate shed. He's such a lover of craft beers that he has multiple fridges running at different temperatures, so he always has his beer of choice available at the optimal temperature.

"He doesn't want to date my mom, does he?" Braden appears beside me, arms crossed, a look of concern on his face. "I don't think she needs to get caught up with another guy in a band. My Dad's bad enough."

I slap Braden on the shoulder, a friendly habit I've gotten into during the time he's been helping with the renovations on his family's house. "He's kind of in love with someone else already, kid. But if he were interested in your mom, I can promise he would treat her right. Johnny has been looking for his Princess Charming his whole life."

Not that I would let him anywhere near Fin. If anyone gets the chance to date her, it's going to be me. I don't think she's ready for that right now, though, anyway. She's still in the middle of a divorce. Not to mention the real estate license she's studying for while working full-time. And she's got three kids. No, it's best for me to keep my distance. Other than helping her with her renovations, that is. But that's not dating, so it's fine.

Right?

"As long as he keeps it friendly," Braden says, turning to look at me. "She'd be much better off with someone like you, anyway. At least you have an actual job. And you show up when you say you will."

Ouch. I knew I was lying to Fin, but I never figured the kids cared this much. Guilt stabs through my chest for lying to Braden now, too.

"I appreciate the vote of confidence, buddy. But who your mom dates, or if she dates at all, is her decision. I know you want to protect her, but she's a strong woman, and she'll make the right choice when the time comes."

He nods, looking off into the distance.

"Come on," I point him to the one board that's been replaced on the steps. "Have a seat and tell me what's really bugging you. It can't only be about whether or not your mom is dating."

I take a seat and he sits next to me. "My dad is supposed to pick us up tonight, but I'm pretty sure he's already canceled. I can tell when Mom looks at her phone if it's him or not by the sad look on her face. I know she's not sad he's gone, but she's sad for us kids. I don't really care. But I think Sarah and Austin do."

He's trying to be tough, and even though he says he doesn't care, I can tell that he does. What twelve-year-old kid wouldn't care if their dad suddenly decided everything else was more important than his own kids?

I take a deep breath. "I don't know your dad, so I couldn't tell you why he's acting the way he is. But I do know you, and you're a great kid. And I am damn proud to call you my friend, and occasional apprentice," I nudge him with my shoulder and he chuckles. "Your mom and my brother should be back any minute with sledgehammers. How do you feel about helping tear this porch apart? I hear smashing stuff is therapeutic."

Braden grins up at me. "Can I really smash it?"

I laugh. "Let me text them to make sure they grab some safety goggles while you put on your work boots. I'll double-check with your mom, but it should be okay, especially if you have some basic safety gear."

He turns to run into the house, remembering at the last second he needs to be careful where he steps. "Thanks, Travis," he says as he makes his way to the door. "You're the best. I wish my dad acted more like you."

Me too, kid. Me too.

8

Things are Getting Heated

Finley

"FLIPPER! IS THAT YOU? I didn't know you lived across from Mom and Pop Donovan." Ryder runs up and hugs me. "What a small world."

He looks around until he spots Travis coming from his parents' place. I've been sitting out on the temporary steps drinking my morning coffee, and Ryder takes a seat right next to me. Thank goodness for Mr. Donovan and his forethought with the steps. I'm glad he was thinking ahead because I certainly had no plan for how we were going to get into the house after we ripped down the porch.

Truthfully, I did very little work. Travis set Braden up with safety gear and my boy smashed boards to his heart's content. He's been feeling down since his dad left and I think this helped him work out a lot of his anger. Poor kid crashed last night and has been asleep for the last ten hours.

Hopefully, the extra rest will get rid of the surly preteen who has taken over my sweet son's body. I'm not ready for the teenage years yet. I still have days when I feel like I'm a teenager; I don't think I'm qualified to guide one into adulthood.

"Hey, Ryder," Travis says when he gets to us. "Thanks for coming. Did you meet Finley yet?"

Ryder throws an arm over my shoulder, pulling me in close. "Who? Oh, you mean Flipper, here? We're old friends. Members of the same club, in fact. Isn't that right, Flipper?"

I shove him off with a laugh. "I thought I told you not to call me that."

Travis looks back and forth between us curiously, no doubt trying to figure out how I know Ryder.

"Our grandmothers both live at the Peaceful Pines retirement community," I explain.

Ryder bursts out laughing as Travis narrows his eyes in confusion. Before he can ask what's so funny, another vehicle pulls up in front of the house. The doors all open at the same time and the strangest assortment of people I've ever seen comes pouring out.

One man is ridiculously tall and very well-muscled but in a Strongman competitor way, rather than a bodybuilder way. There's also a tiny pixie of a woman with short, messy hair and a huge smile, carrying a couple of takeout carafes. Another woman with a messy bun like mine, but dark blonde instead of dark green, follows the pixie woman, balancing boxes of what I really hope are donuts or pastries of some sort on one arm, holding them steady with her other arm, which is in a cast. Johnny and Becca come next, carrying cases of weird-looking beer, of course. Finally, after them, come the last two men, who I'm guessing are the remaining members of the band. One of them looks like he's about to practice yoga right in my front yard and his man-bun rivals my own messy bun for sheer volume. The other man, the one with short, dark hair and nearly as many tattoos as Johnny, runs up and takes the boxes from the woman with the messy bun, kissing her as he does so.

"Finley, these are my friends," Travis says before introducing everyone.

The huge guy, Devon, picks me up in an enormous hug, lifting me right off the ground. Suddenly, a very concerned Austin comes flying out of the house, jumping over the temporary stairs altogether, screeching to a stop right in front of Devon.

"Hey, you put my mom down right now, mister," he tells Devon, shaking his finger at him.

"And who are you, little man?" Devon asks Austin after setting me back on my feet. "I don't believe we've met yet." He sticks his giant hand out for a handshake. "I'm Devon. I'm good friends with Travis and his brother Johnny."

Austin puts his little hand into Devon's and gives it a firm shake. "I'm Austin," he says, giving Devon his best death glare. "And I'm making friends with the ghost that lives in my attic. So you better watch it." He jerks his thumb back at the house.

I snicker a little as Devon raises his eyebrows.

"Really? You have a ghost friend?" He sits on the ground right beside Austin. "That's so cool. How did you meet him? Was he here when you moved in, or did he come with you?"

Austin's face lights up, thrilled at the opportunity to talk to someone new about his favorite topic, ghosts. Devon nods along, letting Austin go on and on. He's the definition of a gentle giant. I leave them to it and walk up to where Travis is talking to the couple, Alex and Connor.

"So, Finley," Connor says when I join them. "How are you liking Westborough so far?"

"I love it," I tell him. "I lived here when I was younger, but I moved away for college and stayed away until recently."

"Oh? What brings you back?" Alex asks. She's wrapped her good arm so tightly around Connor, almost as though she's afraid to let him go. It's cute.

"Umm, divorce?" I chuckle nervously. I don't want to unload my baggage on a couple who is clearly in love, but she asked so...

"My soon-to-be ex-husband went through a midlife crisis and a wife and kids no longer held the same appeal for him."

"Fuck that guy. He sounds like a dickhead," Alex says. "How many kids do you have?"

"Three. Travis has been doing lots of work with my oldest, Braden. He's twelve. Together, they're getting through the list of renovations faster than I ever would have hoped. And Braden is learning so much. Sarah, my middle child, is ten. And the little guy over there with Devon is Austin, and he just turned seven." I look over at Austin and Devon and they're both lying in the grass, eyes closed, arms over their chests and tongues hanging out. "And it looks like he's teaching Devon how to play dead," I snort out a laugh. "Spooky shit fascinates Austin."

He must have heard me say his name because he comes running up to us now.

"Hey, Mom," he says, grabbing my hand. "This guy is great at playing dead. When we put my playroom in the attic, can he come over and help me find more ghost friends? He can pretend to be a corpse to attract the ghosts."

Everyone standing around us laughs. I shake my head and smile.

"Sure, buddy. If we can do a playroom up there, we'll talk about it then. Devon might be pretty busy by the time we can get around to it."

Devon rolls over and reaches out to give Austin a little fist bump. "If I'm in town, I'll be here."

"You'll have to be super extra brave, Austin," the pixie woman, Xena, offers. "Tiny Dancer is a big scaredy-cat. If you two actually find a ghost, he'll probably run away screaming."

"Alright, Princess. We don't need to go around telling everyone that name."

"Oh, fine. I'll stop. You big baby."

Devon turns back to Austin and starts talking to him about scary movies. As soon as he turns his back, Xena mouths the words "tiny dancer" to the rest of us and we all chuckle.

"I saw that," Devon says before continuing his conversation with Austin. "Come on, kid. Let's go over here and let these boring grown-ups get to work building."

Xena shakes her head and laughs.

"Let's finish our coffee and by then we should be able to get started," Travis says. "Dad is on his way back from the hardware store with our lumber order." He pulls a piece of paper from his pocket and unfolds it. "This is the plan that I drew up, based on what we tore down yesterday. Have a look." He passes it to Connor.

I had a look at it last night. It's the same as the porch I had before, but not falling apart. It's perfect. I'm still not pleased that Travis is paying for it right now, though. I hate the thought of owing him money. I hate the thought of owing anyone money.

After everyone has a look at the plan, Travis takes the guys across the street to get extra tools from his dad's place. He already set up the saws and stuff that we'll need, but he said he wanted extras so that anyone who wanted to help could.

While Travis is gone, Mr. Donovan backs up into the driveway in Travis's truck. The box is loaded with wood, cement blocks, and assorted other building materials, including some very cool spindles for the railing. I was planning on the very basics, but I'm glad he chose these instead. They're much nicer than what I would have picked for myself.

"Hey there, Finley," Mr. Donovan says as he hops out of the truck. "Where did everyone go?"

"They're at your place grabbing some extra tools. I wish I had mine here, but my ex fought to keep them for some stupid reason. He doesn't even know how to use them."

He laughs. "He probably wanted to hold on to a reason to get you back. If he has something that important to you, maybe he thinks you'd be willing to go back to him?"

"Fat chance of that happening. I refuse to look the other way while he experiments with his mid-life crisis band and hooks up with dirty tramps in all the surrounding towns."

He walks over and pulls me into a giant bear hug. I haven't had a hug like this in years and I melt into it. Devon's and Ryder's hugs were nice, but this is a world-class dad hug, and there's something special about dad hugs.

"You deserve a good man, Finley, my dear. And your kids deserve a good father. But remember, not every musician is like your ex."

I can only nod. I'm sure he believes that, considering his own son is a musician. Johnny doesn't seem like he'd be one to cheat and lie to his family, but you never really know, do you? I thought Emilio was devoted to me and our family but then he turned thirty and BAM! Suddenly he's reliving his youth, joining a band, traveling to whatever dive bars will let them play, and hooking up with the kinds of women who hook up with any musician they can get their hands on.

"Maybe Travis could go with you to get your tools back?" Mr. Donovan has started unloading the truck, so I move to help him. "He can be very persuasive when he needs to be. Agnes and I will watch the kids for you, in case things get heated."

I feel my face flush. He didn't mean if things get heated between me and Travis, but that's where my mind went immediately. I can picture us driving in his truck, on the way to get my tools when the sexual tension becomes too much to bear, and he pulls over, jumps out and pulls me out of the truck, rips down my pants, and takes me right there, bent over the seat of his truck on the side of the ro—

"You okay, Fin? Do you need some water? You look flushed." Travis is suddenly in front of me, the back of his hand pressed to my forehead. "You don't really have to help today. There are more than enough people here to get this done without you. Maybe you should take a nap if you're not feeling well?"

If only he knew what was really going through my mind right now.

"Oh, no. I'm fine, Travis, really. I drank my coffee too fast, and it warmed me up too quickly." I take off the flannel I'm wearing and tie it around my waist, leaving me in a man's undershirt and jeans. "There, no problem. I'll cool off in no time."

I busy myself by walking into the house, intent on yelling for Braden to wake up and come help, but he surprises me by already being at the bottom of the stairs. He's dressed in his work clothes and looks excited.

"Is Travis here? Can we start? I can't wait to help build the new porch," Braden gushes.

I grab him by the shoulders and smother him in hugs and kisses.

"Ew, Mom." He pushes me, laughing. "Get off. Gross."

"I am so proud of you, Braden," I tell him. "You have been such a big help since we moved here. Not only the help you've been to Travis, either. You've been a big help to me, too." The split between his father and me has been hard on him, but I think it's the move that's really bothering him. Twelve-year-olds can be set in their ways, and Braden really liked his old school and his old friends.

His face turns red, and he looks down at his feet. "Thanks, Mom."

"Now let's get out there and get this thing built. Maybe when it's done, you can carve your initials with someone special's inside a nice big heart?" I tease, putting my arm over his shoulder. "But for now, come meet Travis's friends and the people who will be helping. Your brother has already claimed the big guy. Oh, and when this is all done, I'll need you to help me plan our Halloween decorations. Apparently Halloween is a pretty big deal in this neighborhood and we have nothing to decorate with."

"We need all new decorations, don't we?" Braden asks with a frown. "Everything is still in the old house, isn't it?"

"Don't worry about that, buddy. We'll have a ton of fun shopping for new decorations." When I moved the kids out of the house I shared with Emilio, I only brought the most important things. "Now let's get building. I don't want to leave them without supervision for too long. You and I need to make sure they're building this porch up to our standards."

Braden chuckles and heads down the stairs in front of me. I stop and look out at the people gathered in my yard. Emilio never encouraged a lot of family interaction, and I don't have much extended family, so this is different for me. But I love the feeling of community this weird group of rockstars is giving me.

Funny how a musician ruined my life and now it's a group of them, plus Travis and a few others, who are helping me to build a better, stronger one.

9

That's How I Kiss My Neighbor

Travis

"Again? The kids miss you, Emilio. Is it the drive that's stopping you from seeing them? You know I can bring them to you, right?"

Finley is pacing the driveway. We'd finished saying bye to my friends, thanking them for their help, when her phone rang and she excused herself to answer it. From the sounds of her side of the conversation, it's her ex-husband, and he's canceling on the kids. Again.

"Hey, Braden, buddy. Why don't you run in and grab a shower? You worked harder today than the rest of us combined." I pat him on the shoulder to get his attention. He's focused on his mom on the phone and it's not something he needs to hear again. "You think it would be okay with your mom if I ordered pizza for dinner?" I'd cook something for them if not for two things. Number one: I am filthy from working all day. And number two: I hate cooking and I suck at it. I don't want to risk poisoning her family after they worked so hard today.

He shakes himself and turns to me. "Yeah, pizza is fine. I'm going inside."

I take a few steps closer to Finley, not wanting to intrude, but unable to stop myself from being near in case she needs me.

How can that guy not want to spend time with his kids? I've only spent a little time with them and they're awesome. Braden has grown so much during the last couple of months helping me, both mentally and physically. He works hard, he's clever, and he doesn't give up. What kind of father doesn't want to know a kid like that? Or Sarah? She's unbelievably smart and has this dry sense of humor that takes a minute to settle in, but once it hits you, you can't help but laugh. Her delivery is flawless. And Austin is the coolest little kid. His obsession with death and spooky shit sounds weird, but when he talks about it, he makes it sound cute and fun rather than creepy.

This man had the perfect family, and he walked away. And for what? Smoky bars and desperate women? No matter how I try, I can't see myself or the rest of the guys in Sleeping Dogs throwing away an entire family for that. And I don't think that's because we've been doing it for so long. I know I wouldn't have thrown Fin away, even at the beginning of our career, back when I was wild and crazy.

"They miss you."

...

"Yes, they do. They haven't seen you in months. You've canceled on them pretty much every weekend since I moved back to Westborough."

...

"No, this isn't about me anymore. That ship has sailed. I'm tired of trying to explain to three upset children why their dad isn't coming again. And don't give me that *the band needs me* bullshit. I had the members of a band here today, and every one of them was helping me to build a new porch on my house."

She's not wrong about that. She just doesn't know that I'm also in the band. Yet. I plan to tell her soon. But she knows that all of Sleeping Dogs, plus friends and girlfriends, were here today.

"No, I don't know how successful they are. But I'm willing to bet that it's a lot more successful than you."

I can guarantee that we're more successful than he is.

"Whatever, Emilio. Do you want me to bring the kids tonight or not?"

...

"Yeah, fine. I'm sure I'll be hearing from you again in two weeks, then."

I watch as Finley stabs at her phone with her finger and lets out a strangled yell. "Gah! That asshole."

I walk all the way over and wrap my arms around her. She stiffens for a moment and then sinks into the hug, wrapping her arms around my waist and resting her head on my chest. She's still in her tank top and I took my shirt off a while ago so when we finally release the hug, it's with more of a sticky, peeling apart rather than a simple release. We both laugh.

"Thanks," Fin says, with a shuddering sigh. "I suppose we should shower before we attempt another hug, though."

An image of Finley in the shower with me sears through my brain, sending a rush of blood to my dick.

"I don't know," I say, my voice a full octave lower than usual, with a rawness it doesn't normally possess. "I kind of like having my arms around you while we're both sweaty. Of course, showering with you sounds good, too."

I see her swallow and lick her lips, her pink tongue poking out ever so slightly, moistening the soft skin. Before I can think it through, I pull her against me again, one hand in her hair and the other on her hip, and I lower my lips to hers. I kiss her, brushing her lips with my own, breathing her in. It feels so fucking right. Like everything in my life has been leading to this exact moment. I stop myself before I get too carried away and rest my forehead against hers.

"Go shower," I whisper through rapid breaths. "Pizza will be here soon. Is it... is it okay if I come back for dinner with you guys?"

She nods, a dazed look on her face as she steps back out of my arms.

"I'll bring the kids back with me when I'm showered and changed." I grin and redirect her focus. "I can't wait to see what they've been up to while we've been building."

She laughs. "If I know Austin, I'm going to guess he's planned elaborate funerals for anyone who would let him. Either that or he made skeletons out of whatever building materials your mom had available."

Finley turns and runs up her new stairs, taking a moment to run her hand along the railing. I still need to paint it for her, but at least it's now fully functional for Halloween. Your house is supposed to look scary for Halloween, not actually be scary.

I grab the last of the tools that need to go back to Dad's tool shed and head across the street. This really is a nice, quiet neighborhood. I'm not sure what sort of neighborhood Fin lived in before, but she's in a great spot now.

"Looks good, son," Dad says. He's standing on the front step in his sock feet, holding one of his favorite craft beers. "It's a real nice thing you're doing for that young woman."

I rub the back of my neck before looking at him. "Yeah, well. She's got a lot on her plate right now. I'm being neighborly. Her real estate exam is coming up, they're in a new town, and her ex keeps ditching the kids. I want to help."

Dad gives me a knowing look. "Oh, yeah. Sure, sure," he says with an exaggerated nod. "That's exactly how I kiss my neighbors when I want to be neighborly, too," he adds with a chuckle. "Old Mr. Anderson down the street was particularly appreciative when it was his turn to receive one of those smackers from me, let me tell you. He said he especially liked the feel of my mustache." Dad laughs as he twirls the ends of his admittedly very nice mustache.

I groan and roll my eyes. "Dad. I'm a little too old for you to be teasing me about a girl, don't you think?" I didn't think he was watching or I might have reconsidered that kiss. Then again, I didn't really think before I did it, so maybe not.

Fuck it, I don't regret it. It felt right. No, it felt more than right. It felt perfect.

"Oh, you're never too old for teasing, kiddo." Dad laughs at me, then smacks me on the arm. "Now get in there and shower the stink off you. I don't know how Fin lets you get close when you smell like that. Hooowhee"—He waves his hand in front of his nose—"she must really like you to put up with that stench."

I chuckle and shake my head to myself, leaving dad on the step while I head into the house. I find Sarah and Austin at the kitchen table with my mom, and they're decorating cookies. There's an abundance of black, white, green, purple, orange, and red icing all over the table.

"What are you guys up to here?"

"Hey, Travis," Austin says, grabbing my hand with his little sticky one. "I made a crime scene. Look." He points down to a very gory-looking crime scene, complete with gingerbread men murder victims, ghost policemen, and zombie bystanders, and a LOT of red icing for blood. "This guy"—he points to one victim —"attacked all these other guys with a machete. And then the ghost police had to shoot him. And the zombies are waiting to eat their brains."

I look up at my mom, who's sitting across the table looking both horrified and incredibly amused, a nervous giggle trying to escape her lips. "He has very particular tastes, this one." She shrugs.

"I made normal Halloween cookies," Sarah says, showing me her collection of decorated cookies. "With a lot less blood than Austin used, too."

"We had to make that up special, didn't we, Austin?" Mom says as she squeezes icing onto a bat-shaped cookie on her side of the table. "I don't normally make red icing for Halloween cookies, but Austin informed me we absolutely needed it."

"I can see why," I say with a laugh.

"Did you guys finish the porch?" Sarah asks.

"We did. I'm going to have a quick shower and change my clothes, and then I'll take you guys back over for pizza. Sound good?"

Sarah's face drops. She knows her dad was supposed to be coming today. Out of necessity, Finley stopped telling Austin about the visits in advance. He was getting too upset when Emilio wouldn't show up. But Sarah knew she was supposed to see him today, and I can tell from the look on her face that she's disappointed.

One more reason for me to hate that Emilio fucker.

"That will give us enough time to get some of this mess cleaned up, right kids?" Mom stands up and starts collecting ingredients from the table. "We'll pack up your cookies to bring home and share with your mom and Braden. And I'll save the rest of these for us to decorate on another day."

Mom has a way with kids, probably from having raised seven of her own. Kids rarely, if ever, argue with her. Austin and Sarah are no different, both of them jumping up immediately to help clean.

"Yes, Nana," they say in unison.

I raise my eyebrows at Mom, questioning their use of the name Nana. She shrugs in response. I guess the kids got some extra grandparents out of moving to this neighborhood, too.

And my mom would never complain about having extra grandchildren. Nothing makes her happier than spoiling them all rotten and then sending them home.

Now I just need to figure out how to tell Finley that I'm a musician like her ex-husband, but that I'm also nothing like him at all. Then she and her kids can be a permanent fixture in our family. In our lives. In my life.

Yeah, this shouldn't be difficult at all.

Right.

10

Crime Scenes and Kisses

Finley

"AND THIS IS THE guy who had the machete, and these are the cops who shot him, and these are all the zombies that are waiting to eat everyone's brains."

Austin started explaining his cookie massacre creation as soon as he walked into the house, with Sarah and Travis following not far behind. Sarah's cookies are a little more traditional, which is exactly what I would expect from her. She has a great imagination, but she shies away from spooky stuff. Austin goes over the top with it, as he is proving right now.

"And Nana didn't have any red icing made, but I said 'Nana, I need red for blood'. Then she made some. Because I needed lots of blood."

I look up at Travis and he mouths, "Is that okay?" at me. "If it's okay with your mom" I mouth back. He breaks into a huge grin and nods.

"My mom loves kids, and would make every kid she met her grandchild if there were any way she could actually get away with it."

"That's perfect." I stifle a yawn while setting the table with paper plates I keep for exactly this kind of day. I showered and got dressed as quickly as I could, but after a day of hard work like today, I'm exhausted and even a shower doesn't wake me up. I stretch and wince at a twinge of pain in my lower back. "I need some ibuprofen before my muscles get too sore."

"You got a couple to spare?" Travis asks. "It's been a while since I've done this much manual labor."

That seems like a strange thing for a handyman to say, but maybe he focuses on the hiring of crews and supervising job sites, rather than getting too involved in the day-to-day. Hell, he's probably more of a general contractor than a regular handyman. I suppose I'm really lucky he's been doing all this work around here for me.

"I got you covered." I go to the cabinet in the kitchen and get the bottle out, shaking out pills for the two of us. "Nothing says romance like sharing anti-inflammatory medication."

Travis laughs. "Honestly, I'd rather share ibuprofen and pizza on paper plates with you than go on any date I've ever been on."

A smile creeps up on my face and butterflies hit my stomach. I don't know what's happening with me and Travis, but between that almost kiss the day that I met him and the actual kiss today, I am feeling something. It doesn't hurt that he is so cute, not to mention built like someone who works hard for a living. Every time he moves, my eyes get caught on his flexing muscles. It's sexy in such a subtle way. Drives me crazy every time.

Thankfully, a knock on the door gets my mind off that track before I get too hot and bothered. Travis walks over to answer before I have the chance.

"You could have let me get the pizza," I say, giving him a dirty look when he walks back with the pizzas. "It's the least I can do after you bought all the materials and provided all the labor for building the porch today."

"Don't worry about it," he says, setting the boxes down on the table and turning to me. "It needed to be done, so we got it done. It wasn't that expensive, anyway. And everyone who came today needed the exercise. Except for Aiden. He spends hours every day playing the drums. That guy burns so many calories that his body is basically a furnace. If he ever meets someone who gets him out of his own head long enough to get into a relationship, her body better run really cold or she'll melt from his body heat."

Ugh. I wish I were running cold right now. Ever since that kiss, my skin has been on fire. I take a deep, shuddering breath and force those thoughts from my mind. *Focus, Finley. Feed your kids.*

I pull out slices of pizza for my kids and yell for them to come and get it because I run a classy household like that. They come running and I hand them their plates, letting them go to the living room to watch TV while they eat. It's not something we normally do, but we're all tired and need to relax tonight.

Plus, I really want to talk to Travis alone for a bit about something that isn't renovation related. I feel like I might be starting to have feelings for him, but I know so little about him that there's no way that makes sense. Other than what he looks like, where his parents live, and what he does for a living, the man is a complete mystery to me. A mystery in a sexy-as-hell package.

I flop down into one of the cushioned, upholstered chairs that serve as my dining chairs and point Travis to another. I think I finish an entire piece of pizza before he takes the two steps needed to make it to the chair and sit.

"I'm starving," I say, immediately grabbing another piece from the box closest to me and taking a huge bite. "Construction went faster than I expected it to, but it was still a lot of work."

"Same." Travis shoves a piece of pizza in his mouth, downing half of it in one bite. "We didn't even stop for lunch, did we?"

"I think your mom came over and got Braden for lunch, but the rest of us worked straight through. Thank you again for getting everyone here to help. And for lending me your parents as surrogate grandparents for my kids. My parents are still working a lot and can't get here as often as they'd like and Emilio's parents can't be bothered to reach out, not that they ever really did. The kids have lost not only their dad but also a set of grandparents." I get up and go to the fridge. "Beer?"

"Sure, thanks."

"It's not fancy like your dad's, so you know." I twist the top off the bottle and set it on the table in front of him. "I'm not that sophisticated, I guess."

Travis laughs. "Me neither," he says. "Regular domestic beer is fine for me. It's Johnny and my dad who really love the different craft beers. And Becca, oddly enough. Hopefully, Johnny locks her down soon. He's so in love with her. He has this bad habit of falling in love with every girl he dates, but I'm pretty sure Becca is the real thing. He's never been like this with anyone else."

"It's cool that they're both interested in craft beer. Did one of them get the other into it?"

"No. They met a couple of months ago after our—after the band's last show of the tour. He's been in love since he met her. And she happens to also like craft beer and have tattoos over most of her body like him. He did another tattoo for her recently, actually."

I wipe my mouth with a napkin, finally full after three pieces and a beer. I shouldn't have drank the beer so fast. Then I could have had another piece of pizza, but my thirst got the better of me.

"Johnny did the tattoo, like did the artwork on her? Or he paid for it?"

"He did it. He apprenticed before the band took off. Since then, he volunteers his time and tattoos over the scars of mastectomy patients. It's something he's been passionate about ever since our mom and sister both had double mastectomies because of breast cancer. They were his first mastectomy patient tattoos."

"That's amazing. Being talented in both music and art is pretty impressive." I feel my eyes widen as I say it. "Not that what you do isn't impressive. I mean that it's not often you meet someone who is that good at both music and art."

He laughs. "I understand. Don't worry about it. Johnny is a bit of an odd guy. Would I lose you forever if I told you he's also an excellent baker?"

"Oh, shit. Now that's husband material, right there. Becca is a lucky lady."

"He is a bit of a romantic. I'm sure he'll make someone a wonderful husband. He's also pretty immature, though." A hint of something like jealousy creeps into Travis's voice. "Whoever he marries will have to keep an eye on him constantly or he'll get himself into trouble."

"Hmmm, I'll have to pass, then. I have enough kids, thanks. I don't need another one. Especially not one disguised as a fully grown man."

Almost as if he heard the complaint I was only hinting at, Travis stands up and starts cleaning up the mess from the pizza. He even pokes his head into the living room to ask the kids if they want more pizza before he puts it away. In the past, with Emilio, if I didn't put the leftovers away, they would stay out all night. I can't tell you how many leftovers we wasted on days when my mom brain didn't have room for silly things like remembering to put the food away. It's been so long since anyone helped me without endless nagging beforehand, I almost forgot what it felt like.

"So, what are your plans for tomorrow?" Travis asks, taking a seat opposite me. "My dad offered his babysitting services again.

We were thinking maybe you and I could get your tools back for you. If you still want them?"

"Yes!" I yell, before cringing and adding, more quietly, "Yes, I would love that. Your dad mentioned that to me earlier. Emilio has no need for those tools. He's keeping them out of spite."

"Will we need any extra backup or...?"

"What do you mean, *backup*?"

Travis chuckles at my scrunched-up face. "Will he try to stop us from taking your tools? Should I ask one of the other guys to come with us? I can probably get Devon to come."

"Oh." Shit. I hadn't even thought of that. "I'm not sure. I don't think he would try anything, but then I never thought he'd do half the things he's done the last few years. If he's up for it, maybe it wouldn't be a bad idea to bring Devon. I don't want to inconvenience you guys, though. I feel bad enough having you come with me. What if the band needs him for something?"

"Nah," Travis shakes his head, smiling. "The guys are in the studio these days. They're acting like they're on vacation, though. Ever since Connor found Alex again, he hasn't been able to concentrate on the music for very long. Especially since she broke her hand protecting him from a would-be rapist. He wants to be there to do everything for her. Even if she doesn't want his help."

Alex had told me a shortened version of the attack on Connor when I'd asked about her cast earlier today. Apparently, a stalker drugged Connor and got him alone. She was trying to undress him when Alex stormed in, ripped her off of Connor's bed, and beat the shit out of her. Her grandfather owns a gym, and she's learned a bunch of different fighting techniques over the years and they really came in handy that night. She stopped the attack, but she broke her hand while doing it. Hence the cast.

"And Johnny will probably do something with Becca. It wouldn't surprise me if they end up over at my parents' place.

Becca likes to talk to my dad about their mutual beer obsession, and Johnny takes his role as the favorite uncle seriously."

Travis pulls out his phone and types something.

"There," he says, putting the phone on the table. "We'll see if Devon wants to come. If he's not busy, I'm sure he'll want to. He loves putting the fear of god into people."

His phone buzzes with a notification. Travis looks at the screen and smiles. He holds it up for me to see.

```
Travis- Want to come with us
to get Fin's tools from her
ex tomorrow? She's not sure if
he'll be a dick about it or not.
```

```
Devon- Hell yes, I want to come.
I hope he tries something. This
is going to be fun.
```

I snort out a laugh and pass his phone back. "I guess we're taking a road trip to get my tools. I almost hope Emilio does something, if only so I can see the look on Devon's face."

Travis laughs. "He's like a kid on Christmas when he kicks someone's ass. On such a huge guy, a grin like that looks evil. It's awesome."

Just then, Austin stumbles into the room, rubbing his eyes. I look at the time and see that it's well past his bedtime.

"I'm tired, Mom," he says, climbing up into my lap. "Is it bedtime?"

"Yeah, baby. It's past bedtime. Go brush your teeth and get your jammies on. I'll come to tuck you in shortly."

He jumps off my lap and takes a step toward Travis. "Goodnight, Travis." Travis looks at me with wide eyes when Austin leans in and hugs his arm. "See you in the morning."

Travis and I stand up at the same time as Austin runs out of the room.

"I guess I better go," he says. "I need to get a good night's sleep if we're going to be confronting your ex tomorrow."

He steps into me, his hands cupping my face. He brushes his lips against mine in the barest whisper of a kiss. A shock of tingles shoots from my lips down to my belly. I barely stop myself from grabbing him and shoving my tongue down his throat. The only thing keeping this kiss PG is the thought of my kids in the other room. He presses his lips against mine, and then against my forehead, before letting me go.

"I'll see you tomorrow," he says.

I follow him to the door and out onto the porch. He hops into his truck and I wave as he drives away. My lips still tingle from his kiss as I walk back into the house with a stupid smile on my face.

Tomorrow can't come soon enough.

11

Tool Retrieval and Special Skills

Travis

"So, DID YOUR EX keep your old place?"

I picked Finley up five minutes ago, and other than a quick hello neither of us has said a thing. We've spent some time together while renovating her current house, but we haven't had a lot of time to talk, so I'm hoping this little road trip to pick up her tools will give us a chance to get to know each other better.

Because I can't think of anything I'd like more than getting to know her better.

I'm not sure how well that plan is going to work, though, considering we're on our way to pick up Devon right now, but I'm going to give it my best shot. Maybe if she gets to know me, she won't be as upset when I finally get around to telling her I'm in the band, too.

At least I hope she won't be upset.

"He did. Luckily, my name was never on it. He bought it before we got married, and he owns it outright."

"And you didn't want to fight for it?" I've wondered about this since we met. Why did she and the kids need to move? Her idiot ex-husband should have moved so the kids could keep their home.

"Nah. I want nothing else from him. All I want is for him to see the kids when he says he will. If he could do that with any consistency, then things would be fine."

I keep my eyes on the road, even though what I really want is to look into Fin's eyes and see how she actually feels about the situation. I've never been through a divorce, but I imagine it would be difficult to let go of someone you expected to spend the rest of your life with.

"He had a hard time keeping up with his visits, even when we still lived in the same town, so it shouldn't surprise me that he doesn't follow through with them now that we're in Westborough. He won't give up any of his shows," she says, finger-quoting "shows'. "He thinks if the kids want to see him so badly that I should drive them to wherever he's playing and they can watch him on stage. Because dragging three kids to a smoky bar to watch while their dad plays shitty music and picks up trashy women is exactly what I want to be doing with my weekends. Not to mention, it's not really the sort of family time the kids deserve to have with their dad."

The more Fin tells me about this guy, the more I hate him.

I mean, I get it. I've been there. Playing shitty bars every weekend, hoping you make enough to cover the cost of travel, partying like you've made it when you're nowhere near the big time.

But I was much younger when I did that. I didn't have a wife and kids relying on me when I was driving in a shitty old van with my friends, playing at any venue that would take us, and sleeping on people's couches anywhere we could. Hell, picking up chicks was a way to get a soft bed and a hot shower, with the added bonus of getting off. But again, I was in my late teens and early twenties. That's the stuff guys that age get up to. I couldn't imagine trying to do it all over again now.

I would never betray someone I'd promised to be faithful to. Nor would I turn my back on my kids for the kind of cheap thrills that this guy is chasing. And there's no way anyone he's hooking up with has anything on Fin.

"Do you still have a key?" I ask after a long silence. "Or do we have to break in and hope the neighbors don't call the cops on us? Should I have brought a ski mask?"

She laughs. "No, I still have a key. We probably won't get arrested today. Just in case, though, your brother has no issues bailing us out, right?"

"I have him on speed dial," I tell her. "He owes me many favors, so bailing us out of jail won't be a problem for him."

"Perfect." She picks up her phone from the console and frowns at it. She pushes a button and waits a few moments before typing out a message.

One thing I've noticed about Fin is that she rarely carries a purse. She only ever has her phone and a few cards with her. I don't imagine there are too many places to hang a purse at a construction site, anyway. Since she's been working doing home remodeling with her dad, it makes sense that she wouldn't bother to carry a purse.

"My dad is going to meet us at the house," she says, putting her phone down again. "He thinks Emilio is going to cause a problem."

"Probably not a bad idea," I say. "Even if we are picking up Devon, it could be good for your dad to be there, too. Besides," I say, turning into the parking lot of Devon's building. "I'm sure it has more to do with him wanting to see you than anything else."

"Yeah, I'm sure that's part of it. But I'm also pretty sure he'd love an opportunity to punch Emilio in the face for what he's done to me and the kids."

He and I both. Emilio could do with more than one punch to the face, I'm sure, so I'm not worried about having to share the privilege with Fin's dad. There's more than enough asshole ex to go around.

I pull into a parking spot and text Devon to let him know we're here.

"Well, I'll hold him down if your dad wants to get in a few good shots," I say with a laugh. "From the sounds of it, I wouldn't put it past your ex to try taking some dirty shots at your dad. No man needs his junk kicked for protecting his daughter and his grandkids."

Devon's enormous frame comes ambling out of the building. He's wearing clothes I recognize as his gym gear. His joggers are stretched to their limit across his massive thighs and his t-shirt isn't faring much better. He should probably get some of his clothes custom-made, but he refuses to spend that kind of money on anything but the suits he wears for work. Everything else is strictly utilitarian and off-the-rack, and today is no exception.

"Holy shit," Fin says, her mouth hanging open. "Is he bigger than he was yesterday? Did he grow overnight? That's not possible, is it?"

I glare out the windshield at Devon strolling along, a huge grin spread across his lips. "Devon has the unique ability to make himself appear larger, and more intimidating when it suits him. I think he's showing off right now." And he better fucking stop if he knows what's good for him. Fin's mine.

Or... Well. she's not mine, per se. But I would like her to be. Maybe? I'm interested in exploring the possibility, anyway. And the last thing I need is Devon's huge ass coming along and fucking it all up before anything can start.

"Hey guys," he says, folding himself into the back seat of my truck, directing his casual grin toward Fin after shooting me a wink. Luckily for him, I have the full crew cab, or there'd be no way he could fit back there. As it is, he takes up two-thirds of the bench seat and is blocking out most of the back window. "Fine day for some equipment retrieval, wouldn't you say?"

"Hi, Devon. Nice to see you again. Thanks for agreeing to do this with us." Fin turns around in her seat and sees him hunched, legs spread, so he can fit behind the front seats. "Oh my god. You don't fit there at all. Here, switch with me." She opens the door and gets out, pulling open the back door and motioning for Devon to get out. "Come on, I'm not making you sit back there. It might be less than an hour's drive, but it's long enough that you'll be all cramped up by the time we get there."

Devon opens his mouth to argue, but Fin levels him with a mom look fierce enough to rival even my mom's. And if there's one thing I learned from having a tough mother, it's don't mess with a mom once she's given you that look. Based on how quickly Devon scrambles out of the back seat, it looks like that's a lesson he learned from his mom as well.

Fin climbs into the back seat, sitting in the middle spot. She buckles up and leans back, crossing her arms over her chest, pushing her breasts up so the swells breach the low neck of the t-shirt she's wearing. I swallow hard and Devon clears his throat, getting my attention before Fin notices that I'm staring at her in the rear-view mirror.

"Well, should we get this show on the road?" Devon reaches over to fiddle with the stereo. "Let's get some road music going up in this bitch."

Devon connects his phone to the Bluetooth in my truck, turning on some bluesy rock. I take longer than I care to admit to catch on that it's my brother singing.

"That's Johnny," I blurt, half-surprised. "Where'd you get this?"

"He and Aiden have been messing around a bit. Aiden recorded this at his place a couple of weeks ago. What do you think, Fin?" Devon spins in his seat to look at her. "Johnny's voice is only moderately awful, right?"

She leans forward in her seat, listening intently. "I like it. A lot. Reminds me of something, but I can't put my finger on it. One of those two-man dirty-rock groups that seem to be all over the place right now, but different. Better."

Even I didn't know they were making music like this. Does this mean that they're thinking of going in a different direction? Leaving Sleeping Dogs? If someone else leaves the band, does that mean I'd be off the hook? I don't like the thought of that as much as I thought I would, which is interesting. Maybe I really do still love it.

"Did Aiden give it to you?"

"Nah." Devon grins. "I stole it from his place last time I was there."

I shake my head and grin. Aiden gave us all keys back when we used to rehearse in his garage and he's never taken them back. I haven't used mine in recent years but I know Johnny and Devon still do when the occasion calls for it. Or, apparently, when they feel like stealing something.

"Is that a normal thing?" Finley asks. "Do guys in the band normally do extra stuff on their own? Or are they working stuff out before they bring it to the rest of them?"

"This is nothing like Sleeping Dogs has ever put out before," I explain, carefully avoiding any mention of my involvement in the band. "I'm not sure their fans would be too receptive if their next album had this kind of sound."

The trouble with some fans is that they want you to always put out the same music that made them fall in love you with in the first place. Which is fair, but it is also boring as shit for those of us making the music. We want to grow, change, and explore our sound, and they want us to put out essentially the same songs, album after album, with little to no discernible change. It's frustrating. Makes you feel like you're stagnating. Makes it easier to hate what you're doing.

"I think they're doing it for fun," Devon adds. "They love to play, and they like to keep their skills sharp by changing things up. Aiden practices for hours every day. If he only played one style of music, he'd go crazy. Same for Johnny. He's such a creative guy that he needs to express himself through different styles of music and art. And baking. No one makes better cookies than Johnny."

"Not even Alex?"

"Nope, not even Alex," I say with a smile. "Not that she's been able to do much baking with her arm in that cast. Maybe she'll surge up and take his master baker title from him when she's back in full health. But even if her cookies are better, Johnny won't stop baking. It's the way he relieves stress."

"That's... surprisingly wholesome," Fin says with a snicker.

"My mom got him into it when he was a kid. He used to pull pranks on our sisters and Mom was scared they would retaliate and he'd get hurt." I laugh at the memory of the girls trapping him in the tree house after one particularly mean-spirited prank involving bubble bath and food coloring. If they'd caught him before Mom came out that day, he'd have been as blue as they were, but from bruising, not food dye. "She taught him to put his energy into baking instead of pestering the girls. Cookies pretty much saved his life. If his pranks had gotten much worse, the girls would have skinned him alive."

"And what about you?" Fin asks. "What's your special skill?"

"Yeah, Travis? What's your special skill?" Devons asks, a smirk on his face. "What do you do in your spare time, to help you with the stress of your day-to-day life?"

If Devon doesn't shut up soon, my stress relief is going to be punching him through the damn door of my truck. Maybe it wasn't such a good idea to bring him today. He's going to out me to Fin before she's ready to handle the information, and then I'll have no chance with her at all.

And I refuse to let that happen.

12

Decorations and Better Parking

Finley

"WELL, HERE IT IS," I say, pointing at the contents of the garage at my old house. "All the tools are mine. Let's take whatever we can fit."

Travis already has the truck backed up to the garage door, so it's only a matter of loading the tools in the box. He and Devon get to work immediately while I wander around the garage, taking in part of the home I thought I would be in until my kids were grown.

It's amazing how little I really knew about Emilio after everything was said and done. I thought we were in the same place in our lives, but it seems like he's had another plan for quite a while. I didn't force myself to look too closely into his philandering after I found that g-string in his car. After the first few women, I knew there was no coming back for me. Why punish myself further? I thought I loved him, but maybe I loved the idea of who he was when we met. And he hasn't been that man for a long time if he ever really was.

The sound of a vehicle pulling up gets my attention, and I see my dad parking his truck behind Travis's.

"Hi, honey," he calls to me as he gets out of the truck. "How are you doing, darling?" He reaches me in a few long strides, wrapping me up in his arms and hugging me tightly. "Has that peckerhead shown up yet?" He tips his head up and peers in the garage without letting me go.

"No, Dad," I say, wriggling out of his hug to get some space. "He's not here. Those are my friends."

I walk into the garage, motioning for my dad to follow.

"Hey, guys?" I call out to Devon and Travis. "This is my dad, Aaron Harrison. Dad, this is Travis Donovan, my handyman, and Devon... I'm sorry Devon, I don't even know your last name."

"It's Janes," Devon says, reaching a hand out to my dad. "It's a pleasure to meet you, sir." He shakes my dad's hand. "Your grandson Austin and I had a lovely conversation about ghosts and playing dead yesterday while the rest of our friends built a new porch for your daughter. He's a cool kid."

Dad laughs. He loves how fond Austin is of the weird and creepy side of the world. He's counting down the days until I decide Austin is old enough to listen to some true crime and haunting podcasts with him, so he has someone to break down mysteries with. I think between the two of them they could clear every case in the Unsolved Mysteries playlist.

"He is a cool kid, alright," Dad says, turning to Travis. "And did Fin say you're a Donovan? Is your dad Dennis?"

"Yes, sir. That is his name. How did you know?" Travis shakes dad's hand with a confused look on his face. I'm a little confused myself. How does my dad know Travis's dad?

"I've purchased some custom woodwork items from him in the past." Dad turns to me. "Remember that historic house in Carlisle Creek that we renovated a few years back? I got all the custom woodwork from Dennis."

"That was him? I'm still amazed at how well he matched all the original work in the house. When we were done with that place, it was better than new, mostly because of the custom woodwork."

A look flashes across Travis's face, but before I can identify it, it's gone.

"He does great work," Travis says. "I will mention that I saw you today. He'll be thrilled to know you loved his work so much."

"I didn't know Dennis had a son who is a handyman." Dad looks Travis up and down. "I thought his sons were in a band?"

"That's my brother, Johnny," Travis says, stuffing his hands in his pockets. "He's a guitar player in Sleeping Dogs."

"If you saw Johnny, you'd know he's the rockstar of the two," Devon says, laughing. "He certainly looks the part. More than this tall drink of ginger ale, anyway."

Dad laughs. "I suppose. You don't see a lot of redheads in rock and roll."

"Not many natural redheads, that's for sure." Devon gestures for Dad to follow him. "Come help me grab some of these tools and tell me more about your work. What kind of houses do you restore? Do you focus on historical buildings or would you take on more modern projects as well?"

They continue into the garage with Dad breaking into his favorite subject, historical buildings. I'm sure he'll tell Devon all about the historical projects we've worked on, as that is his passion, but he'll also tell him we do pretty much any restoration that pays the bills.

"Everything okay?" I ask Travis, who's pulled his phone out and is frantically typing a message.

"What? Oh, yeah. No, I'm fine. It's Johnny. He's having a love crisis and I'm talking him down." He puts his phone in his pocket and smiles at me. "Come on, let's get the rest of your stuff. Is there anything inside that you want to get?"

I moved out in a hurry when I discovered the extent of Emilio's betrayal. It's his house, after all. I packed up the kids and some of our things and went back to my parents. There was very little in the house that had much meaning for any of us, anyway. Emilio had it decorated the way he liked, and the kids weren't allowed much leeway in decorating their own rooms. When we left, I made sure I had their clothes and their favorite toys and that's about it.

Still, there is some stuff left in the house that matters to me.

"WHAT IS ALL THIS stuff?" Travis looks around the attic at all the boxes marked "Finley" "Did you keep all your stuff in the attic the whole time you lived here?"

I know what he's thinking because I've been thinking about it a lot lately, too. Was I ever really part of Emilio's life? Or was he playing a role that he tired of too quickly?

"These are all of my decorations. Emilio never wanted to decorate the outside of the house for any holiday, but my Grandma gave me all this cool stuff when she moved into her little cottage at Peaceful Pines. Your dad said that Halloween is a big deal in our new neighborhood, so I thought maybe I could use some of these decorations."

"I'm not sure if we'll have room in my truck for everything this trip," he says. "But we can come back another day for the rest. I have no problem coming back here with you."

Shit. I really don't want to come back, but now that I see these boxes, I'm saddened by the thought of leaving them behind. My grandma used to love decorating for the holidays and I think now that I really have my own house, I would love it too.

"That's okay," I say, looking up at the ceiling to stop the well of tears in my eyes from spilling. "We can leave it. I don't want to come back."

He takes a step closer to me, the dust from the floor of the attic swirling around his feet, dust motes sparkling in beams of light. The air suddenly feels thick, like I can't take a full breath. Travis reaches out and takes my hand, pulling me close. When he wraps his arms around me, I feel like I can finally breathe. He holds me tightly for a few moments before letting go and stepping back.

"No, forget coming back. I have a better plan," he says, grabbing a stack of boxes with my name on them. "We're getting everything that is yours out of here today. We'll rent a truck to get it back to Westborough if that's what we have to do, but you're not stepping foot back in this house again unless you decide you want to."

I can't make any words come out, so I nod, picking up another box. Together, we walk back down the stairs and out the door. Travis sets the boxes down next to his truck and takes his phone out.

"What's all that?" Devon asks, coming up to me. "I thought it was only the tools that you needed. I knew I should have brought the Escalade."

"I had some decorations and things stored in the attic. I had originally planned to cut my losses and leave them here, but I thought, since Halloween is such a big deal in the new neighborhood, maybe I could bring some of them back with me and finally use them. Travis insists we're taking them all today."

"That's good thinking," Dad says, joining us beside Travis's truck. "We've loaded up all the tools."

Travis puts his phone away, a grimace on his face. "Mr. Harrison? Can Finley store some of these things at your place until we can come back for them? I can come to pick them up tomorrow."

"Absolutely, son." Dad grabs Travis by the shoulder, and Devon by the arm. "We'll stack them in the kitchen if we have to. Let's go up and get the rest of it."

"Is there anything else you want to get?" Travis asks. "The truck company doesn't have any rentals available today, but there's no reason for this stuff to stay here any longer."

"No. The stuff in the attic is all I care about. Everything else in the house is his."

Dad throws me his keys. "Back my pickup next to Travis's while we go up and get more boxes, sweetheart."

The three of them turn and head into the house, leaving me in the driveway. After getting dad's truck backed up, and the first load of boxes from the attic loaded into the back, I hop up on the tailgate to wait for them to come back down. Now that I've had the chance to think about it, I'm excited about getting the house ready for Halloween. Grandma's view of spooky stuff is like Austin's, and if I remember correctly, she has some great decorations in those boxes. I can't wait to get them home so I can open them all up and have a look through them.

"This is the last of them," Dad says, shaking me out of my Halloween daydream. "Last chance. Is there anything else in the house that you want?"

As I open my mouth to answer, the sound of a car horn interrupts me. Emilio's beat-up old Porsche Boxster, or should I say my Boxster since I paid for it and my name is on the registration, pulls up and blocks both trucks in the driveway.

"What the hell is going on here?" Emilio yells as he jumps out of the car.

He looks even skeezier than he did the last time I saw him. He's wearing some ridiculous jeans with embellishments all over them, shiny black pointed-toe boots, a silk shirt with nearly all the buttons undone, six or seven chains around his neck, and white-rimmed sunglasses perched on the top of his head, nestled in his overly gelled spiked hair. He looks like he stepped off the set of Jersey Shore. Or like a middle-aged man wearing a shitty rockstar costume.

Which is exactly what he is.

Travis steps around me, blocking me from Emilio's view, with Devon right by his side.

"Why are you taking all of my stuff?" He gives Travis a dirty look. "Who said you could be here?"

"I did." I step around Travis and Emilio finally notices me. "And we're only taking my tools and my boxes of stuff from my grandma. Everything else is exactly where it was."

"I told you I wanted to keep the tools. I need them to do some renovations on the house." Emilio's voice takes on a high-pitched, nasal tone.

"Is that so?" Travis walks to his truck and pulls out a circular saw. He goes to Emilio and holds it out to him. "What's this then?"

Emilio blusters a moment before spitting, "I know what that is. But I don't have to explain anything to you. You're nobody. Do you know who I am?"

"From what I've heard, you're a wannabe musician and a deadbeat dad. Color me not impressed." Devon steps up to Emilio, forcing my ex to look up, way up, to see his face. "We were getting ready to leave. Might I suggest you move your car before I'm forced to move it for you?"

"Now listen here," Emilio screeches, attempting to step away from Devon with little success. "My bitch of an ex-wife is keeping my kids from me. I'm not a deadbeat dad."

Devon laughs in his face and steps closer, making himself look as wide as a house as he does so. *That is such a cool trick.* Emilio must be pissing himself. Hell, I'm way over here and I'm almost pissing myself.

"Alright, I think that's enough," Travis says, shoving Devon and Emilio apart. "Devon, back up. And you," he adds, pointing to Emilio. "You don't say shit about Finley ever again. I've overheard a few of your conversations with her, and I know for a fact she's not keeping those kids from you. And you know what else? The kids know it, too."

"I can't drop everything to come get them whenever she wants me to. My band has gigs booked. It's not like I can skip them."

"I don't give a shit what your little band has booked," Travis sneers, wiggling his fingers at Emilio. "Most of us were smart enough to look for fame and fortune before we got married and had kids. We wouldn't push aside an amazing woman like Finley, or cool-ass kids like Braden, Sarah, and Austin, to chase some sort of mediocre, local notoriety. Grow up, man. And change out of that ridiculous costume. You look stupid."

Devon and my dad burst out laughing, but Emilio looks at Travis with curiosity.

"You look familiar," he says, looking Travis up and down. "How do you know Fin?"

"He's my handyman at my new house. We're fixing the place up together."

"That's right," Travis adds, turning away from Emilio. "And it's time for us to get going."

"Here you go." I hold out the key to the house I shared with Emilio. "Now that I have my tools back, and my grandmother's decorations, I have no reason to come back here. Sign the divorce papers and have your lawyer contact mine. You can keep the shitty car," I say, jerking my thumb toward the Boxster. "It was a gift, after all."

Dad and Devon are in my dad's truck, and Travis is holding the passenger side door of his truck open for me. Once I've climbed in, Travis gets in and opens the driver's side window.

"You have thirty seconds to move your car before Aaron and I move it for you," he says to Emilio. "I suggest you hurry."

Emilio stands in the driveway, making no effort to get in the car and move it.

"Did I hear you correctly? You bought that car? Is it still in your name?"

I nod. "I bought it as a gift for him. For our ten-year wedding anniversary. I always hated that car. I hated it even more when I found some woman's nasty g-string in it. That was the final straw, though. That's what made me push to end the relationship. That nasty g-string was the best thing that ever happened to me." I chuckle and shake my head. I can laugh now, but it hurt at the time. And buying that car is part of the reason I have so little money in my savings now. I wouldn't have had to live with my parents for a year if I hadn't spent a huge chunk of savings on that Boxster.

Travis laughs. "Well, he's not moving and I think our thirty seconds are about up. Are you buckled in?"

I pull out the seat belt to show him it's secure.

He turns to look out his window at my dad's truck. "Ready?" he asks Devon.

I hear Devon and my dad both say "ready".

Travis puts his truck in gear, and Emilio's eyes go wide.

"Too late," Travis says to Emilio. "Time's up."

He and my dad advance on the Boxster at the same time, tapping into the side of it so gently that I don't feel a thing from my seat. And then together they push it out into the street, across two lanes, and onto the shoulder at the other side of the street. When the car hits the gravel, Travis and Dad give it a little extra gas, pushing it right down into the ditch where it tips over, seemingly in slow motion, and lands on its roof. I huff out a surprised laugh as Travis lets off the gas and puts the truck in reverse. My dad backs up and leaves first. Travis backs up and yells out the window at a dumbfounded Emilio, who is standing in the same spot in the driveway.

"That's a much better parking spot for you."

I see Emilio's eyes widen as Travis pulls away, following along after my dad.

"Well?" he asks me with a smile. "How do you like the car now?"

A surprised noise escapes my throat, chased by a laugh.

"That was amazing."

We're both still grinning when we get to my dad's house, where Devon and Dad have already unloaded the boxes of decorations into the back of a black Escalade.

13

Just Jump

Travis

"Remind me again how you two know each other?" Ryder has Fin up off the ground and is squeezing the life out of her in a way that I wish I could. I'm the one who's been spending time with her, so why is he that close to her right now?

"Our grandmothers are neighbors at Peaceful Pines," Ryder says, finally setting Fin down and letting her go. "I met her on one of my midweek visits when I was avoiding the studio."

"You know Gran?" I ask Fin.

Gran is Ryder's grandmother and even though I haven't seen her as often as some of the other guys have, she's infamous. The only woman I know who is more inappropriate and perverse is Gran's best friend, Gladys. She has been trying to see Ryder's dick for years.

"Oh, yeah. Delores is my grandmother's best friend."

I choke on spit, or air, or plain old surprise. I'm not even sure which. Ryder snorts out a laugh, and Devon runs over to pat me on the back.

"Gladys is your grandmother?" I choke out between gasps of air. "Gladys? Are you shitting me?"

"Ummm, yes. She is." Fin looks around, confused. "Is that bad?"

Ryder is laughing hysterically now, pulling in huge gasping breaths and holding onto his stomach. I'm not sure what he thinks he has to laugh about. I've met Delores, and she and Gladys are two peas in a pod. I can see why he feels a certain kinship with Finley.

"Gladys has a bit of a reputation among our friend group," Devon explains, giving me a final smack on the back before walking over to join Finley. "She's been trying to get a look at Ryder's dick for as long as she's known Gran. And together she and Gran get up to some pretty unbelievable pranks and shenanigans over there at Peaceful Pines. Stuff like filling the pool with Jell-O before aqua aerobics class, or old people cage fighting. That one actually sounded kind of fun. The loser was the first to lose their dentures first."

Finley's dad, who's been standing on the porch this whole time, pipes in, "Yeah, that sounds like her alright."

"Dad!" Finley chastises. "She's not that bad."

"She's been like that ever since I was a kid, Fin. I mean, the dirty old lady stuff is relatively new, thank god. I probably would have died of humiliation if she'd talked as much about dicks back then as she does now. But she's always been a troublemaker."

"That's not tr—okay, so maybe it's a little true. She is a bit out there." Finley laughs, a smile on her lips as she admits her grandmother is a bit out there. "She likes it that way, though. And if I'm having that much fun when I'm her age, I'll consider myself lucky."

I'm suddenly struck by an overwhelming need to see it. To see her at that age, to see the fun that she has. I want to be there with her. I want to have fun with her. I can picture us living in our little cottage like the rest of the old folks at Peaceful Pines, taking part in whatever crazy schemes we can come up with, and enjoying each other's company until we die.

Fuck.

I need to squash this feeling.

She's not even really divorced yet, for fuck's sake. And she's probably not even looking for something serious like that if she's even looking at all. Plus, there's the whole thing where I'm lying to her about what I actually do for a living. I doubt she'd look kindly on that if she found out before I told her myself. I should tell her now. But if I tell her now, there's no way she'd ever consider more with me. And the thought of being there when she's old and still having fun is too tempting to ignore.

What am I even thinking? I can't have more with her, anyway.

My priority is the band. I need to remember that. I'm hoping to keep Finley as a friend when this is all over. That's the best I will ever be able to get.

So why can't I stop thinking about kissing her? And why is my dick half-hard whenever she's around? "Travis!" Ryder yells my name, pulling me out of my reverie. "Did you hear me?"

"What?" I blurt.

"Devon and I are leaving now. We'll bring the boxes to Flipper's place and leave them on the deck. I'll let your dad know to keep an eye on them until you guys make it back."

"Yeah, okay. That's good. We'll be right behind you." I look over at Fin. "Unless you want to stay and visit your parents for a bit?"

"Oh, sorry sweetie," Fin's dad says. "Your mother and I have plans tonight. But we were hoping to come see the kids next weekend. If I'd known your asshole ex was going to skip out on his visitation again this weekend, we would have come to visit this weekend, too."

"That's alright, Dad. I don't know why I haven't figured out yet that Emilio won't spend time with the kids at all. He needs to sign the damn divorce papers and give me full custody already.

The kids shouldn't have to deal with this every second weekend. It's not fair to them."

Fin and her dad chat a little longer while I ruminate over what's been said about her ex. Again, I can't believe he would skip out on his weekends with the kids. Well, I guess I believe it a little more now that I've seen the guy. The dude couldn't be more of a douchebag if he tried. I know, I know. Don't judge a book by its cover and all that, but seriously, at some point, you need to trust the advertising.

I wonder if getting my lawyers on it would help at all. Finley isn't made of money. She wanted to wait to fix the porch because she didn't have the money yet. What was it she said about not working as much because she was studying to get her real estate license? Did I ask her what her plan is for that? I thought she was in business with her dad, but maybe she wants to move on to doing something different. It'd be a shame for her to give up construction entirely, though. She was more than competent when we were building her porch yesterday. And she's been excellent with anything she's done with me from her list of house repairs. So what's the deal with the real estate?

Not that it really matters in the long run. She's a grown woman who is more than capable of choosing her own profession. I want her to be happy. I'll support her in whichever direction she wants to take her career. And maybe I can help her in the meantime? It's not like I do much with my money. Hell, I live with my brother in a loft that we own and I spend most of my time at my parents' house when we're not on tour. Even my truck is older.

Shit. Once again, I'm lost in my own thoughts. Luckily, it looks like Fin and her dad are wrapping up their conversation, and I don't think I missed anything.

"You ready?" Fin looks over and asks.

"Whenever you are."

"Bye, Dad. Thanks again for coming over to the house to help clear out my stuff. I can't tell you how good it feels to finally have my tools back. Almost like they're old friends or something. And Grandma's decorations? It's such a relief to have them back. Austin is going to love going through the Halloween stuff, I'm sure."

I chuckle at the thought of Austin tearing through the boxes of Halloween stuff. I can almost see the huge grin on his face as he excitedly describes everything he finds.

"You bet, kiddo. Travis, it's been nice talking to you."

"You too, Mr. Harrison. Come on over to Mom and Dad's next weekend when you visit the kids. I'm sure Dad would love to catch up."

He gives me a nod before hugging Finley and heading into his house.

I get to Finley's door and open it before she does, earning me a smirk and a poke in the arm.

"I can get that myself, you know," she tells me before climbing into the passenger seat.

"I know you can," I say, holding onto the door a moment longer. "But I enjoy doing it for you."

She nods and does up her seat belt, leaving me to close the door.

Once I'm in my seat, and we're on our way back to Westborough, Fin blows out a breath and slumps into her seat.

"Everything okay over there?"

"Yes, more than okay," she says without looking at me. "I'm so relieved to have that over with, finally. You have no idea how it felt to have him holding my tools hostage like that. He never came out and said anything, but it seemed like he thought if he kept them, I would come back. Or something like that. Not that I ever would. He had no intention of becoming a responsible adult, or of stopping his cheating, so there's no way I would entertain the thought of being with him anymore. Once I found that nasty g-string in the car, I was done for good."

"Yeah, I could see how that would put a damper on a relationship."

She laughs. "Not only that, but did you see what he's done to that car? If I'd known he was going to treat it like a demolition derby vehicle, I'd never have given it to him. It was pristine when I bought it a few years ago. I mean, it was a used car, but the previous owner obviously babied it."

"You really bought it? Why don't you have it then?"

"It's not practical for me with three kids," she says, fiddling with her fingernails. "And I bought it as an anniversary gift. Pretty stupid, hey? If I'd known he was going to use it to pick up other women, I'd never have bought it."

"Well, the good news is he won't be using it for much of anything now. Not since we tipped it over into the ditch, anyhow," I give her a huge grin. "You're welcome."

Fin laughs. "How did you guys pull that off, anyway? Did you and my dad plan it ahead of time?"

"Nah."

I don't elaborate for a few moments, letting her sit with her thoughts. We didn't explicitly plan it, but her dad and I definitely seemed to be on the same wavelength. I can't stop a chuckle from escaping my throat.

"Well?" she finally breaks the silence, clearly exasperated.

"Well, what?" I ask, knowing full well she's dying of curiosity. "Oh! How did we both know to push the car at the same time? I may have mentioned to Devon that I was concerned Emilio would try to trap us in the driveway, and what a shame it would be if we needed to push that little car out of the way."

Fin bursts out laughing, the giggles taking over her body. She's borderline hysterical for several minutes before I hear her sucking in giant breaths and forcing her laughs to stop.

"I'm so glad that he didn't have one of his lady friends in the car with him. Not that I could fault someone else for falling for his bullshit. I mean, I married the guy, after all." She heaves a shuddering sigh. "If only my Grandma had told me she hated him before I married him. If anyone could have gotten through to me, it would have been her."

"Somehow, I can't imagine Gladys pulling any punches by not saying exactly what she thought. But she is your grandmother, and she loves you." I shrug. Gladys is a mystery to me. "She probably just wanted you to be happy."

"That's pretty much what she said when she told me how she really felt about Emilio." Fin's smile is gone, the laughter no longer teasing the edges of her voice. "I should have known what kind of person he was right from the start. He told a lot of stories about people that he'd hurt in some way. Not to mention the many odes he sang to his sexual prowess. I can't tell you how many of his stories involved him sleeping around in high school and college."

The thought of that asshole with his hands all over Finley has me white-knuckling the steering wheel. I know he didn't treat her right, and I find myself wishing he'd been in the car before we tipped it into the ditch.

"Before he stopped coming home altogether, I couldn't stand to be around him when he was drinking. If he got drunk enough, he'd start telling stories about sexual conquests that I assumed had happened before he met me. I'm not so sure anymore. It was so humiliating I would race to get drunk before he did, so he'd either be forced to be the responsible one, or I'd at least be drunk enough to not care if he was telling those stupid stories or not. When he stopped hanging around with our friends, it shocked me how infrequently I felt the urge to drink. I didn't need the distraction anymore, and I had way more fun without him."

"You probably had way fewer hangovers, too," I add with a chuckle, forcing myself to loosen my grip on the wheel. "And that's never a bad thing."

She laughs. "Definitely not. Especially now that I'm older and they seem to last longer when I do have one."

"Same. I've had more than enough hangovers for one lifetime, I think."

"Oh, don't even. You've never had a hangover until you have one and still have to get up and take care of your kids at the ass crack of dawn." She laughs. "Six a.m. is a hell of a lot earlier when you didn't get to sleep until four, and when three kids are screaming about breakfast."

"Okay, you win," I say, glancing at her. "I'm glad I have never experienced that. At least I know if I ever have kids now, I've already outgrown all that nonsense. One benefit of being old enough to know better, I guess."

"Is that something that you want?" Fin asks. "You want to have kids?"

It's something I've thought about many times over the years. Being surrounded by groupies and people who are only interested in you for your fame and money doesn't lend itself to starting a family, though. Not to mention all the ways being famous makes it hard to have a normal family.

But it's something I've always dreamed of, even when I knew it wasn't possible for me.

"Yeah, I guess it's something I've always wanted," I finally say. We're back in Westborough now, and in a few minutes, we'll be back at Fin's house. I wish we had longer to spend together today. I really want to discuss my desire to have a family with her. It feels imperative that she knows what kind of family man I would be.

"So why don't you have one?"

"I guess because I've never found the right partner. And because it never seemed like the right time."

She takes a deep breath. "Well, that's one thing I've learned from the disaster my life has become." She looks over at me, a sad smile on her face. "It's never the right time. You just have to jump and hope for the best."

14

Land-Mermaids and Friendly Fire

Finley

SCHOOL PICKUP IS MY least favorite time of the day, I think to myself as I wait on the sidewalk waiting for the bell to ring so the kids can come out. I walked here, for crying out loud. My kids are more than capable of walking home on their own. But until I know for sure that Emilio is out of their lives, I don't feel comfortable letting them walk alone.

Not that I think Emilio would abduct them. He doesn't even want them for a weekend, never mind forever. I'm being paranoid, and I know it. Even the kids would prefer that I let them walk with their friends. But I'm not ready for that yet. Soon, though. I have a feeling that once I pass my licensing exam and get to practice real estate, I'll be too busy to come pick them up every day. I might not have figured out whether I'll be solely practicing real estate or flipping properties with Dad until he retires, but either option will keep me very busy. The kids will need to learn how to walk home on their own eventually, and I will need to learn to be okay with it.

That will probably be for the best for me, too. It hasn't escaped my notice that all the other moms here aren't exactly impressed with me. Besides the comments about my green hair, the word "divorced' has been floating around, as have the words "cheating", and "those poor kids". Not that I really thought we were anything alike, what with me in my usual uniform of green hair, ripped denim shorts, graphic tank, and converse sneakers, and them in their carefully curated athleisure wear and perfectly coiffed, beachy blonde waves, but I at least thought we'd be able to get along because of our kids being in the same school. How silly of me to think that I left high school cliques back in high school.

Speaking of perfect beachy blonde waves, here comes one of the lulu land mermaids now.

"Hi there," she says, and I can practically hear the bubbles in her voice. She's part squeaky, part happy, and part cheerful. If I didn't suspect foul intentions, I'd probably like her. She seems like she could be a fun person to know. But, thanks to Emilio, and a year of very expensive therapy, I've learned to see past the surface of a person, to the deep heart of their intentions. And I'm pretty sure this woman intends to put me in what she feels is my place. "I'm Candace, the president of the PTA here at our lovely school. I've noticed that even though your kids have been registered at South Westborough Elementary for over a month already, you haven't volunteered for anything." She puts on a fake pout. "That's not exactly helpful of you, is it? All the moms at SWE take pride in volunteering for, well, pretty much anything. You do want to be like the rest of us moms here, don't you?" And there it is. The rest of her little speech is dripping with condescension.

Ugh, great. Of course PTA Candace would be the first mom to talk to me. Aren't there any normal moms at this school?

"Hi, Candace. I'm Finley, but I guess you already knew that, didn't you? As the president of the PTA, you must be privy to all sorts of information, right? Like, I'm sure you already know that I'm a single mom, and since I have to work to support my family, I don't have time to volunteer for things here at SWE. And since you already knew that, I'm having a hard time figuring out what exactly you intended by coming over here. So how about this? How about we cut the bullshit, and you tell me whatever it is you and the other moms"—I twiddle my fingers in the direction of the group of women she left behind—"have decided about me, so we can both be on our way?"

"Well," Candace huffs, her perfectly manicured hand clutching her nonexistent pearls. "I can see I was right about you. You're a no-class hussy. You walk around here with your green hair, showing as much skin as you do, and you make it obvious that you're not one of us. You're an embarrassment to the rest of the parents here at SWE. Maybe you should homeschool, so the other moms and all of our children aren't exposed to your unsavory character. And to think, I was going to offer to let you volunteer as a chaperone for the school's Halloween dance."

I snort out a laugh but before I can respond she spins in her expensive sneakers, beachy waves flying dangerously close to my face, and storms back to rejoin the group of lulu land mermaids, no doubt to relay her shock at me denying her oh-so-friendly overtures.

Fake Bitch.

I take it back. I couldn't like her, no matter how fun she seemed she could be at first. Making friends through the kids' school is probably not my best bet. It would be high school all over again, and lord knows I have no interest in repeating that mess. It's not that I was picked on or anything. It's merely that the system of social groups and teen hierarchies exhausted me. I have enough going on in my life right now without trying to navigate social hell two-point-oh.

Good thing I met Travis when I did. I've spent a lot more time over at his parents' place recently, and it seems like Becca is often there at the same time. I wouldn't say we're good friends yet, but we are friendly. And not in the same way that Candace was *nice* to me just now.

Becca is actually fun to talk to, even when she's trying to explain her obsession with craft beer to me. She and Johnny both love the weirdest-tasting beers and I can't get on board. But I listen anyway because she's so passionate about it that it's interesting. Kind of, anyway.

My phone buzzes from my back pocket, so I pull it out and look at the screen before it dies on me again. I really need to get a new phone one of these days. Travis is messaging me about the house. He's done so much work on it, and I still haven't seen a bill from him. I'm worried that I won't be able to pay him after all is said and done. Every time I ask about it he says not to worry, and that we'll talk about it later, but I'm a mom. Worrying is practically my second language.

```
Travis- The windows finally
came in. I'm heading out to pick
them up now. Do you want to
come?
```

I would love to go with Travis to pick up windows, or pretty much anywhere, really. I've been having a great time hanging out with him while we do repairs on the house. Not to mention, he's been starring in my nighttime fantasies since that first day I saw him at his parent's house.

```
Finley- Can't. I'm outside SWE
waiting for the bell to ring
so I can walk the kids home.
I'll keep talking to you for
a bit, though. Just had my
first run-in with the queen
bee of the PTA and now I'm
```

standing here all alone like an
outcast while she's over whispering about with her spandex
minions.

Travis- Be right there.

Oh, shit. He didn't think I was fishing for him to come here and rescue me, did he? That's not good.

Finley- Don't worry about it.
I'm sure the kids will be out
shortly. I can handle a little
gossip.

He doesn't text me back right away, and I'm still waiting for his reply when the bell rings. In a few minutes, kids start pouring out of the school, running to the playground, to meet their parents, or to catch the bus. Before my kids can find me, Travis pulls up next to me in his truck. I laugh. That's how much of an outcast I am. The other parents don't even park where I'm standing.

"Hey," Travis says, rounding his truck to greet me on the sidewalk. He's shirtless and smiling at me. Instead of stopping at a friendly distance, he walks right up to me, pulls me into his arms, and nuzzles his face into my neck. I swear I feel him inhale deeply. "I figured we should give that uptight PTA bitch something to really talk about." He releases me and turns me around.

Another car pulls up right behind Travis' truck, and Johnny and Becca both jump out and join us on the sidewalk. They have their shirts on, at least.

Actually, now that Johnny is a little closer to me, I can see that he is, in fact, not wearing a shirt. He has so many tattoos that it sort of looks like a shirt from a distance.

"Heard you needed some backup," Johnny says, kissing my cheek. "Something about bees in your spandex?"

Becca smacks him on the arm. "Not bees in her spandex, dumbass. Queen bees and spandex minions." She looks at me. "Clearly, he was never a teenage girl. Am I right?"

I laugh. "Yeah. The queen bee has apparently taken a disliking to me. The president of the PTA came over to insinuate that I didn't care enough about my kids or the school to do any volunteering. I told her to cut the bullshit and tell me what she really wanted, which is when she went off about me being a no-class hussy who should homeschool my kids to save everyone the embarrassment of having to see me." I nod my head in her direction, so they can see who I'm talking about. "They've been over there whispering and giggling ever since."

"What a bitch!" Becca sounds angrier than I do. She'd be a good one to have on my side in a fight. Wait. She is on my side right now. I could get used to having backup like this.

Johnny turns and walks directly to Candace, engaging her in a conversation that I can't hear because they're too far away and because there are too many kids running around now. Travis is looking toward the school with a huge grin on his face. I tear my gaze away from Johnny and Candace to see what Travis is looking at, only to discover that he's looking at my kids.

"Travis!" Braden yells, breaking into a slow jog. "I thought we were working on scraping old paint off the shutters today? What are you doing here?"

Travis reaches out and gives my son a fist bump. "I got a call that the windows came in, so I thought I'd stop by and see if you guys wanted to go grab an early dinner and then pick them up with me."

"Can we, Mom? Please. I want to stop at the mall and get some new earrings. Please, please, please." Sarah pleads with me. She's finally good enough about keeping her ear piercings clean that she can wear fun earrings and she's been nothing short of obsessed with the teen store in the mall and all their colorful wares.

"Sure, fine. We can do that." I didn't actually feel like cooking dinner, anyway.

I've only got a couple of weeks left before my real estate licensing exam and I need to spend every available second studying. And with the dishwasher being broken, dinnertime takes twice as long, which takes away from my studying time. Sometimes I wonder if I'm in over my head. Hopefully, this all pays off when I finally have my license. I wanted the extra income stream to give me more time with my family, not less.

Austin is already partaking in his new favorite pastime, talking to Becca about her leg tattoos. She's got a huge Freddy Krueger on one leg, and a gorgeous, yet terrifying, swirly montage of other horror movie villains on the other. Every time Austin sees her, he makes her tell him all about the movies that each one is from, and about any true stories that those movies might be based on. And Becca has the patience of a saint, because she goes through it with him, every time. One of these days, I suppose I'll have to let him watch the movies to satisfy his curiosity. I wonder what kind of mother PTA Candace will think I am then?

"Problem solved," Johnny says as he comes strolling back. "Sleeping Dogs is her husband's favorite band, and I said I'd give her some autographed swag in exchange for not bothering you about volunteering. Oh, and I'm paying for the Halloween party this weekend."

He looks at Travis and winks. I'm missing something there, but I'm too upset with Johnny to look into it now.

"Johnny, you don't need to do that. I can deal with people like her. I've done it countless times."

He looks at me, a frown on his lips, his eyebrows drawn. "You're practically family now, Flipper. I know you can deal with it, but you don't have to. You've got us to help you out now. You're not in this alone anymore."

My breath catches in my chest and I feel my eyes get glassy. Damn it. Who knew the tattooed rockstar was such a softie?

"I, um... thank you. That means a lot."

"And besides," he continues, his voice taking on a joking tone. "We're going to need you to look after Mom and Dad when Sleeping Dogs goes back out on tour," Johnny says with a grin.

Travis coughs and pounds his fist into his chest. "With me. He means you can help look after Mom and Dad with me."

"What?" Johnny looks at Travis. "Oh, yeah. Right. I meant you can help Travis. You know, when he's too busy on job sites and stuff."

"Okay, that's enough of that," Travis jumps in. "Kids? You guys ready? We're burning daylight." He opens the back door of his truck and grabs his shirt, pulling it on while motioning for the kids to climb in. "We'll see you guys later," he says, waving off Johnny and Becca and closing the truck door.

Austin calls out from the truck. He's draped his body across Sarah to hang out the window. "Becca, you're coming too, right? I heard about a scary movie that I want you to tell me about. It's called Saw. Have you seen it?"

Becca laughs and shakes her head, looking to me for permission, so I give her a nod. The kid's got messed up taste and isn't afraid of anything. I gave up trying to shelter him from most scary things years ago when he started sleeping with a skull that was supposed to be a Halloween decoration. He was two years old, and he sleeps with it to this day.

"Sure, Austin. Tell your mom to let us know when you're headed for dinner and we'll meet you and I can tell you about *Saw*."

"Awesome! Best day ever," Austin yells as he pulls himself back through the window.

As I pull myself up into the passenger seat of Travis' truck, I chance a look back at PTA Candace and her minions. They're all staring, mouths open, eyes wide.

Good. Let them be jealous of this no-class hussy. I'll hang out with a member of her husband's favorite band and she can get a t-shirt.

15

Spandex Spidey and a Perfect Ass

Travis

"THIS SUIT IS CLIMBING right up my ass, man." Johnny is standing beside me, trying unsuccessfully to pull the seam of his Captain America costume out of his ass crack. "Tell me again why I agreed to this?"

"Because you found out that Becca has a secret crush on ol' Cap and you got jealous?" I say with a laugh. "Plus, it was your idea to dress up. You didn't have to agree to anything because you came up with this plan all on your own."

Johnny is funding this whole Halloween party at South Westborough Elementary and, because of that, PTA Candace and the school board invited him to attend. I'm waiting for Finley and her family, but they haven't arrived yet.

I look around and admire what Johnny's money made possible. The decorating committee draped all the walls in the school gym in gauzy black fabric with fake spiderwebs stretching wall to wall across the ceiling. Hundreds of helium balloons in black and purple, tied in giant bunches, are interspersed through the assorted stands and booths that take up the floor. They even have fog machines set up, so it looks extra spooky. It's more like a carnival than a party, and it's exactly the kind of thing I would have loved when I was a kid.

And from the looks of it, a lot of these kids today love it, too. I can hardly hear my own thoughts because of all the laughing and screaming. I have to give it up for PTA Candace. She might be a bitch, but she knows how to organize a children's party.

"Okay, fine. You got me there. But that doesn't tell me why your suit isn't crawling up your ass like it's looking for a new place to live." Johnny asks, grabbing his spandex by the inner thighs and yanking downward while wiggling his hips. I can't stop the laugh before it escapes my throat, earning me a dirty look from Johnny.

Fin's daughter, Sarah, convinced me to dress up as Spiderman tonight and to go Trick-or-Treating with them after the Halloween party. And I make a pretty incredible Spidey if I do say so myself.

"I don't know what to tell you, bro. I guess I'm better at filling out my spandex than you."

My phone buzzes from the secret pocket in my Spidey suit.

Finley- Running late. Be there in twenty. Becca is with us.

"Becca's coming, too?"

Johnny shakes his head. "She said she was busy tonight when I asked if she wanted to hang out. I figured she'd be watching a horror movie marathon or something. I was thinking of going over to surprise her with my Cap costume after the party." He wiggles his eyebrows and laughs.

"That's weird. Finley messaged me to say they're running late. And she said Becca is with them."

"Weird. Wonder what that's about?"

"Who knows? But I'm glad Finley has someone to hang out with. I'm over there a lot, but she doesn't have a lot of other friends. And you saw what the other moms at this school are like. I don't think they'll be welcoming her into their little group soon."

Johnny snorts a laugh. "Even if they did, I think Fin has more sense than to get caught up in their den of bitches. She doesn't seem like the type to suffer fools lightly."

I chuckle. "Yeah, you're not wrong about that."

At least she's not anymore. Lord knows he suffered with her fool of an ex long enough. She shouldn't have to deal with any shit like that ever again. Too bad he hasn't signed the divorce papers yet. Sharing kids with him means she'll have to deal with him for the rest of her life. And right now, she also has to deal with the effect his indifference is having on the kids. The guy is such a dickhead. I can only imagine what he did to attract someone like Finley in the first place. My guess is he's a skilled manipulator. That's about the only thing that could explain it.

"Oh, shit. Hide me," Johnny whispers, pulling me in front of him. "That Candace woman is coming this way."

I look ahead and, sure enough, here comes PTA Candace with one of her minions trailing along behind her.

"Johnny, there you are." Candace pushes me out of the way and grabs Johnny's arm. "I can't thank you enough for all of this," she says, gesturing at the gym. "This is the best party our school has ever seen. And it's all thanks to you. Well, and me. We make such a good team." She flutters her eyelashes at him, which probably wouldn't look so ridiculous if she weren't dressed like a bee, complete with crown. I can't wait for Fin to get a look at that. I wonder if she knows that being the queen bee can be considered a bad thing, or if she's oblivious to the social connotations implied by the name. Either way, I'm sure Finley will get a laugh. "Are any of your bandmates joining you this evening? It would be amazing if I could meet all of you."

For a woman who looked at Fin like she wasn't good enough to have her kids at this school because of her green hair, she sure doesn't seem to have a problem with Johnny, whose body is like ninety-five percent ink. Of course, it wouldn't be the first time that a man was judged differently for being covered in tattoos, or having crazy colored hair. Plus, it could be because she knows he's in a band. People seem to expect eccentric looks from musicians. I'm the one who usually stands out from Sleeping Dogs because I'm a normal-looking guy, on stage or off.

I'm extra thankful for my Spiderman costume right now, because there's no way she can recognize that I'm also in Sleeping Dogs. I still haven't worked up the courage to tell Finley and the last thing I need is some woman she dislikes telling her before I get the chance to.

"No, they're all busy with their girlfriends and families tonight. But I brought my brother, Travis."

"Oh, hello," PTA Candace purrs at me. "I didn't see you there." Yeah, right. She didn't see me, yet she pushed me out of the way. How does that work?

"Hey," I say with barely a chin tip, immediately turning to face the entrance. It's been almost twenty minutes and I'm getting anxious about seeing Finley. Sarah picked her mom's costume too, and neither of them would tell me what it is. I can't wait to see what she's dressed as. I know whatever it is, she's going to look amazing.

"But I thought my husband said that your brother is also in the band?"

Shit. She's figured it out. C'mon Johnny, get me out of this.

"Oh yeah, he totally is. That's my other brother, though. Travis is a handyman. He's been doing some work at Finley's house for the last couple of months. That's how we met her." Johnny smiles, and I hope that Candace believes him. Most people who are fans of the band know that Johnny and I are brothers, and they also know that all of our other siblings are women. Candace said that her husband was the fan, so maybe he didn't go into that much detail about Johnny's family dynamics. At least I hope he didn't.

"Oh, yes, of course," she giggles, placing her hand on Johnny's arm. I can see him physically forcing himself to keep his arm still, to stop himself from yanking it away from her. It would be funny if I didn't feel so bad for him. Something about this woman makes my skin crawl, and I can't wait for her to leave. "That makes sense. I couldn't see how anyone of any importance would meet someone like Finley. I knew it had to be something like that."

Yeah, that's enough of that. I'm about to turn around and tell her off, when the doors to the gym fly open and the strangest group of characters enter.

I burst out laughing when I recognize Austin, dressed as the most adorable little Beetlejuice I've ever seen. He's got the white and black striped suit, the greenish colored hair, the white makeup with mossy green spots, and blackened eyes. He's a perfect miniature version of Michael Keaton in that movie.

Braden is dressed as the guy with the shrunken head from the waiting room in the afterlife. I can almost make out the spots in the chest of his costume where his eyes are.

It looks like Sarah went with a Beetlejuice character as well, except she chose Barbara Maitland, the ghostly wife of the movie, when she rearranges her face into a huge beaked thing with eyes resting on a long tongue. Makes me wonder, though, why she insisted I dress as Spiderman, if the rest of them have *Beetlejuice* costumes.

They dressed Becca as Lydia from the movie, the version of the character from the beginning of the movie when she's depressed and all dressed in black. Honestly, if it weren't for the other three, and the very specific way she styled her hair, I might not have known that's what she was going for because she wears a lot of black normally. She looks great, though. They all do.

But I don't see Finley yet. I wonder if she decided on a Beetlejuice character as well, or if she went a completely different direction.

"Hey." Johnny pulls Becca toward him. "You look great. I thought you couldn't come out tonight?" He's completely turned away from PTA Candace and I can hear her huffing. It's hilarious. And why does she care who Johnny talks to, anyway? Isn't she married? Candace stomps her foot and walks away from our little group, finally. "I was going to stop by your place later and see if you wanted to come hand out candy at my parents' house with me. It's my favorite part of Halloween."

"I wasn't going to, but I got a call from this little Beetlejuice earlier today, begging for me to come and be Lydia. How could I turn down a request like that?" She smiles at Austin, and almost ruffles his hair, before thinking better of it. I'm sure whatever is making it that color would transfer to her black lace gloves and make quite the mess. "Plus, this guy's the best looking date I've had in a long while," she adds with a wink for Johnny. He puts his hand on his heart, pretending to be crushed, while Austin laughs.

"Sorry, Johnny. Becca loves creepy stuff, like me. I knew she'd want to come and dress up with us. But you can come too if you want. You don't really match the rest of us, but that's okay. Not everyone can have a cool costume," Austin says with a shrug, before turning and running off to one of the booths. Johnny and Becca both laugh and follow him.

"Well, if it isn't my good pal, Spiderman." I hear Fin say from behind me.

I spin around to see Fin in a subtly sexy Spider Gwen costume. I mean, it's as tight as mine, but hers looks so much better.

"Holy shit. Finley? You look amazing!" I'm glad she can't see how wide my eyes are through my mask. I'm also glad I wore compression shorts under my costume, because my reaction to seeing her in that suit isn't exactly family friendly.

"Not as good as you," she says, gesturing for me to do a spin. "I think I can guess now why Sarah wanted me to be Spider-Gwen, and insisted I call Becca to come and be Lydia."

"She's the one who told me to dress up as Spiderman. I guess she thought you and I needed to match?"

"I hope she's not trying to play matchmaker. Wouldn't that be crazy?" Fin snickers and shakes her head. "Imagine us dating."

Ouch. That hurts. That's not all I'm imagining us doing, but Fin's being pretty transparent about her thoughts on that. She is not interested. At all. I should have known. It's been nothing but friendly and professional.

Except for that kiss. That has to mean something, right?

Interesting. I wonder what Sarah is up to? She hasn't opened up to me as much as Braden and Austin have, but we still talk occasionally. I know she's beyond frustrated with her dad and how he never follows through on what he says he'll do, but I never got any inkling from her that she's trying to get her mother into another relationship. Yeah, that doesn't make sense. She must have noticed how well we work together when we're doing the renovations at their house, and figured we'd have fun dressing up in similar costumes. If that's all she wanted, she could have brought me in on the *Beetlejuice* theme. I could have been Adam Maitland.

Or a sandworm.

"Well? Should we make the rounds and see what kind of stuff your brother's money bought? I hear there are some good prizes at a few of the booths."

"After you." I sweep my arm and let her go ahead. Partly because I'm a gentleman and partly because I want to look at her ass in that skintight suit.

Hey, we can't all be perfect as Finley's ass.

16

Compression Shorts and Halloween Scares

Finley

"What do you say?" Finley yells up the driveway as Austin takes the candy offered by a neighbor and spins around silently.

"Thank you," he yells over his shoulder, already running off to the next house.

Braden and Sarah are both Trick-or-Treating with friends this evening, so now it's only me, Fin, and Austin making our way around her and my parent's neighborhood. Back when I used to think about having a family, this was the sort of thing I hoped for. Sleeping Dogs put a stop to that, though. It's hard to take your kids out on Halloween when you're onstage halfway around the world somewhere.

"You guys weren't kidding when you said Halloween is a big deal on this block. I'm pretty sure every second house is hosting a haunted garage or backyard for the kids to explore. If I didn't have you and your parents advising me, I would have not only missed out on decorating, but I probably wouldn't have allowed my kids to take part in all the fun. You never know with strangers."

"What? You didn't have any trouble letting Braden help me paint the fence the day we met, did you? What's the difference between that and letting the kids explore some stranger's creepy gara—okay, nevermind. I heard myself as I was saying it, and even to me, it sounded weird. And I grew up in this neighborhood surrounded by these people." I shake my head and chuckle. "Why did you let him hang out with me that first day?"

She laughs. "Well, for one thing, you didn't give off any major creep vibes when we were walking around my house. And for another thing, I was watching you out the window the whole time. I thought it was adorable how he took his shirt off like you did, by the way."

"You thought it was adorable that he took his shirt off? How did you feel about it when I took my shirt off?" He stops and looks down at me, his nearness something I'm suddenly very aware of. We've both taken the hoods of our costumes down by now, which I'm currently regretting. Having one's face completely covered makes for moist conversations, but at least I'd be able to contain my embarrassment if I still had it on.

I feel my cheeks burn. If only he knew how many times the vision of him with his shirt off has accompanied me on my dates with B.O.B. He's a good-looking guy, with a good job, and a future ahead of him. I'm sure the last thing he wants to know is that the old mom whose house he's fixing has been lusting after him while she masturbates. Not exactly the most enticing package over here.

I shrug and keep walking. "You had your shirt off when we met, remember? And really, I was praying you remembered to wear sunscreen, Red."

He laughs again, the sound quiet enough that I know it's only for my ears. "I wish you'd said something to me that day. I actually hadn't remembered to get my back. You should have seen how bad the sunburn was. It lasted for a week. Luckily, I know all the tricks and keep a bottle of aloe vera gel in the fridge pretty much everywhere I go. That always cuts down on healing time."

"Mom, Mom, Mom," Austin runs up and grabs my hand. "Can you hold my bag, please? I want to go to that haunted graveyard over there." He points to a house a few doors down.

The house is by far the most decorated on any of the streets we've been on. Not only are there lights, and fog machines, and dozens of Jack-o'-lanterns, but they also have a fake iron fence all around the house with a creepy-looking path leading around the house to the backyard. They win Halloween, for sure.

I look at Travis and raise an eyebrow. "What do you think? You're the expert on this neighborhood's Halloween extravaganza. Is this a safe place for Austin to visit? Or would I be sending him off into a real haunted graveyard to be eaten by zombies and other assorted creatures of the night?"

"Mom," Austin chides, rolling his eyes at me. "Zombies won't eat me. They would only eat my brain, duh."

"He has a point," Travis says with a chuckle. "But he's perfectly safe to go in." Austin doesn't even wait for Travis to finish before he streaks off into the yard. Apparently, Travis' word is as good as mine. I'm not sure whether that's something I should allow, but it's so nice that Austin has someone else looking out for him, I let it slide this time. "That's the Anderson's place. They never had children of their own and they live to do stuff like this for the neighborhood kids. Wait until Christmas," he adds with a wink. "That's when the really intense decorations come out."

"Well, I might enlist your help for putting up the Christmas decorations," I say, taking a step closer. "I wouldn't want to be the only one on the block with no Christmas cheer."

"Anything you want, babe." He reaches out and tucks a strand of hair behind my ear, causing a pleasant shiver to climb my spine. "Did I tell you how much I love the color of your hair?

Or how amazing you look in this costume?" His hand settles on the back of my neck, his thumb tracing along my jawline, and he pulls me closer.

Holy shit, is this really happening? Is Travis going to kiss me? I lick my lips and lean in as he lowers his face to mine. With my eyes closed, all I feel is his hand pulling me closer, and the warmth of his breath on my lips before he seals his mouth to mine. Heat floods my body, tingles run through my chest and stomach. This kiss feels different from those that have come before. Maybe he is interested in the old mom across the street? I wrap my arms around his waist and his free hand slides down, grabs my hip, and drags my body against him. A groan escapes me at the feel of his hard length pressed into my stomach. Desire pools in my core and my breaths come quickly as Travis slips between my lips, slowly massaging my tongue in a gentle rhythm. I run my hands down, taking full advantage of his skin tight costume to feel every muscle and curve of his back and ass. I squeeze his butt with both hands and I'm met with a groan from Travis. I slide my hand to his front, wanting to stroke him and feel him beneath my hand, when he grabs both of my hands with his, stopping me before I can touch him.

"Stop, stop," he says, panting. "We need to stop."

My stomach falls, and I'm suddenly nauseated, my cheeks flaming in embarrassment. He doesn't really want me, after all. He got caught up in the moment. I should have known.

"My compression shorts can only hide so much and we still have a lot of Trick-or-Treating to do." He leans down and kisses me chastely on the lips and rests his forehead against mine. "You have no idea what you do to me. I've never been this hard."

"Huh?" I blurt. "You're not stopping because you don't actually want me?"

"What?!" He chuckles. "Are you insane? I have thought of nothing but you since the day we met."

"Seriously?" I'm stunned. I hoped he might find me desirable, but I knew it was highly unlikely. I'm a nearly divorced mom of three, after all. What do I even have to offer?

"Yes, Fin. I am serious."

"Huh." I must look puzzled, because he chuckles when he sees my face.

We stand together quietly for a moment while I try to wrap my head around this information and he tries to get his dick under control.

"Are you okay?" I ask, gesturing to the general area of his dick. "Compression shorts?"

"I didn't want everything on display in front of a bunch of kids. I wear them when I go to the gym with Ryder and Connor. They can help keep a jock strap in place or, like I'm wearing them now, they can act like a dick girdle. They keep everything together." He groans uncomfortably and adjusts himself.

I risk a quick peek at the area in question and see no evidence of the monster that was pressing into my stomach a few moments ago. I wonder what he had to think about to make it go down that quickly. Or are the compression shorts tight enough to smooth it all out like that?

I'm about to ask him when a man dressed as Hagrid from *Harry Potter*, walking what appears to be a three-headed dog with six ears so long they drag on the ground, approaches us from the direction of the haunted graveyard, halting my train of thought. He smiles when he sees Travis.

"Travis, my boy. I haven't seen you in ages." He holds out his arms and Travis steps into his embrace. He must have a lot of trust in his compression shorts or he's calmed himself down in record time. Travis looks back at me and mouths, "that was close". I cover my laugh with a cough.

"Mr. Anderson, still spooking up the neighborhood, I see." Travis squats down to pet the dog, opting for the middle head and being rewarded with a slobbery kiss up the side of his face. "I can't say this is the scariest costume you've ever worn, though."

"Oh, you know me. I love Halloween and the scarier it is, the better. But I heard there were some new kids in the neighborhood this year and figured I'd try something a little less horrifying. Nevermind that. Aren't you going to introduce me to this lovely lady friend of yours?"

I reach out a hand and introduce myself. "I'm Finley, and at least three of those new kids you heard about are mine. That little Beetlejuice who ran by you is my youngest. We recently moved in across the street from Travis's parents."

"Into Gladys' old rental property? Oh, honey. I hope you got a good deal on it. It's fallen into quite a bit of disrepair these last few years, you know."

"Well, I suppose that depends on whether you think free is a good deal." I say with a laugh. "Gladys is my grandmother, and she gave it to me when I found myself in need of a new place to live and a fresh start. Travis has been doing some repairs for me to help make it more liveable,"

He smiles ear to ear. "I'd say that's a damn good deal. How is old Gladys doing these days, anyway? I haven't seen her since the last of my seniors's chair burlesque classes she attended. Has she figured out how to loosen those hips up a little? Poor dear looked like she was being electrocuted when I had the class doing hip rolls."

Travis pinches the bridge of his nose and releases a pained laugh. "I did not need that mental image, Mr. Anderson. Thanks a lot."

The man in front of us laughs. "Oh, come now, Travis. All you need to do is turn your head and look at this ravishing Spider-woman you have beside you and that image will fly away without quarrel." He winks at me and there's no way he can't see how red my cheeks are. Moist mask be damned. I'm about ready to pull this hood up again so I can regain some of my dignity. I can already tell that this man is going to take pleasure in teasing me. "Besides," he adds, "a woman owning her sexuality even when she's getting on in years is a beautiful thing."

Mr. Anderson hooks his arm through mine and pulls me along. "Come then, my dear. Let us go around to the back and see if we can't find Mrs. Anderson trying to scare your son. With how excited he was to run in here, I think Jenny will have to work extra hard at it, wouldn't you say?"

I allow Mr. Anderson to drag me through the fence into the fog covered graveyard with Travis following close behind. He doesn't seem to mind all that much, though. At some point during our conversation, he ended up with the leash so he's walking along, happy as can be, with a three-headed basset hound for company.

"What is your dog's name, Mr. Anderson?"

"Who, him? We call him Happy."

I turn and look at the big Basset Hound, with his droopy ears and eyes, and he looks anything but happy to me. I think that might be what they look like, though, because he's walking along energetically enough with Travis in the lead.

"It's sort of a joke," he explains further when he catches me looking back. "Because he looks like such a sad sack."

I chuckle. "Okay, yeah. That makes sense."

Travis bends down and grabs Happy's squishy face between his large hands. "You're not a sad sack, are you, boy? You're a cheerful guy. You can't help if you have a droopy face. It's those ears. They're so long they pull your face down and make you look sad. Isn't that right, Happy? Who's a good boy? Who's the best boy?" Travis says to Happy in a silly sounding baby voice. Happy answers by flopping down on the ground with a phwump and laying his head on his paws.

Mr. Anderson snickers. "You're not getting him up now," he tells Travis and reaches for the leash. "Let me take him and you two head on back to catch up with that boy of yours. I'll join you in a few minutes when I can convince this lump of dog to get up again."

"Thanks, Mr. Anderson. I forgot how Happy likes to take breaks in the middle of a walk, no matter how short that walk may be."

"I think that means you need to come around more often, Travis. How long are you boys home for this time?" Mr. Anderson asks while setting up a trail of treats for Happy. He has them placed six inches apart and Happy drags his body forward inch by inch without getting off the ground. You have to admire his dedication to taking this break, even with the treats he's being offered.

I see Travis flinch ever so slightly. That seems odd..

"Johnny's home for at least six months this time, Mr. Anderson," he answers before turning to me. "Should we go check on Austin? It wouldn't surprise me if he's the one scaring Mrs. Anderson instead of the other way around."

"Oh, yeah. Sure. That's probably a good idea. See you back there," I say to Mr. Anderson. "Good luck getting Happy on board."

He nods and gives me an absentminded little wave, his focus on dropping a path of treats for Happy.

"So, Johnny is home for six months? Why did Mr. Anderson ask about how long you're going to be home, too?"

"Oh, uh. I'm not too sure about that. I traveled with Johnny for a little on one tour. Maybe that's why?"

"Hmm, I guess that makes sense." It's a reasonable explanation, but I'm still getting a weird vibe from Travis. Whatever it is, it's not like he owes me an explanation. He's been helping me fix my house, not inviting me to share his life, despite what seems like his interest in sharing his bed with me.

"Mom, you gotta see this. Check out this cool zombie Mrs. Anderson made," Austin giggles from somewhere off in the fog. "It's so awesome."

I heave a sigh. "You know this is a trap, right?"

"I had a feeling." Travis grabs my hand, lacing his fingers with mine. My stomach drops and I get tingly in my chest at the contact. "Shall we?"

He walks us around the back of the house, where Austin and a woman, who I assume is Mrs. Anderson, dressed as a zombie, jump out at us and scream right in our faces.

Travis and I both react appropriately, screaming at the top of our lungs and pretending to run. Travis goes so far as to fall down and attempt to scramble away while on his back. Austin and Mrs. Anderson erupt into peals of laughter, their night made by Travis's antics. And I can't say he hasn't had the same effect on me. I wonder if he knows how hot I find him when he plays along with my kid's attempts at connection?

17

Close Calls and Phone Calls

Travis

"Do you want to come in?"

Finley's kids are sleeping at my parents' house tonight with all of my sisters' kids. It's a Halloween tradition that only happens when Halloween is on a weekend, and my mom invited Fin's kids to stay over too, when we finally made it to Trick-or-Treat at her place with Austin. They all sit around and go through their candy together, making trades and barters for their favorites, and then they watch a scary, but not too scary, movie before sleeping all together in the living room on mattresses they pull out from every bedroom. We did it with our cousins when we were kids, too, and I can attest to how much fun it is.

But it's got nothing on Fin asking me to come in right now.

I walked her home after she said goodnight to her kids and we're standing together on her new porch.

"Really?"

Fin's face falls, her tentative smile dropping at my question. She looks down at her feet. "Oh, yeah, umm. Nevermind, sorry. I just—"

I reach out and tilt her chin up, forcing her to look at me. "That's not what I meant, Finley. I want nothing more than to come inside with you right now. I wanted to make sure that you are sure. Because if I come in with you right now, I don't know that I'll be able to keep my hands off of you."

"Oh, thank god." Her chest and face flush red and she quickly turns to unlock the door.

I can't hold myself back anymore, so I take this opportunity to wrap my arms around her waist and nuzzle my face into her neck. She smells so fucking good. I'm already rock hard and, as she struggles to get the door open, her round ass pushes against me, making me groan.

"Fuck, Fin. You're killing me."

She chuckles, looking back at me. "Sorry. The door is stuck again."

Fucking door. That moves to the top of the list right now. I'll fix it first thing tomorrow. For now, though, I move Finley out of the way to force it open myself. One turn of the knob, and a not altogether comfortable shove with my shoulder later, and we're inside.

Finley reaches up and wraps her hands around behind my neck, pulling me down for a kiss. My hands run through her hair again, the silky strands slipping between my fingers while we kiss. She tastes like the candies she stole from Austin's bag while we were Trick-or-Treating, sweet and a little fruity. Which reminds me. It's still relatively early on Halloween night. I'm not positive, but I think I even hear someone yelling Trick-or-Treat in the distance. Shit.

"Hold on one sec," I groan against her lips. "We need to turn out the lights and decorations or kids will be knocking on the door all night."

She nods and pulls herself away, trying to walk to the door.

"What do you think you're doing?"

"Going out to turn off the lights in the pumpkins? Isn't that what we were talking about?" She looks around with a confused look on her face. "Did I imagine that?"

I chuckle and pull her toward me again, burying my face in her neck. "No, Fin. Not you. I meant I would go do it. I have to grab a change of clothes from my truck, anyway. I'm dying to get out of this costume." I emphasize my point by tugging at the crotch of my costume. I don't know what old Spidey gets up to in his suit, but after wearing this one tonight, I'm pretty sure it never involves having an erection.

She raises up on her toes and kisses me softly. "I thought that was the whole point of you coming in?" she whispers before spinning around in my arms with a sigh. "But getting out of this costume sounds like a brilliant idea. Unzip me?" She holds her hair up, giving me access to the zipper that runs the length of her back. "I can't reach it myself."

A jolt of desire zings through my body when I see the first inch of smooth flesh revealed by the lowering zipper, and I get even harder than I already am, which makes the compression shorts I'm wearing even more uncomfortable. Dragging my hand along her back as I lower the zipper doesn't help my situation, but Finley shivers against me, so I'll take it.

"You are so fucking beautiful," I whisper against her neck. "I can't get enough of touching you." I slide my hands inside the zipper and around to her stomach, the skin under my rough hands softer than I could have imagined. "What are the chances that anyone's going to come knocking on the door now, anyway? It's got to be what? Nine o'clock? Shouldn't all the kids be home stuffing their faces by now?"

Fin trembles under my hands as I slowly slide them up, my fingers hovering at her bra line, my thumbs caressing the swell of her tits. I lick the pulse point in her neck, and I'm rewarded with a whimper as she drops her head back. Sliding a hand up, I pull one side of her bra down, freeing her breast so I can roll her nipple between my finger and thumb, holding her tightly to my chest. Her breath quickens, and she reaches back with both hands and grips my hair. With my free hand, I trace a line down, past her belly button, and tease the hem of her panties, dipping my fingers in slightly before retreating to skim the lace along the edge, over and over, until Finley is whispering my name.

"Travis, please," she whimpers, rubbing my dick through my pants with her ass as she writhes against me. "Touch me."

I oblige, plunging my hand into her panties, teasing my fingers through the damp curls to get to her slick pussy. A groan crawls up my throat. "Fuck. You're so fucking wet, babe." If she keeps pushing her ass against me, I'm going to come in my costume like a horny teenager.

A knock at the door startles me, stopping me before I plunge my fingers into her slick pussy.

"Trick-or-Treat,"is the muffled call we hear through the door.

Fin jumps, a little gasp escaping her before she laughs.

"Ugh, I jinxed it," I say, placing another kiss on her neck, sliding my hands out of her clothes, regretting the absence immediately. "I'll get them some candy and then shut everything off. You relax. I'm not done with you yet." I spin her around, kissing her deeply, not letting up until she's melting against me and the kids outside are yelling *Trick-or-Treat* again. "Fucking Halloween," I grumble as I let her go, which Fin meets with another laugh.

I turn and force the door open to hand candy out to the kids on the porch. When Fin took the kids out earlier this evening, she'd left a bowl of candy on the porch with a note telling kids to take one, but that's long gone. I find her stash of extra treats sitting on a table beside the door, and give the last three kids of the night extra large handfuls before sending them on their way. Once they've made it down the stairs and on to the next house, I turn off the porch light and go out, closing the door behind me. Fin and her kids made several Jack-o'-lanterns, so I take a minute to turn off the battery operated candles she lit them with before going to my truck to get my clothes.

There aren't many kids out now, so we probably would have been fine to leave the lights on, but I want nothing to interrupt us when I finally get Fin to myself. I've been fantasizing about her since that first day when she walked up to me and asked me for my card. She's exactly the kind of person I could see myself settling down with, if I could find some way to make it happen. I can't help but wonder how much of my attraction to her stems from the fact that she has no idea who I am.

Everything with Fin is so normal, so comfortable.

Well, other than the giant hard-on I'm sporting in these damn compression shorts right now, that is. That certainly isn't comfortable. All the more reason to get my clothes and hurry back to Fin's place. If I don't get out of these shorts soon, I might suffer permanent damage. I'm too fond of my dick to let that happen.

I grab the bag with my change of clothes from the back seat and hurry back across the street to Fin's house. Without knocking, I open the door and let myself in. And right away I can tell something is wrong. Fin's yelling and it doesn't take more than a second for me to figure out who she's yelling at.

"I don't give a fuck. You were supposed to spend this weekend with the kids. I didn't even bother telling them anything because I knew you wouldn't show up."

I walk toward the sound of her voice until I find her standing in the living room, still in her unzipped costume, phone to her ear. She's as far from relaxed as I've ever seen her. I can feel the tightness of her muscles just by looking at her. Should I go to her? Would that help her relax? Or would my nearness make it worse?

"No. No. I don't want to hear it. The kids don't care about your stupid band. You're a middle-aged man who dumped his family to chase fame. I'm all for chasing your dreams, but they need to be realistic when you have a family to consider. And newsflash, you're not going to get this dream. You guys aren't any good, and you don't know anyone in the business."

She's gesturing wildly with her free hand, her frustration showing itself in the way she grabs her hair and runs her hand down her face. I walk up behind her and wrap my arms around her waist, resting my chin on her shoulder. She takes her free hand and places it over my arms, squeezing slightly. I hate that she has to deal with this all the time. And I hate that the kids don't get to see their dad. Even if he is a useless piece of shit.

"No! Jesus, Emilio. I didn't even ask who they were. All that mattered is they were here and ready to help me. I don't care what the name of their band is. It has nothing to do with why I talk to any of them."

Oh, shit. I figured this would happen eventually. I know the kids still talk to him on the phone occasionally, so I'm sure this guy heard about the band from one of them. He's probably looking for confirmation. I can guarantee that none of us will help him, that's for sure. Even if they were any good, which from what Fin said, is unlikely, we wouldn't help him because he's a fucking douchebag who abandoned his family.

"Hell no," Fin says with a cruel laugh. "But hey, who knows? Maybe they'll be around next time you come to pick up the kids. Gotta go. Bye." Fin stabs at the end call button and throws her phone onto the couch. "How could I have married such a prick?! You know, he probably will show up now. And he'll look for excuses to hang around to find out if the guys in the band can help him."

Shit. I didn't think of that. Sticking it to her ex might come with unintended consequences for Finley. Not to mention that having him around increases the chances of her finding out that I'm not the handyman I told her I was.

As much as I want to tell her the truth, I don't think we're there yet. And as much as it kills me to say it, spending the night with her probably isn't the best idea. At least, not until I've told her the truth about me. If she's still interested when she finds out I've lied to her about being in the band this whole time, then we can talk about getting more physical.

Yeah, I know. My dick hates me, too.

"You want a beer?" she asks, stepping out of my arms and walking to the kitchen. "I think I need a drink after that conversation."

"Sure," I say, following her into the kitchen. "I'm going to change. I'll be right back." Regardless of what happens between us tonight, I can't handle this costume for another minute.

18

Snuggles and Snacks

Finley

LEAVE IT TO EMILIO to call and ruin the mood. My panties have been wet enough to swim in since Travis undid my zipper and explored my body with his hands, and now it's all for nothing. He'd started to show me how good he is with his hands when those kids came knocking for candy. Some day, when I tell this story to my friends, I'll say that knock was the beginning of the end. And then, to drive the final nail in the coffin, my dickhead of an ex-husband had to call and wreck everything.

Fucking Emilio.

He ruined our marriage. Tried to ruin my life. And ruined what I'm positive would have been the best orgasm of my life.

Now I'm too irritated to be turned on, and I can't imagine Travis is doing much better. What single guy wants a reminder that the woman he's about to have sex with has three kids and is in the middle of a messy divorce? I'm surprised he only went to change instead of immediately running from the house screaming.

Wait, he probably needed to change into more comfortable running clothes. Then he'll run. That would be in keeping with how this evening is going so far.

I grumble to myself all the way up the stairs on my way to change. If there's anything worse than sitting around in wet underwear, with no orgasm in sight, it's sitting around in wet underwear underneath a skin tight one piece spandex costume.

It gives new meaning to the term 'swamp ass', that's for sure.

I wonder if I have time for a quick shower?

Not that anything is going to happen with my downstairs tonight, but I'd feel better with a quick rinse. After taking out my contacts, I decide to risk it, jumping into the shower of my ensuite bathroom and soaping myself up. I don't bother washing my hair, tying it in a knot on top of my head instead. I don't feel like suffering through the shockingly cold water rinse needed for it to keep its forest green color vibrant.

Five minutes is all it takes to wash off the sweat of the day and then I'm drying off and changing into cotton sleep shorts and a loose racer back tank. Despite how much fun I've had today hanging out with my kids and Travis, after talking to Emilio I'm suddenly hit with bone deep exhaustion. I yawn so deeply, I worry for a second my jaw might get stuck, and make my way back down to the living room.

Travis is sitting on the couch, drinking the beer that he must have grabbed from the kitchen himself, considering I never gave it to him, looking as sexy in gray sweats and a black t-shirt as he did in his tight costume. Maybe even more so, because the gray sweatpants let me see what he's working with more than the compression shorts did.

"Hey," he says when he sees me. "I grabbed you a beer, too." He leans forward and grabs the other bottle off of the coffee table and holds it up for me.

I walk around to the front of the couch and flop down next to him. Immediately, Travis puts his arm around me, pulling me against his warm chest. He kisses my temple and for a moment, the only sensations I'm aware of are the softness of his lips, his hard body against mine, and the warmth of his breath against my skin. I relax fully, sinking into him, resting my head on his shoulder and closing my eyes.

Ugh, I should ensure he knows nothing is going to happen tonight, but it's hard to remember why when it feels so good to be next to him like this. But I know if we sleep together now, I'll regret it tomorrow. Maybe. Probably not, but I don't want to risk it. I like him too much for that.

"Listen, Travis," I say. "Maybe the kids coming knocking and my ex calling was a sign that we should slow things down a bit? I mean, I still can't get Emilio to sign the divorce papers. I'm not so sure I should be starting up with someone new right now. Is that okay?"

He squeezes me with the arm over my shoulder and tilts my chin up with his other hand. "Look at me, Fin," he says, running his thumb over my bottom lip, setting it to tingling. "Of course it's okay. I'm a little hurt, and a little angry at your ex, that you would even think you needed to ask that. You get to decide whether this ever goes further between us." He brushes his lips over mine. "But for the record, I was sort of thinking the same thing. I had the feeling that what you really needed after that phone call was a drink, a cuddle on the couch, and then a good night's sleep. How close am I?"

I chuckle a little, surprised at his understanding. "You're pretty much spot on," I say. "The only thing you missed was the snack."

He laughs. "Well, let me fix that right now." Travis takes his arm out from behind me and stands up, heading for the kitchen. "Anything in particular you're wanting to snack on, or should I surprise you?"

I can't remember the last time anyone got me something without my asking first. And since it's usually my kids that I'm asking, I've had to ask more than once. I could get used to this.

"Surprise me."

"You got it. Why don't you pick out something you want to watch and I'll bring it to you when I've got it ready? It might take me a few minutes to figure out where you keep everything in your kitchen."

Fuck, this man is amazing. Why couldn't I have married someone like him, instead of Emilio? A nice, stable guy with a good job, who also is sweet. And who could forget that sexy body? A girl could do a lot worse.

And I did, hence the divorce I'm trying to get.

Why is a catch like Travis single, anyway? It doesn't make sense to me that someone who is obviously the total package would be single. Maybe Becca knows something or can find out from Johnny for me. Or I could ask his mom. I'm sure she'd jump at the chance to tell me all about him, if the baby pictures she showed me last time I was there for dinner are any sign.

"Leaving me in charge of the show? Yikes. You don't know what you're in for, buddy," I tease.

"Anything is fine with me. I get to snuggle up to a beautiful woman while we watch so I couldn't care less what show it is. Now quit distracting me. I need to concentrate on making this snack."

Thinking of Travis in the kitchen, making me something to eat, makes me all warm and fuzzy, something that I've never personally experienced and had long suspected to be a bunch of bullshit people made up. I'm a little concerned about his snack-making abilities, though. I've never seen him do any cooking, not even at his parents' house when Johnny, Becca, and I all pitch in. I have a sneaking suspicion that he doesn't know how to cook, and somehow that makes his offer of making me a snack that much sweeter.

That doesn't mean I'm going to go easy on him when I choose a show to watch, though. After years of going along with whatever Emilio wanted, I deserve to choose some things for myself. Even if it's a stupid TV show to watch while I snuggle up with my scorching hot handyman while eating the snack that he made especially for me.

So Brooklyn 99 it is. It never fails to make me laugh, and I think Travis will like it, too. Hey, it's not like I said I wouldn't take him into consideration.

"Alright, for better or worse, your snack is ready." Travis holds a plate out for me to grab. It's loaded with crackers and cheese, a peanut butter sandwich, a couple of packages of fruit snacks, a whole carrot, and a stack of salami.

"Awww, it's like a Lunchable and a charcuterie board had a baby," I chuckle, barely able to contain my laughter. "I love it. Thank you."

Travis rubs his neck. "Yeah, I probably should have mentioned that I don't really get along with kitchens. But it's all edible, so that's something."

I pat the couch beside me, urging him to sit. "It's perfect. Come on, let's watch a show."

He sits next to me, his body pressed up against me, and wraps his arm around me again. I could get used to this. Not that I should even think about it before my divorce is finalized. It's probably best if I keep Travis firmly locked in the spank bank file for date nights with B.O.B. for the foreseeable future. It's safer that way.

"Brooklyn 99? This show is hilarious." Travis steals a pack of fruit snacks from my plate. "What season are you on? Or should we start over at the beginning?"

"I was planning on starting over." This may or may not be my fourth watch-through of the series, but I'm not about to tell Travis that. A lady has to have some secrets and the watch status of her favorite comfort show is one of those.

"Perfect," he says, working his body lower into the couch and resting his feet on the coffee table. "I haven't seen it in a while, so I could use a refresher."

"I've seen it so many times. Some women like to watch and rewatch Gilmore Girls over and over, but I prefer this instead. I find it so much funnier. Plus, the thought of being best friends with my kids gives me the willies. Just, no."

He chuckles. "Yeah, I love my parents, but the thought of either of them being my best friend when I was a teenager is terrifying. How do you get up to no good with your parents always in your business?"

"Oh, I think you still get up to no good. Plus, it's not like your parents didn't know you were doing stuff you weren't supposed to when you were young."

"You're probably right. But I wasn't that bad. I spent most of my time looking out for Johnny, really. He's the one who was doing all the underage drinking and sneaking into bars. I tagged along to look after him, like I always do." Travis' lips thin into a frown.

"Why were you always looking out for him?" I can't imagine having to be the babysitter for an older sibling. Luckily, my two sisters were the more responsible of our trio, not that I was bad or anything. "He doesn't seem like he has it in him to be all that bad."

"I'm not really sure," he says. "I've done it ever since I can remember. When he was really young, like maybe three or four, he would do dangerous things like climbing onto the house, or running off down the street, and I sort of took it upon myself to keep him safe. I would do all the same things he did and keep an eye on him at the same time. And it's been like that ever since."

My jaw drops. "But... he's a year older than you. You were two years old and stopping him from jumping off the house?

Sounds like you've been looking after him for your whole life. How does he manage when he's out on tour and you're here?"

"Oh, yeah, um." He squeezes my shoulder and laughs. "The other guys look after him, and so does Denise, the band's manager. He hasn't had any major injuries so far, so I guess they do alright."

"Yeah, I kind of get that vibe from them. Especially Devon. He doesn't seem like he'd let anyone fuck with the band."

Travis chuckles again and leans back against the couch, his eyes glued to the TV. Something about what he said about him looking out for Johnny is bothering me, but I can't quite put my finger on it. I'm sure it will come to me.

I snuggle closer to Travis and turn my face to the TV. This night started out with much different intentions but the way it's ending feels so good, and so right.

19

Emilio to Milo and Back Again

Travis

"I CAN'T KEEP DOING this, man." I'm sitting at a table with Johnny. We finished our performance with Connor a little while ago and he and Alex have already left to celebrate alone, leaving the rest of us at Rough Mix to enjoy their engagement party without them. "I can't keep lying to Fin. If she knew I was in the band, and not really a handyman, I could have brought her with me tonight."

"Maybe. If she didn't hate your stupid fucking face for lying to her about it in the first place, after you finally told her the truth," Becca says, pointing her beer bottle at me. She makes a face. "This stuff is disgusting. I wonder if Bill would stock some better beer for when we come in? I'm going to go ask him." She kisses Johnny before she goes, shocking the hell out of me.

"Whoa, what's that all about?" I didn't think they were actually together, at least not the kind of together that warrants kisses before stepping away for a moment. I suppose I have been preoccupied with Finley lately, though, so it's possible I didn't notice they'd been getting serious.

"Don't change the subject. Why are you still lying to Fin?"

I blow out a breath and throw up a hand. "Her ex is a massive dickhead. He's been pretty much M.I.A. for years because his version of a mid-life crisis was joining a band and banging groupies while they were still married."

"And? What does that have to do with you?"

Is he fucking with me? He has to be. Does he really not understand? "Uh, because she wants nothing to do with musicians. And I am a musician."

"Are you sure about that?" Johnny asks, his tone suddenly serious.

"Yeah, I am. I'm in the band, aren't I?"

He shrugs. "You are, but do you really want to be? I've been watching you for a long time, Travis, and you've been going through the motions for years. You only really look like you're enjoying yourself when you're building something. When we all helped build Finley's porch, I swear you smiled more than you have in the last five years. Of course, that could have been because you were doing something nice for Fin."

"I love working with my hands. You know that. But that doesn't mean I don't love playing with you guys and being in the band."

"Yes, I do. But do you know that? Really?" He stands up and puts a hand on my shoulder. "You should take some time to really think about what you want from life before you resign yourself to something you're not completely sure about. Don't miss out on something that could be great because you're scared to let go of something that isn't serving you anymore. Besides, you haven't given her a chance to make up her own mind. You've been lying to her since you met her, and I think that is going to affect her opinion of you more than you being in the band will. Not every musician behaves like her ex. I'd bet he was an asshole before he started his band, and he'll still be an asshole long after they're done."

I drop my head down to the sticky tabletop and make a noise that's a cross between a grunt and groan. Johnny doesn't get it.

Becca's ex was so horrible to her there's no way Johnny has to worry about being in the same predicament. As long as he acts like a decent human being, there's no way Becca could think he's the same as him.

Finley, though, her ex joined a band and started fucking around on her. And it's not like musicians haven't been known to sleep around a lot, especially while on tour. I mean, shit. I've heard about dudes back in the day sticking their dicks in breakfast burritos before going home to their wives and girlfriends to get rid of the smell of whatever strange vaginas they'd been in that day.

"How could Finley possibly believe that I'm not the kind of guy who would cheat on her? You know how so many guys in our business are. Women love musicians, and they throw themselves at us all the time. Just because I don't take them up on it anymore, doesn't mean that other guys in the industry won't be giving me a bad name through association."

"Who gives a fuck what those assholes do? They're not you, just like they're not me. She'll believe you if she trusts you. But you're not even giving her the chance to trust you. That's what me and the guys have been trying to tell you. Look at Alex. She's been cheated on so many times, and all those guys were normal assholes. And tonight, she accepted Connor's proposal. She trusts him. There's no reason Fin couldn't trust you." He raps his knuckles on the table, fixes me with a look, then turns and leaves.

I stare after him, stunned, watching as he walks over to Becca and joins her in talking to Bill at the bar.

How did he know how I've been feeling about the band? He's never been much good at reading my mind with our fake twin thing, but I think it's safe to say he's nailed this.

Shit.

My conversation with Johnny leaves a sour taste in my mouth, so I say my goodbyes and take myself home to think about how badly I fucked this up.

"You'll never guess who I ran into."

"Devon?" I rub my eyes and try to see the time on my phone. It's after midnight and I was sleeping peacefully on the couch until my phone rang, startling me awake.

I couldn't sleep at all last night, too busy thinking about what Johnny said at the engagement party to allow my brain to rest. And today, after setting up the surprise baby shower for Denise, and then the surprise wedding for Denise and Ryder, and then attending the wedding and reception, my eyes closed as soon as I got home and sat down. Stress and physical labor will knock me out every time.

"Yes, it's me, asshole. So, guess." Devon's laughing, enjoying this little guessing game he's having me play.

"I don't know, man. Why don't you tell me?"

"Xena was right, you're no fun."

"I'm fun when I've gotten enough sleep. And I hate guessing games."

"Ugh, fine. I saw Finley's ex-husband at Maggie's Diner tonight."

That makes me sit up, fully alert now.

"Here in town. What the hell is he doing here? Did he come see the kids?"

"I don't think so. He was with a couple of other guys. Probably his bullshit band. But that's not the crazy part. Are you ready for this?"

For one moment, a vision of Fin flashes through my head, and in it she's kissing Emilio because they've gotten back together. My stomach roils. God, I hope to fuck it's not that.

"Tell me already. I can't handle the tension. Was Fin with him?"

Devon splutters. *"What? No! Of course not. Dude. Give her some credit. Hell, give me some credit, too. I would not call you in the middle of the night with that kind of news. I'd come over with a bottle of whiskey and break it to you in person."*

I heave a sigh of relief. Not that I really think Finley would go back to the asshole, but you never know. She married him. She must've loved him at some point. Thinking of her loving him, even in the past, sends a pain to my chest and I'm left rubbing my hand over my heart. That can't be good.

"Okay, good. So what, then?"

"Geez, man. I still can't believe you think I'd call you up with that kind of information. I know I'm technically an employee, but we're still friends first. You really hurt my feelings." I can hear the pout in his tone.

"Okay, okay. I'm sorry. I know you wouldn't do that. I panicked for a second."

"Alright. I forgive you."

Fucking Devon. Why is he dragging this out? I open and clench my free hand repeatedly, wishing I could reach through the phone and slap him.

"Devon. Please, tell me already."

"Oh, yeah, right. Sorry. Okay, so Xena and I went to get some food after the wedding because she got trashed and needed to eat before she went to sleep. Apparently, Johnny and Becca had the same idea because they were there, too."

"Okay... and?"

"And Emilio was also there. Only he was calling Becca Freddy, and Becca was calling him Milo. He's Becca's shitty ex-boyfriend

who took a topless picture of her and gave her the Freddy Krueger nickname."

What? My phone clatters to the floor, and I scramble to pick it up.

"Wait, what?! For real? Does Becca know they're the same person?"

"She didn't say anything like that, so I don't think so. Are you going to tell Finley?"

Shit, am I? I probably should. She already knows he's a dick. Does she need to know about something he did before she even met him? She's friends with Becca, though. Would it be better or worse for them to find out that Milo and Emilio are the same person accidentally? Or for someone to break it to both of them at the same time?

"Wow," I release a long breath and scrub a hand over my face. "I have no fucking idea. What do you think?"

"That's a tough one, man. I don't know Finley that well, or Becca either, for that matter. But somehow I think it would be worse if they stumbled on the information, you know?"

"Yeah, you have a point. Did he recognize you?"

"Oh yeah. So much so that he pissed himself and I had to escort him from the building for that little waitress. You know the one. I think her name's Ivy. The one who compulsively gives out her phone number?"

I burst out laughing. Of course, that little fucker pissed himself.

"I lifted him up by his shirt and carried him outside. It was hilarious."

"Devon, have I told you recently that you're the best? I can't believe he pissed himself and you carried him outside."

"Well, I couldn't leave him there and let him get piss everywhere. That wouldn't be fair to the people working. Xena told me that once a customer at Bump & Grind had an accident and

trailed it around the shop before he left. She had to close for the rest of the day and have a biological waste cleaning crew come in."

"No. No, I guess you couldn't. Thanks for calling to let me know. I'll let you know what I decide about telling Fin. Can you hold off on telling Becca until we talk again?"

"*Sure, man. No problem. Let me know what you decide. I got to go now, anyway. Talk to you later.*"

"Thanks. Bye."

I hit the end call button and put my phone in my pocket.

Emilio is Milo. Milo is Emilio.

What the fuck?

I would never have guessed that. I thought the dude was only some guy having a midlife crisis, but with what he did to Becca when she was a teenager, I'm suspecting he's got more serious issues than that. It's no wonder Finley fell for him. He could probably be whatever she wanted him to be for the first little while. It was only after a few years that he showed his true colors. He must've gotten a lot better at manipulating people in between Becca and Fin. And now she's stuck with him in her life forever because of the kids.

I know I need to tell Finley. It's the right thing to do, especially if she's going to continue getting closer to Becca like she has been.

But how do I tell her? And when?

20

Coffee Dates and Conversations

Finley

"HEY, THANKS FOR COMING over. My ex *actually* picked up the kids for his weekend for once and I've been going crazy trying to figure out what to do with myself. I haven't had girlfriends in so long I wasn't sure if invitations to come over for coffee was still a thing people did."

"Anything that involves coffee is something I need to be invited to," Alex says, grabbing a cup and curling up on the couch. "After this past weekend, I will take all the coffee I can get."

Becca is halfway to sitting when she suddenly jumps up. "Wait! Did you say your ex had the kids this weekend? You could have come?"

"Come where?"

Alex and Becca give each other a look and then Becca turns back to me. "Alex and Connor got engaged on Saturday, and then Denise and Ryder got married last night. It's been a crazy ass weekend. Wait until you hear what Denise's ex did."

My stomach takes a dive, and a hint of jealousy pokes its ugly head into my thoughts. An engagement and a wedding in one weekend? Seems like everyone is busy falling in love while I'm trying to navigate the aftermath of a divorce that I can't even get my ex to sign papers for. But that's not who I am. I can be happy for my friends even if I'm not exactly where I want to be in life. It's not my fault that my marriage didn't work out and it's not their fault either. Shit happens. It sucks that for the last year, it seems like the shit is always happening to me. I can have a pity party later. I won't let my misery bring these women down with me. I take a deep breath and calm myself.

"Congratulations, Alex. That's so exciting. Tell me everything about the proposal. I can't wait to hear all about it," I say, plastering my brightest smile on my face. Alex's answering grin is all I need to know how she feels about being engaged.

"You bet, but there's something even more exciting that you should probably hear about first."

She settles into the couch and picks up her own coffee as my phone buzzes from my pocket. I take a look and see it's my grandmother. "Oh, crap. Don't start yet. I need to take this, if that's okay? It's my grandmother."

Becca's eyes go wide and Alex chokes on her coffee. Weird. I press the answer call button on my phone, shaking my head at the two women on my couch who are suddenly still.

"Hey, Grandma,"

"Flipper, kiddo. Before you hear it from somewhere else, Delores and I are fine. We took care of that little dickhead. He won't do something like that again, that's for sure."

I spin back to Alex and Becca. I have a feeling whatever this is, it has something to do with what they were about to tell me.

"What do you mean, you took care of that little dickhead? What little dickhead?"

"Well, Ryder got married last night, you know? It was a lovely ceremony, and I should know. I performed it myself. Too bad you missed your chance with him. But that's not why I called. Yesterday afternoon, Denise's ex-boyfriend came here. Denise is the woman who Ryder married. Anyway, her ex-boyfriend came here and tried to get Delores. Can you believe it?"

"Oh my god, Grandma. Are you sure you guys are okay? Do you want me to come over?"

"Right as rain, Flipper. But that dickhead sure isn't. I zapped him in the nuts with my stun-gun and Delores tied him up with her fancy pink rope. It was outstanding. We're crime fighting grannies. They're probably going to ask us to join the police force to help take down all the criminals in this town." The sound of laughter pours from the phone, and I can tell it's more than my Grandma laughing. She has an audience, which doesn't surprise me. She's probably told this story to anyone who would listen at least a hundred times since yesterday. *"I wanted to let you know that there's no need to worry. We took care of it. You don't need to make a special trip today to check on me."*

I choke on a laugh. Of course my grandma electrocuted a man in the testicles. That's not even the weirdest thing I have heard of her doing. Just another day in the life of Gladys Harrison. "Okay, Grandma, thanks for letting me know. I have some friends over now so I'll talk to you later, alright?"

"You bet, Flipper. Next time you come over, me and Delores will do a reenactment for you. You're going to love it. Gotta go, sweetheart. Our friends at Peaceful Pines are throwing us a big party to celebrate. Bye-bye Flipper."

The line goes dead. With a sigh, I put my phone back in my pocket and sit back down.

"Well, that was my grandma." I pinch my lips together and nod. "She and Delores got into some trouble yesterday, and she zapped a man in the testicles with her stun-gun. She wanted to let me know she's okay."

After a beat of silence, Alex, Becca, and I all burst into laughter at the same time.

"That's what I was going to tell you," Becca gasps. "I keep forgetting that Gladys is your grandma. She and Delores are my heroes. I want to be like them when I'm older."

"They're something else, alright," Alex chuckles, regaining her composure. "It's always a good time when they're around."

We sit and drink coffee for the next while and Becca and Alex tell me everything they know about the events of the previous day. It sounds like Delores and my grandmother are quite the heroes, in more ways than one. They even pulled off a surprise wedding for Ryder and Denise on the same day as all this other stuff happened.

All I managed to do yesterday was put some new flooring in Austin's bedroom and start a load of laundry, and I thought I was doing pretty good. Talk about feeling inadequate now.

"Oh, and then after the wedding, Johnny and I went for pancakes and you'll never guess who was there. My ex! Can you believe it?"

"Umm, no?" I say, confused. I don't know much about these women, so I'm not sure how surprised I should be by this revelation. "Is that bad?"

She laughs. "Actually, it was more hilarious than anything. I came back from the bathroom to find him fan-boying all over Johnny, but before anything else could happen, Devon and Xena came in. You should have seen how scared my ex was. He actually pissed himself. Devon picked him up by the shirt, then carried him outside. It was awesome."

I chuckle a little at how happy Becca seems to be about this, but I still don't really understand. "I don't get it. Is he, like, a terrible guy? Did he hurt you?"

Becca stops laughing. "I didn't tell you this yet? It feels like after so many years of hiding shit that I've finally told everyone. Okay, this is the short version. I had an accident when I was a kid and I got burned over a good portion of my body. Other kids made fun of me because I would wear clothes that covered me head-to-toe, so I could hide my scars. This guy convinced me he liked me, then when he got me partly undressed, he snapped a picture. After that, he and everyone at school started calling me Freddy, for Freddy Krueger, because of my burns."

I stare, open-mouthed. "What a dick." Something about her story niggles at me, but I can't put my finger on what.

"Oh yeah, completely. But his uncle is the person who gave me my first tattoo, the giant Freddy Krueger, on my thigh. And he—his uncle, not my ex—and his husband are both like family to me now, so I guess it wasn't all bad. I still wish Devon would have punched him in the dick, though."

Alex laughs. "I'm sure he would have, if the asshole hadn't pissed himself first. Devon's good like that. He and Ryder beat the shit out of my ex for showing up at my apartment and trying to beg forgiveness for cheating on me. Well, that and he had accidentally hit me in the face with my door, trying to stop Connor from closing it on him."

"Sounds like Devon is an excellent protector," I say. "And that he got into the right profession."

"And Xena sure lucked out, too. For such a tiny girl, she has a big mouth and the attitude to match. He's wrapped right around her finger and neither of them wants to admit it. But she needs someone like him around to help her out when her mouth gets her into trouble."

"What? Why?" Every time I've seen them together, they look pretty close. They didn't look like they're trying to deny anything, anyway.

Becca leans back, pulling her legs up onto the couch. "From what I could make out last night, Devon is friends with Xena's older brother. So he likes to pretend that he thinks of her like a little sister and that's why he looks out for her."

"He looks at her like he wants to get into her tiny pixie pants. Nothing brotherly about that," Alex laughs. "But they're so cute together, so I'm really hoping they work it out. Of course, when the older brother of the woman you're interested in happens to also be a cop..."

"Ooh, yeah, that could be an issue." I get up and gesture to the kitchen. "You guys want more coffee?"

They both say they're fine, so I go to the kitchen and pour myself a cup. When I get back into the living room, I don't even get my ass into the chair before the questions start.

"But now that we're here, and there are no men with us, tell us what's up with you and Travis?"

"Yeah, you've been spending a lot of time together. Johnny says he's never at home anymore," Becca adds. "What's going on with you two?"

Instantly my cheeks heat. "What? Nothing. Nothing's going on."

"Yeah, uh-huh. I totally believe you." Alex's eyes are comically wide as she purses her lips and nods her head. "That didn't sound suspicious at all."

I feel my cheeks flame and I'm sure I look redder than the eighteen bottles of fake blood Austin insisted we stock up on after Halloween. "Seriously, nothing is going on. We sort of kissed the other night, but it didn't go farther than that." Not for lack of trying. If it weren't for the interference of those kids showing up at the door at the wrong time, and my ex calling right after, I'm sure we would have wound up in bed together. That's what I was hoping for, anyway.

"Oh, yeah. I believe you, sure. But I'm thinking that maybe, even if nothing is happening now, you want something to happen soon."

"You want that ginger beefcake to show you his ham candle. Come on. Tell the truth. You picture him when you have quality time by yourself, don't you?"

My mouth opens and closes repeatedly while I do my best impression of a fish, but no words come out. How did they know that? "Ham candle?" I finally splutter.

"Becca means you think about him when you masturbate. And from how your face just went from red to burgundy, I'm going to say that she's right. Travis is a good guy. You should go for it."

"Plus, if he's anything like Johnny, he's packing some serious hardware. And I'd be willing to bet he even knows how to use it." Becca leans back and laughs. "That's what really matters, after all."

My mind immediately flashes back again to Halloween night, and what I could feel pressed against me when Travis was getting friendly with my downstairs kitty-cat. Even with the compression shorts he said he was wearing, it felt impressive. And, once again, I'm pissed at Emilio for calling and ruining everything that night.

"Look at the way her eyes glazed over," Alex laughs. "Something has to be happening between them."

"Between who?"

I jump at the sound of Travis' voice. I was so lost in my memory of the other night that I guess I didn't hear the door open when he came in.

How long has he been standing there, anyway?

21

Eavesdropping and Hardwood

Travis

I LET MYSELF INTO Finley's house and silently congratulate myself on finally getting the door fixed. It opens so smoothly now it barely even makes a sound. I guess Halloween night wasn't a complete bust. I got to snuggle up with Finley and I got the door repaired.

As I'm about to yell out to let Fin know I'm here, I hear voices coming from the living room. Sounds like she has some company. Either that or her kids somehow all became adult women over the course of the weekend.

"Becca is saying that you think about him when you masturbate. And from how your face just went from red to burgundy, I'm going to say that she's right. Travis is a good guy. You should go for it."

Holy shit. That's Alex. And it sounds to me like she's saying Fin thinks about me when she gets herself off. No, that can't be true. I mean, sure, we almost did something on Halloween night, but that doesn't mean she thinks about me all the time. Does it?

"Plus, if he's anything like Johnny, he's packing some serious hardware. And I'd be willing to bet he even knows how to use it. That's what really matters, after all."

That's Becca. Fin still hasn't responded. I need to get in there before they say anything more and I'm caught standing here eavesdropping.

"Look at the way her eyes glazed over," Alex laughs. "Something has to be happening between them."

I take the last few steps to the living room and pause at the entrance. "Between who? Becca and Johnny? We all know that already." All three women startle in their seats and Finley looks like I caught her doing something wrong.

"Hey, wow, is that the time already? We better get going, Becca." Alex gets up from her spot. "Thanks for coffee, Finley. Seriously, call me anytime. I'm always up for a coffee date."

"Same," says Becca. "I'm still not getting as many bookings as I'd like for my photography business, so I've got lots of time on my hands."

"See you later, Travis."

"Bye, Trav."

Finley walks Alex and Becca to the door to see them off while I make myself useful by cleaning up the coffee cups left in the living room and bringing them to the kitchen. My imagination is working overtime, sending me images of Finley touching herself, whispering my name, calling out her release to thoughts of me, and I don't hear her when she comes to stand beside me until she speaks.

"Travis," she yells, finally getting my attention. "Are you alright? Where'd you go there?" she asks with a laugh.

All traces of redness have left her face and now she's back to her normal self. She's as beautiful as ever, especially when she laughs. The guys gave me shit when I left the studio early again, but when I walked in and saw Finley, I knew instantly I made the right choice. She's the only thing I've been able to think about all morning, and I'd have gone crazy if I'd waited even longer to see her. I'm digging myself into such a deep hole with her, but I can't seem to stop myself. We're not even together, and I can't be away from her for more than a few days. How the hell am I ever going to survive going on tour?

"Sorry, I was thinking about the job I was doing this morning." Not exactly a lie, but not quite the truth, either. That's the other thing the guys keep giving me shit about, continuing to lie to Fin. I should tell her the truth, I know I should, but I can't stand the thought of her never speaking to me again after I tell her. There has to be some way to tell her the truth and not have to give her up completely. If only I could figure out what that way is. "I'm having some trouble figuring out how I'm going to do it, is all. That's why I came here. So you can tell me what to do."

She smiles and pushes me with her shoulder. "I do like bossing you around. Hey, I thought that today maybe you could help me rip up some old carpet? The one in my bedroom has got to go. I don't even care what's under it anymore, as long as it's not more of the disgusting mustard yellow shag that's in there right now."

"Let's do it," I say. "I'll grab my tools and meet you up there."

"Sounds good."

"OH MY GOD, LOOK at this. Look at it." Finley ripped up a corner of the filthy carpet, and its underlay, before I got back with my tools and she's practically vibrating with excitement. She gets down into a low squat, grabs the edge of the carpet, and yanks, scrambling to get her balance when it gives, revealing another chunk of what's beneath. "Ha! Can you believe someone covered this with carpet? What is wrong with people?"

I step over the loose carpet and look down to see a gorgeous honey colored hardwood. In this spot, at least, it even looks to be in good shape.

"Damn, Fin. You Hulked out and ripped this up with no tools? That's pretty impressive," I laugh. "And it looks like you lucked out in the flooring department, too. It's probably a good thing for you that someone was dumb enough to cover this hardwood. If they hadn't, I doubt it would look this good now." Every time we work on the house together, I'm more amazed at everything Fin can do. She doesn't shy away from the hard stuff.

"You're not kidding. Look at how good these floors look. I can't believe it. I was sure we'd be renting a drum sander and redoing the whole thing. Not today, obviously, but at some point. Depending on what it looks like under the rest of this god awful carpet, we might not have to do any restoration at all. This is great."

Finley's excitement is getting the best of her, and she's right back to pulling on the enormous piece of carpet, trying to reveal more of the beautiful flooring underneath. She's about reached the limits of her strength, though, because fifty-year-old shag carpeting that's seen better days isn't exactly light.

"Here, Let me cut some of that off and take it out to my truck. After that, it should be easier to pull off more carpet." I grab my utility blade and start cutting to remove the piece of carpeting she's already pulled up. She rolls it up as I cut, and I can't help but marvel at how seamlessly we work together. I didn't even need to ask before she started doing exactly what needed to be done. And it's a little weird how much that turns me on.

Finley and I continue to work side by side for the rest of the afternoon, until finally, we get every last bit of carpet, underlay, and tacking out of her bedroom. The carpet and underlay were the easy part, especially since whoever laid it didn't glue down any of the underlay. We were even able to pull some nails and staples out with the carpet, so we had fewer to remove when it got to that point.

I'm down on my hands and knees on the far side of the room, removing a small patch of underlay that is stuck to the floor, when Finley's kids yell from downstairs.

"We're home," Braden yells. "What's for dinner?"

Finley laughs. "Hi, mom, I missed you. How was your weekend?" She imitates Braden's voice as she stands and dusts her hands off on her pants. "Hey guys," she yells. "I'm upstairs in my bedroom. Come and look." She stops and looks over at me. "You want to stay for dinner? Not sure what I'm making, but I promise it will be edible. Or at least not poisonous."

I stand up. "Yeah, I'd love to. How about you let me order dinner, though? We've both worked too hard at ripping out this carpet to be required to cook on top of it." I pull my phone out to start our order. No matter her answer, I'm ordering dinner tonight. I can't sit here and let her cook for me after she's worked so hard. And if I attempted to cook, no doubt whatever I made would be barely edible. The kitchen and I have never gotten along, and I don't think we ever will. It's much safer if I leave the cooking to the experts.

"Are you sure? I can cook. I don't want you spending even more money on us. I still haven't paid for any of the work you've done."

"Don't worry about that. We'll square up later." Well, we won't, but I'm not ready to tell her about that yet. She still thinks I'm a handyman who makes my money doing jobs like this, when really, the money I've spent on her renovation hasn't made a dent in my bank account. "We'll call this a business dinner, if that makes you feel better."

"Wow." Austin runs into the bedroom first and jumps up on Fin's bed. "Where'd that gross carpet go? This is way better."

"Isn't it nice? We need to check what's under the carpet in your bedrooms, too," I tell the kids. "I have a feeling there's also a nice floor under those." And if there's not, we'll install some. Before I go back on tour, I plan to have this house finished to Finley's liking. It's the only way I can look after her and I plan to do it.

Austin jumps off the bed and sprints from the room. "Let's do it now," he yells as he runs.

Finley laughs, "We're having dinner soon. We'll have to work on your floor another day."

"Aw, man. No fair. How come your bedroom gets to look cool and mine still looks like a bunch of ugly old puppets died on the floor?" Austin whines. I think this is the first time I've heard him complain about it looking like something died anywhere near him. Normally, he loves that stuff. Poor kid. Life's rough when you're the youngest.

Finley follows Austin to his room, probably to talk to him about the carpet thing, and to make sure he's not too upset. I know it bothers her she hasn't been able to finish all the renovations on the house yet, but for it being only the two of us, plus Braden, doing all the work, we're moving along pretty quickly.

Not that I want the work to be over yet. I need to keep my reason for seeing Finley, after all. Once the work is done and she doesn't need me anymore, I don't know what I'll do. But I'm beginning to think not seeing her isn't going to be an option for me. Not if I want to be even the tiniest bit happy.

22

Rose-Colored Glasses and Candy

Finley

"GIRLS, LOOK WHO FINALLY showed up to a meeting. Nice to see you, Finley. Not that we couldn't see you. It's certainly hard to miss you with that... interesting hair."

Don't punch her, Finley. She would definitely sue you.

Of course Candace has to be a bitch to me immediately. I guess it would have been too much to ask for a little common courtesy from her, simply based on the fact that I'm a human being, too.

"Hi, Candace. I had some time available, so I thought I'd come to the meeting and see if I can help with the Christmas show."

PTA Candace graces me with a condescending frown. "Oh no, did you lose your job? What are you going to do now?"

"No, Candace. I still have my job, but thanks for your concern," I say sweetly. Kill them with kindness, right? I don't think it's going to work, but I need to try for my kids' sake. I can't have them being ostracized because their mom can't get along with the alpha-mom of the school. "I'm taking my real estate licensing test tomorrow. I'm going to have some free time coming up since I won't be studying anymore. I thought maybe I could help while I can. You know, pitch in for good old South Westborough Elementary." I make a fist, and pump my arm in an *aw shucks* motion, hoping she'll interpret it as enthusiasm, instead of the sarcasm it really is.

Instead, she looks down her nose at me. "Yes, well. I don't suppose Johnny Donovan will come and bail you out this time. I'm sure he's realized his money is better spent somewhere else, somewhere other than helping you."

It's okay, Finley. Breathe. You knew she would bring him up. You knew she would try to rub your nose in it.

"Well, he wanted to, of course. But I told him that wasn't necessary. There are so many well-off parents at SWE that we'd be able to fundraise the money. No problem. I know you and your husband won't have any problem at least matching what Johnny spent on the Halloween party, will you? You're generous like that, right?"

"Well, I, uh... Yes, well, I have to go get the meeting started."

I watch Candace walk to the front of the room. The delusional woman actually has a judge's gavel that she bangs on the table to get everyone's attention. She takes this PTA thing way too seriously, and from the way all the other parents face the front of the room and stop talking immediately, they do, too.

I roll my eyes and shake my head. Why did I come here? I'm sure the kids can make friends without needing me to volunteer with the Stepford moms of the South Westborough Elementary PTA.

"Saw that."

I turn toward the speaker to see another mom beside me, leaning back against the wall, tossing popcorn into her mouth. Her bright copper hair is piled on top of her head in a knot similar to mine, and she's the only other person here wearing beat up sneakers besides me. Could she be a kindred spirit amidst this gaggle of try-hards?

"Excuse me?"

"I said, I saw that. I saw you roll your eyes." She points at me with a paper bag filled with popcorn while she chews. "Actually, you rolled them so hard I think I might have even heard it."

"Uhhh…"

"Oh, don't worry. I used to roll my eyes, too. I had to train myself to stop because I'd do it so much during these meetings I'd leave with a migraine after every one."

"Uh huh," I drawl. "Not a fan of PTA meetings?"

"Oh no, I love 'em. Watch," she says with a grin before throwing another handful of popcorn into her mouth. "Want some?" She holds the bag out.

"No, thanks."

"We go over this every meeting, Rose. You can't bring popcorn in here." Candace raises her voice so it carries all the way to the back of the room where I'm standing. "Why must you continue to defy me?"

"Uh oh. Busted," the woman next to me stage-whispers. "Hold this. I'll show you why I love PTA meetings so much." She passes me her popcorn bag and dusts off her hands. "Oh, come on now, Candy." She smirks as a look of horror crosses Candace's face. "How the hell can you expect me to make it to the end of this bullshit meeting without snacks?"

Huh. I guess my new friend is the Rose who Candace was talking to. She seems fun. I think I like her.

I grab a handful of popcorn and throw it in my mouth, looking between Rose and Candace, waiting to see how this plays out. If this is the type of entertainment I can expect, maybe these PTA meetings won't be so bad after all?

"Rose," Candace says, holding the bridge of her nose. "I am the president of the PTA. You need to listen to me, or else."

Rose snorts a laugh. "Or else what? You'll fire me from my voluntary position? You'll refuse my monetary help? You and your husband will do all the heavy lifting by yourselves?"

"Well, umm..."

"Yeah, that's what I thought. Why don't you run your little meeting and leave me alone with my popcorn?"

Candace turns to speak to a woman at the front of the room with her. There's some nodding, some whispering, and finally Candace stands up straight and pats down her hair. She smacks her little gavel on the table again, calling the room to attention, and starts the meeting.

"That was impressive." I tell Rose while handing her popcorn back. "She's been nothing but trouble to me since my kids started coming here."

"Meh, she's a bitch, but she's harmless. I think she likes to make herself feel important. I'd tell her there are much better ways to feel important than lording over the PTA, but she already hates me. So fuck her," Rose laughs.

"I think you and I are going to get along just fine, Rose. I'm Finley."

"Oh, I know," she says with a wink. "Travis is my brother."

She laughs as my mouth drops and my eyes go wide. How did the hair not tip me off? Few people have that vibrant shade of copper. "Wait. Aren't you Tyson's mom?"

"Yup, I hear he and Braden have become good friends over the last little while. I've seen Braden at my parents' place, but I always seem to miss you. I was on the verge of forcing Travis to give me your phone number, but it looks like I won't have to do that anymore."

"Yes, oh my god! Tyson has been amazing for Braden. He was so unhappy with the move. He was sure he wouldn't make any friends, but then he met Tyson before school even started and it helped him so much. Now he's back to just being angry at me for the divorce, instead of the divorce *and* making him lose all his friends."

"Ladies? Will you be taking part in this meeting or not? Your chatter is very distracting." Candace stands with her hands on her hips, glaring at me and Rose. Ha! She's even tapping her foot. She must be furious.

Rose snickers in Candace's direction and turns to face me again. "Want to get out of here? Grab coffee or something? I'm sure Candy can handle this on her own. Isn't that right, Candy? You'll let us know what you need help with, right? You don't need us here while you pretend to hear everyone else's ideas before ultimately forcing us to do whatever stupid thing you've already decided on, right? Okay, great. Buh-bye, then."

Rose grabs my arms and pulls me to the door, giggling the entire way. She pulls the door open with a flourish and we both burst into the hallway as peals of laughter escape our mouths.

"That was so great," I gasp. "She really hates you, doesn't she?"

"Oh, yeah. Hates me with a passion. It's awesome. She has great ideas, though. The events she puts on for the kids are better than I've ever seen. If she wasn't such a bitch, we could probably be friends. Alas, she is a bitch and so I must spend PTA meetings knocking her down a few pegs."

"It's certainly entertaining for me. Watching you eviscerate her was the highlight of my week."

"Why thank you, dear lady," she laughs with a bow. "I live to serve. Now come on. Let's get a ridiculously overpriced, blended, caffeinated monstrosity of a beverage and you can tell me all about what's going on with you and my brother."

"I—what? No. There's nothing go—"

"Before you say nothing is going on, I think it's only fair to tell you I have three kids and I can smell lies."

I shake my head at her and chuckle. "That's good skill to have. I have three kids, too, and they are much too good at lying for me to be able to tell anything."

She laughs. "Now, I know that's not true. Mom's always know, even when we don't. Remember that. Come on. I have my car, I'll drive."

I nod and follow her to the parking lot, my mind suddenly elsewhere. What *is* going on with me and Travis? Is it something? Is it nothing? Do I even have the mental capacity for it to be something? I groan internally. I haven't felt this conflicted about a guy since high school. And as a mom to three kids, I don't have the luxury of jumping in and out of relationships. In fact, it's probably best for me to stick to friendships only in the foreseeable future.

Menstruation Man - A New Kind of Hero

Travis

"Hello?"

"Hi, um, is this Travis?"

"Sarah?" What? What's Finley's daughter doing calling me in the middle of a school day? My heart pounds so hard I can hear it, and suddenly my palms are sweaty. "Is everything okay?"

I can hear her sniffle through the phone, *"Um, kind of? I tried calling my mom, but she's doing her test today and she didn't answer. And my dad didn't answer either. Then I called Nana, but she has all the little kids today and she doesn't have enough car seats for them to drive anywhere. She said I should call you."*

"Okay, honey. That's okay. I'll help you. Tell me what's wrong."

The guys all stopped playing when I answered my phone, probably surprised that I would stop a rehearsal for a phone call, but too bad. When the call display told me it was the school calling, there was no way in hell I wasn't going to answer.

"It's so embarrassing. I don't want to say."

Shit, hold on for a minute. How old is Sarah, again? Ten? Yeah, ten, almost eleven. I have a sneaking suspicion I know what this is about. And I think I know how to feel a little more comfortable telling me about it.

"Hey, Sarah? Did you know that I have five sisters?"

"I know your mom has a ton of grandkids."

I chuckle. Well, here goes nothing. If she's not calling for what I think she is, then this is going to be weird as shit. "Yeah, that she does. But that's not what I was saying. I have five sisters who are all older than me. Do you want to take a guess at how many times in my life I've had to run to the store to buy pads and other products that they needed because they got their period unexpectedly? I'll give you a hint. It was a lot."

Now she's laughing into the phone, her sniffles coming less frequently. Bingo! Looks like my leap of faith paid off. *"You did?"*

"I sure did. I did it so many times I'm practically an expert at shopping for that stuff. So what do you need, sweetie? I've got my keys in my hand and I'm ready to go. Tell me what to bring and I'll go get it for you."

"Umm, well, that's part of the problem. I don't really know what I need." She chokes back a small sob. *"I do need clean clothes, though."*

The guys are all staring at me with puzzled looks on their faces as I rush around, trying to put away my equipment and gather up my stuff. I stop dead in my tracks when what Sarah says sinks in.

"Sarah, is this your first, uh, your first time? First period?"

"Yes."

Fuck. This changes things a little.

Okay, I'm not really qualified for this. Running errands and gathering supplies is one thing. Figuring out what she needs on my own is another thing completely. I'm going to need backup.

"Okay, that's okay. No problem. Hold on one second, okay, sweetie?" I hold my phone away from my mouth without waiting for an answer. "Connor, is Alex home? Can you get her in here?"

"Sure, man. Whatever you need." He must hear the panic in my voice because he wastes no time running off, intent on tracking Alex down wherever she is in the house. I put my phone back up to my ear.

"Sarah? I'll be there shortly, okay? Do you remember my friend, Alex? She's going to come with me to make sure I get all the right things. Don't worry about a thing, alright? We'll be there soon."

"Okay Travis, thanks."

"No problem, kiddo. I'm happy to help. See you soon."

Sarah says goodbye and then hangs up.

"What the fuck, man? You're bringing a kid shit for her period? What are you, some kind of Menstruation Man?" Ryder laughs.

"Fuck off, Ryder. She's ten years old. She's scared. Don't be a dick," I snap at Ryder while I gather up my stuff. "Have some compassion."

"Oh, shit. That's young, isn't it?" Ryder looks chastened by my outburst. Good.

"I don't know. I think so? All I know is she's freaked out and her mom is sitting for her real estate licensing exam and can't even answer the phone. And my mom can't leave with all the kids she has at her house, so she told Sarah to call me. And Sarah's useless excuse for a dad didn't answer his phone."

"Here she is," Connor says, dragging Alex behind him.

"Slow down. What the hell, Connor?" Alex pulls her hand from his. "I have stuff in the oven."

"Sorry, Alex. I need your help. My friend Finley's daughter got her first period at school, and through the process of elimination, she called me for help. I can grab pads and tampons when I'm told exactly what to get, but she doesn't know what she needs, and I'm lost. Can you come with me?"

"Oh, that poor kid. I'll grab my phone and meet you outside." Alex doesn't run as quickly as Connor when she leaves, but I appreciate that she's walking faster than normal.

I know getting your period isn't technically an emergency, but to get your first one and not have your own mom or dad there to help has to be a little scary. Not that I think Emilio would be much help in a case like this. I have a feeling that he wouldn't even want to buy the supplies Sarah needs.

Asshole.

Now that I know he's the one who caused Becca so much trouble when she was younger, I hate him even more.

But that doesn't matter right now; right now I need to go take care of Sarah.

"I'll see you guys later," I say with a wave, and head out the door.

Once at my truck, I pull out my phone again and text Finley.

Travis- Hey. Sarah called me. She's had her first period and needs supplies. I'm taking care of it. Call me when you finish your test.

"Hey. Ready." Alex climbs into the passenger seat and buckles up. "We need to stop at Bump & Grind right before we go to the school. I called Xena, and she's putting together a surprise."

"A surprise?"

"Oh, yeah. Periods are a big deal for a little girl. We're going to throw her a period party when her mom gets home. Xena has cupcakes for us. And we're going to get Sarah a decaf frappuccino while we're there."

"Okay, so where to first, then?"

"The drugstore."

"Done," I say, putting the truck in gear and driving. "She'll need a change of clothes too, but we can grab that at her house. Finley gave me a key for when I'm doing renovations."

"HI THERE, I'M LOOKING for Sarah?"

"Travis! You came." Sarah comes running from the school's office and throws her arms around my waist, hugging me tightly. She has two shirts tied around her waist, one in front and one in back, and she's waddling a little, like she's trying not to let her legs touch each other.

"You're Travis Donovan?" There is a receptionist behind a long counter style desk looking at me over the top of her glasses. "Mrs. Donovan called me and said you'd be coming to school to help Sarah. You're not an emergency contact. How do you know Sarah?"

"He's my mom's friend, like I already told you," Sarah huffs and rolls her eyes. "His mom is my Nana. She's the one who called you to say he was coming. She's Mrs. Donovan."

" One minute please, Sarah. I'd like to talk to"—I squint to read the name plaque on the far end of the counter—"Ms. Cohen for a sec. Can you wait over there?" I point to an area off to the side of the office door. "I'll only be a minute."

Sarah nods and with one last eye roll for Ms. Cohen, she walks over and takes a seat.

"What she said was correct. My parents live across the street from Sarah and her family, and I'm friends with her mom. I've been doing renovations on their house since they moved in."

"I understand that, Mr. Donovan, but you're not on the emergency contact list. She can't leave with you."

I clench my fists and take a deep breath. I know this isn't Ms. Cohen's fault, but I'm sure Sarah would love to go home and have a shower before she gets into clean clothes.

"Can you call Mrs. Donovan back and have her vouch for me? She's an emergency contact, right?"

"Yes, but she can't authorize another person to take Sarah home. Only her mother and father can do that."

For fuck's sake. If her mother and father were available, I wouldn't be here. I know I wasn't Sarah's first choice.

"Sarah?" I call her over. "What's your dad's phone number?"

"I have it here, Mr. Donovan."

"I understand that, Ms. Cohen, but I'd like to talk to him to explain the situation, if possible."

She ignores me and dials the number on the ancient office phone propped up on the counter. I thought this school was supposed to be well-funded? Why is the receptionist using a phone that looks like it went out of production in the early '80s?

"Hello, yes. Mr. Mathews? I have Sarah here in the office at the school. She's had a little problem and needed someone to pick up feminine hygiene products, and your wife was unavailable. Sarah's other emergency contact was also unavailable, but she sent her son, a friend of your wife's, to take care of the situation. Is it alright if Travis Donovan drives your daughter home?"

Ms. Cohen's eyes get rounder and rounder as the voice on the other end of the line gets louder and louder. There's a mixture of laughter and yelling that I can't make out, but it seems Ms. Cohen is none too impressed.

"There's no need for that kind of language, Mr. Mathews. A simple 'yes' would have sufficed."

She pulls the receiver away from her ear and gives it a dirty look before slamming it back into the cradle.

"Well... that was uncalled for. I won't repeat what he said, but you are clear to escort Sarah home. Sarah, please call the school when you get home and let me know that you have arrived safely. This goes against my better judgment, but since your father seems to be okay with it, I will allow it. I would like to see your identification first, please, Mr. Donovan." I grab ID out of my wallet and pass it over to her. She seems satisfied, and after a moment, she passes it back to me. I'm glad she thought to ask for it.

"Thank you so much, Ms. Cohen," Sarah says. "I really just want to go home and get cleaned up. I'll be glad when this is all over."

Ms. Cohen raises an eyebrow and looks at me. I answer with a shrug. I don't know what Finley has already talked to Sarah about, but it seems she might have missed the part about how this is going to happen every month for the next thirty or forty years. I know I'm not going to be the one to fill in that little piece of information. No way.

"Thank you, Ms. Cohen. I will have Finley call you to confirm you made the right choice today. And who knows? Maybe she'll add me as an emergency contact to prevent any complications in the future." I wink at her and give her my best grin. "Then I'll get to come in and see you again."

Ms. Cohen snorts a laugh and waves us off. "Get out of here before I change my mind, you two. And Sarah? Ibuprofen and a heating pad will help with the cramps, sweetie." The smile she gives Sarah is one of actual caring, so I suppose I can forgive her for giving me a hard time. She's only doing her job, and she seems to really care.

Now onto the really awkward part of this adventure. At least I still have Alex with me. She's in the truck, but she's going to be the one teaching Sarah how to use all the products I insisted on buying.

I swear, when I walked up to the checkout with my entire shopping cart full of assorted feminine products, all the other customers thought I was crazy. I know Alex did when I filled that cart so full to begin with. She tried telling me that Sarah wouldn't need all of it, but I wanted to be sure that she had options. If NASA thinks a woman needs a hundred tampons for seven days in space, who am I to decide that a ten-year-old doesn't need a shopping cart full of pads for her first period?

"I'm so glad you convinced Ms. Cohen to let me come with you. Everyone was already laughing at me once today. I need a night to recover before I go back."

"Even the girls laughed?" You would think that another girl would have more sympathy than that, unless…

"I don't think anyone else in my class has had this happen yet," Sarah says with a shrug. "It doesn't matter, anyway. Kids are dumb."

I choke back a laugh. "Yeah, some kids are dumb. But sometimes that can be fun. When we were kids, my brother Johnny did dumb stuff all the time. It was kind of irritating to me, because I was always trying to look out for him, but the other kids thought it was hilarious. Sometimes dumb is just mean, like today when they laughed at you for something that can happen to anyone, and probably will happen to a lot of them at some point. Other times, dumb is pretty funny. Unless it's dangerous. Don't do dangerous dumb stuff. Uh… Maybe call your mom and ask before you do anything too dumb? Shit, I don't know. I'm not very good at this, am I?" I run my hand through my hair and chuckle. "I guess there's a reason I don't have kids yet. I don't have the necessary skill set."

Sarah puts her hand on my arm. "I think you're doing okay, Travis. Thanks for coming today. My dad didn't even answer the phone when I called. Hey, Alex. Is that for me?" Her attention shifts suddenly. She climbs up into the back seat of the truck and reaches forward to grab the frappuccino Alex picked up for her. "This is so good. Thank you."

I look up suddenly when she says Alex's name. I've been so busy talking to Sarah while we walked, I didn't even notice we had made it to the truck already. And what was that she said about her dad not even answering when she called? What the fuck is with that?

I hate this guy more and more every day.

24

Period Parties and Sangria

Finley

I FINISHED MY TEST in record time and I'm pretty confident I earned my real estate license. I should be a licensed realtor in time for the start of the new year. But that doesn't even matter to me right now because my girl got her first period and I wasn't there for her.

My stupid phone turned itself off again, and I missed calls from the school, and Mrs. Donovan, and a text from Travis.

Sarah left me several panicked messages and then went radio silent. I couldn't even call her back because I haven't allowed her to have a cell phone. At least when I contacted the school, they let me know Travis picked her up. Apparently, they contacted Emilio, and he gave the okay for that. I let the school receptionist know that she made the right call and told her she could add Travis to the emergency contact list to be prepared in case something ever happened again. I'll go in tomorrow to sign the form to make it official. After I've taken care of Sarah and thanked Travis for being there for her, that is.

Right now, I'm on my way home, trying not to break any traffic laws as I rush to my girl's side. Or at least not get caught breaking them, anyhow.

I can't believe I missed being there for the start of her first period. I wanted to do a cute little period party like you see some kids having these days. I would have given her a cute period pack, with a fun little case, and all the supplies she'd need for when it started at school again. There would have been balloons, and cake, and maybe party hats, and definitely some chocolate.

I don't have time to stop for any of that stuff now, though. It's been over an hour since she first called me and I want to get home as quickly as possible. We can have a party another day, I suppose. If I'd thought it was happening this soon, I would have had some things prepared. But I never thought she'd get her first period at ten years old, so I don't have so much as a boxed cake mix or packet of balloons. I'm feeling like a pretty shitty mom right now.

I pull onto our street, after what feels like the longest drive in existence, and notice that the Donovans have company again, and I feel a twinge of jealousy. I envy them for their large, close-knit family. They have someone visiting them almost every day. They'd always have a family member available to help if one of their kids ran into trouble at school.

My parents are still too far away for everyday visits, but I've been trying to wear them down and convince them to buy in Westborough. When Dad retires, there's no reason for them to stay where they are.

My attention veers away from my thoughts when I notice something a little off as I get closer to my house. It takes a minute for my brain to register all the red balloons and streamers decorating my porch.

Did Travis do that?

I pull into the driveway, jump out of the car, and run into the house. Inside are even more balloons, all red, but all different sizes. And streamers hang from every fixed surface, other than the floor. The inside of my house looks like a festive crime scene.

"Mom!" Sarah runs out of the living room, straight into my arms. "Isn't this cool? Travis did it."

"It wasn't only me. I had a lot of help. Alex actually did most of it," Travis says, close behind Sarah. "And now that you're here, we can get the party started. Come on into the living room. Everyone else is here already."

"Everyone?"

Sarah grabs my hand and drags me to the living room.

"Finley, dear. How did your test go?" Travis's mom asks, coming over and pulling me into a hug. "Can you believe all this? I wish I had a party like this when I got my first period. I was taught to keep it secret and given the impression that it was dirty. This is a much better way of welcoming a girl into the club."

I laugh. "I definitely would have preferred this, too. My mom didn't teach me to keep it a secret, but I wasn't exactly encouraged to talk about it."

The sound of talking and laughter surrounds me, and I take my first proper look around the room. Travis wasn't kidding when he said everyone was here. The whole band is here, even, but I can't imagine that they're staying. They must've come to help decorate.

"You finally made it," my new friend, Rose, yells from across the room. "Time to get this party started. Bring on the red velvet cake and sangria."

"It's non-alcoholic," Travis whispers to me. "We don't need a bunch of drunk idiots at your daughter's party."

"This is more of a party than I ever could have imagined. I was thinking it would end up being me and the kids, and maybe a cake and some balloons."

"Oh, shit. I'm so sorry. I should have asked you first." Travis frowns, his eyebrows drawn. "I should have known you would have planned something already. It sounded interesting when Alex mentioned it and I got carried away. Is this okay?"

I step out of the living room and gesture for Travis to follow. "Travis, I'm not upset at all. This is one of the nicest things anyone has ever done for me. And the other nicest things are the porch you and your friends helped me build, the school function that Johnny funded entirely with his own money, and your parents always stepping up to help me with the kids. I don't know how I can ever thank you all." My eyes feel wet by the end of my little speech, as I realize that Travis' family is the kind of family I always wanted.

Travis pulls me into a hug. "No thanks necessary. We help because we want to." He lets me go, holding on to my shoulders and bending a little to look me in the eye. "We care about you. I care about you. And your family. Okay?"

I look down, tears threatening to spill from my eyes, suddenly overwhelmed with too many feelings. "Yeah, okay." I force out. "I'm going to run up and change. I'll be there in a minute. Don't start without me."

"Yeah, you bet." He leans in and kisses my forehead. I don't even wait for him to go back into the living room before turning and heading for the stairs, tears streaming down my face the entire way.

Once in my room, I search through my drawers for a fresh shirt to wear, to lend credibility to the reason I gave Travis when I said I was coming up here. I strip off the shirt I'm wearing and go into my bathroom to wash my face.

I can't believe I would cry from what Travis said. It's not like he said he loved me. He didn't even say anything revolutionary. But telling me they all care about me and my family hit that spot in my heart that I've been protecting for so long. Emilio never showed that he cared, and as I looked back at our relationship over the last year that we've been separated, I can see that he never did. I've shored myself up, acted as a shield for my kids, to lessen the impact of his not caring, so they didn't feel the full effect of his disinterest. And it doesn't need to be that way anymore.

Travis, and his family and friends have welcomed us with open arms. And being cared for in this way feels too good. It's too much.

But it's also not a good time for me to sit with it, and break it all down.

I take a few deep breaths and look at myself in the mirror. A little concealer and some mascara and I'm good as new. I'll investigate this feeling later, after my little girl's period party.

Bring on the cake and sangria. Maybe Rose has some wine to add to our sangria, because I could use a drink or two.

25

Homework Help and Family Dinner

Travis

"OKAY, ONE MINUTE." I put down my guitar and go to the kitchen to grab some water for the kids. "You guys sound good. This is going to be the best Christmas concert South Westborough Elementary has ever seen."

"Yeah, right," Braden says, following behind me. "We sound like a bunch of dying cats."

I chuckle. "I wouldn't go that far."

They're really not that bad. I don't think any of them have a future as a professional singer, but they're certainly good enough to muddle their way through a song during their elementary school concert at the end of this week. Especially since they're each going to be singing with their entire class. A room full of untrained kids all belting out a song at the same time? Nothing says Christmas spirit more than having to sit through that. And I can't explain how excited I am that I get to be there.

I fill three glasses of water and pass one to Braden to carry.

"Yeah, well, I wouldn't want to be in the audience on Friday night. It's a good thing winter break starts the next day. It will give all us kids time to forget how terrible we sound. Why do teachers think parents want to listen to a bunch of kids sing? If I ever have kids, I'm going to boycott the Christmas concert. I'll refuse to let my kids take part and we'll stay home and have hot chocolate instead."

"Oh, Braden. Something tells me that when you're a parent, you'll have a different opinion." After all, I've never had an interest in listening to kids sing, not even my nieces and nephews, as much as I love them, until I met Finley and her kids. Now, I wouldn't miss hearing Braden, Sarah, and Austin sing at this concert for anything.

Not that I'm their parent. I feel invested because I'm helping them learn their songs. Yeah, that's all.

Once back in the living room, after the kids have had a little water, we work on the songs again. Luckily, we have a pretty easy line-up of "Jingle Bells" for Austin, "We Wish You a Merry Christmas" for Sarah, and a rousing rendition of "Deck the Halls" for Braden. We make it through nearly perfect rehearsals for Braden and Sarah before we move on to Austin. Again.

Now, Austin is a very... enthusiastic singer, and in his mind "Jingle Bells" must be screamed at the top of one's lungs and no amount of attempting to convince him otherwise has been successful. And it's for this reason that we all don't hear the front door open, or Fin walking in, until she yells from out in the hallway.

"Why is there a herd of dying cats singing 'Jingle Bells' in my house?" She peeks around the entryway to the living room, her hands covering her ears. "Oh, it's you guys. Phew. I thought we were under attack by a pack of stray Christmas cats."

"See? Told you," Braden whispers to me.

"Uh, Mom? A group of cats is actually called a clowder." Sarah says with an air of certainty. "Although, sometimes, if the cats are unsure of each other, they could be called a glaring. I would imagine a group of strays would be unsure of each other, so, if anything, we would most likely be under attack by a glaring of Christmas cats. You know, if accuracy is of any concern."

I burst out laughing. Sarah is one of the smartest kids I've ever met. She retains information in such a way that I wonder what it's like inside her head. It's packed full of random information, such as what to call a group of cats in varying circumstances.

Braden shakes his head, looking older than his twelve years, but I can see a small upturn at the corners of his lips. He thinks his sister is funny, too, but he doesn't want to let on while he's enjoying having his mother confirm his "dying cats" assessment of their singing.

"Well, now. We're working on it. Isn't that right, guys? Austin is having a hard time convincing us you need to scream "Jingle Bells", though. This was his last attempt to convince us, before he agreed to sing at a normal volume."

"Oh, of course," Fin looks at me with a raised eyebrow. "Well, Austin. I don't think you've convinced anyone. Better try it again at a normal volume." She sits next to me where I'm perched on the coffee table. "I didn't know you played guitar."

"It's something I do for fun." A twinge of guilt rolls through my stomach, but I'm not technically lying since I play bass guitar in the band, and this is a regular acoustic guitar. Extra strings, a higher octave for tuning, and I never play it on stage. So it is for fun, *technically*. "I thought it might help these guys practice their songs for the concert. We've been working on it in secret for weeks. So congratulations on coming home early and ruining the surprise."

She looks at me with a grin and wraps an arm around my back, giving me a quick squeeze before letting go. "I don't know what I'd do without you. You're always stepping in and helping us out. Thank you."

"It's my pleasure. I love hanging out with you guys. You're awesome." I relish the hint of red that creeps into her cheeks. Teasing her is the best part of my day.

"Okay, can we do this already? I'll sing normally. I guess." Austin stands with his little arms crossed over his chest, his foot tapping his impatience. "I want to get this over with."

Fin and I both laugh.

"You bet, kid. Let's do it."

Fin stands up, rubbing her hands on her thighs. "I'll get dinner started. Do you want to join us?"

I've stayed a few times when Fin and I were working on the house, but this will be the first time that I'm here for a normal weeknight dinner. "I'd love to."

And the truth is, I'd love nothing more.

So where does that leave me?

26

Kindness and Christmas Concerts

Finley

TRAVIS AND I ARE rushing into the school's gym turned concert hall, looking around trying to find seats, and from the looks of things, we may be out of luck. We finished dropping the kids off in their respective classrooms, and Travis gave each of them a pep talk, so we're a little later than I would have liked to be. It's going to be tricky to find somewhere with two seats together.

Not that I have to sit with Travis, but after all the help he's given the kids with their performances, it would be nice to see his reaction to the results. Plus, he was nice enough to come with me. The least I can do is keep him company while his ears get assaulted. My kids may sound better than they ever have, but I've been to too many of these things to have high hopes for the rest of the performers. After all the regular schoolwork, homework, sports, and other activities they take part in, most of them have zero time left to practice singing. And no one like Travis to help them.

"Guys. Over here." Johnny is standing up in the front row of the school's gym turned concert hall, doing his best impersonation of the wavy arm balloon guy from a car dealership, oblivious to the stares he gets from some parents in the gym. "We saved seats for you."

A quick look down the front row shows me that all the guys from the band are here. Here with them are Alex, Becca, Denise, Devon, and Devon's friend, Xena. And down at the end of the row sit my parents next to Travis' parents.

"You did this?" I ask him with a smile. There's a strange heat in my chest that I can't seem to rub away. "You invited everyone to come watch my kids' Christmas concert?" Why would he do something like this? Something this big? And why would they all want to come to something like this? For people they hardly even know?

"Well, they've been working so hard this last month. I couldn't let all that go to waste, could I? They need an audience who will appreciate all the work they've put in." He smiles down at me and laces his fingers through mine, causing a swarm of butterflies to fly through me. "Let's get to our seats before the show starts."

We take our seats at the center of the row, Travis not letting go of my hand, and I look up and down the row on either side of us. Every seat in the front row is full of Travis' family and friends. Our family and friends, I guess. But one chair is empty.

"Who's missing?" I lean close and whisper to Travis. "Why is there an empty chair?"

"Oh, um." Travis clears his throat. "I told them to save a spot for Emilio, too. I figured he'd be coming tonight and thought it would be nice if he could sit up close."

My stomach flops as I recall the phone conversation I had with Emilio before Travis picked me up tonight. "Hell no, I'm not going. I'm a serious musician," he'd said. "Why would I want to sit and watch a bunch of kids sing stupid Christmas songs?"

"He's not coming," I mumble. "He made that *quite* clear on the phone earlier."

"Shit," he breathes, sounding almost disappointed. "Do the kids know?"

"No. I didn't tell them. I didn't want it to ruin their night before it even started."

He puts his arm around me and pulls me into his side. "I'm sorry, Fin."

I release a deep breath and lean in a little closer. At least everyone else made it. It may not be the same thing as having your dad here to see you perform, but having more than a dozen people who want to watch you? That has to feel pretty good, too.

Not for the first time since we moved, I find myself grateful for the gift my Grandma gave us when she gifted me the house. Whether she knew it or not, she gave me not only a home, but a whole family. Grateful doesn't even come close to how I'm feeling as the stage lights come up.

"Well," says Johnny, as we're filing out of the gym after the concert. "That was... interesting."

I snort a laugh.

"I can't believe he screamed the entire song. Still. After all our rehearsals." Travis shakes his head. "I thought he agreed he was going to sing it normally? Isn't that what he decided?" He looks to me for confirmation.

"Hey, don't look at me. I tried to convince him, but it's Austin. He's always been a little different. I have a feeling that's never going to change."

Travis snickers a little, still shaking his head. "I suppose you're right. He was the only kid up there wearing all black for a

Christmas concert. And when it came time for the ugly Christmas sweaters, his was the only one with a skeleton on it."

Becca walks up beside us. "You mean like this?" She gestures to her body where she's wearing the same style of sweater as Austin. It's all black but for a full skeleton wearing reindeer antlers. "I bought it for him so we could be twins. Your kid is so damn cool, Fin. If I could be assured of having a kid like that, it might tempt me to procreate."

Johnny's eyes nearly pop out of his head, his excitement shining from his smile. I can tell he's thinking about how badly he wants to be the dad in that scenario. Poor guy. I don't know exactly what's going on with those two, but it's easy to tell that Johnny is madly in love with her.

I laugh. "You say that now, but when he wakes you up at three in the morning conducting seances in the kitchen, you might change your mind."

Her eyes widen in surprise. "Are you serious? That's amazing. Austin is the fucking coolest kid."

Becca walks away, still giggling to herself, with Johnny right beside her, and they make their toward the exit of the gym with everyone else. I told the kids to meet us out at the front of the school after the show so that I wouldn't have to fight my way through the crowded hallways again. After Candace and her PTA gang refused my help because I escaped with Rose during the last meeting, I have no interest in seeing her any more than I have to.

"I was thinking we could all go out for dessert?" Travis asks. "Once the kids are out."

"Yeah, they would love that, I think."

"Great, I'll go see who else wants to come."

Travis squeezes my hand, which he's been holding since before the concert started, before letting go and going to talk to the others. In all the excitement of the concert, I forgot to be nervous about how sweaty my hands were, but now that he's let me go, I can feel that nervousness sinking in. While I'm waving my hands dry and waiting for the kids, my parents come over to say hello.

"We have a few minutes to chat, but then we need to get on the road."

"Oh, that's too bad, Dad. Are you sure you don't want to come out with us for dessert? Travis is asking everyone right now."

"We'd love to, sweetheart, but we really do need to be getting home. Maybe we can come back later this week?"

I heave a disappointed sigh, laying the guilt on thick, but smile anyway. "Yeah, that sounds good. Love you guys," I say, hugging Mom first, and then Dad. "Drive safe. Text me when you get home."

"Yes, Mom," they reply in unison with a laugh.

"You're going to stick around a few more minutes to say bye to the kids before you go, right?" I ask. "Emilio didn't show up. Again. They'd be heartbroken if you two left before they got to see you."

"Of course we will," Dad says, giving me another hug. "We're their biggest fans, after all."

"Hey now," Travis says, coming back to join us. "You might need to fight my parents for the title of 'the biggest fans'. They're over there gushing over how good they all were. Even Austin." He grins at my parents. "Mr. and Mrs. Harrison, it's great to see you again. Tell the truth now. What did you think of the kids' performances?"

"They were lovely. And Austin was very," Dad looks around, trying to find the right word.

"Austin was very loud?" Travis offers.

Dad laughs. "Yes, that he was. We sure could hear him over everyone else."

Just then, the kids come running up beside us. Austin jumps up into my arms for a hug and Sarah and Braden hug their grandparents hello.

"Where's Dad?" Austin asks, his head swiveling as he searches the crowd for Emilio. "He said he would be here."

The frowns form instantaneously on my parents and Travis. They all know that Emilio isn't coming, and I'm stuck trying to make excuses for him again, without making him sound like the asshole he is.

"Your dad said he's sorry, but he couldn't make it, after all. I'm sorry, buddy," I tell him with an extra squeeze. "We're going to go out for some dessert now, though. Doesn't that sound good?"

"Yeah, I guess." He pushes away from me, so I set him down.

"Hey, kiddo. Why don't you come with me so we can find Becca? I want to get a picture of you two in your matching sweaters." Travis reaches out and places a hand on Austin's shoulder. "I still can't believe she found the same skeleton Christmas sweater for both of you. Heck, I'm not sure I would have believed skeleton Christmas sweaters even existed if it weren't for the two of you."

Austin laughs, "That's silly, Travis. Of course there's skeleton Christmas sweaters. Skeletons like Christmas too, you know." He hugs my parents goodbye before going off with Travis, telling him all about what kinds of scary creatures like Christmas.

"Okay, now we really do need to get going," Mom says. "Have fun tonight, kids. You did a great job at your concert. I can't wait to print out all the pictures I took."

"Grandma, you don't have to do that. I know we sucked. No matter how much time Travis spent practicing with us, we never got any better."

Dad looks at me and mouths, "Travis?" And I give him a combination shrug slash nod that I'm sure isn't very informative. He gets a quizzical look on his face, but says nothing else.

"I thought you kids were wonderful." Mom hugs and kisses me and the kids once more, and then my parents turn and go.

Braden comes to stand beside me and Sarah goes off to find Travis and Austin.

"So," Braden says, looking straight ahead with his hands in his pockets. "No Dad again, huh? I wish he would get out of our lives for good. We'd all be better off." Braden doesn't wait for a response. He doesn't even look back as he walks over to Travis' parents, leaving me stunned.

I knew this divorce would be hard on the kids, but I had no idea it would be this hard.

Actually, I just never knew Emilio would make it harder than it needed to be.

27

Secrets and Santa

Travis

"WHAT'S ALL THIS?"

Johnny gestures to the pile of wrapping paper, tape, and gift boxes I have spread out on the island in our kitchen. We're home in our loft, together, for the first time in what feels like months. It's Christmas Eve and I'm standing here, attempting to wrap the mountain of gifts that I bought for Finley and the kids. The gifts I bought for my family are already wrapped and at my parents' house, ready for tomorrow morning when everyone goes over. The mountain of gifts in their living room reminded me of Fin's Christmas tree and made me want to add some gifts from me to the assortment already laid out there.

I may have gone a little overboard.

"What's it look like? I'm wrapping gifts to bring over to Finley's. I have a feeling her shithead ex-husband won't be doing much in the way of gifts for the kids, and I don't think they should miss out because he's a dick."

I've been at the house too many times when Emilio called to have faith that he will actually do anything for the kids for Christmas. I can't even bring myself to hope that he'll call. And they deserve so much better than that.

"You're spending a lot of time with her," Johnny says, grabbing a roll of wrapping paper and a gift, a book about the most haunted hotels in the world. I could barely stop myself from making reservations at the one nearest to Westborough, but I finally realized that would probably be a little much. "Who's this one for?"

"That's for Austin."

"Ah, I should have guessed," he laughs. "Becca would love this, too. Those two are like two weird peas in a pod, aren't they? Becca said she's been over to visit Fin and Austin's roped her into watching ghost hunting shows with him. Not that he had to do much to convince her, I'm sure."

I chuckle. "It is strange how similar their interests are. When Austin grows up, you'll have to do a horror icon tattoo for him like the one you did for Becca."

"Maybe. I don't know if Finley would go for that. He's a little young right now to be planning out future tattoos, anyway. But quit trying to change the subject. I know something's going on with you and Fin. You were awfully cozy at the kids' Christmas concert. Oh, and then there's the fact that you got us all there for it. I think you care about her, and I know for a fact you care about those kids. What's going on?"

It's times like these that I'm glad Johnny's faux-twin telepathy thing doesn't work as well as mine. I can tell with one hundred percent certainty that he's in love with Becca, but he doesn't know how strong my feelings for Finley are. And I need to make sure I keep it that way. It will hurt less when I have to leave if no one knows.

"Nothing's going on. We're good friends, that's all. I've been helping with her house renovations and doing the odd favor with the kids. That's it."

He drops the scissors he was using to cut the paper with and nails me with a look. "Yeah, right. You expect me to believe that? Try again."

I finish the gift I'm working on, and add a name tag before adding it to the box with the rest of the already wrapped gifts. I grab another gift and get the paper ready to wrap it before I answer.

"It's nothing. It can't be anything. Drop it."

"What do you mean, *it can't be anything*? She seems interested in you, too. And Becca says she's not hung up on her ex still. What's the issue?"

I slam the gift down on the counter. "Damn it, Johnny. It can't be anything. Leave it alone."

I turn and storm to the couch, dropping myself into the farthest corner of it with a huff. I reach forward to grab the remote, but before I get my fingers on it, Johnny is there, grabbing it first. He throws it into a chair on the other side of the room and stands in front of me.

"Yeah, like I'm letting your ignore this, little brother. You like her. A lot, if it's even close to what your face shows every time you're near her. So now you're going to stop pouting like a goddamn child long enough for you to tell me why you think nothing can happen, and then I'm going to tell you why you're an idiot. After that, you can thank me, and then get your ass over to Finley's and tell her how you feel."

I jump to my feet and push Johnny, the smug bastard, shoving him back with a hand to the middle of his chest. Why can't he let this be? I'm torn up enough about it without having him come along and try to tell me it's possible when I know it fucking isn't. "Fuck off, Johnny. Leave it alone." The backs of his legs bump the coffee table, causing him to stumble and sit down heavily. His face contorts with an expression somewhere between shock and rage. When he stands up, shoving the coffee table across the room, he drives his shoulder into my stomach without warning, knocking the wind out of me. I fall onto the couch and he jumps on me, pushing me down, resting a knee on my chest, pinning me to the couch, while I try like hell to suck in a breath.

He slaps me on the side of the head and says, "Grow up, dumbass. I know why you think nothing can happen, and you're wrong. Don't be stupid. You can't let someone like Finley get away. You'll never get another one like her."

I suck wind while Johnny pins me down, nodding along with what he's saying, to get him to ease up. When he takes some of his weight off me, and I can breathe again, I sit up quickly, throwing my shoulder into him, rolling him off of me and onto the floor beside the couch. His breath escapes in a whoosh, and I take pleasure in listening to him struggle to take in a breath just as hard as I did a second ago.

We lay there, me on the couch and him on the floor, the only sounds our matching raspy breaths. I stare up at the mix of old wooden beams, ductwork, pipes, and several huge, industrial light fixtures that make up our ceiling, going over in my head exactly why Finley and I can't work. The number one reason being, I am a musician and I am leaving soon. We have six months, maybe eight if we're lucky, before we have to be on tour again, and that's not enough time. I can't have the family I want, and be leaving for months at a time. I won't do that to her. Or the kids.

"Well, as fun as that was, I think it's time for you to listen up." Oh, here we go. Sounds like Johnny finally caught his breath. "I will tell you this once, fuckface, and I want you to really think about this before you commit to something stupid, like denying what you feel for Finley and those kids. Are you listening?"

I sit up and reach out a hand to pull him up beside me. "Yeah, I'm listening."

"Good. I know you think you need to look after me. I know you've been doing it your whole life. And I also know that, until recently, I probably needed at least a little looking after. So I appreciate what you've done for me. But I've watched you get progressively more miserable in the life that I've led you into, and I can't do it anymore."

"That's not wha—"

"Shut up and listen. I'm not done." Something in his tone tells me he's actually serious.

"Fuck. Fine."

"You're like me." I shoot him a look, and he laughs. "A little, anyway. You want the family and everything that goes with it, like I do. So maybe you haven't been looking for your one and only like I have, but that doesn't mean it's not something you've hoped for all the same. Somewhere along the way, you got it into your head that you can't have that family if you have the band. But you can. Plenty of artists make it work. Hell, Ryder and Denise are going to do it. They don't know how yet, but they'll figure it out. And if you really want that with Finley, then you guys can figure it out, too." Johnny slaps my leg a little harder than necessary and stands up. "But I think you already know that much, at least. So why don't we finish wrapping these gifts and you can tell me what the real problem is? And before you try to tell me there isn't anything else, keep in mind that me and the rest of the guys are still keeping it secret from Fin that you're in the band, and I'm pretty sure the reason isn't that her ex is a musician."

He walks back to the counter where all the wrapping paper and gifts are, and starts on a new box, leaving me on the couch with my mouth hanging open.

Did I say that Johnny's faux twin telepathy didn't work as well as mine? I am beginning to think maybe it works even better, and he's been hiding it all along.

Fuck.

28

Special Deliveries

Finley

CHRISTMAS EVE, AGAIN.

The second without my husband, the first with me and the kids in our new house. We've been decorating and wrapping gifts all day, and now that the kids are finally in bed, I'm planning to sit down with a drink, a book, and the fireplace channel on TV. Momma needs some relaxation before the chaos of Christmas wakes me up way too early tomorrow morning.

I know what you're thinking. The fireplace channel doesn't have quite the same charm as the actual fireplace, but it's been so warm this year that I refuse to light a fire. Not that I even have any firewood to start a fire with if I wanted to. I'll need to ask Travis if he knows of a good place to get some.

Maybe I can convince him to chop some for me. Shirtless.

And that image goes right in the spank bank.

I let out a sigh and snuggle myself further into the couch cushions. Like Travis isn't the only resident in my spank bank lately, anyway. It's been like that for the last few months, since the day I worked up enough courage to cross the street and ask for his card. I'm still a little disappointed that I didn't jump him on Halloween. Even with Emilio ruining the mood by calling, I don't think it would have been too difficult to get back on track.

And it probably would have been a hell of a lot more satisfying than using my imagination and B.O.B. like I have been.

I reach over and grab my throw blanket, pulling it up over my legs, and flip to the last page I was reading in my book. It's one of those romance novels with the shirtless man on the cover who you know is going to be some kind of muscular Prince Charming. The type of guy that can't possibly exist in real life. Usually the guys who look like that end up being total dickheads. And the guys who act like Prince Charming are doing just that, acting.

Fictional men don't forget to aim when they pee, or forget to put the toilet seat down when they're done. They say the sweetest things and always think of great ways to show their girl how much they love them. And unless you buy a very specific sort of book, you won't find another woman's dirty g-string in your fictional man's car.

I personally don't buy those books, because I've had enough heartbreak in my real life, thank you very much. I'll keep my fiction happy and carefree until my life calms down a little. If it ever does.

It doesn't appear that it will calm down anytime soon, though.

After only a few minutes of reading, there's a soft banging at the door that makes me jump. That better not be Emilio, not after he already made me tell the kids that they wouldn't be spending Christmas with him after all. We had agreed to alternate years, but he decided, again, that something to do with the band was more important. And he waited until the last minute to tell me, too. So if he's at the door now, thinking he's taking the kids to his place after all... I'm going to punch him in the dick and send him on his way.

I get up and make my way to the door, taking a calming breath before pulling it open, ready to give Emilio a piece of my mind. But the sight that greets me at the door isn't Emilio.

It doesn't look like anyone, really, just a pair of legs under a stack of boxes.

"Hey," says a voice from behind the boxes. "I hope I didn't wake you."

"Travis? Is that you under there?"

"Uh, yeah. Hi, Fin. Can I come in?" he asks, turning sideways to look at me around the large boxes he's holding. The grin on his face is infectious and I can't help but smile.

I stand back and swing the door open wide, taking one box from Travis so he can see.

"Thanks," he says, going directly to the living room. "I didn't think I had so much stuff, but once I got it all into the boxes, it became pretty apparent that I was wrong. I should have taken more than one trip, but it's like groceries. I would have had to forfeit my man card if I did that," he says with a chuckle.

I follow him into the dimly lit living room, where the only light is coming from the Christmas tree. The kids and I decorated it, using some decorations we found in the boxes we brought over from the old house. Turns out my grandmother had more than Halloween decorations stored away. Good thing, too, because I wouldn't have been able to afford presents *and* decorations this year.

Travis goes straight to the Christmas tree and sets his boxes down. I put my box down on the coffee table. One by one, he pulls gifts from the first box and starts placing them under the tree.

"What's all this?"

He stands up straight, still holding a gift, and looks around before looking at me. "Is this a trick question? They're Christmas gifts."

I laugh. "Obviously, they're Christmas gifts. I can see that. I have eyes. But why are you bringing them here? Where did they come from?"

"From Santa?" he says with a shrug. He turns back to his task, finishing the first box and moving onto the second.

It's a good thing Austin is asleep and didn't hear Travis talking about Santa. The kid loves all things spooky, creepy, and downright horrifying, but one thing he cannot handle is Santa. The fat man in the red suit is Austin's Achilles heel. It's the only thing that really terrifies him. Ever since that first fateful trip to sit on Santa's lap at the mall, Austin has been afraid of him. It's taken me years to get him to believe that Santa Claus isn't real, and to teach him not to spoil the fun for the other kids.

I was telling Travis the other day that I was worried the kids wouldn't have as good a Christmas as I'd like to give them due to me taking time off to get my real estate license. Even with Grandma giving us this house, money has been tight for the last little while. Now that I have my real estate license, that should hopefully change soon, but it's been hard keeping up with the bills.

"Travis, you didn't have to do that. I already owe you so much for all the help with my renovations. I haven't paid for a single thing yet, and at this rate, it's going to take me years to pay you back."

"Whoa, whoa, whoa." He comes over and grabs me by the shoulders. "Don't worry about that. I've told you before, I don't care about the money. I have more than enough to get me by, and I like helping you. We'll settle up when you're in a better position to do so. It's no big deal. And this is just a few gifts for the kids. Nothing you have to worry about paying back."

I jerk out of his grasp. "It is a big deal. It's a big deal to me. I hate owing you. I don't want to rely on anyone. I relied on Emilio and look where that got me. I had to live with my parents for an entire year when we split up, because my name wasn't even on the deed for the house we shared. And I only have this place now because my grandmother gave it to me."

He looks at me, eyebrows drawn, and shakes his head. "Finley, you don't owe me. At least not in the way you're thinking. You've met my family, you know how we are. When someone we care about needs help, we help them. Besides, I didn't bring these gifts over to help you. I brought them over because I wanted to give you guys gifts. And if there's a lot? Well, that's because I have no control when it comes to buying presents. And actually, some of them probably have Johnny's name written on them, considering he helped get them all wrapped up to bring them over here. I never would have finished otherwise." He gives me a small smile.

"That's what gift bags are for," I say, with possibly a little too much snark. "Stuff a gift in a bag and top it with tissue. Voila, a wrapped gift in a hurry."

"Where was that information three hours and six rolls of gift wrap ago?" He laughs. "You could have saved me a *ton* of paper cuts."

I take a deep breath and release it slowly. Maybe he's right. Maybe I don't have to worry so much about owing him for every little thing. But I really hate feeling like I'm not doing this on my own. It's bad enough that he's been fronting the costs of most of my renovations without him coming over bearing a truckload of gifts. I've been racking my brain to find a reason he would do this much for me, and I can't make any sense of it.

But maybe it's finally time to stop being too afraid to ask why.

"Travis?"

29

All I Want for Christmas

Travis

"Travis? Why are you doing all this? Why are you helping me so much? It doesn't make sense."

The sound of Finley's voice makes me freeze on the spot. I should have known this was coming. I've been acting more like a boyfriend than a friend to Finley pretty much since we met, and at some point or another, it was bound to incite her curiosity. I guess me bringing all these presents over finally pushed her over the edge.

Fuck. I was hoping I'd have more time before I'd need to explain myself. But it looks like time is up.

I might not have a reason that makes sense, but I have to tell her something.

I stand up, abandoning the gifts I'm unpacking, and turn around to face Finley. I didn't notice when I came in, but she's clearly dressed for a relaxing evening at home, wearing flannel pajama pants, a tank top, and a giant fuzzy gray cardigan that hangs down to her knees. A quick look at the end table behind her shows me a full glass of wine and a paperback lying open face-down beside it. She was definitely planning on having a quiet Christmas Eve alone, and then I came along and threw confusion at her instead.

God, I'm such a dick.

I run a hand through my hair and rub the back of my neck. If I don't say this right, Finley might tell me to leave and never come back. I can't risk that. I don't know what I would do if I couldn't see her as often as I do now. It's bad enough when we're in the studio for a full day and I can't see her until after.

What the hell am I going to do when it comes time to go on tour?

"Travis?"

Shit. I've been rambling in my mind for too long. Finley looks worried.

"Sorry. I think I zoned out a little there," I say, walking over to sit on the couch, patting the spot next to me for her to sit, too. "There... There isn't *one* reason I've been helping you as much as I have. Part of it, I guess, is that I feel bad Emilio has been jerking you and the kids around and I want to make sure you all know that someone cares enough to help. And part of it is that my parents would probably kill me if I didn't do everything in my power to keep you and the kids around. They've become quite attached to you guys, and they worry." I force a chuckle to lighten the mood, but I have a feeling things are about to get serious, anyway. I blow out a breath. Here goes nothing. "But mostly it's that I really like spending time with you, and I think you're amazing, and you deserve everything I've done for you and more."

She barks a laugh. "You think I'm amazing? Why? You remember that I'm a single mom with three kids who can't even get her ex to sign the divorce papers, right? That I haven't been able to pay any of my bills in full for over a year?" She sits next to me and looks down at her hands.

My mouth drops open and I walk over to her. "Fin, why didn't you tell me? I would have helped you."

She spins away from me and yells, "You shouldn't have to help me, that's the problem. I'm a grown ass woman with three kids.

I should be able to take care of my own family without relying on help from someone I barely know."

I turn her to face me, holding her shoulders and staring into her eyes. "Finley, you know me. Sometimes I think you know me better than anyone." Other than the one tiny detail of me being in the band. Other than that, she knows me better than anyone else.

"Hmph." She crosses her arms and looks toward the Christmas tree. "I doubt that."

"Why? I spend all of my time with you. I spend every spare second I have with you or your kids. And the rest of the time I'm thinking of you. You know me, you know my family, and you know my friends. What more is there to know?"

"Just what I already asked you," she says. "Why are you always helping me? Helping us? You spend more time with my kids than their own father does. You do the kinds of things with them their dad should be doing. You pay for my renovations, and the materials for them, and you do most of the work. And let's not forget about how you brought my kids all these gifts." She throws her hands up and chuckles ruefully. "I don't get it."

She's right. I can see how she would be confused. I'm acting like her boyfriend, but I've been trying my damndest to keep it platonic. Okay, so I've slipped a few times. We've kissed more than once, we hold hands all the time, and then there's what nearly happened on Halloween night. I don't know how much longer I can, or even want to, keep it strictly platonic.

"You even rescued Sarah when she got her first period at school. And then you threw her a period party and invited everyone you know. Most guys wouldn't have done the rescuing, never mind throwing the party."

She's frustrated with me and it makes her even more beautiful. Fuck. I'm so tired of trying to stay away from her. Not that I do a wonderful job of that.

"Finley, do you really not understand why I would do all this for you? Why I would spend every possible minute I can with you?" I turn her face toward me, looking into her eyes again, my heart beating so wildly I can feel it trying to jump from my chest. "I care about you. I can't stop thinking about you," I whisper.

"You can't mean that. You haven't thought it through. I have three kids, Travis. Three. Kids. You're a good-looking guy with a decent job. You can have any woman you want. There's no need for you to burden yourself with a thirty-two-year-old single mom of three kids who can't even get divorced properly. Find someone better."

"You're not understanding me, Finley. There is no one better." I lean in slowly, cupping her jaw with my hand, and whisper, "I only want you."

Her breath catches. She reaches in and grabs my shirt in her fists.

"I can't pretend with you anymore. I knew I wouldn't be able to stay away for long after I got to touch you on Halloween. I want to be a good guy, and give you more time to get over your ex, and deal with your divorce, but every time I see you, it gets harder and harder to keep my hands off of you." I kiss the hollow of her neck, behind her ear, and her pulse quickens beneath my lips. My dick swells at the taste of her skin. "Tell me to keep my hands off of you, Finley, if that's what you want. But do it quickly because I'm dying to touch you."

She shivers against me, but doesn't tell me to stop. I leave a trail of soft kisses along her jaw, making my way to her mouth where I stop, hovering a hair's breadth away, feeling her breath on my lips. "Do you want me to stop? Do you want me to keep my hands off of you?"

She shakes her head, her eyes closed, her breath rapid.

"I need to hear it, Finley. I need to know that you understand." I brush my lips against hers, feeling their softness and the way she melts against me, her hands pulling me closer. "Tell me you want me to kiss you here"—I kiss her lips—"and here"—I suck the pulse point in her neck—"and here." I trail my fingers down the swell of her breasts. "Or tell me you want me to stop. Because if you don't, I'm going to spend the next few hours with my face buried between your legs before finally getting you underneath me and sliding my dick into your wet, hot pussy."

Finley gasps at the filthiness of my words, then opens her eyes and looks into mine. "Don't stop," she whispers. "Never fucking stop." She releases her hold on my shirt, reaches up and wraps her arms around my neck, and plants her lips on mine.

Finley is kissing me, her tongue sweeping into my mouth, exploring me with abandon. I wrap my arm around her waist and pull her tightly against me, my heart beating so hard it's threatening to beat right out of my chest. With one hand around her waist and the other in her hair, I turn us and sit down on the couch, pulling her so she straddles my lap. Finley instantly rocks her hips against me and I groan into her mouth. She's killing me with how good she feels against me.

"Fu-uck, Fin. That feels so good."

She rocks against me again, and I already feel an orgasm building in the base of my spine, causing my balls to tighten and my dick to swell even more. I've never been this hard. And I've never been this close to coming from a little dry-humping. I need to get control of this before I embarrass myself and make a mess in my pants. I grip Finley around the waist again, shifting us until she's lying beneath me on the couch.

"You're too fucking sexy, sweetheart. I need to slow this down a little before I disappoint you."

She chuckles a little. "I don't think you could ever disappoint me," she says. "You've seen what I've worked with in the past. You're definitely an upgrade."

Wait a minute. Is she saying what I think she's saying? Emilio... was her only lover?

"Finley? You've only ever been with him?"

"Uh, yeah. Is that bad?"

I shake my head. Of course it's not bad. It makes me feel a little... dirty, though. I've slept with many women in my life, but none of them compared to Finley. What's done is done, I guess. I can only hope that I learned enough from them to make this the best experience Finley has ever had.

"Not bad at all, sweetheart. It makes me wish I'd been a little more discerning when I was younger, is all."

She laughs. "I wouldn't worry about that. As long as you understand that if you're sleeping with me, you're not sleeping with anyone else, then we're fine." She lifts her head and kisses me. "That's non-negotiable, of course."

I tip my head back and look into her eyes. "I don't want anyone but you, Fin. I wouldn't betray you. I'm not that kind of guy."

"Good. Now that that's settled, come down here and kiss me."

I smile. "Oh, I'm going to do more than that, Fin. I hope you're ready," I say, and then take her lips in a deep kiss. "I can't wait to do all the things I've been thinking of doing to you. I think you're going to like them, too."

"Oh yeah? I like the sound of that," she says, pulling my face to hers and capturing me in another deep kiss. I can't believe we waited this long.

After tonight, I'm never going to go back to being just friends with Finley. I couldn't even if I wanted to. She already means too much to me.

30

Mom Body-ody-ody

Finley

SOMEWHERE BETWEEN MAKING OUT like a couple of teenagers and an enthusiastic bout of grinding against each other, Travis and I decide we should probably take this to my bedroom. Neither of us wants to chance the kids walking in on us. It's not until after he gives me an orgasm with his fingers, though, that we actually get up and make our way there.

As soon as we get in the room, I turn off the lights. I've had three kids and my body shows it. I've got a few extra pounds, a bunch of stretch marks, and a belly pooch, none of which I want Travis to get a clear look at.

Travis turns them back on.

I turn them off again. What the hell? Why doesn't he get that I don't want him seeing my mom-body in a well-lit room.

"What are you doing, Fin? Why do you keep turning the lights off?"

"I just want them off, okay?" I wrap my arms around myself, hugging tightly. I can't show Travis all my flaws. I can barely look at my flabby stomach and many stretch marks in the mirror after a shower. How I can let Travis, the man with a perfect body, see that mess?

Travis closes and locks the door behind him, and follows me further into the room. "Finley," he says. "I want to see you."

"You really don't." I try to force a laugh, but it comes off sounding like exactly that. A forced laugh. "There's a lot happening under these clothes that someone who looks like you doesn't want to see, I promise. Not everything is as high and tight as it was when I was younger." Something Emilio liked to remind me of every chance he got. "I'm far from perfect. I don't want you to be disappointed."

He sits on the end of my bed and pats the spot next to him, motioning for me to sit down. I perch my ass on the very edge of the bed and look at him, but he takes a deep breath and wraps me in a giant hug. I exhale a long, slow breath and melt into his arms. When my body relaxes, he leans away to look at me.

"I'm not sure where you got the idea that you're anything but perfect, but it's now my mission to make you believe you are. You're perfect to me, Fin. I don't care if your body isn't the same as it used to be. We didn't even know each other back then, so why would that matter? Plus, I already know your body made three amazing kids. There's no way you could do that and come out of it unchanged. That's one more thing that makes you amazing." He scrubs a hand down his face. "But never mind all that. You and your body have fueled all of my jerking-off since we met. I'm talking a LOT of jerking off."

I bark out a laugh. "That's... surprisingly helpful."

"I live to serve. And it's the truth. You're so fucking hot I spend every second around you actively trying to kill my boner."

Listening to him say these things, hearing how he feels about my body, it does something to me. My chest feels a little tight, my stomach is fluttering, and I'm blinking away tears that have no reason to be there. Who'd have thought him telling me he jerks off to thoughts of me would be so sexy?

"Where did you come from? You say all these things to me, and I have such a hard time believing you could actually mean them."

"Oh, Finley. I mean them. And if I have to kiss every inch of your beautiful body all night to make you understand that, well, that's a sacrifice I'm happy to make." He laughs and kisses my forehead. "In all seriousness, though, if I ever see Emilio again, I am going to have so many things to say to him about how he treated you. After I beat the shit out of him for it. For you to not know how truly beautiful, and sexy, you are? That's another major fuck up on his part. I promise you, I will not make that same mistake."

He threads his hands into my hair and lowers his lips to mine, kissing me while lowering my back to the bed. His hands make quick work of the elastic holding up my messy bun, and soon my hair is loose and spread out against my green duvet. I laugh when he sits up, grabs me by the hips and throws me farther up the bed. The laugh dies in my throat when he leans over and turns on my bedside lamp.

"Is this okay?" he asks.

I take a breath and nod. I'm still terrified that he'll see my body and it will disgust him, but I know I can't let that hold me back. Not if I want this to actually happen. And dear lord, do I ever want this to happen. He smiles so widely I can't help but smile right back.

When he grabs my old flannel pajama pants by the waistband and rips them all the way down my legs before throwing them across the room, I laugh.

"Someone's a little eager," I say, still laughing. "Been a while?"

"Since I've had my fill of the sexiest woman I've ever seen? Only my entire life." He reaches for my hand and pulls me to sit so he can slide my shirt off. "I hope you weren't hoping to get a lot of sleep tonight. Because I plan on taking my time with you."

A ripple of pleasure runs through me, settling in my core, making me clench with anticipation of what's to come. I know Travis is good with his hands, and tonight I get to experience it first-hand. But I know I won't feel comfortable if I'm the only one with no clothes on. Travis seems to sense this, because before I do more than open my mouth to tell him, he reaches back and pulls his shirt over his head in one smooth motion.

His body is even better than I remember it. I feel a little guilty knowing it's because of all the extra work he's been putting in working on my house, but I still appreciate the result. It's not enough, though, and I sit up and start unbuckling his belt. I need him naked with me. My hands are shaking, making it hard for me to get hold of the button of his jeans, so Travis takes pity on me and does it himself. He stands up, and with a hand on each hip, he pushes off both his pants and boxers, leaving him completely nude.

"Holy shit, where the fuck were you keeping that?" I blurt. "I mean, where? How? What?" I think my brain malfunctions. Becca was right. He is packing some serious hardware. Those compression shorts on Halloween must've been doing a stellar job of compressing, because if I thought his dick felt impressive that night, there are no words to describe how much more impressive it is now that I can see it in all its glory.

And let me tell you, it is glorious. It's the most beautiful penis I've ever seen. Okay, sure, maybe I've only been with Emilio, but it's not like I've never seen porn, and Travis's dick? Better than porn-worthy. Better than every fantasy I've ever had. Better than I ever thought I'd get to be near.

I shoot up and slide to the edge of the bed, grabbing Travis by the hips and pulling him closer to me. I know for a fact that monster will barely fit, but I need to get my mouth on it before the drool runs down my chin. Despite what Travis says about my looks, I know openly drooling out of my mouth would not be attractive. Already I'm wet at the thought of getting up and close and personal with it.

I lean forward and lick him from base to tip. The moan that comes from him can only be described as pornographic, and it turns me on so much that I'm sure there's a wet patch forming underneath me. I don't even care. I slowly lick around the head, tasting the salty pre-come from the tip, and moan at the taste. I take his dick in one hand, relishing the hiss Travis makes when I grip him, the soft skin feeling velvety under my fingers, and attempt to put him into my mouth.

"Fuck, babe. Your mouth feels so fucking good. You gotta stop or I'm going to come," he says as I get my mouth around him and slowly suck him into me. He groans louder this time, and if my mouth wasn't full of dick, I'd be smiling ear-to-ear. I'm pretty impressed with myself for making him feel good. "Okay, okay, okay," he says, taking his dick from me. "That's enough of that. We'll definitely be revisiting that later, though. Tonight it's my turn to play."

He bends and grabs me by the hips, again pushing me up closer to the headboard on the bed. I move to spread my legs, to give him access, but to my surprise, he closes them and straddles me. I feel the heat of his hard cock on my thigh as he leans in to kiss me. He thrusts against my leg as he pushes his tongue into my mouth and grips my hair in his fist.

"Promise you'll stay still, Fin. Can you do that?" he whispers in my ear.

I frantically nod my head, not sure I can stay still, but desperately willing to try. He has me so turned on I'm pretty sure I would come if I only wiggled my legs together a little. I briefly think about trying it, but I'm too caught up in what Travis is doing to me to risk moving and making him stop.

Like he promised earlier, he takes up kissing me head-to-toe. His warm lips and soft tongue leave almost no spot untouched and soon I'm thrashing my hips up, trying to find a little contact somewhere, to ease this orgasm that's been building and building inside me. He avoids the one spot I need him to be, though, until I'm whimpering and pressing my hands to my eyes.

"Poor Finley," he says, kissing a line up my inner thigh. "Didn't you like that? Do you want me to start all over again?" He moves like he's going to come up and kiss my face again to start the entire process over when he stops inches away from my clit. "Oh, but wait," he whispers, his voice gravelly, his breath nearly sending me over the edge. "I think I missed this spot"—he kisses my hip—"right"—he kisses the crease of my thigh—"over"—he kisses the tiny patch of hair above my clit—"here."

He finally lowers his mouth to my slit, licking a languorous path from entrance to clit before sucking that small bundle into his mouth and grazing it with his teeth. He slides a finger inside, finding that perfect little spot, causing me to immediately clamp down, and his mouth latches onto me, sucking me through my orgasm as I writhe and whimper and grab his hair, holding him to me while I ride his face, my thighs locked tight to his shoulders. He licks and sucks and nibbles me until fireworks light up behind my eyelids and my body rises from the mattress and his name bursts free from my mouth. Wave after wave of ecstasy rolls through me as I make animalistic moans into the semi-darkness of my room, the orgasm renewing with each suck on my clit.

When the stars behind my eyes finally stop sparkling and the throbbing inside slows, I relax my grip on his hair and let my legs fall open because I can't do anything else with them. Travis turned them into jelly. He gives me another long lick from entrance to clit, sending another aftershock through me even though I can't even move, and then kisses a trail up to my mouth.

My eyes are closed, but I feel him kiss me before his weight leaves the bed. The sound of crinkling foil tells me he's putting on a condom. It's not long, though, before he's resting his body over mine again, his skin burning as hot as my own. I open my eyes to see him lying over me, staring at my face with a small smile on his lips.

"You're even more perfect than I thought, Finley. Watching you come was so fucking sexy." I grunt a reply, too sated to make actual words. "I don't even care that you pulled out half my hair," he adds with a chuckle. "If I run out of hair for you to hold on to, I guess you'll have to sit right on my face so I can pull you down onto my mouth myself."

I snicker a little at that. "I didn't rip any hair out."

"Not yet," he whispers against my lips. "But we're not quite done, are we?" He lines himself up with my entrance, nudging against the hole with his tip, and he moans. "You're so fucking wet, Fin," he says, sliding in inch by inch. "You feel too good. If I don't last long, please forgive me. And then give me a few minutes to get ready for another round. I know once with you will never be enough."

Travis lifts himself up, grabbing my headboard and staring down at where we're connected. I look down too, and watch as he slides himself all the way in, inch by inch, burying himself to the root inside me, and slowly slipping back out again. He pushes himself in once more, slower than the last time, and I feel my orgasm already building again, the fullness adding to the pleasure.

"Travis," I whisper, not even sure what I'm going to say, but needing to say something. "This feels..." I trail off, not having the right words for how amazing, and monumental, this feels.

"I know, babe," he says. "Me too."

Travis lowers a hand to my belly, pressing down just above my pubic bone, and suddenly every stroke he makes feels a thousand times more intense. I'm rocketing toward another orgasm and Travis is smiling down on me like he hasn't ruined me for sex with anyone else. Not that I was looking for sex with anyone else, but now I'm really not looking, not even a little bit.

A groan escapes Travis as he looks into my eyes. "God, Fin. I can feel how much you like that. I love the way you're squeezing my dick; it feels so fucking good. Give me another one, babe. Come for me."

Travis thrusts, slamming into me even harder, and my hands fly down to his ass, my nails digging into his skin, as I start to pulse around him. I arch my back, my toes curl, and I pull Travis into me with more force, as my release tears thorough me again. The fireworks are blinding flashes of light this time, and wetness surges out of me, coating us both as the orgasm to end all orgasms threatens to kill me with delicious pleasure.

"Oh, fuck yes, Fin. Good girl. Fu-u-uck." Travis stutters, his thrusts become less rhythmic, before he stills. I can feel his pumping release inside me as he lowers his face to mine and takes me in a deep kiss. He still tastes like me.

We continue to kiss as we both come down from our orgasm highs, the pulses from where we're connected slowing in time with our heartbeats until finally, we fall apart. Travis places a chaste kiss on my lips before sliding away from me and standing up.

What? Where's he going? He must sense my confusion because, before he turns away, he says, "Relax for a minute. I'm going to get rid of the condom and get something to clean you up. Be right back."

I look down and notice I'm lying in a huge puddle, but I'm too boneless to care right now. Fuck the puddle. It'll dry eventually. I'm going to lie here and enjoy this feeling. This effortless relaxation. My eyes are already drifting closed.

"Yeah, that's what I mean. I'll get new sheets, too," he says.

I watch as he removes the condom and ties it off, disposing of it in the trash can beside my bed, before sliding his boxers and jeans back on. How does he look as sexy getting dressed as he does getting undressed? It ought to be against the law. I think I make an 'mmmmm' noise as I appreciate his body. He chuckles and leans over the bed, kissing me deeply again.

"I probably could say the same about you, but I don't plan to let you get dressed anytime soon to find out." Oh, shit. I guess I said all that out loud. He kisses me again before leaving the room.

A yawn comes unbidden, and I close my eyes and wait for Travis to come back.

I'll just have a little cat nap before Travis while I wait, and if I'm lucky, we can do that again.

31

Scared of Santa?

Travis

FIN IS IN THE same spot she was when I left the room a few minutes ago, looking as though her eyes will open and she'll ogle me all over again. I can hear her even breaths and faint snores as I get closer to the bed. She hasn't moved a muscle, not that I'm surprised. I think we're both pretty worn out after what I can only describe as the best sex I've ever had.

Seriously. The. Best. The way she clenched around me as she came? Fucking heaven.

Judging from the wet spot surrounding her, I'd say she had a pretty good time, too. Feeling that rush of liquid splashing my dick and balls was a surprise at first, but fuck if it wasn't the hottest thing I ever experienced. Thinking about it now is making me hard again, already.

Down, boy. You already had your fun. Let her sleep.

I drop the fresh sheets and spare towels I brought from downstairs onto the bench at the end of the bed and use a damp washcloth to clean Fin up. I go slowly, doing my best not to wake her. She fell asleep quickly, so she must need the rest. I wasn't totally serious about keeping her up all night, despite my dick's pleas to get inside her again right now. It takes everything in me to get Fin cleaned up and get the sheets changed without waking her up with at least a kiss, but seeing her laying there so peacefully afterward makes it worth it.

After she's tucked in, I venture back downstairs to the living room to finish unpacking the presents I brought over. Once I see them all under the tree, and surrounding the tree, and climbing the walls at the sides of the room, I realize maybe Johnny had a point about the number of presents I brought. Looking at them all together like this, it looks a little excessive. But then I remember that they're likely not getting anything from their own father, and I put that thought out of my mind. I have the means and the desire, so if I want to spoil them, I will. I mean, as long as Fin says it's okay, of course.

I take another quick look around, checking to make sure Finley has everything ready for the kids for Christmas morning, and of course, she does. Before heading back upstairs to her room, I set the alarm on my phone for six in the morning, which should give me plenty of time to get out of here before the kids wake up. I'm not sure what Fin wants to tell them and I refuse to force her hand by being here on Christmas morning and deciding for her. I walk softly back up the stairs, turning the bedroom doorknob when closing it behind me so the latch doesn't click too loudly, before stripping to my boxers and climbing into bed. Fin immediately rolls over and lays her head on my chest, throwing an arm and a leg over me, her smooth skin warm from the blankets.

I could get used to this.

"*Ahhhhhhh.*"

A blood-curdling scream cuts through my dreams and startles me awake. Before I can think, I jump out of bed in a panic and run down the stairs in Fin's house, toward the screaming, only to find Austin in the living room holding a gift and screaming bloody murder.

"Austin, what's wrong? Are you okay?" I run over and grab him by the shoulders, bending down to look into his eyes. "Are you hurt? Where are you bleeding?"

Austin blinks a few times, the scream dying in his throat. His eyebrows are drawn. "Travis?"

"Yeah, buddy. What's wrong?" My heart is beating overtime, and this kid is staring at me like he wasn't the one screaming the house down in the middle of the night.

"He's coming for me. I knew he'd find me here. It's not safe. Mom lied."

"What?" I'm confused. But more than that, I'm standing in Finley's living room, in my underwear, talking to her kid while he freaks out about a gift. And my alarm hasn't even gone off yet. I guess six a.m. wasn't early enough after all.

"Austin, what are you doing up so early? What's all the yelling about?" Finley is stumbling down the stairs, rubbing the sleep from her eyes. Looks like she, at least, had the sense to put her clothes back on before she came down. She even pulled her hair up into a knot on top of her head.

Austin drops the gift he's holding and sprints to Finley, immediately jumping into her arms. He buries his face into her neck and cries, "Santa found me. I told you he was real. You lied to me."

Finley's eyes go wide and she looks at me. She makes a sad smile, and I can tell she's holding in a laugh. She sits on the couch with Austin in her arms, rocking him back and forth, and motions for me to sit beside her.

"Austin, honey. There's nothing to be afraid of. Those gifts are not from Santa," Fin says, lifting Austin's head so he can look at her. "They're from Travis. I didn't lie to you. Santa isn't real."

Holy shit. Suddenly it hits me. The kid who loves all things spooky, who conducts middle of the night seances alone in his kitchen, who talks about horror movies constantly, and who still wishes he lived in a haunted house, is afraid of jolly old Saint Nick. This is... unexpected.

Austin turns to look at me, and scrunches up his nose, sniffling back his tears. "Is that true?"

"Uh, yeah, buddy. It's true. Well, they're from me and Johnny."

A huge shuddering sob racks his body. "But it says it's from Santa? Lots of them do. Why would you do that?"

I look at Fin, so confused it must show on my face. She mouths, "I told him Santa's not real".

Shit. *Santa* might not be real, but *I* am a real asshole. I scared the crap out of a child by writing Santa on some gifts.

Austin is such a unique kid.

"I'm so sorry, Austin. I wasn't thinking. I thought all kids liked gifts from Santa. I went a little crazy when I went shopping for you guys and felt silly writing my name on so many gifts."

His little body shudders in Fin's lap, making her and the couch move with the force of it. Like the thought of getting gifts from Santa is the most disgusting thing he could think of.

"Why would anyone want anything to do with Santa?" Austin screws up his face and in a funny, deep voice, he says, *"Hey, kid. Come sit on my lap and I'll give you some candy. And if you're really good, I'll break into your house and give you presents. Oh, yeah. I also watch you when you're sleeping."* He stops and takes a deep, shuddering breath. "Does that sound like fun? Or does that sound like the stuff a stranger danger creep would do?"

He's glaring at me now, and if I didn't feel so bad, I'd probably have to laugh. He looks so cute, but I know he's mad and trying to look mean. He probably wouldn't appreciate it if I laughed at him.

I rub my hand down my face, physically wiping the grin away. "When you put it like that? No. It doesn't sound fun at all."

"Yeah," he says, hopping off his mom's lap to stand on the floor directly in front of me. "Are you positive Santa isn't real?" he whispers. "Do you promise?"

"Cross my heart, kiddo. I wouldn't lie to you. Santa is not real. I bought those gifts and Johnny and I both wrote that some of them were from Santa because our nieces and nephews like to get gifts from Santa. Believing in the magic of it helps them to be in the Christmas spirit."

He bunches his eyebrows at me, back to his normal self. "That's not the magic of Christmas, Travis. The magic of Christmas is spending time with your family and friends who love you."

I laugh. This kid is too smart. "You're absolutely right. Sometimes I forget that. Thanks for the reminder."

"You're welcome," he says, turning to grab the gift he dropped. "Maybe after you put some clothes on I can open some of these presents? Better do it before Braden wakes up, though. I remember how mad he was that first time you were here naked."

I laugh again, Fin joining in from beside me on the couch.

"Listen, I wasn't naked that first time, and I'm not naked now," I say with a chuckle. "But I will go put some clothes on because I feel weird. So there." I stick my tongue out at him and he laughs, returning the gesture.

God, I love that kid.

Come to think of it, I love the other two as well.

And I'd be lying to myself if I don't admit that I might be falling in love with their mom, too.

32

New Dishwasher and a New Babysitter

Finley

"Oooh, looky here, Delores, Lana. My little Flipper is finally getting some dick. And from the looks of her, it's some good dick at that." Grandma waves to me from her porch, telling Delores and anyone else within earshot about the good dick she seems to think I'm getting.

I mean, I am, but it's not like she actually knows that.

My hands fly to my cheeks. With the heat suddenly coming off of me, I'm positive that I've burst into flames, but my hands come away unscathed. No flames then, just embarrassment.

Delores and another woman step out onto the porch from inside my Grandma's house.

"It's about time, dear," Delores says. "We were worried about you."

"Yeah, pretty soon you'll be old like us and then there'll be only three kinds of dick available to you." Grandma holds a finger up for each item. "Rubber dick that you buy and operate yourself, look but don't touch dick that you pay for, and little blue pill dick that's almost as wrinkly when hard as it is when soft."

"The rubber dick is my first choice," says the woman who came out with Delores. "They never change what they're doing when it starts to work. And even better, rubber dicks don't open their mouths and say something stupid when you're done."

My jaw drops and I stare at the newcomer. Has my grandmother finally met her match? Delores comes close, but I think this woman is even more like my grandma than Delores is.

"Oh, Flipper, you haven't met Lana yet, have you? Lana, this is my granddaughter, Finley. Finley, Lana used to babysit Ryder and his brother, Hunter, when they were little. She's our newest neighbor."

"And she's the newest member of our gang." Delores lifts her hands, palms up and fingers spread, to about waist height and moves her fingers in slight squeezing motion. "The Titty Club."

My grandma does a similar movement with her hands a little higher, and Lana pats her chest with her hands flat and her fingers together. They're making boob squeezing motions at the height their own boobs are and I can't help but laugh.

"I had mine cut off," Lana explains. "No big deal, though. I might not have titties, but I have some sweet tattoos. And, as an added bonus, no more breast cancer." She holds her hand up for a high five, which I, of course, give her. Beating cancer is a big deal and should be celebrated at every opportunity.

Grandma corrals us and leads us over to Delores's house. "My place is full of dicks," she says, with no further explanation.

I'm not even sure I want one at this point. My grandmother's life is way more interesting than mine, and that's sad. I started having great sex with the hottest man alive, and my grandmother still has more going on than I do. But all I can do is laugh. I want to be like her when I grow up. Not sure I'll be able to pull off the whole *perverted old lady* bit she's got going on, though. At least, not as well as she does.

We go into Delores's cottage and take a seat at the small dining table she has at the back of the living room while Delores makes herself busy in the kitchen. Grandma reaches over and squeezes my hand, her skin papery and cold compared to mine. It's one of the few reminders I get that she's not getting any younger, despite her sometimes childish behavior.

"So, Flipper, what brings you by today?"

"Just visiting. The kids are all at their friends' houses and I couldn't think of a better way to spend the afternoon than hanging out with you."

"Oh, you flatterer you. But I don't believe you for a second. What's the truth?"

I chuckle. "I have some time to kill before I meet with potential new clients who are thinking about listing their house. I was hoping you would calm me down before I freak out about it. They're the sixth couple I've met with since getting my license, and all the others chose not to use me. Maybe I'm cursed."

"Nonsense. They're stupid if they're not using your services. You're clearly the best option out of any realtor in this city." My Grandma is always on my side, even when there's no actual proof to back up the way she feels. That's why I came to her for a confidence boost. She believes in me so much that I almost have to believe in myself. It's nice after so many years of Emilio thinking I couldn't do anything right. "I'll let all my friends know to call you if they need real estate help. Do you have any business cards I can give out?"

I don't think many of the residents here at Peaceful Pines will require my services, but it can't hurt to give Grandma a few business cards. "Here you go," I say, passing her a small stack from the card holder I keep in my pocket.

I wonder if carrying a purse will make me look more professional? I have one, but I'm always more comfortable keeping things in my pockets. That's why the number one feature I look for in pants is pockets. Something I've recently discovered most women's dress clothes don't have. Because women who need to dress professionally don't need to put things in their pockets, I guess.

Delores comes back from her kitchen and, with a grin, passes me a big coffee mug with the word "ball-buster" on the side. I grin. I've seen her collection of sweary teacups many times, but this is the first time I'm seeing this mug.

"I had a set of coffee mugs specially made, because not everyone likes tea," Delores explains. "Not even when it's proper tea instead of the whiskey the girls and I usually drink."

"This is great, Delores. Thanks." A look in the cup confirms she's actually given me coffee, which is a relief. Not that I think she would pour me a proper drink when she knows I'm off to meet clients, but it's still good to be sure.

"Great," she says, sitting in the chair opposite me. "Now that we've all got drinks, why don't you go ahead and fill us in on this new man in your life? What's his name? Where'd you meet?"

"And, more importantly, does he know what to do with his meat stick?"

"Gladys!" Lana shakes her head at my grandmother, but all I do is laugh. I suspected this question was coming as soon as she announced to Delores and Lana that I've been having sex again. How she knows these things is still a mystery to me.

"His name is Travis, and he's the handyman I hired to help me with the renovations on the house. And yes, he uses his meat stick very well, Grandma. But you're not getting any more details than that."

"Boo, you're no fun." Grandma takes a sip of whiskey from her teacup. Today hers reads *dickhead* while Delores and Lana have *asshole* and *bitchtits* respectively. "How can I live vicariously through you when you won't give me any details about your sex life?"

"Yeah, um… you can't. That's kind of the point." We all laugh, except for Grandma.

"Well, you leave me no choice then. I suppose I'll have to take my chances with one of the old boys at bingo. Looks like it's going to be strictly blue-pill, wrinkly dick for me from now on." The frown on her face causes the rest of us to burst into laughter, which makes Grandma laugh too.

"A handyman, hey?" Delores asks. "Too bad my Ryder and his friends are all pairing off these days. You could have snagged yourself a real live rockstar. I hear they're all quite good with their meat sticks, too."

I snort out a laugh, my coffee spilling out of my mouth and running down my shirt. Great. Now I'll have to run home and change before my meeting.

"No way. No rock stars for me. Emilio and his stupid little band have given me enough of a taste of rock star behavior to last a lifetime. I will not be involving myself with any more of those." Delores raises an eyebrow at me. "Except as friends. Your grandson Ryder and the other guys have helped me a lot in the last while. They've all really come through for me. But I don't think a relationship with a rockstar is in the cards for me. As much as I like those guys, they're all a little much for me, you know?"

"You never know who you'll fall in love with, darling," Grandma says, a strange gleam in her eye. "Don't turn someone away because you had a terrible experience with someone else who had a similar job." She pats my hand again. "But to get back to the subject at hand, which wrinkly-dicked old codger should I set my sights on. It's almost bingo time."

The three ladies discuss the merits of dating any of the men who live in the Peaceful Pines community, gossiping like teenage girls, and I pull my phone out of my pocket to check the time. Damn it. The stupid thing powered itself off again.

I push the power button and wait impatiently. I really need to get myself a new phone one of these days. What if a client wants to list with me and then they can't get in contact with me because my stupid phone constantly turns itself off? It's not very professional of me to not have a working phone.

When it finally turns back on, the lock screen shows notifications for three missed text messages, one from Emilio and two from Travis.

Travis- I'm at your place. New dishwasher finally came in. I figured you'd want it put in right away.

Finally, we've been waiting for that dishwasher since before Halloween. I can't wait to no longer need to wash dishes by hand.

Travis- Kids have been home for a while, but no sign of Emilio yet. Have you heard anything?

Travis agreed to go to my place and wait for Emilio to pick up the kids before he even heard that the dishwasher was here. I was going to go straight to my meeting from here. Even with going home to change, I won't have time to hang out and wait for Emilio to show up. Something tells me I should have checked his text before Travis's.

Emilio- Change of plans. Can't take kids tonight.

Oh, for fuck's sake. Not again. Today is the worst day for him to pull this. I was counting on him being with the kids while I had my meeting. But maybe there's another way.

    Finley- Emilio canceled. I have a huge favor to ask.

33

Chilling with Children

Travis

"You are a lifesaver. I can't thank you enough for doing this for me." Finley runs around her house, grabbing her keys and the purse I've never seen her carry before, before kissing the kids on the head. "I'm so sorry that Emilio's poor life choices are affecting your life now, too."

"Enough, Finley. You've already thanked me. I'm happy to do it. The kids and I will find something fun to do. You'll have a great meeting and book some clients, and you'll be home before you know it. It's no big deal."

"Well, I'm still sorry. I'm sorry you had to miss going out with Johnny. He probably gets all the special treatment at the clubs. That could have been fun."

"Nah, he's fine. He's going to look for Becca. Apparently, her mother set her up on a date and he needs to go see the guy. He says Becca has a no relationships rule or something, and he's pretty heartbroken over it. He would have ditched me there the second he found her, and I hate dance clubs, so there's no way I'd want to be there alone."

Fin came home to change her shirt after I'd agreed to watch the kids tonight, and I took the opportunity to rush Johnny over to Aiden's place. It's only a few blocks away, so I wasn't gone long, but Finley used it to her advantage. I didn't notice when she first came in, but she's wearing a tight, knee-length skirt that shows off her ass to full advantage, and her makeup is a lot fancier than she normally wears it. And she's wearing high heels. I love the way she looks in the sneakers she usually wears, but these heels are really doing something for me.

I wonder if she'd wear them to bed if I asked really nicely?

That's enough of that line of thinking. It's not the time for that.

"No relationships? I wonder why."

"Probably has something to do with her ex. He's a piece of work, from what I hear." *Exactly like your ex. Because they're the same person and I still haven't told you.* I groan internally. *You're such a coward, Travis.* I don't know why I haven't told her. It shouldn't make much of a difference to her or to Becca. So why haven't I told her?

Fin laughs. "Yeah, I know what that's like."

I cringe. I hate that Emilio hurt her so badly. I'd love to be the one to show her what love can be like, but first I need to tell her the truth about me. I'm not quite ready to risk the possible fallout from that, though. I want to be with her for as long as I can before I risk losing her. But I swear I'll tell her soon.

Probably.

Fin throws her coat on and reaches under her hair to slide it up and out of the back, making my dick swell slightly. I love when women do that. It's such an unintentionally sexy move. Fin's definitely not doing it to be sexy now, considering she's going out to meet potential clients, and I'm here to babysit her three kids, but it's sexy, nonetheless. Then again, I think everything she does is sexy; this hair move is merely kicking it up a notch.

"Good luck, Mom," Sarah says, squeezing Finley in a tight hug. "This couple will be the one. I have a good feeling about them."

"Yeah, me too," Austin adds. "They will see that you're the awesomest house-seller that ever lived and then they'll want you to sell their house."

"You got this, Mom." Braden holds his fist out and Fin bumps it. "I made a playlist for you to pump you up on the drive there. Make sure you listen to it, okay?"

The grin on Finley's face doesn't hide the fact that tears are forming in her eyes. She fans her hands in front of her face and looks up at the ceiling. "Okay, guys. That's enough. New rule: no making Mom cry when she's walking out the door to meet clients." She waves at them once more before turning to walk to the door. I follow along behind her, watching the way her ass swings with each step she takes in her high heels. I've never seen her dressed up like this before and I gotta say, I am thoroughly enjoying it.

"Okay, I'm off then." Finley looks up at me. Even with heels on, she's still a little shorter than me.

I take her hand and lead her out onto the porch, closing the door behind us. This feels good, sending her off to work like this, while I stay home and watch the kids. It feels like the family I thought I could never have. I'm still not sure I can have it for real, but my heart aches with how good it feels to have it for now.

Fin wraps her fists in my t-shirt, pulling me close. I wrap my arms around her.

"You look beautiful," I whisper. "Will you wear those shoes to bed tonight?"

She tips her head back and laughs. "What?"

I lean in close, my mouth touching her ear, and I whisper, "All I can think of is stripping you out of these clothes, bending you over the side of the bed, and slamming my dick into your sweet pussy while you wear these heels and nothing else." I feel her shiver, and I know I'm turning her on. "And after that, I'm going to throw you on the bed, bury my face between your legs, and lick you until you're screaming my name and coming all over my tongue." I give her a quick kiss on her lips, and another on her forehead, before letting her go and stepping aside. "Now, get going. You don't want to be late for your meeting, do you?" I swat her on the ass and she jumps.

"Not fair, Travis," she says with a laugh, turning to walk away. "You're going to pay for that later."

"The smack? Or the rest?" I call out as she walks down the driveway.

"Both." She turns and blows me a kiss. "See you later."

"Ill be here waiting."

"Counting on it."

"So what was all that about this couple being the one?"

The kids and I are sitting in front of the TV, watching some sort of musical cartoon, eating pizza I ordered for dinner. I still haven't mastered that whole cooking thing. If I'm going to be spending a lot of time with the kids, maybe I should learn how to cook, so we're not always eating takeout. I wonder if Alex would teach me?

"Mom hasn't booked any clients yet," Braden says through a mouthful of pepperoni pizza. "She's been doing a lot of work with Grandpa during the day, but she said it would be nice to get someone to list with her. I heard her say to her friend Rose that she wants to let Grandpa retire. She thinks he keeps working just so she can have a job."

Kids really do hear everything.

"So she hasn't had any clients at all? No one wants to list their house with her, or have her help them buy a house?" That seems odd to me. Fin would be excellent at helping someone buy a house, considering all the experience she has renovating and remodeling houses. If I were in the market to buy a place, she's the realtor I'd want, and not only because I have feelings for her. She's beyond qualified. "Has she had a lot of meetings?" It's only been a couple of months since she got her license, I suppose. Maybe that's it?

"Not many, and one has booked with her yet."

Too bad I don't know anyone in the market.

34

New Friends and First Clients

Finley

"So, then what happened?"

"Uh, well, after that?"

"Yes, after Travis brought over all the gifts and you freaked out. What happened then?" Alex is sitting on my couch, shoveling cake and ice cream into her face, and looking to me to distract her from her newly discovered pregnancy with gossip about Travis and me. She showed up about an hour ago with one shopping bag full of pregnancy tests and another full of cake and ice cream, just as I was about to get a glass of wine and sit down to read my book.

Apparently, Becca left town after a fight with Johnny, Denise is busy with her search for a new assistant, and I'm the next person on Alex's list of girlfriends who's available to offer support. Not that she seems to need much. She walked into my house, dropped her bag of cake and ice cream onto my kitchen table, then took herself to my bathroom, with barely a hello. I only knew what she was doing after she came out and told me we'd have to wait three minutes for the test results. It was all very calm and business-like. Hell, she hardly reacted when every test came back positive.

I don't even know why she needs me to distract her when the cake she's currently massacring with a fork is a very lifelike replica of a soda-can-sized penis and the ice cream sitting on the plate beside it looks like two hairy testicles. You'd think that would be enough of a distraction for her. I know I'll never look at chocolate sprinkles the same way after this. When I asked about it, she mentioned something about a dick decorating party and leftovers, but I couldn't get anything more out of her. The curiosity is nearly killing me.

That will have to wait, though. Right now, she's staring at me, waiting for an answer.

"Um, well." I cover my mouth, fake a cough, and say, "He stayed the night."

She drops her plate to the coffee table, the poor cake dick flopping over and rolling away from his balls. "He stayed over! That's fantastic. I knew the two of you would get together."

I roll my eyes. "Don't get too excited. We've been together a few times since then, but it's hard with the kids around. And after that first time, he seems less interested in staying too long after. I want to say it's because he doesn't want to get caught with his pants down again, but I'm not sure. I've got a weird feeling about all of it."

"Wait, wait, wait. What do you mean *caught with his pants down*? Oh my god, did your kids walk in on you? Are they scarred for life now?" She laughs through a bite of ice cream.

"What? No. Of course not," I laugh. "He ran downstairs early the next morning when Austin woke him up with his screaming." I take a few minutes to explain Austin's fear of Santa Claus and Travis's great idea to write *from Santa* on some of the gifts he bought, and by the time I finish, Alex and I both have tears streaming down our faces from laughing too hard.

"He ran down in his underwear? What the hell was he thinking?" She's sucking in breaths and holding her belly while she laughs. Meanwhile, I'm busy trying to wipe tears from my eyes and stop the horrible, braying laugh from escaping my mouth anymore. My neighbors will think I'm keeping farm animals in here if I keep laughing like this. "Did you run out in your underwear, too?"

"No," I say with a laugh. "I had to get dressed before I left the room because I was still completely naked. I don't remember him putting his boxers on, even. He must've done it right after, I guess?" I was completely out of it after that last orgasm. I fell asleep almost instantly.

Alex leans back, snuggling into my overstuffed couch, and pulls her feet up, crossing her legs beneath her. Her cake and ice cream sit on the table, the plate a messy puddle, but she seems to have lost interest in it, for now.

"I don't get it," she says. " Because Austin caught him in his underwear once he's decided not to spend the night anymore? Seems weird."

"You're telling me," I say. I push out a breath and slap my hands on my legs. "But let's forget about him for now. Let's get to the real reason for your visit. You've had a dick cake, a few bites of ice cream balls, and a lot of laughs. Are you ready to talk about it now?"

She releases a slow exhale and rubs a circle on her still-flat belly with one hand.

"I'm surprised, I guess. It's not that we didn't want it to happen, but I certainly didn't think it would happen so soon. We only got engaged a couple of months ago, for fuck's sake. I haven't even thought about a wedding, and now I'm jumping right into having a baby? It's just... it's a lot."

I get up from the armchair and sit beside Alex on the couch. It can be scary finding out you're pregnant, especially when the father of the baby isn't with you when you find out. What I want to know is why Alex came here to take her tests instead of going home to Connor. I think she's worried about more than being pregnant, and that's the real reason she came here to see me.

"That makes sense," I tell her, wrapping my arm around her shoulders. "I bet it feels like it's moving so fast. Are you afraid to have a baby? Because, I gotta tell you, when you saw those pink lines, and blue lines, and plus signs, and the word pregna—" Something dawns on me. "You bought every kind of test the drugstore had, didn't you?"

She laughs. "I wanted to be sure."

"I think you can be sure now." I smile. "As I was saying, you saw all those positives, and it's like they didn't even phase you. So what's really bothering you? Because I don't think being pregnant is scaring you all that much."

She looks at me, a tear sliding down her cheek. "Connor," she says. "How do I know he won't do to me what the other guys did? How do I know he won't cheat? He's the lead singer in a band. It's not like he wouldn't have plenty of opportunities if he were looking to hook up with someone. When they finish this album, they're going on tour again. I was going to go with them, but this whole pregnancy thing has me rethinking that plan."

My breath leaves me in a rush of air, her words hitting me in a spot that I was sure wasn't hurting anymore. She thought she should come to me with this issue? Does she know what Emilio did to me? I'm sure she knows. She must.

"I don't know if I'm the best person to answer that, Alex. My ex pursued music and he couldn't resist the women who threw themselves at him, and he only ever played tiny, local bars. I can't imagine what it would have been like if he'd actually had some success."

She wilts in front of me, clearly disappointed with that answer. "I forgot about that. I'm sorry for bringing it up. Are you doing okay?"

"What? Oh, yeah. It's fine. It hurt a lot at first, but when I realized he'd never been who I thought he was... Well, let's just say I knew I was better off without him." Alex brightens a little. "I've thought about it a lot, though. When Travis introduced me to Johnny, and to the rest of the guys in the band, I thought long and hard about whether Emilio cheated because he was pursuing a career in music, or whether it was something else. And you know what I discovered? Emilio cheated because he's Emilio. Because he's an asshole." I laugh. "If I could have been bothered to look back a little further, I'm sure I would have found that he'd cheated long before he joined his stupid little band. But I was glad to be rid of him. I'm disappointed that it took finding someone else's underwear in his car for me to finally walk away."

Alex gets a strange look on her face and she sits up straight, her head on a swivel. "Wait a minute. Where are your kids?"

I laugh. "Emilio picked them up for the weekend. I'm sure they'll be back soon, though. He rarely keeps them overnight. I don't know why he insists on the visitation schedule; he never follows it. It's so hard on the kids, you know?"

She breathes a sight of relief. "Oh, good. I didn't think you were the kind of person who'd say shit about a kid's dad where they could hear it, but I wanted to be sure." She smiles at me. "Glad to see that I was right."

"Sadly, my kids have come to their own conclusions about Emilio, all based on his own behavior. I never say bad things in front of them. He's still their dad, even if it seems like he'd rather not be."

Alex grabs her plate of leftover cake and ice cream, standing up. All that's left on the plate is mushy cake and ice cream soup, and she carefully balances it as she carries it to the kitchen. She puts the plate in the sink and washes it before placing it in the dishwasher.

"Thank you so much for talking me down," she says. "If Becca hadn't up and gone to Vegas without warning, she could have come with me and you would have had someone to share the burden."

"You're not a burden. And for what it's worth, I think Connor is the real deal. You don't have to worry. I can't think of a single time I've seen him when he wasn't looking at you like you hung the moon. The guy's so in love it drives him to distraction." I pull her in for a hug. "I can't wait to hear how he reacts to the baby news. Make sure you call me and let me know how it goes, okay?"

She laughs. "Okay. I will." She hugs me one more time before walking to the front door. "Thanks, again. Talk to you soon."

I nod and open the door for her. She walks out and waves before she gets into her car and drives away. I close and lock the door, and go to the kitchen to pour myself a glass of wine. Time to relax and get into my book.

As soon as I sit in my favorite spot on the couch, book in one hand, wineglass in the other, my phone buzzes from its spot on the coffee table. I huff a sigh and set everything down. Guess there will be no relaxing tonight.

Unknown- Hi, Finley. This is Aiden. I got your number from Travis. My girlfriend and I need a realtor, and fast. Can I call you?

Finley- Of course! I'd love to talk to you about that.

Things are looking up.

I program Aiden's number into my contacts. I didn't even realize he had a girlfriend, and now they need a realtor? This could be a really big deal for me.

Yet another thing I'll have to thank Travis for later.

35

Never So Scared or Humbled

Travis

"Hello?"

It's three in the morning and my phone's ringing woke me up from a restless sleep. I've been tossing and turning for the last two hours, stuck on the edges of a bad dream that I can't remember. I'm actually glad for the interruption of a middle of the night phone call.

"Travis? Travis Donovan? That you, kid?"

It takes a second to shake the cobwebs out of my head before I can place the voice on the end of the line.

"Bill?" Bill has never called me before. He usually deals with Denise when we want to play a show at Rough Mix. A chill runs through me. "What's going on, man? Is everything okay?" I bolt up, swinging my legs out of bed and putting my feet on the floor. I rub my eyes with the heel of my hand, forcing myself to wake up more. "How'd you get my number?"

"Oh, good. I'm glad it's actually you. I thought they might be messing with me. Listen. I just finished closing up the bar, and was getting ready to go home, when I found these kids peeking in the front door. They couldn't get hold of their mom and they asked me to call you."

My stomach drops all the way to the floor, and I feel sick. I know exactly who he's talking about and it's not any of my nieces or nephews. I jump to my feet and scramble around, looking for pants. "Three kids? Two boys and a girl, right? Braden, Sarah, and Austin?"

"That's them. I'd bring 'em to ya', but I only have my bike. I could probably fit one kid on it, but definitely not three."

"No, no. It's fine. I'll be there in, like, ten minutes. Please don't leave them alone." I tug on a pair of jogging pants with one hand while pulling a shirt out of my dresser.

"What the hell kind of guy do you think I am, kid? You can't really believe I'd leave children alone, in front of a bar, at three in the morning, do ya?"

I pull a t-shirt over my head one-handed, and grab my keys from my nightstand. "No, Bill. I know you wouldn't do that. But if I'm right about who left them there, and you knew about it, you'd understand why I'd want to make sure."

"Oh yeah, Trav. I know. The kids told me." Bill lowers his voice, and whispers, *"Between you and me, even if he shows up before you do, I'm not letting them go with him."*

"Thanks, Bill. I owe you. See you in a few." I punch the end call button with my finger as I run through the loft. My heart is pounding out of my chest and adrenaline courses through me, my body preparing for a fight. I shoot off a quick text to Devon, telling him to meet me at the bar, in case Emilio shows up. I'd get Johnny to join me, but he's not even here. Something about Becca leaving town has him spooked, so he's been running around trying to track her down or something.

I smash the elevator button with the side of my fist, sending thanks to the universe when the door opens right away. I pull open the gate with a little more force than necessary, and slam my palm against the parkade level button, pulling the gate closed behind me. I pace the inside of the tiny elevator for the duration of the entire ride, which I know from experience is very short, but tonight it seems to last for hours.

When I see that fucking dickhead Emilio again, I am going to crush his fucking skull. What the hell was he thinking? How did he leave his kids? I need him to explain to me exactly how his kids came to be standing outside a bar, alone, at three in the morning. Thank god it was Rough Mix, or who knows what could have happened to them.

I PULL UP IN front of Rough Mix at three-twenty and Devon is already there. He's got Austin sitting on his shoulders and Braden and Sarah sitting in the Escalade. Bill is still there, too, telling Austin a story from the looks of how hard they're both laughing. I release a long breath and focus on relaxing my muscles, preparing to put on a calm face for the kids before I get out of my truck. They can't see how angry I am. It's not their fault their father is a fucking idiot who deserves to be beaten within an inch of his life.

"Hey, guys," I say, stepping out of my truck. My voice couldn't sound any faker if I tried. Pretending to be calm and cheerful is not a good look on me. "Ready to go home?"

"Hi, Travis," Austin says from Devon's shoulders. He pats the big guy on the head. "I think I need to go home so I can go to bed now. It's way past my bedtime."

"You're not wrong, buddy. It is so far past your bedtime it's almost time to get up again. I have a feeling the three of you will sleep in tomorrow."

Devon swings Austin down and sets him on the sidewalk. "It was good seeing you, little man," he says, giving Austin a fist bump. "We have to hang out more often, and not in the middle of the night like this."

Austin looks up at him, his eyebrows scrunched down. "But that's the best time for seances and ghost-hunting," he says. "How would we ever find a ghost in the daytime?" He puts his fists on his hips and squints up at Devon. "You're not very good at this, are you?"

Devon laughs and ruffles Austin's hair. "No, I guess I'm not. You'll have to teach me, I suppose."

"Yeah, I guess I can do that." Austin turns to Devon's Escalade and motions to his brother and sister to come out. "But not tonight. I'm way too tired right now."

"I hear you, little man. I didn't expect to be out and about this time of the night tonight, either. I'll be sure to have a nap first next time."

"Hey, Travis," Sarah gets out of the vehicle and walks up to my side, wrapping one arm around my waist and giving me a side hug. "Thanks for coming to get us. Mom's phone went straight to voicemail."

I wrap my arms around her for a quick hug and kiss her on the top of the head. "No problem at all, sweetie. You guys can call me anytime, you know that. I'll always come running if you need me."

She nods and I drop my arms, letting her get into the truck. I can tell by the way she's dragging her feet that she's exhausted. Ten-year-old girls should not be out at three in the morning without an adult. Even with an adult. They should be home, cozy in their beds at this time of the night.

Braden walks up to me next, and without hesitation, he throws both arms around me and buries his face in my chest. There's an instant feeling of wetness on my shirt, his tears soaking into the material as quickly as he sheds them. I'm sure this incident tonight had him scared beyond belief, but he's such a good big brother that I'll bet this is the first time he's showing how badly it has affected him. No twelve-year-old should have to worry about taking care of their siblings in the middle of the night in an unfamiliar city. It's not fair to him. And it's another reason I'm going to find Emilio and make him regret being born.

"You did good, Braden. Austin and Sarah don't look scared at all. Not only did you solve the problem, you kept them calm the whole time. You have no idea how proud of you I am. No idea." I squeeze him tightly, comforting him now that he feels safe enough to be afraid. And comforting myself, too, if I'm being honest. Until I set eyes on them tonight, I was more scared than I've ever been in my life. "It was quick thinking to call me when you couldn't get in touch with your mom. And I'm so glad you were here at Rough Mix, because I know Bill is a good guy. He would have stayed with you for as long as it took. You're safe. Everything is going to be okay."

Braden shudders in my arms. "Dad said he was playing here tonight. He gave me money to go to the movies and said he'd meet us outside the movie theater after. He wasn't there when the movie was over and I don't have my own phone, so I couldn't even call him. We waited there for a long time before finally coming here to find him. Except he wasn't here, and the doors were locked." He sniffles and wipes his face on his sleeve. "We waited for a long time before Bill came out, too. I could see him moving through the dark window on the door, though, so I knew someone was here."

"You did great, Braden." I give him another squeeze and then let go. "I need to talk to Bill for a second, okay? Can you go sit in the truck and let your brother and sister know we'll leave in a couple of minutes? I don't want them to worry that I'll take too long. You guys all look exhausted. We need to get you home to bed."

"Okay, Travis." Braden turns, wiping his face with his sleeves, and gets into the truck. I wait until I see all the doors and windows are closed before I walk over to Bill.

"Hey, man. Thanks again for hanging out with the kids until I could get here." I shake his hand and pull him into a quick hug. "Their dad is a piece of shit."

"No problem. I'm probably going to hang around for a bit now, anyway. If he comes back, do you want me to tell him anything? Or let him think he lost his kids?"

"Let me know if he shows up, but don't say anything about the kids unless he asks. I want to see if he even realizes he forgot them. And I want to see if he calls the cops when he realizes they're missing."

Devon chuckles. "My money is on him not remembering."

"Me too," says Bill. "He seemed like a fuck-up when I met the guy. I can tell you another thing, too. They'll never play here again. Even if this didn't happen, they're not good enough to get another chance with me."

We all laugh at that. Bill let us play here when we started out and I'm sure we weren't that great. But we were basically nice kids, so he was always happy to have us back. And now that people pay to come see us? Well, let's say, we've happily repaid that favor several times over.

"One more thing. Once their mom finds out about this, I'm sure she'll get her lawyers and the cops involved. They'll probably want to talk to you about what happened tonight, too."

"You bet, kid. You know where I am. I'll do whatever the little lady needs."

"Thanks, Bill. I owe you."

He nods and walks back into the bar.

"Thanks for coming, Devon. I wasn't sure if I'd be walking into an ambush. I didn't want to have to fight Fin's ex to get the kids away from him, but I would have."

He punches me in the arm as gently as is possible for a huge guy like him. "You got it. I'll probably hang around here, too. For a little while, at least. I kind of want to see if he pisses himself when seeing me now." Devon lets out a rumble of a laugh. "It'd be like Pavlov's dogs, only instead of a bell and drool, it will be my ugly mug and that idiot pissing his pants."

I shake my head and chuckle. "Okay, well, let me know if you see him. I'm going to get these kids home to bed and break the news to Finley."

"Good luck, brother. Stand back a little when that Mama Bear temper gets activated. You don't want to be taken out in the crossfire. I'd hate to lose you like that."

I walk around and get into my truck, still shaking my head. "Well, what do you guys think? Should we get you home now?" I ask the kids as I pull away from the curb.

Soft breaths and slight snores are my only answer. I look around the truck and see all three kids are fast asleep. They've been awake so long that it only makes sense they'd sleep now, but it still feels good to know they feel safe enough with me to fall asleep after such a scary ordeal.

It feels damn good.

36

Unsupervised Visitation

Finley

I WAKE UP TO the feeling of someone climbing onto my bed.

"What's going on?" I mumble, sitting up. I fumble for my glasses on my nightstand, knocking them to the floor accidentally. Someone picks them up and places them in my hand. "Travis?" I slip my glasses on at the same time Travis turns on the lamp. "What are you doing here? What time is it?"

"Hey, babe," he says, kissing me on the cheek. "It's early. I made you a coffee." He helps me prop myself up against the headboard.

I grab my phone from the nightstand to check the time and notice that the power is off again. "Damn it. Not again. Stupid fucking phone." I press the power button to turn it back on and put it back on the nightstand. While I'm waiting for it to power up, I take my coffee mug from Travis. "Thanks."

"So, there's something I need to tell you," he says, looking down at his lap. "But before I tell you, you need to know that the kids are here and in bed."

"What?!" All residual sleepiness vanishes and I'm suddenly alert. I push past Travis, letting him take my cup from me, and jump out of bed, running down the hall to check the kids' rooms. He's right. All three kids are here, asleep in their beds. But how can that be when last I saw them they were getting into Emilio's beat-up old van, going to spend the weekend with him?

"Shhhh," Travis whispers, walking up behind me as I stare into Braden's room. "They've had a rough night. They fell asleep a few minutes before I came to get you. I wanted to wake you up first, but all three of them zombie-walked straight to their rooms from my truck and went straight to bed."

He takes my hand and leads me back to my room. Travis gets me settled up against the headboard again and gives me back my coffee. I take a deep drink and look at my phone again. It's nearly four in the morning.

"What happened?" I finally ask. I won't like the answer, no matter what it is, but I need to know. Now.

"I got a call from my friend Bill. He owns a bar called Rough Mix and when he was locking up and leaving for the night, he found your kids at his door, looking for Emilio. His band played there tonight. Braden told me that Emilio gave them money and sent them to the movies, saying he'd pick them up after, but he didn't show. They waited for a long time and he never came back."

My temper flares, my guts churning with a burning anger I haven't felt since I found out Emilio cheated. Actually, scratch that. That anger was nothing compared to this. I'm going to find him and I'm going to bury him alive.

"The movie theater was already closed by that time, and the kids didn't have a phone, so they walked to Rough Mix to find him. I'm sure you can see where this is going. He wasn't there, and the doors were locked already. Luckily, they could see movement inside, so they smartly waited until the person came out. Not long after that, Bill found them. He tried calling you," he says, gesturing to my phone, "but it went straight to voicemail. Then Braden asked Bill to call me."

Shit! I grab my phone from the nightstand, and sure enough, there's a voicemail from an unknown number. I open the screen and press the icon to listen to the message. The voice on the other end of the line tells me his name is Bill, and that my kids have been left at his bar. I hear Braden in the background telling Bill to say that he'll call Travis Donovan next. The last thing I hear is Bill asking how the kids know someone from Sleeping Dogs before the message ends. It strikes me how dangerous the situation could have been, and how lucky I am to have Travis in my life, how lucky my kids are to have him in their lives.

"I... thank you." I throw my arms around him and squeeze him tightly, pulling him against me. "Thank you for being there for my kids." The fear of what could have been makes the tears well up in my eyes. They spill down my cheeks, leaving wet trails in their wake.

He wraps his arms around me and squeezes me back, running his hand over my hair and lowering his face to rest his cheek on mine. "Always, Finley. I'll always be here for you." He slides his hands to my cheeks, wiping my tears away with his thumbs. "I told the kids the same thing. If they ever need anything, they can call me."

The adrenaline coursing through me slows, and I relax into Travis. I can tell he means every word, and the relief I feel is immense. Even when I was with Emilio, I never felt like we could count on him. I always felt like I was doing it all alone. Here I've known Travis for a few months and I already trust him way more than I ever trusted Emilio. And it's sounding like my kids trust him, too.

"There's one more thing, Fin. It's something that I've been meaning to tell you about your ex," Travis says after a few moments of silence. "I found this out a little while ago, and I've been trying to find a good time to tell you, but there never was one. And compared to what happened tonight, it barely seems worth mentioning."

I lean back and raise my eyebrows at him. "Okay," I drawl. "What is it?"

He blows out a breath and runs his fingers through his copper hair. "Did Becca tell you about her Freddy tattoo? About the ex that inspired it?"

"She told me a little. That some guy started calling her Freddy because of some scarring. Why?"

"Well, he took a topless photo of her and then got the entire school calling her Freddy. His uncle is the one who gave her that first Freddy Krueger tattoo, and most of her other tattoos, to help her take back the name and start covering up some scarring to help her feel more confident."

"Okay. But what does that have to do with Emilio?"

"Did you know Emilio lived here in Westborough when he went to high school?"

"Yeah. He played baseball. He got a scholarship to college. That's where we met." I get a sick feeling in my stomach. I think I know where this is going, but I really, really hope I'm wrong.

"Well, back then, Emilio called himself Milo. And he's the guy who did all this to Becca."

The words slam into me with physical force. My stomach drops and I'm gripped by swirling nausea. I frantically wave one hand while covering my mouth with the other. Thankfully, Travis gets the hint and passes me the trash can from next to my bed. I throw up what's left in my stomach, mostly a little coffee from this morning and the half a glass of wine I drank last night.

"You alright?" Travis asks. He holds my hair back as the dry heaves taper off. I nod my head and he takes the trash can from me and places it on the floor. "That was surprising."

"You're telling me," I say, grabbing a tissue and wiping my mouth. I pick up my coffee and take a swallow to get rid of the vomit taste. "I didn't even have that strong of a reaction when I found out about the cheating. Cheating seems almost... I don't know, boring? Unimaginative? Compared to what he did to Becca. Does she know?"

Travis shakes his head. "Devon knows, and he only told me. Johnny is familiar with what Milo, or Emilio, or whatever his name is, did to Becca, but he doesn't know that he's also the guy who hurt you and the kids. He's not known for being calm and rational in situations like this, so we weren't sure if he should know before you and Becca did."

"Why didn't you tell me right away?"

He messes with the fringe on a blanket, avoiding my eyes. I push him with my foot, forcing him to look at me.

"Tell me why you didn't tell me, Travis."

"I wanted to. But I wanted to tell you and Becca together, and I never found a good time to do it. And then, the more I thought about it, the more I realized maybe it would be better if you guys didn't know? It's not like it would make a difference to either of you now, right? Becca has nothing to do with him, except that one night she ran into him when she was out. And you only deal with him as much as you need to for the kids. What good would come from bringing it up? From making that connection?"

My breath catches in my throat, my brain zeroing in on only one part of what Travis just told me. "Becca saw him? When?" I can hear my heart beating inside my ears. "When did she see him, exactly?"

"Uh, pretty sure it was the weekend of Alex and Connor's engagement and Denise and Ryder's wedding. I think Devon said it was after the wedding. They went to a diner for pancakes and when Becca went to the bathroom..."

"Milo sat with Johnny and started fawning all over him?" Shit. Fuck. I pick up my phone to check the dates and confirm my suspicions. "Dead again? Fuck this phone," I whisper, pressing the power button, yet again.

"Yeah. How'd you know?"

"I had Becca and Alex over for coffee one morning when Emilio had the kids and she mentioned it. She also mentioned that she was upset no one knew Emilio had the kids or someone would have invited me to everything that was going on that weekend."

Travis's head jerks up, and he stares into my eyes. He blinks several times and then shakes his head.

"Wait. Are you saying that last night wasn't the first time Emilio left the kids unsupervised?"

I release a breath. Even though in my heart I know that's what happened, I have no proof that he didn't get a babysitter that night.

"I need to call my lawyer." I jump out of bed and head to the bathroom to wash up and get ready for the day. "I have a feeling this thing with Emilio is going to get a lot worse before it gets better."

37

They're Right. It's Time.

Travis

BETWEEN DEALING WITH LAWYERS and working on the sale of Aiden's old house and the purchase of his and Rhea's new properties, Finley has had very little time to see me in the last couple of weeks. I've been working on her house every chance I get, and hanging out with the kids a lot, but Fin is as good as a ghost.

I miss her.

I'm not sure if she's avoiding me, or if she really is that busy. I have a sneaking suspicion it's the former, though, and that scares me.

"Hey, what crawled up your butt?" Connor drops beside me on the floor. I've been laying here for the last twenty minutes, trying to work out what I'm going to do about Finley. Johnny didn't show up today, and neither did Aiden, so we're not getting much done, anyway. It's not like I'm interrupting a good studio day, or anything. "You've been moping around for weeks."

Oh. I guess it's not only my laying on the floor today that has him concerned. That makes sense.

"Nothing. I'm fine." I sit up. "I'm thinking."

"Bullshit." Ryder sits beside us on the floor and offers me a piece of red licorice. I feel like a kid sitting around a campfire.

"You're not stealing your pregnant wife's licorice, are you?" I ask. If having five sisters, most of whom have kids, has taught me anything, it's that you don't steal a pregnant woman's food. *Especially* when it's her main craving.

"Nah," he says, making a face at me. "I may be dumb, but I'm not that fucking stupid. She'd stab me with one of her pointy heels if I did that. Denise is off licorice right now. She says she never wants to see it again." He takes a big bite. "So now I have to dispose of every bit of licorice in the house. It's a tough job, but I'm man enough to do it." He bites off another huge piece of licorice and grins.

"You're going to be in deep shit when she changes her mind and suddenly there's no licorice to be found," Connor laughs. "Thank god Alex hasn't gotten too demanding yet. I don't know how I'll be able to deal with the cravings of a chef, you know?"

Connor's face lights up and he smiles. He found out a couple of weeks ago that Alex is pregnant and he is so fucking excited. It's kind of adorable. You know, in a completely masculine, grown man kind of way.

"Can't you hire someone to go get whatever she wants? That's kind of the point of having all this money, isn't it?"

"I could. But I'd rather provide it myself, you know? I want to be the only one making sure she gets what she needs."

I nod at him. I get that, I really do. When I sent my lawyers to confer with Finley's lawyer to help with her custody case, I felt like I was on top of the world. It might not have been me doing the work, but I provided it, and that made me feel pretty damn good. And the fact that my lawyers have helped speed up the process makes me feel even better.

Just then, Devon walks in. I was actually hoping he'd show up today. He was going to the police station to make a statement about the night we picked up the kids outside Rough Mix, and

I want to know how it went. I went and gave my statement yesterday.

"What the hell are you guys doing sitting on the floor all criss-cross-applesauce? Did I miss a memo? Are we going back to kindergarten?" He spins around, pretending to look for whatever he thinks would make this a kindergarten classroom instead of the music studio it is. "Nope. Can't be kindergarten," he says, pulling up a chair and spinning it around to sit backwards on it. "Not enough finger paintings."

"How'd it go at the station?" I ask, unable to wait even a second longer. "Does it sound like Emilio will be charged with child endangerment, or anything?"

Devons shakes his head and gives me a sad smile. "I don't really know, man. I think we'll have to wait and see what the lawyers come up with."

"Have you asked Flipper?" Ryder is hanging onto that nickname for dear life, rubbing in the fact that his Gran and Fin's Grandma are best friends so he's seen her more recently than I have, when he's been visiting at Peaceful Pines. I'm almost tempted to put myself through a visit with those crazy women if it means I'll get a chance to see Finley for a few minutes.

I shake my head. "No, I haven't seen her much since the night we picked up the kids. She got up and started dealing with the problem immediately, and hasn't really stopped since then. When she's not in meetings with lawyers, she was working at getting Aiden and Rhea the property they wanted."

"Oh yeah," Ryder laughs. "Aiden said she went to every house around the lake, knocked on doors, and talked to the home-owners in person to explain the details of the offer. It worked, though. She found two properties side-by-side for Rhea and Aiden to buy. I can't wait until the housewarming party to see what they've chosen. They made me promise to stay away until then."

"How does that work? You live out there."

"No idea. I'm guessing they won't be right next door to us, maybe? I haven't seen much traffic at either of our neighbors' properties, anyway."

"When's the party? Will Finley be there?" Maybe I can see her then.

"I'm sure she will be. At least, I'm sure Aiden and Rhea invited her. After the amount of work she's done to get them this deal, Rhea would have kicked Aiden's ass if he hadn't invited her." Connor laughs. "Hell, after seeing all she's done for them, I'm thinking it's time to sell this place and get a place for me and Alex at the lake, too. If anyone could find me what I want, it's Fin."

My heart swells with pride at his comment. Finley is amazing, and it's time that other people see it. More than that, though, it's time for her to see it for herself. Hopefully, after pulling off this deal for Aiden and Rhea, she gains some confidence in her abilities. It will be sad to see her give up the construction aspect, though. She's so good with house restorations it would be amazing if she could do both.

"Speaking of Finley," Devon says, tipping forward in his chair. "Have you told her about you yet?"

I groan and run a hand through my hair. "No, not yet. It was hard enough telling her that Emilio and Milo are the same guy. How am I supposed to tell her I'm not really a handyman? That I'm actually in the band that I told her I wasn't in?"

"Especially right now, while she's going through this thing with her ex-husband leaving her kids alone in the middle of the night so he could play a gig?"

I shoot a glare at Ryder. "Thanks, man. That's real helpful."

He grins at me, and chomps at his licorice. "No problem. That's what I'm here for."

"You need to fucking tell her," Connor says. "Quit putting it off."

I huff out a breath and lie back on the floor, my hands folded under my head. I know I need to tell her, but would it be so bad if I waited? We still don't know what's happening with the tour now that Ryder and Connor's significant others are both pregnant. What if we don't even go? I would never have to tell Finley at all. What if I tell her, she gets mad at me, and then we don't go? I would have made her mad, possibly lost her entirely, for nothing.

"We all know what you're thinking," Connor interrupts my thoughts. "You have to tell her whether or not the tour happens."

"Fuck, man." I close my eyes and run a hand over my face.

"You know it's true."

"What if I tell her, and she can't handle it?"

Ryder reaches over and punches me in the leg. "Then she can't handle it. But that's for her to decide. Not you."

"Tell her after the party. Then you know at least one thing she's been focusing on won't be an issue. Tell her and let her make up her own mind."

I sit up again. "I hate you guys."

Devon laughs. "No, you don't. You love us. You're just mad that we're right."

Yeah, that sums it up. They are right. And I wish to god they weren't.

Because I can't help thinking that I've fucked myself by waiting this long to tell her.

38

Good News and Bad News

Finley

"Okay, guys. Get a move on. We're going to be late."

It's the night of Aiden and Rhea's house party and my kids are moving as quickly as a herd of turtles stampeding through peanut butter. I swear, they're acting like they've never even heard of shoes before, let alone have pairs of their own and know how to put them on.

"What kind of party is this?" Braden asks. "You won't leave us, right?"

My heart cracks at that, and I step away from the door where I've been tapping my foot impatiently and give Braden a hug. Ever since that night when Travis picked them up at Rough Mix and brought them home to me, Braden hasn't let me out of his sight. With lawyer meetings and getting the properties for Rhea and Aiden, he's had to be away from me more than he likes. Travis told me how brave Braden was that night, and how well he looked after Sarah and Austin, but the price he's had to pay for that bravery is a prolonged recovery period. He's been spooked ever since that night.

"I promise, Braden. I will not leave you." I squeeze him tighter. "I will never leave you."

He relaxes into my arms and releases a breath. "I know, Mom. I just... I love you." This kid. I think my heart is melting.

"I love you too," I say, kissing his forehead. "But if we don't get out of this house in the next three minutes, I'm going to take the three of you, tie your feet together, and make you hop all the way to Aiden and Rhea's house." I spin him around and push him toward the door.

Mom threats. You're not going to follow through with them anyway, so you may as well make them totally ridiculous.

"Yeah right, Mom," Austin says from the door. "Are you ready yet? I've been waiting here for hours." He snickers behind his hand. "And Sarah is already outside."

Braden laughs and slips his shoes on.

"You little shits," I say with a laugh. "You're making me crazy, you know that? There's a reason I dye my hair green and you want to know what it is?" I ask as I shoo them out the door. "It's to cover all the grays you guys are giving me. Come on. Let's get out of here."

"THAT WAS QUITE THE entrance." Travis pulls me to the side of the party. "It feels like I haven't seen you in ages."

The kids brought the party to a halt with the game of screaming tag they played to announce our arrival, but now they're occupied with my Grandma and Delores, and their two friends, Lana and Cathy. Every time I turn around, their little gang of geriatric misfits gets bigger. I'm still laughing inside because Aiden thought he needed to warn me to keep the kids away from the grannies because they're such a bad influence. I guess he's the last to find out that Gladys is my grandmother, and she is the worst offender of them all.

"It's been a while. I've been so busy with the lawyers, and with helping Aiden and Rhea make this party possible, that I've barely even had time to see the kids. Braden's not doing so well since that night you picked them up. He can't bear to be away from me for too long." I nod my head to where Braden sits with Grandma. "See how he keeps looking over here? He asked me before we left the house tonight to promise that I wouldn't leave him."

"Oh, fuck." Travis rubs a hand over his chest. "I really hate your ex, you know?"

"Oh, believe me. I know how that feels. If the lawyers weren't doing such a great job of making sure he never gets to be alone with the kids again, I'd have probably found a way to make him disappear forever."

Travis laughs. "I'd have brought the shovel."

"Oh, no. Don't worry about that. Your mom already told me about your great uncle's pig farm. Plus, I have access to industrial freezers and a wood chipper. No one would ever find him."

We both laugh. I'd never kill anyone, not really. Not even Emilio. But it's nice to joke about it with someone who seems to hate him as much as I do.

"You really do have big lady-balls. Aiden and Rhea were telling everyone before you got here all about how you marched around the lake and made offers on every property until you found people who were willing to sell."

My cheeks heat. "Well, to be fair, I didn't actually march. I drove." I smile up at him. "And Braden came with me some-times, too."

Travis smiles and touches my arm. "Don't downplay it, Fin-ley. What you accomplished in only three weeks? Well, it would be amazing even if you weren't dealing with the lawyers and Emilio, too."

His fingers send zips of electricity up my arm. I almost forgot that being near him was so intense. The loneliness of the last few weeks rushes up to swallow me all at once, and I wrap my arms around Travis's waist and pull him into a hug.

"Thank you," I say, burying my face in his chest. "I missed you so much."

His arms wrap me in his warmth and I feel his lips on my head. "I missed you too, Fin." He exhales, his warm breath blowing through my hair. "Listen, can I come over after this? We really need to talk."

My stomach drops. I don't like the sound of that. I unwind my arms from his waist and look up at him. "Uh-oh," I say with a frown. "That doesn't sound ominous or anything."

He smiles and runs a hand through his hair. "It's important, but I wouldn't say it's ominous."

My stomach flutters, but not in the good way. I get a queasy sort of feeling, like maybe I should be more worried about this conversation than I already am. "Do you want to go outside and talk now? Maybe we should get this over with and rip off the bandage?"

"What? No, Finley. It's not like that." He grabs my hand. "I promise."

Aiden and Rhea stand together at the side of the room and Aiden speaks to get his guests' attention. "Hey, everyone. Thanks so much for coming tonight to celebrate with us in our new home." He raises his glass a little and gives a small nod.

"And thank you for accepting me into your lives the way you have. I've had very few friends and family around me throughout my life, and having you all here means so much to me." Rhea's eyes glisten with unshed tears. I know she grew up in foster care, moved around to several foster homes. I can't even imagine what it would feel like to have her own home with Aiden now. A place to settle down and grow roots.

"There's one more thing we wanted to celebrate, since we are all here together." Aiden smiles at Rhea and pulls her tightly to his side. "Shortly before you all arrived tonight, I asked Rhea to marry me."

"And I said yes!" Rhea's smile is enormous as she holds up her left hand to show off the ring.

I feel a sad sting, as I realize my proposal is far behind me, and I didn't end up with the happily ever after I'd envisioned when it happened. Emilio, or Milo, since I'm not even sure which is his real name, never intended to follow through with any of the promises he made to me. He was looking out for himself all along. And that's what hurts more than anything. Because he had me completely fooled.

Travis is still beside me, but his attention is on his phone now. He tilts it toward me and I look at the screen. He's playing a video and in it Johnny and Becca are standing on a stage, in front of... Elvis?

"Is this...?" Travis nods, anticipating my question. "Really? Now?"

"He just sent it to me. Said he walked off stage at Becca's dads's drag club in Vegas and got his phone back from someone named Regina Rhymes? Wait. I thought Becca didn't know who her dad was? I have so many questions."

I snort a laugh. "You mean Ruhj-Eye-nah. It's a long 'I' sound."

He scrunches his eyebrows in question. "Isn't that what I said?"

"No, you said 'Reh-JEE-nah'. It's Ruhj-Eye-nah. The joke is that *Regina rhymes* with heaven."

He takes a second before he catches on, then he barks out a laugh. "Ha! Regina rhymes with vagina. That's great. Kind of a weird name for a drag queen, though."

"I don't know. Drag queens have some pretty cool names."

"Don't move, okay?" Travis gestures with his phone to where some of the guys are standing. "I need to go show them this. But I still need to talk to you after."

I nod, and he walks to the group, which includes my Grandma. I see them stand around in a circle, all taking in the video on his phone. I can't believe Johnny and Becca got married, and it looks like it's taken everyone else by surprise, too.

Several moments of silence pass in the group before I hear my Grandma's voice. "Well, shit. Better get over here and unzip those pants, Travis. Looks like you're my last chance," she says to him. "I need to see someone's rockstar dick before I die and it looks like you're the last rockstar standing."

Travis's eyes are as big as dinner plates when he spins and faces me. "Oh, I... uhh... umm..."

"Oh, no, Grandma," I say, jumping to Travis's rescue. "Travis is the handyman I was telling you about. It's his brother, Johnny, that's in the band."

The room is silent as everyone stares at me.

Travis looks at me with guilt in his eyes.

And that's when it hits me.

Travis is in the band.

Travis is in the band, and he's lied to me about it all along.

And everyone else knew.

39

Just Crazy Enough to Work

Travis

"Fin, wait. Please. I can explain." I follow Finley as she herds the kids out to her car. "I wanted to tell you."

She spins around and jabs a finger into my chest. "Then why didn't you, Travis? Huh? Why did I find out now, in front of a room full of people who apparently all knew? You made me look like an idiot." She punctuates every question with a finger jab. It hurts, but I deserve it.

She checks to be sure the kids are all in the car, closing the door behind Austin.

"Oh my god." She slaps a hand to her forehead. "It all makes sense now. Playing guitar for the kids, the little slips of people thinking Johnny's brother was in the band too, your sister saying neither you nor Johnny had mentioned how the album was coming along." A sardonic laugh breaks free from her mouth, and it hurts more than her jabbing me in the chest did. "And you made them all lie to me about it, too. I can't believe I was so stupid."

"I'm so sorry, Finley. I've been arguing with myself since we met, trying to convince myself to own up to it. But I couldn't risk losing you completely. I... I think I'm in love with you."

Her eyes widen in surprise. "That's ridiculous, Travis." She huffs out a breath. "You don't lie to someone you love for months. Tell Aiden and Rhea I'm sorry to rush out like this." She walks to the driver's side door and opens it, stopping to look at me before she gets in. "And send me a bill for the work and materials on the house. I should be able to pay at least some of it with this commission." And with that, she climbs in the car and drives off. When Austin waves to me out the window as they go, my heart breaks.

"FUUCCKK!" I yell, kicking the gravel in the driveway. "Motherfucker."

"Well, now I can die knowing what a real fucking asshole looks like. It's not rockstar dick, but it's something."

I turn around and see Gladys walking toward me from the house. She has a beer in each hand and holds one out for me. I twist the cap off and take a long drink. The sound of the door closing tells me someone else is coming out, but I refuse to look. The last thing I need is someone else telling me how stupid I am. I already know.

"Hey there, boy." Alex's Pops comes up and puts a hand on my shoulder. "Seems like you screwed up pretty big with that lady of yours."

"Yeah, I don't think the word 'big' quite demonstrates the enormity of how much I screwed up." I walk over to the stone fence lining the driveway and take a seat on the rough surface. "This was a monumental fuck up on my part."

Pops laughs. "No, you're right. I was trying to be nice. It was easier when your brother showed up at my gym all heartbroken and hungover. I made him work out until he puked and that seems to have turned out alright for him. He married the girl he was heartbroken over, after all."

"That's different, I think. I'm pretty sure Johnny hasn't been lying to Becca for months like I have to Finley. I told her I was a handyman. I've been working on her house." I suck back the rest of the beer.

"Why would you do something dumb like that?" Gladys asks. "It's not like she holds being in the band against the rest of you idiots. She'd have still been friends with you." She raises an eyebrow at me. "Unless...?"

"I'm in love with her. I'm in love with her, and I know how much that dumb fuck Emilio hurt when he joined a band and turned into an asshole." I sigh. "I liked the way she looked at me when we met, when she thought I was a handyman. She made me feel normal. Like I could have a family, a real one, like I had growing up. I guess I wanted to pretend that it was a possibility for a while."

"Jesus, you're more of a dumbass than I thought," Pops says, and cuffs me on the back of the head.

"Ow, what was that for?"

"Weren't you listening? For being a dumbass."

"Didn't you guys come out here to help me and make me feel better? Because if you did, you're doing a shit job. So far, you're just calling me names and slapping me around." I rub the sore spot on my head. "You're not very good at this cheering up business."

Gladys laughs. "Why would I cheer you up? I watched you break my granddaughter's heart. I came out here to fuck you up a little before I tell you how to make it right."

"And I came out here to watch her fuck you up," Pops laughs. "I always did like me a woman who could fight," he adds, with a wink in Gladys' direction, and I see the woman blush.

"Oh, stop that," she says to Pops before turning to me. "Okay, first, Emilio was a scumbag all along. I never liked him, not from day one. I still kick myself for not telling Finley back then, even though I know it wouldn't have done any good. She only saw what he wanted her to see."

"I kind of thought the same thing. Did you know it turns out Emilio is also Becca's old ex from high school? The one who got all the kids calling her Freddy?"

She nods. "Ryder told me and the girls one day when he was visiting Delores. Such a little dickhead that Emilio was. What I wouldn't give to get after his testicles with my taser." She unzips her ever-present fanny pack and pulls out a small pink stun-gun, giving it a test zap. Pops and I both instinctively cover our crotches. We've both heard of Gladys' accuracy when it comes to zapping men in the berries and we want no part of it. "Denise's ex got a taste of my lighting. It only makes sense that Emilio should, too."

"If only," I say, blowing out a breath. "I don't know how that's going to work now, though. I don't think he's going to be around much longer. It sounds like he's going to wind up with supervised visits with the kids, and I have a feeling he's not going to care enough about them to bother with that."

Gladys puts her little stun gun away and zips up her fanny pack. "Enough about that little piss-stain. Let the law deal with him. We need to figure out how you're going to get my Flipper back. You may be an idiot, but I can see how much you love her, and how much you love those kids, so I'm going to tell you exactly what you need to do."

I must either be completely desperate or completely insane, because I'm going to listen to her, and then I'm going to do exactly what she says. What other hope do I have?

"WELL, YOU'VE REALLY DONE it now, haven't you?" I'm not even out of my truck before Mom starts in on me. She leans in my passenger window and continues chastising me. "I told you to stop lying to that girl, and now look at what you've done. Poor girl only leaves the house to go to court. It's been weeks, Travis. *Weeks.*"

I release a shaky breath and step out of the truck, stealing a quick glance at Fin's place. It looks the same as it did before the party, but now I'm not welcome there. Shaking my head, freeing myself of those gloomy thoughts, I walk around the truck and pull my mom into a hug.

"You're absolutely right, Mom. That's why I'm here. I need your help."

She looks up at me with a raised eyebrow. "What do you have in mind, son?"

"Let's get Dad, too. We need to go shopping."

40

Penance Party

Finley

"YOU LOOK LIKE SHIT," Rose says with a grin. I try to close the door in her face, but she gets her foot in the way before I can do it. "Oh, come on now. You know you look like shit. It's not like this is new information."

She's right. It's not new information. I glimpsed my reflection in the side of the toaster earlier today and let's just say my, well, my everything, has seen better days. My hair is only half contained in a messy top knot. I'm wearing worn out pajama pants, and a sweatshirt that's more holes than fabric. I'm also pretty sure I could pack enough clothes for a month-long vacation in the bags under my eyes.

I do not look my best. Which makes sense, because I don't feel my best either.

I turn around and walk back to the living, back to my nest of blankets on the couch and the coffee with liberal amounts of cream liqueur added. I pull the blankets up to my neck and grab my mug.

Rose comes a moment later, carrying her own cup of coffee. "So, how long are you going to mope around like this? Because I have orders to take you out somewhere and not let you come back until late tonight."

"I have to pick the kids up from school. I can't go anywhere." And I don't want to go anywhere. I'm fine here, wallowing in my blanket prison.

"My parents are taking care of that. You and I are going out on the town. I have a limitless credit card and an entire day to use it. The only stipulation is that you have to come with me, and we have to have fun. So finish your coffee, get your ass up, and get into the shower. And if you come back down in those same ratty pajamas you've been wearing for the last week, there's going to be trouble. Don't make me call the rest of the Donovan sisters to come wrestle you into submission." She laughs. "They won't be nearly as nice as I am about this. They'll drag you into the yard, strip you down, and spray you with the hose. You don't want that, do you?"

"Fucking Donovans," I grumble. "Y'all have no boundaries." I chug the rest of my coffee and heave myself off the couch. "You know I hate you right now, right?"

"What's that? You love me? Yeah, I know you do. Now get moving before I get the hose ready for my sisters."

"Wʜᴀᴛ ɪs ᴛʜɪs ᴘʟᴀᴄᴇ? Is this a salon? A spa?"

Rose laughs. "Yup. You need some pampering, and this is the best place to do it. We're meeting the rest of our group here."

The rest of our group? Oh god, did she call her sisters, after all? I showered and got dressed like she said. What the hell else are they going to make me do?

Fucking Donovans.

We leave her car in the parking lot and walk to the front of the building. Standing there is the rest of our party.

"Flipper!" Ryder yells, running over, picking me up in a big bear hug, and carrying me back to the group. "I knew Rose would be the one to get you out of the house. She threatened you with her sisters, didn't she? That's how we got Aiden here, too." He sets me down in the middle of the most ragtag group of people you could ever see.

We've got tattooed rockstars, ex-cops, giant bodyguards, and old ladies wearing matching tracksuits and fanny packs.

"Hey, Fin. Just so you know, if you don't take Travis back after this, I'm going to be pretty upset." Johnny is back from Vegas, sporting a shiny new wedding band and the biggest grin I've ever seen. By his side is Becca, a matching grin gracing her face. "I only agreed to do this because I knew if I didn't, my sisters would hold me down and do it themselves, and I'd prefer a professional be the one using hot wax on my man-bits."

I look around, a little stunned, to be honest. I've been in the house for the last week, leaving only to pick the kids up from school and to see my lawyers. I forgot all these people were interested in my life.

Actually, that's not true. I remembered they were interested, but not interested enough to tell me the truth. I'm still a little pissed at that.

"I'm still mad at all of you," I say, crossing my arms over my chest. I'm sure I'm giving Austin a run for his money with the pout on my lips, too. "You all knew, and not one of you told me. Not even you," I turn and point an accusing finger at my Grandma. "You knew how I felt about musicians and you let me fall for Travis, anyway. Why would you do that?"

Grandma has the nerve to laugh, and the new lady in their group smacks her arm. I think I like her. "Listen, Flipper. You and I both know being a musician had nothing to do with your bad feelings toward Emilio. He is the way he is because he's a sociopathic, pencil-dick, piss-stain, loser asshole, not because he joined a band at the same time his lies fell apart around him."

"But…"

"No, I know if you think about it, you can see that he changed well before the whole band thing came about. It was a convenient excuse for why he did it. But believe me when I say he was always a bad guy." Grandma has tears in her eyes. "I wish I'd told you before you married him. Maybe I could have saved you all this trouble."

"No, Grandma. I wouldn't change it. I got the kids out of the whole mess, after all. There's no way I can regret that. Even if they can be little shits at times." She laughs and wipes her eyes, nodding in agreement. "But you should have told me about Travis."

Becca steps over to me and links her arm with mine. "Let's go inside and see what we've got in store for us. While we wait, I can tell you all about my ex, Milo, who I've recently discovered is a mutual acquaintance of ours." She gives me a sad smile. "I think I can shed some light on what kind of person he's always been."

Becca leads me inside, and the rest of our party follows behind. Ryder steps up to the counter with the rest of the guys right behind him.

"Good afternoon, my lovely lady. I believe my beautiful wife has booked the four of us in for special treatments today. Under the name 'Penance Party'?" The woman behind the counter nods. "Perfect," Ryder holds his hand out and Rose passes him a credit card. "And Travis Donovan called and confirmed payment was to go on his card? Okay, perfect. Glad that's taken care of."

"What is happening? Penance Party?" I ask, looking around in confusion. "What is a penance party?"

Connor and Aiden both shake their heads while Ryder laughs. "We are here to apologize to you. We told Travis to tell you the truth when you first met, but we should have forced the issue. We knew he was being an idiot, and that it wasn't fair to you, but we should have tried harder to make him tell you."

"So to tell you we're sorry, we're getting the full-body special, while you watch, to show you how truly sorry we are." Johnny has a grimace on his face and Becca is barely holding back a laugh from where she stands beside me, still holding my arm. "And after you've had your fill of listening to our pained screams, you, and any of the other women who want to, will stay and partake in any services you like, all paid for by Travis, of course."

I'm still a little confused. "What exactly is the full-body special?"

Rose steps up to me, phone in hand. "This," she says, as she presses the play button on a voice memo. Suddenly Travis's voice comes from the little speaker, loud enough for everyone in the lobby to hear.

"Hey, Fin," his voice says through the speaker. *"I couldn't be there with the rest of the guys to take part in the Penance Party, so I went in earlier to have the full-body special. It's not nearly enough to prove how sorry I am, but I hope you enjoy listening to the recording I made for you. Rose will send it to you after so you can hear it wherever you need a little pick me up."*

What follows is several long minutes of pained grunts and squeals, along with several strings of very creative expletives. I can't help but laugh despite myself.

"It goes on for like, twenty minutes," Rose says. "Let me skip to the end. Here."

"So that was what it sounds like for me to have my whole body waxed. It was not fun. Not at all. I'm going to petition for any man who comments on a woman's body hair to go through this themselves, and then we'll see if they have anything to say.

Anyway, Finley, I am truly sorry I lied to you about being in the band. I have more apologies coming soon, but for now, enjoy this recording as often as you need to. I hope listening to it brings you as much pleasure as making it gave me pain. See you later. Oh, and Fin? I love you."

"That was insane," I say, wiping tears from my eyes. Jury's still out on whether those are from laughter or sadness, but either way, I'm happy to have the recording. "Does it make me a bad person to say that it makes me feel a little better?"

"Not at all, Fin," Ryder says. "That just makes you one of us."

"Okay, let's go get this over with," Aiden says, cupping himself through his jeans and wincing. "Listening to that didn't make me feel any better about this whole scenario."

The guys follow an esthetician down a hallway, each of them sporting some sort of grimace of pain, while the rest of us follow along, laughing as we go.

I've only ever had my legs waxed, and it hurt enough that I knew I'd never do it again. Pretty sure after these guys have their whole body waxed, I'm going to have to forgive them.

Not Travis, though. Not yet. He has more groveling to do before I'll even consider it.

The recording of him screaming his way through a full-body wax is a good start, though.

41

Penance Party Part Two

Travis

"How did it go?"

The guys all pile out of the Escalade into Finley's driveway, looking a little tender in the downstairs region. I owe them big for going along with this plan.

"It was great," Ryder says. "Not nearly as bad as the first time I had it done. Plus, I got to listen to the rest of these guys scream and cry."

"I only cried a little," Devon says, walking way more bow-legged than usual. "Those are very sensitive areas. The woman slapped my taint after she ripped the wax strip off. SHE SLAPPED IT!"

I snicker, but only a little. That part really does hurt.

"Well, I owe you guys. Thank you for going through with it."

"We didn't do it for you, dumbass," Johnny says. "We did it for Finley, because we all feel like shit for lying to her right along with you. She deserves better than that."

I nod my head. "I know she does. And I'm going to do everything in my power to give her better from now on. Starting with finishing her yard. That's why you guys are here." I point to the sod I had delivered this morning while they were getting their bodies waxed. "To speed things up, I hired a crew to remove the old lawn for me, and all that's left is to lay the new sod."

"Why didn't you keep the crew to lay the sod, too?" Johnny whines. "This looks like hard work."

"It is hard work. That's why I will do that part myself. I was hoping you guys could put together the new furniture I bought for the porch. The kids are at my parents' house helping put together some flowering planters and stuff, so I might need some help to bring those over after, too. I wouldn't ask for even this much help if time weren't a factor. I know this is all my fault, and I deserve to fix it all myself, but I would appreciate it if you could help me get it all done before Finley gets home."

The guys nod and get to work. Despite my intent to do the hardest work alone, the guys take turns pitching in and helping. Minutes turn to hours until I return to the pallet to grab more sod, only to see there's none to be found. I look up, shocked to see that we've finished the entire yard.

"Thanks, guys," I say when we've all gathered in my parents' kitchen for a celebratory beer. "I couldn't have finished this without you."

"No, you couldn't have," Ryder says, flexing his biceps. "You don't have the strength needed to finish a project this big in such a short amount of time. It's a good thing you have all of us to lean on when times get tough."

"And maybe next time, when we tell you not to lie to the woman you love, you'll listen. Instead of thinking you know what's best for her, you can let her make up her own mind. It wouldn't be a bad thing if you let your big brother take care of you every once in a while, either. Oh, and I'll also be fine if you decide to let me take care of myself." He winks. He's letting me know he doesn't need me to look after him anymore. Here, or on the road.

I nod. "You're right, Johnny. If I'd listened to you guys in the first place, I wouldn't be in this mess. I only hope she can forgive me."

We finish up our beers, and then the guys head out. They may have helped with the yard, but the apology is something I need to do on my own. I grab a change of clothes from my truck and take a quick shower. When I emerge from the bathroom, my parents are there to greet me in the hallway.

"There's a couple of pots left in the backyard, Trav," Dad says. "Don't forget to take them back over with you."

"Sure thing, Dad. Thanks."

"And you better fix this," Mom adds, grabbing my cheek. "I love that girl and I love those kids. You best make sure they're sticking around to be part of our family, you hear?"

I smile down at her. "Yes, Mom. I will do my best. I love that girl and those kids, too, you know."

From the back of my parents' house, I grab the last of the flower pots before walking back to Fin's place with Braden by my side.

"You know, my mom really likes you," Braden says. "And I talked to Sarah and Austin, and we really like you, too. That's why we never told her about you."

My mouth drops open and I stop in my tracks. "You knew?"

Braden chuckles. "We're kids with access to the internet." He shrugs. "I googled you that first day after we painted the fence at your parents' house and told Sarah and Austin who you were. We decided not to tell Mom after we saw how she smiled when you were around. She tried keeping us out of everything involving our Dad, but it was hard to hide how sad she was when she thought we weren't looking. She didn't look so sad after she met you." He shrugs again. "We figured we'd give you a chance to tell your secret on your own time."

This kid. How did he get so smart at twelve-years-old? "Thanks, Braden. That means a lot."

"Don't thank me. You really dropped the ball here. But I do hope your plan works out. We really like you."

"I really like you guys, too," I say. "I screwed up pretty badly, though. I'm trying to make it right, and I hope your mom forgives me, but even if she doesn't, that doesn't change how I feel about you guys. You're a great kid, Braden. I've really enjoyed all the time we've spent working on the house together."

"My dad never did anything like that with me," he says. "He never really did anything with me, or my brother and sister."

I starat walking again and don't stop until we reach the bottom of the porch stairs at Finley's and put down the pots I'm carrying. I turn to Braden and grab his shoulders, getting down to look right into his eyes. "That has nothing to do with you, and everything to do with him, Braden. I don't want you to worry for a second that you did something wrong to make him treat you that way. Your dad couldn't see how cool of a kid you are because he's too caught up in his own bullshit to see what was right in front of him."

He nods at me and sniffles a little. "I know that. I guess I wanted to say thank you for actually seeing me and wanting to hang out with me. If it weren't for that, I might have believed my dad being this way was my fault. But you wanted to spend time with me, so I know I can't be that bad. And that's how I knew you weren't bad guy, even if you are in a band."

I chuckle and shake my head at him. I can't help it; I pull him into a hug. "You're not bad at all, Braden. You're cool as shit, and I'm so glad I've had the chance to get to know you these last few months."

My phone buzzes and interrupts the moment. Rose has been keeping me updated on their progress at the salon all day, and before I know it, she's texting to let me know they're on their way back to the house. We only have a few minutes for finishing touches.

"Hey. Can you help me with one last thing?"

"Sure. What do you want me to do?"

"Come up on the porch and I'll show you."

Together, we hang the porch swing on the hooks I installed earlier in the day. Fin's always snuggling up with blankets and a glass of wine or a cup of coffee, and I'm hoping the porch swing becomes a cozy place for her to relax. Even if she doesn't forgive me, I hope she enjoys this space for years to come.

42

More Clients and a New Look

Finley

"Wow, Finley. Your color looks amazing." Becca says as I step away from the stylist's chair. "How do you look like you were born with green hair? Whenever I've tried any color other than my natural black, I end up looking like I'm wearing a bad Halloween wig."

I laugh. This green is a lot richer than the one I usually do at home, and I'm in love with it, too. I know it's because of the professional products applied by a professional stylist, though, so I won't feel bad about the results I get at home. I'll enjoy this lush green while it lasts and remember it fondly when it's gone.

"I don't know what to tell you. When I used to use different colors, I always felt the same way. Like I was wearing a bad wig. Then one day I tried green and I haven't gone back. It makes me feel like a forest nymph, or something. It makes me feel more like me."

"Well, whatever it is, it suits you." Grandma walks over from her stylist's chair, sporting a purple fauxhawk that, naturally, looks amazing on her. "*Yer dead sexy.*"

We all laugh at the *Austin Powers'* reference. Good thing I know my Grandma well enough to know that she's not telling me I look like the Fat Bastard character who said that line.

The ladies in the Titty club are all sporting different colored faux-hawks, each more vibrant than the last. The newest member, Cathy, is thrilled with her wild pink mane.

"My husband would have never let me do something like this," she says, reverently touching the very tips of her fauxhawk. "He would have been furious."

"Yes, well. We all know your husband is a grade A, diseased dicksicle, don't we girls?" Delores claims, looking around for support. Every single woman here, including me now that I've heard the story of her husband, who was not only abusive toward Cathy but also tried to destroy Rhea's career, nods her head and says some variation of "hell yeah". "How's the yard looking, anyway? I haven't driven by recently."

Cathy laughs. "I went over yesterday to make arrangements for the contents of the house before I sell. It still looks like a giant dicks-co ball. The way those glitter dicks sparkle in the sunshine," she sighs happily, a small smile on her lips. "Just gorgeous. Now I need to hire a realtor and then I'll list."

"I know a great realtor, if you're interested," my Grandma says. "Finley here is brilliant. Isn't that right, Rhea?"

"You got that right. I've got my dream property; now we need to turn one of the houses into our dream home. I want to renovate rather than rebuild. I was looking into the history of the houses and apparently one of them used to belong to one of the most notorious bootleggers for miles around back during prohibition. You can't tear down that kind of history."

"In that case, I also happen to know some of the best restoration contractors in town. Isn't that right, Flipper?"

Rhea spins her head to look at me. "You do restorations too? That's perfect. You're like a one stop shop. I can't wait to tell Aiden." She pulls her phone out and starts tapping on the screen. "He was worried we wouldn't be able to find someone who would understand the importance of restoring as much as possible." She walks away, tapping away on her phone the whole time.

"Looks like business is picking up, hey Flipper?" Grandma wiggles her brows at me.

"Yeah, Grandma. Looks like it is."

Rose comes up to me and places an arm around my shoulders. "Well? Ready to head home and see what that idiot brother of mine dreamed up next?"

Shit. I forgot Travis was cooking up more apologies. I'm not sure there's anything he can do that will make up for all the lies, but I'm also not sure I can stand to stay away from him. I guess what I really need to know is whether *everything* he told me was a lie, or if some of it was true?

WE PULL UP IN front of my house and I see Travis sitting on the front steps with Braden. They're both smiling and talking, reminding me so much of that first day, when I sent Braden to apologize to Travis, and Travis wound up enlisting Braden's help in painting his parents' fence. They look like they're having fun, and I feel a little guilty that I'm going to have to break it up.

"You know," Rose says as I reach for the door handle. "Travis talks about you guys non-stop. Not only about you, but about the kids, too. If you ask me, and you should, because I'm the oldest of seven kids and I'm basically the smartest person around these parts, Travis is in love, not only with you, but with your kids, too."

I nod. I suspected as much. "But I can't keep someone around who isn't good for me, to make the kids happy. I did that with Emilio and we all know how that turned out."

"I know that," Rose agrees. "But we both know that Trav is nothing like your deadbeat ex. He thinks no one knows this about him, but the only thing he's ever wanted is a family. A wife, some kids, a place to call home. But then he followed Johnny into the band, and as much as he loves it, he knows it's not an easy life to bring a family into. He'd never want his kids to suffer the kind of instability a life on the road sometimes offers. He would do everything in his power to keep everything as normal as possible for his family. Hell, the guys have kept us out of the spotlight so well, most people think we're their dates if they see us together. It's hilarious. And disgusting." She shudders, then chuckles.

I never thought of it that way. Emilio would have never wanted us with him because it would interfere with his silly rock star lifestyle. Travis wouldn't want a family to live a life on the road because he knows that kids need stability and routine to thrive.

"He doesn't realize, though, that trips can be fun occasionally. And even if he spends a lot of time on the road, that doesn't mean that any family he had couldn't still live a nice stable life at home. Especially if that family also lives right across the street from his incredibly helpful parents, and near his many helpful siblings." Rose laughs, then whispers behind her hand, "That's because, as the youngest of seven children, sometimes he can be a bit of a dumbass."

I laugh. "Yeah, I've seen that firsthand."

"Do me a favor, and don't hold his dumbassery against him because your ex is a scumbag. Travis lied, yes, but he has never been malicious or tried to hurt you. He's done nothing without thinking of you first. Even if he went about it all wrong."

"You're a good big sister," I tell her, finally opening the door. "And you're not half bad as a friend, either." I get out, closing the door behind me.

Rose opens the window and yells, "Ha! I'm the best friend, bitch, and you know it. Now tell Braden to get his butt in the car. He's spending the night at our house. Tyson has been texting me all day, asking when I was bringing Braden over."

I wave to Rose before I turn to walk to the house. Braden and Travis both stand to greet me.

"Hey, Braden. Rose informed me in no uncertain terms that you're staying over at Tyson's tonight. Go grab your stuff so you can have a sleepover."

Braden hops down the steps and gives me a giant hug. "Thanks, Mom." he turns and runs into the house, returning less than a minute later with his backpack in hand. "I packed already.." He gives me another hug and runs to Rose's car. "Love you, Mom. Good luck, Travis."

Travis runs a hand through his hair, a sheepish look on his face. "Um, hey Fin. Uh, do you like the yard?" he asks.

I turn and look, expecting to see the same old, sparse patch of weeds that's been growing there since we moved in, but instead, I'm surprised to see an actual lawn. *How did I not notice that as we drove up?* Travis laid new sod, and it must've taken nearly all day to do. In fact, looking around now, I can see he's done more than the lawn. Pots overflowing with flowers line the porch and hang from the roof over it, perfuming the air. He's set up new patio furniture, too. Best of all, though, is the swing hanging at one end of the porch.

"I thought you might like a nice, cozy outdoor reading spot," Travis says when I take a step in that direction. "Braden helped me hang it right before you got home."

I settle on the swing and pat the seat beside me, inviting Travis to join me. "I think we should have that talk now."

43

This is my Confession

Travis

I SUCK IN A breath and sit beside Finley. The swing beneath us sways slightly with my added weight. Seconds become minutes as we both wait for the other to start. At least, that's what I'm waiting for. I'm suddenly terrified that I haven't done enough. Not only that, I'm terrified that I don't have the words to make her understand I wasn't trying to hurt her with my lies.

"Here," I hand her the gift bag I had hidden behind a cushion on the swing. "Before we get started, I want you to have these."

"Nice wrapping job." She raises an eyebrow at me, taking the bag from my hands. Upon removing the tissue paper, she sees four brand new cell phones, each labeled with the name of someone in her family. "Travis, I can't—"

"But, before you say no, listen. I've been scared out of my mind since that night Emilio left the kids." I choke out a humorless laugh. "I wake up from nightmares where my phone is ringing and I can't answer it in time. I know it's overkill, and I know kids have survived hundreds of years without being in constant contact with their parents. But your phone has a power issue, so you needed a new one, anyway. And I'll sleep better knowing the kids have a way to get in touch with you in the event they're separated from you again. Please say you'll take them."

"Travis, this is so nice of you. I appreciate it so much, and I will keep one for me since my phone has proven itself to fit only for the trash bin. But I can't afford the bill on four cell phones. I can barely afford the bill on one. That's why I hadn't replaced my phone yet."

"Okay, I know you won't like this, but I will automatically pay all the bills with my credit card. It's already set up. When the real estate picks up a little more, you can pay me back. I'd prefer if you didn't, but something tells me you won't like that." I look up and she nods.

"Fine. I'll keep them. But only because I've been just as scared. My phone doesn't ring in my nightmares, though." She laughs. "Even in my dreams, it's broken."

I chuckle. "Okay, good. Thank you." We sit quietly together, side by side on the swing, not quite touching. That sliver of space between us feels enormous, and it kills me.

Finally, Finley turns to face me, and puts me out of my misery. "So... You're in the band?"

I grimace at the question. I was kind of hoping we could start with something else, like maybe, "hey, you did the lawn". Or, "nice work on the flowers".

"Yeah, I am. I should have told you right away. I'm so sorry, Fin. I should have trusted you with that information."

"You're damn right you should have."

Ouch. She's still really mad. I deserve it, though.

"I'm an ass."

She laughs. "Yeah, you are." She pushes off the floor with her feet and makes the swing move a little more, tilting her head back and sighing. "So, what do you do in the band? Play guitar? Is that why you knew how to play when you were helping the kids with the Christmas concert?"

"Uh, I play bass." Oof. I'm not exactly eloquent tonight. I had all these things I'd planned to say if Fin agreed to talk, but now that she's here beside me, I'm tongue-tied.

"Do you like it?"

I think for a minute. *Do* I like it? I don't think anyone's seriously asked me that before. "Yeah, I like most of it," I say. "I enjoy playing music. I like the adrenaline I get from playing a show in front of thousands of people. I really like being with my brother and my friends. I don't much like touring anymore. That part I don't like."

"Why not?"

I see her shiver from the corner of my eye. The sun's going down, and the temperature is going down with it. I reach into the basket on the floor next to me and pull out a fuzzy blanket, stretching it across her lap. She mouths a thank you to me.

"I hate being away from home for that long, I guess. It's hard being in a new place every night. Being on the bus isn't great. And since I met you, I've been dreading the thought of going back on tour even more than I used to."

Finley crosses her legs beneath her and pulls the blanket up to her chin. "Why did you tell me you were a handyman? Why didn't you correct me?"

I exhale slowly. This is where the lie started. If I don't explain this right, I'll never get Fin to trust me again. "Because I liked the way you looked at me. I loved feeling like a normal guy. When you walked up to me that first day, I thought you were a fan. Did you know that? It shocked me when that wasn't the case. And I got caught up in the feeling of being normal. The fame and stuff is nice, I guess, but you never know if someone really sees you, or if they only see the carefully curated public image of you. When you thought I was a handyman and wanted to hire me to fix your house, you saw me. You saw Travis, the regular guy. And I loved spending time with you as Travis, the regular guy."

We swing quietly for a moment, listening to the sound of the breeze.

"Would you quit?"

"Would I quit the band?"

"Yeah. If you want the life of a regular guy, you could quit the band. You could have the family you've always wanted. Without the band, you could have a normal life, with a normal, stable family."

"In a heartbeat," I say without hesitation. "If I had you, I would quit in a heartbeat."

The sun has dropped below the horizon now, and I can only see Fin thanks to the illumination of the streetlight a few houses down. *I need to remember to buy some solar lights for the porch. Maybe some of those tiny fairy lights that lit the arch at Ryder and Denise's wedding.*

"Okay."

Finley's voice is barely audible. Did she say okay?

"Okay?"

"Okay."

I don't know what that means. Looking down at my feet, I try to think through what she could possibly mean by the word okay. Is she okay? Is it okay if I quit? Does she want me to quit? Is she saying she'll be with me if I quit? Or is she saying she forgives me? Okay is too broad of a word. It could mean anything, really. Or nothing. Shit. What if she's saying that we're done talking, and she doesn't forgive me?

"Are you okay over there?" Fin startles me out of my thoughts.

"Huh?" I look around. "What?"

She chuckles at me. Fuck, I've missed that sound this past week. I didn't realize how much I loved hearing her laugh every day until I didn't get to hear it anymore.

"Travis. Tell me why you lied. Tell me why you kept on lying."

This is it. All or nothing.

"Because I enjoyed feeling like I could have a chance with you. I liked pretending like this could go somewhere. If I were a handyman, you and I could be together for real, without the threat of a tour looming over us. Without you thinking that I might be like Emilio, and that thought threatening to destroy any trust you could have for me. If I were Travis, the regular guy, I could fall in love with you and you could fall in love with me, too."

"Hmmm."

"Yeah."

I push the swing back with my legs, lifting them and letting the momentum carry us forward. I wait until the swing settles to a standstill and repeat the motion; push us back with my legs, lift my legs, and let the momentum carry us forward. The anxiety eats at my stomach, and my heart beats furiously against my ribcage. Push back with legs, lift legs, let momentum carry us forward.

Push back with legs, lift legs, let momentum carry us forward.

Push back with legs, lift legs, let momentum carry us forward.

"Well, I did fall in love with Travis, the regular guy."

I slam my feet down on the floor of the porch, making the swing come to an unsteady halt.

"Whoa," Fin says, uncrossing her legs from under her, and dropping her feet to the floor right before she's thrown off the swing. "Warn a girl, would you?"

"Sorry, sorry. Are you alright?"

"Yeah," she says with a snicker. "I'm fine."

"Oh. Okay, good then. Good."

She reaches out and touches my arm. "Travis?" I look up into her eyes, and she smiles. "I understand."

"You understand?"

"I understand why you lied. And I forgive you."

A grin tries to creep onto my face. "You do?"

"On one condition."

"I'll quit the band first thing in the morning." I blurt without hesitation. "I'll go to the studio and let the guys know all at once, then I'll get the lawyers working on how to get me out of the contract for the next tour."

"What? No. I don't want you to quit for me. That's crazy."

"But..." I'm confused again. That seems to be the theme of the evening. *Travis is confused. Surprise, surprise.* "I thought that was what you wanted. You asked me if I would quit?"

"Yeah, I asked if you would. I didn't ask you to do it. I could never. No matter what you say about not enjoying going out on tour, this is something you've been doing for what? Almost twenty years? I wouldn't ask you to stop."

I stand up from the swing and take a step, stopping directly in front of Finley. She stands to meet me, her body pressed close to mine.

"What is the one condition? I'll do anything." I push a hand into her hair, letting the vibrant green strands slip through my fingers. "Whatever you want, I'll do it."

"Promise me you won't lie to me," she whispers, staring into my eyes.

"I promise I will never lie to you again."

"Okay."

"Okay?" I ask with a smile.

"Okay," she whispers. She reaches up, wraps her arms around my neck, and pulls me down into a kiss. A kiss that I thought I'd never get to experience again. And it's the best kiss I've ever had. Well, other than the one that comes next. And the one after that.

"Wait," I pull back, suddenly remembering something she said. Fin's eyes go wide with shock. "What about this Travis?"

"Huh?" It's Finley's turn to be eloquent.

"You said you fell in love with Travis, the regular guy. What about this Travis?" I ask, pointing to my chest. I'm scared to hear it, but I need to know the answer.

She laughs. "Travis the regular guy and this Travis are the same," she says, pulling me down to meet her lips. "And I love you both," she whispers against my mouth, before kissing me deeply.

I pull her tightly against, gripping her hair in one hand, and tilt her to deepen the kiss. Turning our bodies, I take small steps toward the door, letting us inside when I finally reach the doorknob.

"I love you," I whisper. "I will spend the rest of my life trying to show you how much."

"Good," she smirks. "You can start tonight. Take me to bed, Travis. I've missed you."

44

Happily Ever After

Finley

"Come on, guys. You're killing me. Let's go, let's go, let's go. We're already late. Please tell me you know where your shoes are."

The kids are nowhere to be found. I'm standing in the entryway of our new house at the lake, a summertime extravagance I never thought I'd have, waiting for the kids to come down so we can walk out to the ceremony together.

"Braden is already outside with Travis," Sarah says, finally making her way down the stairs. "And Austin is somewhere with Johnny and Becca. I'm the last one."

I smile at her. No matter how late she was, I would wait for her before we started. How could I get married without my maid of honor?

"Ugh, you smudged your lipstick," she says, pulling a tube of pink gloss out of her tiny purse. "Let me fix you up."

She's been practicing her makeup skills so much over the last year that she's nearly an expert. I still don't allow her to wear it at school, but her YouTube tutorials have millions of views. How could I say no to her when she asked to do my makeup for the wedding?

"There, much better."

"Thanks, baby. I don't know what I'd do without you."

"Well, your makeup wouldn't look half as good, that's for sure," she laughs.

"Shall we, ladies?" My dad stands in the doorway, waiting to escort me down the aisle. "You need to get out there, Sarah. Here you go." He hands her a bouquet. "See you shortly."

She kisses my cheek and goes outside to join everyone else.

"Well, Dad. Any last words?" I'm not making the same mistake as when I married Emilio. "If you have anything to tell me about Travis, now is the time. I can still pull a runner if I need to."

He laughs. "No, darling. I knew Travis was the one for you the very first day I met him. Any man who's willing to push a Porsche into a ditch for the woman he loves is a good man in my book. That he's such a great dad to my grandkids is a bonus in my eyes."

Emilio is no longer in our lives. He signed away his rights after the police discovered how often he'd left the kids unsupervised during visits. It took a long time for me to come to terms with it, partly because someone I'd once loved could do that to our children, and partly because it hurt that the kids didn't talk to me about it. We've talked about it a lot since then, though, and I now know it was their misguided attempt at protecting their dad. The whole thing's been hard on them, but we have an excellent family therapist helping us work through it all in a healthy way.

Travis has helped immeasurably, always willing to drop everything to be there for us. No one was happier than the kids when he asked me to marry him. Except maybe my Grandma.

"Okay," I say. "That's pretty much what Grandma said, too." I breathe in deeply. Grandma never liked my ex and look how that turned out. Her love for Travis is all I needed to know that I made the right choice this time. "I guess it's time to get this show on the road then, isn't it?"

Dad leads me outside, and the music starts. As he walks me down the aisle, to where Travis is waiting on the beach, my eyes catch on his best man. I spin my head to look at my dad with my mouth wide open. He chuckles at me. Braden is standing up as Travis's best man. And the tears that I swore I wouldn't cry come spilling down my cheeks.

Damn it. Sarah's going to be mad that she has to fix me up again already.

As if Travis asking Braden to be his best man wasn't enough to have me sobbing like a baby, now another amazing surprise now catches my attention. A soft voice fills the air with a beautiful falsetto, singing one of my favorite songs, Bob Dylan's "You belong to Me." Austin stands to the side of the altar singing his little heart out, at a completely reasonable volume, while Johnny accompanies him on guitar. The tears are streaming now.

Not fair. These assholes ganged up on me.

When we get to the altar where Travis waits, Dad kisses my cheek and sits down next to my mother. Thank goodness this is going to be the shortest ceremony in the history of weddings, because I don't want to be up here crying in front of all our friends and family for too long.

"Well, kids. Here we are again. It's becoming a bit of a tradition for me to marry you youngsters, isn't it?" Grandma says. She's performing the ceremony for us, like she did for Ryder and Denise, Aiden and Rhea, and Alex and Connor. We're the last of the group to take the plunge. "Of course, Johnny and Becca had to elope in Vegas, but if anyone could do almost as well as me, it's the Elvis impersonator who performed their ceremony. She's a credit to the wedding industry, that one."

Whimpers and soft cries start up from the crowd, and I know we have a brief window left where we can do this without it having a background track of crying babies. So many babies.

Alex and Connor's twin girls, Allie and Mollie, are almost seven months old, and Denise and Ryder's baby girl, Cole, is ten months old. But there are even more babies here today. Aiden and Rhea recently adopted a sibling trio who they were fostering, so they have a three-year-old boy, Jackson, a two-year-old boy, Baron, and a six-month-old girl, Ella.

With that many babies in the crowd, this could get real ugly, real fast.

"Pick up the pace a little, Grandma," I say. "The babies are about to revolt."

Travis smiles down at me, and then at my hands in his. "I'm ready."

"Well, okay then. We've signed all the paperwork, so this is only for showing off our fancy clothes, anyway. Travis, do you take Finley to be your wife?"

"I do."

"Finley, do you take Travis to be your husband?"

"I do."

"Well then, as two wise men once said, 'be excellent to each other'. You can smooch each other's faces off now. But not too much tongue. There are children present."

Travis bends down, cradling my face in his hands. "I love you, Finley," he whispers, before kissing me softly.

"I love you, Travis."

I wrap my arms around his neck and kiss him again. We kiss until the crowd's cheers dissipate and the crying babies quiet.

Okay, so maybe they aren't quiet, but the noise disappears as I enjoy kissing my new husband. I may have been way off base with the last one, but this time, I definitely got it right.

"WELL, THAT WAS THE shortest wedding reception I've ever attended. Pretty disappointing if you ask me," Grandma says as Travis helps her and her friends to the Uber waiting for them in the driveway. "It's a good thing I planned an after-party at Peaceful Pines for tonight."

I snicker from my place on my porch swing, an identical version of the one hanging at our house in town, already wrapped up in a cozy blanket and ready to snuggle up with my new husband. Leave it to my eighty-year-old grandmother to complain about a party being too tame. I'm not sure what she was expecting. Over half the guests were in diapers. And no, I don't mean those who are probably three days away from needing the adult variety. When you're older, and you and all your friends have young kids, your wedding reception looks very different. It's less dancing and debauchery and more stealing desserts and sticky fingers.

"Yes, Gladys. It's a good thing you thought ahead. What kind of party do you have planned? Jell-O wrestling? Strip poker? Naked pillow fight club?"

Grandma snorts a laugh. "Come on now, Travis. The first rule of naked pillow fight club is, we don't talk about naked pillow fight club." She pats his cheek. "But no. It's none of those things. Me and the rest of the Titty Club are having a plain old tea party to discuss what we need to do moving forward."

"Moving forward?" Travis asks.

"Yes. Moving forward. I'm off of rockstar dicks now. You've all gone off and gotten married, so there's nothing left for me to see. Besides that, when I saw Ryder's, I wasn't that impressed. It's time to move on."

I choke on a laugh. Grandma's been trying to see the Sleeping Dogs guys' dicks for so long I thought she'd never give up. Something about her tone tells me I'm not going to like what she's considering next.

"Cathy's grandson plays for the Wombats. I'm thinking it might be time to become a football fan."

"You can't see my grandson's dick, Gladys." Cathy yells from her seat in the car. "He has teammates, though."

Travis massages his temples with one hand and holds the car door open with the other. "Okay, that's enough of this conversation. Get in the car, Gladys. It's time for me to enjoy my wedding night with my new wife."

"Oh, I see how it is. You can talk about banging my granddaughter, but I say one little thing about looking at dicks and you turn into a prude? Well. That's plain rude."

"Grandma, get in the car. You can tell me all about your new football obsession next time I see you. I'm kind of partial to their quarterback, myself."

"Oh, yes. I've heard he's packing. I'll go on the google as soon as I get home to see what I can find out." She slides into the car. "Don't just stand there, Travis. Close the door. You've got a wife to please. Better not slack off, either. I hear the quarterback isn't the only Wombat with something to offer a lady."

Travis grumbles as he closes the door and watches the car drive off with the last of our guests before stalking back to me. With one hand, he loosens his tie and unbuttons the top two buttons of his shirt. I swallow hard.

Since the first day I saw Travis, shirtless and painting the fence at his parent's house, he's been a repeat performer in my spank bank playlist. That I get to be with him, in person, and have him fill the role my battery operated boyfriend used to hold... Well, that's a dream come true.

And the way he's looking at me now, his pupils blown with lust, the bulge in his pants rapidly growing, tells me my dreams are about to come true. Again.

"Partial to their quarterback, huh?" he asks while he lifts the blanket from my lap and kneels in front of me, a twinkle of mischief in his eye. "What's so great about him?"

"Oh, uh. You know. I hear he's got good hands." I already can't concentrate because of the way he's looking at me. Heat floods my core and my heart beats faster.

"Good hands?" Travis pulls my legs down on either side of him, grazing his fingers along my calves. "What else?"

"He always rises to the occasion."

Travis leans over me and traces kisses along my jaw and neck-line. "And?"

"He knows how to place his balls?" I gasp, his heated kisses

"Mm-hmm?" He slides his hands up my legs, hooks his fingers into the sides of panties and slides them down.

"He has great pocket presence?"

"Is that right?" He lifts the hem of my dress over the back of his head, shoves his hands under my ass, and slides me to the edge of the set. His lips hover over me, and I feel his breath ghost over my clit. "What else?" He swipes his tongue from entrance to clit and nearly orgasm right there.

"Oh, fuck if I care. Don't stop."

He chuckles against me, and the vibration nearly does me in. "That's what I thought. Now be a good girl and open wider for me. I want to spend some time getting to know this sweet pussy again."

"Oh, fuck. Yes."

After bringing me to orgasm, twice, Travis finally takes his head out from under my dress, shoves his pants down, and fills me with one exquisitely slow thrust, the swing moving beneath me.

"Fuck, Fin. You feel so good." He leans in and kisses me. "How did I ever get so lucky?"

Still boneless from his excellent tongue work, I lazily tangle my fingers in his hair, kissing him as he slowly pumps into me, working another orgasm from me like only he can. With a groan, he follows me over the edge, before stilling and resting his head against mine. We sit like that for a moment before Travis tucks himself back into his pants, pulls my dress down over my legs, and drags me to my feet as I try to stifle a yawn.

"I think now would be a good time for me to get my new wife to bed." He cuts me off as I nod. "Unless you'd like to stay out here and tell more about the Wombats quarter-back?" He waggles his brows as he leads me into the house and up the stairs to our bedroom. "If I'd know you were such a fan, I'd have invited him to the wedding. Davis and I go way back."

I screech to a halt, my mouth dropping. "Wait. Are you saying you're friends with Davis Avery? Like the real Davis Avery? The quarterback Davis Avery?"

He barks a laugh. "Are you that much of a fan? You're telling me you had no idea who I was when you first saw me, but you know who Davis Avery is?"

I stick my chin out and stand facing him, fists on my hips. "And? What's your point? Football players are way cooler than rockstars," I tease. Really, the only reason I know anything about Davis Avery is because Braden knows *everything* about Davis Avery. "*Of course* I know who he is."

Travis shoots a wicked grin in my direction. "Cooler? Is that so?" He shrugs. "Well, that makes sense. I never thought the guys and I were very cool, anyway." He wraps his arms around me and kisses the top of my head. "I guess I can take you to a game one of these days and introduce you. We've had a good run." His chuckle tells me he's teasing.

I sigh into his chest. "You caught me. I don't care about Davis Avery, but Braden would love to go to a game."

"And I can't wait to take him."

That's why Travis is the right man for me. Because he's also the right man for my kids. And it doesn't matter at all that he's a rockstar.

THE END

Keep Reading Sneak Peek of Santa's Baby (coming late 2023)

Chapter One

PHOEBE

Of all the ways I ever imagined spending the Christmas of my thirty-first year I can say with certainty tracking down the Santa Claus who impregnated me was not one of them.

Yet here we are.

"This place is nice, Phoebe," Gavin says, walking into the living room and setting down a box marked "Lincoln." "Maybe the owners won't ever come back from their trip abroad so you can buy it. The furniture is pretty sweet." My idiot brother then flops face down on my fully furnished rental's overstuffed blue velvet couch and groans obscenely. "Oh, man. I could do dirty things to this couch."

It's not every day I rent a place sight unseen, so you can imagine the relief I felt when we got here and the place looked exactly like it had in the photos. That I could find a fully furnished place on such short notice, right before the holidays, was a miracle in itself. Finding a nice place in a safe neighborhood? Yeah, there had to have been some divine intervention involved for that to happen.

"Ew, don't be gross Gavin. And get your stinky ass off the couch. You're filthy."

"Is that any way to treat the guy who helped you move?" He dragged himself off the couch. "Speaking of which, didn't you promise me pizza and beer as payment for that help?"

"Ha! Nice try, kid. I'll order pizza but you're sticking with soda until you're of legal age. Plus, you still need to drive home so I wouldn't let you drink even if you were old enough."

Gavin is eighteen, my much younger sibling from my mom's second marriage. My bio dad left mom when Lane was born and I was still a few months shy of two years old. Needless to say, after being with such a bastion of paternal fortitude, it took Mom a long time to find another man worth taking a chance on. I was twelve when she started seeing Dennis, and fourteen when they married and Gavin was born.

Like most teenage boys, Gavin's all raging hormones and unrestrained snark. But, despite his many annoying traits, he has the biggest heart and he's one of my favorite people. When I found myself left at the altar almost a year ago no one was angrier than Gavin. He stormed around the hotel, hoping to run into my newly ex-fiance so he could unleash his teenage fury. It's probably a good thing he never found him, though. I doubt it would have been a fair fight.

Seventeen-year-old Gavin was a short, scrawny little shit. Eighteen-year-old Gavin is almost six and a half feet tall and packed with muscle. He's never said so, but I'm pretty sure he started working out after the wedding disaster so he'd be ready if he ever saw my ex again. After a year of protein shakes and lifting weights, not to mention a huge growth spurt, Gavin is formidable. It still wouldn't be a fair fight, but the advantage would go to Gavin, not Webster.

I almost feel guilty for not being as upset as he was about the situation. It was a shock when I got the text telling me he wasn't coming, but not marrying Webster Day was for the best. It was a dick move, but in the end, he made the best decision for both of us.

"No way, Lane said she would drive home." Gavin jumps up off the couch and yells down the back hallway, "Isn't that right, Lane?"

Oh, shit. Despite being one of my favorite people, I may have to murder Gavin if he wakes up Lincoln. That thing they say about never waking a sleeping baby? Yeah, that's totally true.

"Shhh. Will you shut up already?." I slap my hand over his mouth. "Lincoln is sleeping."

He looks so sheepish I might actually believe he felt bad about it if I didn't know better. There's no way Gavin would leave here without saying goodbye to his nephew, even if said nephew is barely old enough to see past his own fist. Gavin is sure Lincoln recognizes him, though, and is so proud of that fact. I believe it, too. Lincoln always seems calmer when his Uncle Gavin is holding him. And Gavin never misses a chance to hold him, even if he has to make his own chances.

"Too late," Lane says, coming out of the back hallway with a tiny baby snuggled in her arms. "Little guy was awake when I tried to sneak into his room to drop off a box. I think he sensed me because as soon as I walked in an unholy rumbling started coming out of his little rear end. You need to do laundry, by the way. I rinsed everything and left it to pre-soak." She looks down at Lincoln with a grin and singsongs, "Isn't that right, Linky? Mommy has to do laundry. Yes, she does. She's lucky Auntie Lane changed you and the sheets instead of running away and letting her deal with it."

My heart swells watching my little sister snuggle my baby and not for the first time since I came up with the plan, I second-guess my decision to move back to Westborough. What am I going to do without my family around to help me for the next three months? This was a terrible idea. But if I want Lincoln to at least have the chance to meet his father, this is where I need to be. And my sense of right and wrong won't let me entertain the thought of not trying to find his father. There's a man out there who doesn't know he has a son, and that doesn't sit right with me. I want him to at least have the choice of whether to be involved in Lincoln's life, even if he ends up being a dickhead like my father and chooses to have nothing to do with him.

"Hey, hey. I can see your brain working from here." Gavin is back on the couch, getting his sweaty teenage boy smell all over it. Whatever, I'll Febreze it when he leaves. He can't stink it up too badly in such a short time, can he? "Everything is going to be fine. Tell her your news, Lane. I can't handle seeing her cry."

I reach up and touch my cheeks, and sure enough, they're wet. "Sorry if my feelings offend you, you little twerp. I'm going to miss you guys, that's all. I'm allowed to be sad about that."

He jumps up off the couch and wraps me in a sweaty hug. "I'm going to miss you too, Feeble," he says, using the nickname he called me when he was little and couldn't quite get his little mouth to say Phoebe. "But you won't have to miss Lane."

I blink a few times and pull myself out of his embrace. "What's he talking about?" I ask Lane. "What are you talking about?"

Gavin takes Lincoln from Lane, snuggling him tightly to his chest, and takes him into the kitchen. I hear the cupboard doors open and close and the water runs in the sink. Sounds like Uncle Gavin is making his nephew a bottle.

"I didn't tell you because I knew you'd try to talk me out of it, but I'm staying with you. You have the third bedroom I can sleep in. I even got myself a part-time job at a coffee shop. I'm staying to help you with Lincoln so you can focus on finding his dad. It will be easier to track him down if you don't have to bring Lincoln with you everywhere you go. Plus, I can't be away from you guys for that long." Lane's eyes are shiny with unshed tears. "I just can't get enough of those midnight feedings," she jokes.

I chuckle. "Are you sure? You don't have to put your life on hold for me, Lane. I love you for wanting to do this, but you don't have to stay."

"I know that," she says, wrapping her arms around me. "I want to stay."

"You're the best sister I could ever ask for," I choke through a sob. "I couldn't have made it this far without you."

And it's true. The seemingly endless months of my pregnancy with Lincoln would have been so much harder if it hadn't been for the help of my brother and sister, and, of course, my mom and stepdad. I won't tell Lane and Gavin, but after living back home with my parents for the last year, and having my family around all the time, I was a little scared to be on my own with Lincoln in the city. I loved living here with Webster, but being on my own with a baby is different. The excitement of Westborough seems almost scary when I think about protecting my son from unseen dangers. I tried to play it cool, but I'm thinking I didn't do such a good job of it if Lane secretly arranged to move here with me. I've never been so happy to be such a shitty liar.

"Are you guys done with all the girly feelings out there? Me and the big guy want to come chill on that sweet-ass couch but we don't want your emotional breakdowns cramping our manly style."

Lane and I both burst into laughter. After one more squeeze, I let her go.

"Yeah, we're done," I call out. "I'll order that pizza now so you can get on the road."

"About that," he says, walking back to the living room with my son in the crook of his arm. "Mom told me to spend the night and drive back in the morning. She doesn't want me driving alone at night in the winter. I don't know what she thinks I do after work at home. It's usually pretty late by the time I get out of the market."

Lane sits next to him on the couch, her eyes on Lincoln. "There's a big difference between driving five minutes in Fallbridge at ten at night and driving on the highway at two in the morning. Especially in the middle of winter."

"Yeah, yeah. Okay, Mom," he teases. "I'm already staying the night. Happy?"

"You bet," she says while ruffling his hair, taking advantage of the fact that he has his hands full feeding Lincoln. "We just wuv you so much, Gavvers," she adds in a baby voice. "We would hate it if anything happened to you."

"Hey, no fair. Hands off my hair. Do you know how long it took to get it like that?"

They sit side by side, alternating between cooing over Lincoln and bickering with each other while I busy myself with ordering the pizzas and unpacking some boxes. The best part about finding a fully furnished rental is how little I had to pack to come here. It would have sucked if I'd had to move my furniture out of storage for such a short stay. Three months isn't long enough to justify renting a moving van. With this rental house, all I needed was some boxes in the back of Gavin's truck and I was ready to move in.

I just hope three months is long enough to find Lincoln's dad.

The doorbell rings, and Gavin hops up to grab the pizzas. "Oh, thank god. I'm starving," he says, spreading the boxes down on the coffee table and flipping one open. "I'm a growing boy, you know." He grabs two slices and stacks them.

I bring plates and napkins out from the kitchen. "We know, Gavin. You tell us every time you get even the tiniest bit hungry."

He wiggles his eyebrows, and grins before shoving the pizza sandwich in his mouth.

"So, Phoebe. Why don't you tell me how you plan on finding this guy? All you said before we came was that you're moving here for three months to look for him. Do you even have any idea where he is?"

I heave a sigh. This is the biggest problem with my plan. It sucks. When you get blind drunk after being left at the altar and hook up with someone you just met, it would be a lot easier to move on with your life if you didn't get yourself pregnant in the process. Failing that, it would be nice if you remember the name of the person or any detail about them other than he'd been dressed as Santa Claus for a Christmas party that was being held at the same hotel as your wedding. The only things I have to go on are the big red velvet coat I stole when I crept out of there in the wee hours of the morning, still drunk from the night before, and a picture I snapped of him with his face mashed so far into the pillow you can't tell with any accuracy what he looks like.

Why did I take his jacket, you ask? I guess I thought my walk of shame would feel less shameful if I covered my wedding dress with Santa's jacket. It didn't. But I made it back to the room without being seen, packed up, and headed home with no one finding out I spent what should have been my wedding night with a stranger.

Until a month and a half later when I got the shock of a lifetime, ensuring that *everyone* would eventually know *exactly* how I spent that night.

That's right.

My fiancé left me at the altar and the first thing I did was run out and get impregnated by Santa Claus.

Talk about Ho Ho Ho.

WANT TO KNOW WHEN Santa's Baby is available? Get the Roomie Review. Sign up at chantalroome.com/newsletter

Start the Sleeping Dogs series over at the beginning

Second Chance (Sleeping Dogs Book 1) Chapter One

ALEX

"Son of a bitch." I stomp my way to my car after slamming the door behind me. I rip off my chef's jacket and throw it into the passenger seat, along with my knife roll. These assholes may have sent me home, but I should have left long ago. Not just today, but permanently.***

I've had it up to my ass with my latest personal chef clients, the dirty old pervert and his not-quite-young-enough-to-be-a-trophy wife. He keeps trying to grab my ass, and she keeps trying to blame me for it. I really need this job, but I'm not sure how much longer I'll be able to keep my mouth shut about the harassment.

I pull my hair out of its high bun and scratch my fingers along my scalp to help ease some tension. It's amazing the stress a tight hairstyle can cause. Once I'm mostly calm, I turn on some angry music to finish soothing me (what can I say? Angry music calms me) and drive home to the apartment I share with my boyfriend.

Well, it's probably more accurate to say I live in his apartment, rather than share it with him, considering he's been there for years and I only recently moved in. It doesn't feel much like mine since almost everything in it belongs to him, anyway.

I stop to check the mail in the lobby on my way in before taking the elevator to the 4th floor where our apartment is. Since I'm off work early, I think I may as well put the time to good use. I'm distracted with thoughts of the hot bath I'm going to take and the amazing meal I'm going to cook when I put the key in the lock of my apartment door and find there is no resistance when I turn it. That's weird. I'm pretty sure I locked it when I left the house this morning. Or am I remembering yesterday?

A loud bang from inside the apartment makes me jump.

Oh Shit! Someone's in there! I'm being robbed! What do I do? I can't let someone take all of Derek's stuff that he's worked so hard for. Holding my breath, I reach for my phone as quietly as I can and call my best friend Becca.

"Becca, it's me. I just got home and there's someone in my apartment. I think I'm being robbed," I whisper.

I inch open the door and creep in, reaching for the first weapon-like item I can find. The cute ladybug umbrella I keep for rainy days is about to see a different kind of action. I suppose I could use one of the knives I'm already carrying, but like hell I'm going to get dirty burglar blood on one of my professional knives and risk it being locked up as evidence.

I couldn't afford to replace it if that happened. Working as a personal chef hasn't been as lucrative as I'd hoped, but it sure beats the long hours of grueling labor I'd have to put in working in some other chef's kitchen. When you're not partaking in illegal stimulants, kitchen hours are unmanageable and, unfortunately, I've always preferred coffee to cocaine.

"What? Did you call the police? Get out of there, you're going to get hurt. I'm serious. Don't do anything stupid."

"I'm fine," I whisper, hoisting up my umbrella. "I have a weapon."

"Like what? I know for a fact you won't dirty up one of your work knives, and that's the only thing you'd have with you that could work." She knows me too well.

"I have an umbrella. I'll be fine, promise."

I hear another loud bang coming from somewhere in the back of the apartment, so I tiptoe in that direction.

"An umbrella? Have you lost your mind? Get out of there, Alex. I swear to god if you die trying to catch a burglar, I'm going to kill you!" Becca shrieks as she attempts to talk me out of what I'm about to do.

Also, threatening to kill me if I die? Not the smartest thing she's ever said. Of course, attempting to catch a burglar in the act instead of waiting for the police is far from the smartest thing I've ever done, so I'd say we're even.

"Shhhh, he'll hear you, and I need to catch this asshole intruder by surprise." Nobody messes with me and Derek and gets away with it. "This guy's going to feel my wrath and that of my ladybug umbrella."

I creep forward, choosing the placement of each foot carefully so I make the least amount of noise. A giggling sound stops me dead in my tracks. It's coming from further back in the apartment, like from the bedroom.

I groan inwardly and lower my umbrella. *Oh, come on, not again. I thought Derek was different. I mean, sure, he works a lot and barely has time for me and he thinks my cooking is a hobby, but still. He asked me to move in. I thought he was serious about me. But apparently he's just like all the rest of them.*

My mind quickly races through all the boyfriends who've cheated on me. Which is all of them, in case you were wondering. I refuse to relive the shitty details, but yes, I caught most of them in the act, and yes, I ended it with all of them.

It's just as depressing as it sounds.

And now Derek is fucking someone in our bed when he's supposed to be at work. When we're both supposed to be at work.

"That motherfucker," I whisper yell into the phone. "Becca, come over, now."

"I'm already on my way. What is it? What's wrong? Are you hurt? Should I call 911?" Becca is freaking out. If she doesn't lower her voice, all the neighborhood dogs will come running. Actually, now that I think about it, that could benefit me. I've never had a pack of dogs attack a cheating boyfriend before. It might be fun to watch.

You might hear that and think I'm being callous and, well, you would be right. I am. I've been through this so many times now that I almost find it enjoyable to find new and clever ways to get back at the cheaters once I've caught them. Not that I want it to keep happening for that reason, but you know what they say. When life hands you cheating lemons, beat the shit out of them until you get lemonade. Or something like that. I'm not great with sayings. The point is, putting my heart on the line just for the chance of getting revenge isn't something that interests me. Sadly, I actually kind of like the guys before they end up cheating. I just suck at picking them.

Becca's car revs in the background. Good. If this is actually happening, I'm going to need backup. I creep up to the bedroom door and stop just outside of it. I force myself to stop breathing and try to listen closely, my ear pressed to the door.

"You like that, huh? You like my cock in you, you dirty slut?"

Well, fuck. That's Derek, alright. He likes to talk dirty, even though I've never thought he's all that great at it. My body gets numb all over, and then a burning rage sears a hole in my chest. You think I'd be completely numb to this by now, but the betrayal always hurts at least a little.

"Becca? It's happening again."

"That asshole! I'm five minutes away, Alex. Make sure you save some for me. I'm going to take pleasure in beating his ass."

"He won't last another five minutes, Becca. I need to go in now. He just doesn't have that kind of stamina. Believe me, my less-than-satisfying love life is proof of that."

She chuckles a little at my confession. Maybe she thinks I'm making a joke at Derek's expense, but I'm really not. He's not quite a two-pump chump, but he's pretty damn close.

"Yeah, Derek, harder, harder! It feels so good, your cock is so big," the dirty slut, his words, not mine, screams as I continue to listen at the door. Derek's dick is mediocre on a good day so either this chick has the tightest pussy on earth or she's lying.

I'm going with lying.

No one's pussy is *that* tight. Plus, I'm pretty sure I can hear a hint of sarcasm in her voice even from out here.

"Are you gonna come for me, baby?"

Shit, that's Derek's way of saying 'I'm coming soon and if you don't, that's your problem.' Ever the selfless lover, that Derek is. That means if I want to surprise him in the act, I need to get in there fast.

"Becca, are you almost here?"

"On my way up. Is the door unlocked?"

"Yup, come right in. I'll be the one in the bedroom swinging the umbrella."

I turn the doorknob to the bedroom, careful not to make any noise. It opens to the sound of moans and grunts. Fucking Derek and his grunting. He's facing away from the door, pumping into Miss dirty slut from behind, so I sneak up on him while raising my ladybug umbrella. From this angle, I can see his hairy balls flopping around. Gross. I can't believe I actually found him attractive. And that was just this morning.

"It's happening baby, I'm gonna come now, it's happening... ungh, ungghhh," he groans obscenely.

I creep closer to the bed as Derek thrusts erratically and grunts some more. This angle is not exactly flattering and again I wonder what I ever saw in him. Whatever. That doesn't matter now. What matters is teaching him a lesson. I grip the top of the umbrella with both hands, step right into it, and swing that ladybug like I'm Babe Ruth, nearly breaking the handle off on Derek's cheating ass.

"And it's a home run! The crowd goes wild!" Becca yells from behind me. Looks like she got here just in time. She puts her hands up like a megaphone and imitates the sounds of a crowd cheering for me. Derek's screaming nearly drowns her out, though. He throws himself off the bed, leaving Miss dirty slut exposed. She's just as scared as Derek is, but I'm guessing her reason differs from his.

Becca is in the room, still cheering as she pretends to run the bases while collecting the other woman's clothes from the floor.

"You have a girlfriend?" miss dirty slut screams at Derek. She frantically tries to cover herself with the sheet. "You fucker!"

"He *had* a girlfriend," I correct her, while Becca passes her clothes to her. "But good news. It looks like we just broke up. He's yours if you want him. Though, I have a feeling that you no longer do."

Derek's eyes are wide and he looks like a fish with the way he keeps opening and shutting his mouth. He's sitting on his hip on the floor while he rubs his umbrella-imprinted ass cheek gingerly, wincing every time his hand grazes the hook mark left by the handle. Good. I hope he can't sit for a month.

"I am *so* sorry," the girl says to me. Her eyes are wide and her lip quivers a little. "I didn't realize he had a girlfriend. This is what I get for day drinking to forget my problems, I guess."

"No worries," I tell her, heaving a sigh of relief. It's so much easier when the other woman feels bad about being the other woman. "I've been through this enough times that I know the side chick is rarely aware of the situation. I can't blame you for trying to have an orgasm with someone who told you he was available. All the blame lies with that asshole over there." I point the broken carcass of my umbrella, all bent metal and ripped canvas, at Derek. "Isn't that right, Dickhead?"

Derek flinches a little and scoots back while I point at him. He probably thinks I'm going to break the rest of this umbrella over him, which, I have to admit, he sorely deserves. The girl stands up, holding her clothes to cover her body as best she can.

"Um, so yeah. I think I'm just going to get dressed in the hallway and go if that's cool with you?" She points to the door behind me and I nod. "So, I'll just leave you and Derek to work this out." She looks over at Derek. "Don't call me," she says. "Ever."

She takes tiny shuffling steps past both me and Becca to get out the bedroom door. I hear her stop and get dressed in the hallway, and shortly after that, the door to the apartment opens and closes as she leaves.

"Alright, let's get to work, shall we?"

"You bet," says Becca, shooting a dirty look at Derek. "Be right back."

"Please don't hurt me Alex. I'm sorry, I love you. I'll never do it again. I didn't mean to do it. She meant nothing to me."

Tears fall down Derek's cheeks as he crawls around looking for his underwear while continuing to spew the typical cheater's bullshit apology: *I love you, I'm sorry, it was an accident; I tripped and landed dick-first in her vagina. Blah, blah, blah.* I've heard it all before. I kick his boxers over, not because I care about his dignity, but because I don't want to see his dick and balls flopping around anymore. I can't believe I ever thought he was cute.

Of course, crawling around on the floor while crying probably isn't a good look on anyone.

"Quit being a little bitch, Derek. I'm not going to hurt you more than I already have. Probably. One never really can tell what I'll do once I've discovered my boyfriend cheated on me. But then again, I've already ruined a perfectly good umbrella. I don't really feel the need to break anything else trying to teach you a lesson that I don't actually care if you learn. I'm sure you will cheat again, because once a cheater, always a cheater. But I can guarantee you won't ever cheat on me again. Want to know why?" I taunt him by spinning what's left of the umbrella around my wrist. "Because I won't give you that chance. Now get the fuck out, I have packing to do. I'll leave the keys with security."

All the boyfriends I've ever had may have cheated on me, but at least I'm smart enough to never give them a second chance.

Now, if only I could figure out what it is about me that makes them cheat on me in the first place, I'd know what to avoid next time.

Derek begins to protest just as Becca returns with some boxes and a little something extra.

"Here slugger, catch." She winks and tosses me a baseball bat and I drop the umbrella to catch it. "You know, in case you're not done with batting practice."

I bounce the bat up and down, testing the weight of it, before making a practice swing. "Nice. Thanks."

That kicks Derek into high gear. He scrambles to pick up his clothes and keep an eye on me at the same before practically sprinting from the apartment in only his boxers. "I'm going, I'm going," he's saying as the door closes behind him.

"I've got a few more boxes in my car. I'll grab them and make sure he leaves at the same time."

"Hey Becca?" I call out, causing her to turn around before she gets to the door. "Thanks."

"No problem, girl, that's what besties are for," she says with a sad smile.

I nod and turn away. I can't stand to see the pity in her eyes. Again.

I'm not sure why Becca had boxes in her car, but I'm thankful she did. I'll be able to pack and get out of here right now, and I'll never have to come back. I should have known Derek would cheat.

Because in my experience, they all do.

"Well, look on the bright side," Becca says, while packing my clothes into a box. "A few more shitty boyfriends and your batting skills will be good enough to join a major league baseball team." She can barely contain her laughter.

Becca's been my best friend ever since I moved to this city when I was 16, and she's been there to help me through my breakups with all my previous unfaithful boyfriends. Not to mention Connor, the boy I had to leave when we moved. My first boyfriend and first love. And the only man who never cheated on me. Despite how it ended, he's the only boyfriend I ever look back on fondly.

"I can't believe you broke an umbrella over his ass. That shit was hilarious. He's going to have a hook shaped mark on his cheeks for at least a month."

I snicker a little at that. "I feel kind of bad for the girl. I'm amazed she actually apologized. Usually they get embarrassed and run. She seemed pretty cool. I mean, it's not her fault Derek fucked her while he was still living with me, right?"

"Funny you should mention that. I ran into her outside when I went to grab more boxes from my car. She was waiting on her cab out front. She asked me to apologize to you again." Shit. That is cool. Under other, less adulterous, circumstances, she might be fun to hang out with. "And then Derek came over." I look over at her like she's about to tell me that miss dirty slut (yes, I know, it's not nice to call her that. Sue me, I just found out my boyfriend was cheating. I can't help that I didn't get her name) had made up with him, but I see Becca struggling not to laugh. "And then she kicked him in balls and kneed him in the face!"

A snort of laughter escapes me, and I double over. Fucking Derek totally deserved that. That chick *is* so cool. Now I really regret not getting her name. I laugh until my stomach hurts before I get myself back under control.

"Okay," I say, pulling my long hair up into a messy bun on top of my head. "Let's get the rest of this shit packed up. You know the drill, all my kitchen shit, clothes, bathroom stuff, and recipe books."

"Got it, boss." Becca gives a salute while kicking her boots together, like some kind of army cadet. Not that she'd ever join the army. She's way too punk rock for that. I swear that girl has more ink than regular skin. When I met her, she was only 16 and already had two full sleeves and a chest piece. Now she's 35, and most of the rest of her body is tattooed as well. I've noticed some scarring under the color, but I've never asked her about it. It's not my business unless she wants to tell me, so for now I admire the artwork and hope it's helping her.

Becca grabs a big box and takes it to the kitchen to get started on the pots and pans. I paid a shit ton of money for them and they come with me every time I move. I always work professional cookware into my contracts for working as a personal chef, too. It's hard to prepare food exactly the way I want it when I don't have the right tools. I could do it if I had to, but it's much more enjoyable with the right gear.

"So where are we moving this stuff to, anyway?" Not sure why Becca is asking. She already knows the answer to this question. "Want to be roomies again? I promise I won't cheat on you like all these dudes. Well, unless some sexy tattooed guy comes along and waves his big fat pierced cock in my face. No promises then." She waggles her eyebrows at me.

"I wouldn't blame you at that point. I might just cheat on myself if that happened to me." I laugh.

The rest of the packing goes quickly and I'm completely moved out of the apartment in less than an hour. We have an absurd amount of practice with moving me out of places, which is pretty sad, but it makes for much faster moves when the time comes. How I always get myself into these relationships is beyond me. I seem to attract all the assholes and then I move in with them. I guess I just love love and love really hates me.

"Let's go back to your place and just chill for the rest of the day. You know, the usual breakup routine of bashing men, eating ice cream, drinking too much, and watching chick flicks." This is literally the last thing I want to be doing today, but it's become a sort of tradition. Becca has been with me through all my break-ups and if she wants to get shit-faced and eat ice cream with me, I won't argue.

Becca's phone rings from where she left it on the counter. Probably a client. She has her own photography business and makes most of her money shooting weddings, but occasionally she's booked for other things. She talks on the phone for a few minutes while I double check I have all my stuff. I refuse to see Derek ever again, so I don't plan on forgetting anything.

"Change of plans, Alex; no pity party today. I have to go shoot a promotional thing for the radio station tonight. Some local band is doing the last show of their tour and having a special meet and greet afterward. The station wants me to shoot the meets for people who won some call-in contest."

"Oh, no worries. I'm sure I can find something to do" I'm a little relieved. This has happened to me so many times now that I don't even care about the breakup ritual. It's like my heart doesn't break anymore, it's too strong. Either that or it's been broken since the first time and has stayed that way ever since.

She grins at me. "Actually, I convinced them I will need to bring extra equipment so they're giving me an extra press pass for my 'assistant'."

"But you don't have an assistant," I point out, confused.

"Congratulations," she says to me, throwing fake confetti. "You're hired. There is no pay, and the boss is a huge bitch. What do you think?"

I laugh, finally figuring out what the hell she's talking about. "That sounds like a much better breakup ritual. Thanks."

"No problem. Now let's get this shit back to our place and figure out a plan for after the show. Oooh, you can have hot rebound sex with someone in the band. I'm sure they fuck a lot, so it's possible they're awesome at it." She wiggles her eyebrows at me while walking backward toward her car. "Of course, it's also possible they're terrible and groupies are just telling them what they want to hear. It could go either way."

"Ha, yeah right!" I flip her off as I get into my vehicle. "I'm not exactly rockstar girlfriend material."

"Who said anything about girlfriend? I said rebound sex. Get your mind *into* the gutter, girl," she yells from her open window while pulling out of the lot.

I shake my head and chuckle. She's such a bitch. That must be why I love her.

Hopefully, this band tonight is good. I might not be completely heartbroken, but I could use something to distract me from sitting around trying to figure out why I've been cheated on yet again.

Keep reading in Second Chance (Sleeping Dogs Book 1)

Books by Chantal Roome

Sleeping Dogs the complete collection
The men of Sleeping Dogs have had their fair share of women, but now that they're a little older, and a little wiser, they're looking for something more meaningful than the one-night stands typical of their past.

Second Chance (Sleeping Dogs Book 1)
She's an unemployed chef afraid of being burned by love again. He's a world-weary rock star tired of being used. Can a second chance at first love heal them both?

Face the Music (Sleeping Dogs Book 2)
She's a serious control freak of a band manager. He's a jaded joker of a rock star. Will a jealous ex and surprise pregnancy tear them apart before they start?

Skip a Beat (Sleeping Dogs Book 3)
She's a disgraced ex-cop looking for a career change. He's a moody drummer trying to keep his demons at bay. Can vandalism and ill-conceived revenge plans be the glue that mends their lives and binds them to each other?

Only the Best (Sleeping Dogs Book 4)

He's a romantic, guitar-playing tattoo artist looking for true love. She's an emotionally and physically scarred photographer who keeps people at a distance. When one wants true love and the other wants one night, can friendship and a fake relationship ever be enough?

Way off Base (Sleeping Dogs Book 5)

She's a single mom struggling to rebuild her life. He's a reluctant rock star tired of being alone. Can they repair a foundation of lies to build the life they both want?

CHANTAL ROOME WRITES CONTEMPORARY romantic comedies and is the author of the Sleeping Dogs series of cinnamon roll rock star rom-coms. She loves writing love stories with just the right mix of sweetness, humour, and sex. When she isn't writing, she's drinking way too much coffee, binge reading romance, and living out her own second chance romance with her husband. She's also a mediocre mom to two frustrating, but hilarious and endlessly loveable kids, and one dog who has eaten every toy he's ever been given.

Keep in touch with Chantal on social media

Visit Chantal's website at: www.chantalroome.com

Get the Roomie Review Newsletter chantalroome.com/roomiereview

Join my readers' group facebook.com/groups/theromcomroome

f   facebook.com/chantalroomeauthor

    instagram.com/chantalroomeauthor

    pinterest.com/chantalroome

    tiktok.com/chantalroomeauthor

    twitter.com/croomeauthor

g   goodreads.com/chantalroome

BB   bookbub.com/authors/chantal-roome

Thank you

Thank you for joining me on this Sleeping Dogs journey. This project started when I had the idea to write a low-angst rockstar romance after reading one too many rockstar romances that ripped my heart out. I wanted something where the guys in the band were ooey gooey cinnamon rolls who loved their women more than anything, and would do anything to show them, and I like to think I succeeded.

Keep your eyes open for future releases featuring some of the side-characters from this series *cough* Devon and Xena *cough*